Cathy Wo█████████████████████ █ her young
family. A former vet, Cathy is now a full-time writer.
Her debut novel, UNDER THE BONNET, was joint
winner of the Harry Bowling First Novel Award.

UNDER THE BONNET

Cathy Woodman

First published in 2004
by HEADLINE BOOK PUBLISHING

First published in paperback in 2004
by HEADLINE BOOK PUBLISHING

4

ISBN 0 7553 0956 1

Typeset in Times by Palimpsest Book Production Limited,
Polmont, Stirlingshire

Printed and bound in Great Britain by
Mackays of Chatham plc, Chatham, Kent

Papers and cover board used by Headline are natural, recyclable
products made from wood grown in sustainable forests. The manu-
facturing processes conform to the environmental regulations of the
country of origin

HEADLINE BOOK PUBLISHING
A division of Hodder Headline
338 Euston Road
LONDON NW1 3BH

www.headline.co.uk
www.hodderheadline.com

To Graham, Tamsin and Will

Acknowledgements

I should like to thank all those involved with the Harry Bowling Award, my agent, Laura Longrigg at MBA, and my editor, Sherise Hobbs at Headline, for their encouragement and support.

Chapter One

This is a delicate operation in more ways than one. Lorraine is tugging strands of my hair through the holes in the plastic cap on my head while I try to distract myself from the exquisite pain by eating the filling of a creme egg with a teaspoon.

If I glance up I can see Lorraine's reflection in the mirror. (I don't like to look at my own.) Lorraine is my best friend and next-door neighbour. She's thirty-seven, two years younger than me. She's tall and she has the kind of figure Kate Moss would envy. Her blonde hair waves softly down to her shoulders, and she has green or blue eyes, depending on which pair of contact lenses she is wearing. Today they are blue. Am I jealous? *Can fish swim?*

'Haven't you finished yet?' I mutter through a mouth-ful of sickly-sweet fondant.

'Oh Juliet, I've hardly started.'

It is hot in Lorraine's kitchen, but chilly outside. The kitchen is what *Changing Rooms* would term 'contemporary eclectic'. Rustic oak units are teamed with pale blue paint and contrasting flushes of pink tiles. It's as hideous as it sounds, and I've been trying to persuade Lorraine to go 1970s' funk on the basis that it couldn't be any worse.

There is a photo of the current season's Crystal Palace football team on the cork board beside the kitchen door. Next to it is a crudely drawn picture: Mummy and Daddy with big heads and skinny limbs and no bodies. It is signed with a scribble, but there is no doubting the artist. Tyler is Lorraine's three-year-old daughter, and her drawing is more realistic, more recognisable than anything my own daughter Emily can do, yet Tyler and Emily are the same age, almost twins, having been born within half an hour of each other on the same day. Not that I'm a particularly competitive mother. Emily does have other gifts, although I have to confess as I suck on my spoon that I can't think of any offhand.

There is a second photograph pinned to the board. It is identical to the one that hangs resplendent in a gilt frame in the sitting room, but much smaller, and it's of Lorraine and Joe on their wedding day. When I first met Joe I assumed that because he worked in computers he had to be a bit of a nerd, but he isn't like that at all. Joe has sandy hair, brown eyes and a grin more wicked than Robbie Williams's.

In the photo Lorraine and Joe stand side by side against a backdrop of blurred fountains and autumn leaves at some country hotel. Joe, dressed in a dark morning suit and blue bow tie, has his arm around Lorraine. Lorraine, boasting a fantastic tan and even more fantastic cleavage, clutches a bouquet of white roses. The happy couple are both smiling. I haven't seen them smile like that for a while – at least, not in each other's company.

I take another scraping of fondant. I shouldn't really – I'm nine stone one before breakfast and without my dressing-gown, and I'm not as tall as Lorraine, only five foot two. Creme eggs have never sat well on my thighs.

Lorraine takes another tug. I wince.

'You have done this before, haven't you?' I ask nervously.

Lorraine pauses. 'Stop fussing, Juliet. Have another egg.'

'I'm still eating this one, thanks.' I place the spoon on the towel in my lap, and begin to peel the wrapper from the chocolate that is left. It is the first time I've let Lorraine near my hair since last summer, when she cut it too short around my ears which stick out a fraction too much to be considered one of my more attractive features. When she offered to colour it for me, I accepted because she had recently attended a day course on colouring for aspiring hair and beauty therapists, and we had just shared the dregs of a bottle of white rum from her understairs cupboard.

Lorraine takes two more tugs, pulling my eyebrows halfway up my forehead. 'That's the last one. Now I can do the best bit – the colours.'

'Colours?' I say, panicking. 'I thought you said one colour.'

'No, two. Copper and Honey Gold to complement your natural shade.'

My hair is brown. Some call it mousy brown, but I have never seen a mouse this colour.

'Does this hide grey?' I ask as Lorraine shifts to the worktop beside the sink. She slips a plastic apron over her white coat, and begins pouring and mixing potions in dishes with coloured spatulas, like some kind of witch. I hope she's better with the instructions on the boxes than she is with Jamie Oliver. She has some certificates, and she has all the gear, including a couch in the spare room out the back. She and Joe have extended. We – that's me and my husband Andy – haven't.

Lorraine and I live in adjacent houses in an Edwardian terrace in Ross Road, South Norwood. Before we moved here nine years ago, the name Norwood conjured up pictures of a pretty stone church with a mossy porch, and acres of beechwood, friendly local people who stop to exchange benign gossip, and a single shop selling everything from greengage jam to lottery tickets. Then Andy showed me where it was, on page 124 of the *London A–Z*.

Was I disappointed? Not really. This area has a buzz

about it, people moving in and out. I remember think-ing, this is the kind of place where anything could happen.

We're within shouting distance of the football ground, and we were so busy dashing about that we lived next door to Lorraine and Joe for five years without doing more than give a little wave when we put the bins out. That was when Andy had bought the business – a secondhand-car dealership on the Whitehorse Road that was going for a song. We soon found out why. The owner appeared very successful, selling to the luxury end of the market in what might in retrospect be considered a rundown area. However, it turned out he had a sideline laundering drugs money. He's banged up in Belmarsh now.

I recall walking across the forecourt for the first time. Andy was pushing Jamie's buggy. We stopped at the entrance to the showroom where I caught sight of my reflection in a broken pane of glass. My hair, run through with natural auburn highlights, was tied back, and I was wearing a cream T-shirt with a long navy skirt picked out with tiny cream flowers. I had cheekbones. I had a waist. I had a confident smile.

'Well, my gorgeous wife?' said Andy, slipping an arm around my shoulder. 'What do you think?'

I turned to face him and hesitated, detecting from his expression that he had already made up his mind. I knew how much this venture mattered to him. To us. The fulfil-ment of a dream.

'I want you to look past what you see here and imagine what we could do with it,' Andy went on.

'Knock it down?' I suggested. Andy fell silent. I elbowed him gently in the ribs. 'I'm pulling your leg. I can see it has potential.'

'Should we go for it, Jules?'

I nodded, and Andy's eyes lit up with boyish excitement.

'Welcome to Wyevale Autos,' he grinned. 'Welcome to our future.'

It was rough. No one came here to buy a car, that was for sure. The yard was full of rubbish, and the windows smashed, but we worked twenty-four hours a day, seven days a week, to turn it around. I was receptionist, book-keeper and valet then, and fulltime mum, keeping an eye on Jamie as he toddled around the showroom.

It isn't easy running your own business, as I keep telling Lorraine. She would like one of those little shops down on the Portland Road – La Bagel Queen, or the London Piercing Clinic, or the Afro-Caribbean Food Store where you can get mangoes and spiced muffins all year round. She'd like one for herself so she can rent out stand-up tanning cubicles, and employ a nail technician.

Lorraine picks up one of the boxes and peers at it, cross-eyed.

'Here we are. Yes, it'll cover grey. Hey, you didn't tell me you had grey hairs.'

'I haven't,' I lie. I have two. I plucked them out this morning – one from my left eyebrow and one from above my right ear. They're tough and springy, and incredibly well embedded in my scalp.

'Why did you ask then?'

'For the future,' I say, picking off the last of the creme egg wrapper. My pulse quickens slightly. What will the future bring? Two days ago, the future was calm and monochrome, like the surface of South Norwood Lake on a quiet day.

My eyes return to Tyler's picture of Mummy and Daddy, and I am torn between telling Lorraine about Joe, and not telling her. I tell her everything, you see – apart from about the grey hairs – yet I don't know how she will react to this. I mean, should you tell your best friend that her husband has the hots for you? Should you risk breaking up a happy home, and a beautiful friendship? If I keep it to myself it will be like keeping Joe's dirty little secret. It will make me feel guilty, as if I have taken pity on him. He said he would die if I wouldn't let him make love to me, but you don't die if you don't have sex, do you?

Look at me and Andy. We'd be six foot under if that was the case. Anyway, Lorraine and I have always promised each other that if we found out that our men were playing away, not watching footie or drinking down at the Portmanor, then we would tell each other.

What can I tell her? As usual, I open my mouth before

the words have unscrambled in my brain but, before I can make a mess of things, I am interrupted by the sight of my son, Jamie, almost falling through the kitchen doorway, closely followed by Tyler and Emily.

'Mummy! Mummy!' Jamie shouts. 'Look outside. The rabbit's playing football.'

I sigh. I had almost forgotten the children, they've been so quiet playing upstairs. It's the week after Easter, so Jamie's not at school. My son is six, and he is the spit of his father, even down to the way he speaks with a strong South London accent. Andy is his father, in case you're wondering. I've been immaculately monogamous since I met him. I had thought that that was my natural, instinctive state, but the events of the past couple of days have made me wonder. Jamie is quite tall for his age, and an excitable temperament lurks behind his serious blue eyes. He's wearing combat trousers, a lime green T-shirt, and socks with footballs on them.

'Mummy!' Emily follows. She has dark hair like Jamie. She wears dungarees over a pink shirt, and a shiny bangle around one chubby wrist. She lives life like a rollercoaster. One minute she can be laughing fit to burst, yet in the time it takes a cloud to block the sun, she can be writhing on the pavement in the middle of the High Street, sobbing and screaming that she hates me.

I feel a restraining tug on my hair.

'Look!' Tyler wriggles between Emily and Jamie –

she worships him. Tyler is small and delicate. She has big brown eyes, pretty blonde ringlets, and dimpled cheeks. She also has asthma which is why the rabbit lives outside and why Lorraine has laminate flooring throughout the house.

The three children eye me suspiciously.

'You look like an alien.' Jamie grins, revealing the gap where one of his top teeth has fallen out.

'Why are you wearing that funny hat?' says Emily.

'Because Lorraine's doing my hair.' I stand up quickly so I can see out of the window, and the spoon in my lap clatters to the floor.

'What are you eating?' Jamie asks.

'Nothing. Where's this rabbit?'

'He not a rabbit. He Ronnie,' Tyler announces, pronouncing the Rs as Ws. Lorraine picks Tyler up and sits her on the worktop so she can see.

'I can't see,' wails Emily.

I feel the sticky remains of the creme egg between my fingers. I can't pick her up. I begin to giggle. Lorraine picks her up for me.

'Look at the rabbit!' says Jamie.

'No, don't,' I say.

The rabbit, grey and white, is on the lawn alongside the daffodils, and it's doing something I can't find the words to describe to a football. I bite my lip.

'What's he doing, Mummy?' says Jamie, frowning as he peers over the worktop.

Lorraine laughs out loud. 'He's shagging the football,' she says.

'What's shagging?' asks Jamie.

'It's a football term – ask your father,' I say quickly.

'That's right. He's playing football,' says Lorraine. 'He's scoring goals, in a manner of speaking. Now, off you go and play.'

'There's nothing to play with. I'm bored,' says Jamie.

'Hasn't Tyler got a new dolls-house?' I say.

'That's girls' stuff.'

'You brought your Lego.' I know he did because I had to carry it thirty-two steps down to the pavement and thirty-three steps back up to Lorraine's house this morning. 'You can show the girls your Jedi Starfighter.'

Lorraine and I listen for the children to climb the stairs out of earshot. Lorraine grins at me.

'It's spring,' she explains. 'Joe said Ronnie was frustrated, so I should put a ball out for him, give him something to relate to.'

'You could at least have put a pair of ears on it. Can't you speak to the vet and have him neutered or something?'

'Who – Joe?' Lorraine chuckles. 'I should have thought of that before.'

I don't want to talk about Joe right now. Lorraine doesn't know what she is saying, but to me, it's too close to the truth.

'I must buy some more of those Thomas the Tank

Engine vitamins for Jamie,' I say, licking chocolate from my fingers.

'I thought he was looking pale again,' says Lorraine, directing me back to my seat. 'Did you take him to the doctor?'

I shake my head. Jamie has been looking tired recently, yet I've put it down to school, and Beavers and swimming. I should have called the doctor to make an appointment for him, but I've had so much on my mind lately, and each time I'm about to pick up the phone, something else comes along to distract me. Emily starts crying because she can't find her doll, or she's got herself stuck on the kitchen worktop trying to pinch a breadstick when I've already told her she can't have one because she'll spoil her lunch.

Not only do I feel guilty about not taking Jamie to the doctor, but I also feel guilty that I haven't been able to bring myself to tell Lorraine about Joe. Two days have passed since he propositioned me, two days since the party I had for my thirty-ninth birthday.

It wasn't exactly a party, just Lorraine and Joe and Tyler who was in bed in Emily's room upstairs so they didn't have to find a babysitter. They found their last one asleep in their bed when they came home. She was alone, but dressed only in her underwear. They gave her a second chance, but the next morning Lorraine found a girl's top in the tumble-dryer, and three empty wine bottles in the bin. She was nineteen, very pretty, and Joe said he offered to have her round to babysit him. I thought he was joking, but now I'm not so sure.

Lorraine begins to dab colour from her dishes onto my hair. I can tell from her frown that she is concentrating and this wouldn't be a good time to talk. I don't want to end up Honey Gold all over.

We were having a takeaway – Chinese with melt-in-the-mouth prawn crackers and crispy fried seaweed – and wine, of course. Lorraine followed me into the kitchen.

'Did you find it? Your wedding ring?'

'Shhh,' I warned.

'Have you told Andy yet?'

I shook my head.

'You said you were going to. Hasn't he noticed it's missing?'

'He doesn't notice anything much any more,' I said glumly as I fetched plates down from the shelf. 'The wife's body, or the bodywork of some old BMW? To Andy, there's no contest.'

'He'll notice you when I've coloured your hair next week,' said Lorraine.

'For all the right reasons, I hope.'

'I could wax your eyebrows too, if you like.'

'No, thanks. The wineglasses are in the dishwasher.' We returned to the sitting room where Andy and Joe, surrounded by four-packs of lager, were unwrapping foil dishes on the coffee table and sniffing at the contents, trying to distinguish king prawn from pork chop suey. I parked the plates on the floor and crashed onto the sofa, watching Lorraine sort out the wine and the glasses.

There were birthday cards on the mantelpiece – a drawing of a cat that looks like it might have been run over from Emily, and a family card from Andy with a picture of a woman with wrinkles. There was a card from my sister that read, *Almost 40*, and one of a sailing scene from my parents. I want to burn them all, along with my presents, apart from the chocolates I had from the children.

Andy bought me a watch which only reminds me of how time is passing. Lorraine gave me homemade vouchers for some of her beauty treatments which make me feel even more of a dog than I already am. I had more vouchers from my parents because they don't know me well enough any more to be sure of my likes and dislikes, and a copy of Delia from my mother-in-law which is the one we gave her for Christmas – the splash of coffee which I dropped on the flyleaf while I was wrapping it up is still there.

'You're the king prawn chop suey, aren't you, Jules?' said Andy, handing me a plate of steaming noodles.

'Am I?'

'They've given us three bags of prawn crackers. I asked for four,' Joe complained. 'Where's the crispy duck? Can't anyone get anything right nowadays?'

'Have some wine,' said Lorraine, handing Joe a glass. I noticed how he pushed it away sharply so that the wine slopped over the rim.

'You know I prefer lager,' he said quietly, and with that an atmosphere of discord descended upon my birthday party. Lorraine sat on the sofa beside me, looking gorgeous in a shimmering green top and black trousers. And there I was in a black sleeveless number and my slippers because I forgot to change into my shoes. Andy remained on the floor with Joe.

Andy's lucky. He's gone before me, passed the milestone of forty without the need for Prozac or counselling, almost without noticing a couple of years ago.

He's changed physically since the photo that sits slightly askew in its frame on the low bookcase behind the television was taken, but he's coped with it. David, Andy's brother – not the professional photographer Andy would have had if he'd married the woman his mother wanted him to – took the photo. Andy, with his hair gelled back, and muscular shoulders threatening to burst from his suit, stands beside a slim woman dressed in a red jacket, and holding a teddy bear. From the way she is smiling, you'd guess that Andy is pinching her bottom. In fact, I know he is because that woman is me on my wedding day which seems a very long time ago.

Most of Andy's hair has gone from his head now, and seems to have migrated to his chest and back. His features have rounded and softened with age, too many calories and not enough exercise. He plays football as a veteran, and veterans don't chase all round the pitch. They prefer to stand in one place, and pass the ball to each other.

Tonight he was wearing chinos and a soft blue shirt, in contrast to Joe, who was wearing a red and blue Crystal Palace shirt, and jeans with a hole in the knee.

'So what's it like to be thirty-nine, Juliet?' Joe said suddenly. 'Happy Birthday, by the way.'

'Er, thanks,' I said, taken aback that he wasn't asking me for my opinion on last Saturday's game.

'You know, you don't look thirty-nine,' he persisted. 'She doesn't, does she, Andy?'

'Juliet has good skin,' observed Lorraine.

I noticed Andy didn't comment. He had a lot on his mind. He always has a lot on his mind. In fact, I was surprised he'd found time to mark my birthday. If he's not on the forecourt with his cars, he's in the office, or chasing off after cheap deals. I shouldn't grumble, but sometimes I feel terribly neglected. Maybe Andy would prefer me to be a car, a nice little runaround he could park up when it wasn't needed. Sometimes I feel like a car – not some stream-lined sporty number, but a cut and shut. Sometimes I feel as if I'm not really married.

I cast an envious look towards Lorraine. I'm sure she and Joe have a better relationship than we do. I know they make love more often – she told me.

There was a strange noise from upstairs. Silence. Then uproar. Joe reached for a can of lager. Andy sat immobile while a red globule of sweet and sour trickled down his chin. Lorraine and I rushed upstairs. One of the children was screaming. I groped for the switch in the girls' room, and turned on the light.

'Mummy!' Emily cried. 'Tyler's been sick.'

Tyler was on the top bunk, hanging over the edge.

'Mummy, she's been sick on my head.'

There was chaos, during which I found myself questioning the wisdom of buying bunkbeds for prospective sleepovers.

'I'm sorry,' groaned Lorraine.

'Must have been those sherbert-filled saucers,' I said. I'd gone into the newsagent's to buy a newspaper, and come out with four packets of sweets. I don't eat them myself (liar) so I gave them to the children.

'It's pink sick,' shrieked Emily. She wanted a hug, but she had strings of vomit in her hair, and hugging wasn't an appetising prospect. Lorraine called down for more wine, as we stripped the beds and bathed the girls, and Jamie, who joined in.

'Our dinner will be cold,' I observed as I returned from Jamie's room where I had tucked him up in bed.

'We can put it in the microwave,' said Lorraine.

'I'm not hungry any more,' I said, pouring more wine into the glasses that we'd left on the landing while Lorraine gave Tyler a goodnight kiss.

'See you in a minute,' I called, and I carried the dirty sheets and pyjamas downstairs. Passing the sitting-room door, I noticed Andy and Joe were engaged in conversation – football or Kylie, I guessed – and mine and Lorraine's dinners were still on the coffee table where we'd left them, congealing masses of monosodium glutamate and glue. In the kitchen, I began to stuff the sheets into the washing machine. I was aware of the click of a door behind me, and the sound of breathing. As I rummaged about for a tablet to go in the net, I felt the pressure of a hand on my waist, and a dry desert heat on the back of my neck. Andy? My heart quickened until I realised I could smell aftershave, and it was the wrong one. It was Joe.

Instinctively, I did the housewifely thing, and threw net and tablet into the drum and slammed the door. As I straightened, I turned to face him. Joe was pushing me back. My fingers searched for the button for the correct programme. 40C. Deep fill. The machine gave a shudder. I heard a valve snap open.

'Joe, what are you doing?' I hissed over the sound of running water.

'I want you,' he muttered. He stared at me, his pupils dark and dilated, the muscle in his cheek tautening and relaxing. I stared back in disbelief. 'Please . . .' Joe went on. 'I'll die if you won't let me make love to you.'

'I d-didn't realise,' I stammered. What about Lorraine? What about Andy? What about me? Joe might be

17

goodlooking, but I didn't fancy him, certainly not enough to save his life. The drum turned. Wet sheets slapped about behind us.

'You don't realise what a bloody attractive woman you are, Juliet. You drive me mad when you pretend you don't notice me.'

'But I'm not pretending.'

'Please, Juliet. We've been friends for a long time.'

'I don't sleep with my friends,' I protested. I thought I could hear footsteps. 'Someone's coming,' I said, pushing Joe away.

'It could be you . . . and me,' he said plaintively, but I was hardly listening. My eyes were fixed on the opening door, and my heart was jumping about all over the place, but it wasn't Lorraine about to yell and scream at me for jumping on her husband. It was Andy.

'Juliet's been having a spot of bother with the machine,' Joe said. 'You should buy her a new one.'

'I'm not made of money,' Andy said. 'It's going now, isn't it?'

I nodded furiously, my face burning even though I wasn't the guilty one. What did Andy see when he walked in that door? Apparently just Joe helping me start the washing machine in a friendly sort of way, because he strolled over to the fridge, opened the door and pulled out more lager. As I made to follow him back out of the kitchen, I heard Joe's low whisper.

'Don't let me die, Juliet.'

Later Andy and I stood on our doorstep, me with my arms folded, Andy with one arm loosely around my shoulders, and we watched Joe and Lorraine make their way home. Joe jumped and Lorraine stumbled in her high-heeled boots over the mini white picket fence the people before us had put between our precipitous gardens. It doesn't do anything except mark the line between two territories. It is symbolic perhaps of the line that has to exist between two married couples if they are to remain friends. Funny how it has always been Joe who wants to take the picket fence down . . .

A car drove by, accelerating up the hill between rows of parked vehicles, their roofs shiny in the moonlight. The brightest was the white van that belongs to a plumber based in Anerley. I think he's having an affair with a girl in one of the flats further down the road. The trees opposite seemed to ripple and bend, but it wasn't just the wine . . . I leaned into Andy, feeling the warmth from his body flooding through mine. My chest tightened, and the unfamiliar sensation of desire flickered deep in my belly like an ember in a dying fire. What was happening to me? Whatever it was, I welcomed it, and I turned to Andy and whispered, 'Shall we go to bed?'

It was all right in principle, but not such a good idea in practice. Upstairs, I made sure all the lights were off before I undressed, and settled back on the bed. Andy arrived, clambering on top of me. He gave a little gasp while I reminded myself that I must take the sausages out of the freezer first thing tomorrow. He gasped again, and it was all over before I could decide whether to fantasise over Colin Firth, or Leonardo DiCaprio. (Yes, it turned out that, like me, Lorraine saw *Titanic* four times when it first came out. She gave me the video for Christmas a couple of years ago.)

'That was wonderful, darling,' Andy sighed as he pulled the duvet up over our shoulders.

'You were great,' I said, unmoved. How can I tell Andy that I don't feel the same way about him as I used to? How can I begin to explain when I don't understand myself how we have allowed the jar of hot spice that was our marriage to be pushed into the back of a cupboard behind the everyday tins of chopped tomatoes and baked beans?

'I don't know why we don't do it more often.'

'Mm,' I said. Maybe this was a good time to mention the fact that I had been unable to find my wedding ring for the past few days. 'Andy?' He was lying alongside me, facing away. I rubbed at his back, catching curly hairs between my fingers, but the only response was a deep, lager-induced snore. Restless, I got up to check on the children. It wasn't the drink, but I knocked into the shelving unit in Emily's room, waking the Furby which belched and yawned. Andy bought it for Jamie ages ago, when he was far too young to appreciate it.

'Play with me,' the Furby begged. Chirpy-Chi, the interactive plastic bird, joined in with the theme to Beethoven's Ninth Symphony (I only know that because

I read the instruction leaflet that came with it). I held my palm over the Furby's eyes until it fell asleep again. If only children were that easy.

Emily was breathing lightly with her eyes closed and a smile on her face. Tyler was asleep too, clutching a damp teddy bear. The air around them smelled faintly of sherbert and sick. I love the children, all of them, including Tyler who is like a cousin to my two. I am proud of them, but not so proud of myself.

Standing in the dark, which wasn't strictly dark because there was light coming through the chink in the curtains – the sky glows orange all night here – I wondered what I was doing here. One more year and I would be forty, and I would never have had that great romance, like Kate and Leonardo on that ship . . .

'Fancy a coffee?'

I jump in my seat. I'm back in Lorraine's kitchen in the bright light of day. I must have been dozing. Lorraine is staring at me.

'You've hardly said a word this morning, Juliet. Everything all right between you and Andy?'

'He's fine, same as usual.' I must tell Lorraine about the party. I must tell her about Joe, but how? 'Would you ever consider having an affair?' I ask.

'Me? What brought this on?'

'I was thinking about love and marriage and constancy. Did you know psychiatrists say true love lasts three and a half years?'

'You've been watching too much of *This Morning*,' Lorraine chuckles as she peels the cap from my head, moves over to drop it in the sink, and returns to massage my scalp. 'Bit deep, isn't it? Anyway, when I married Joe, I meant every word of those vows. Till death and all that.'

'Oh? So did I – when I married Andy – but people change, don't they?'

'You're not thinking?'

My neck grows hot. 'I love Andy,' I say, 'but I'm not *in* love with him. He's comforting, like a mug of hot chocolate. He's safe.'

'So is Joe.'

I don't think I can do this to Lorraine. I don't think I can bring myself to tell her, so I launch into, 'Have I told you about the man I saw in the newsagent's?'

'Several times,' Lorraine says, picking up the mirror and bringing it closer so I can see the fine lines that splay from the corners of my eyes and those that rise vertically from my upper lip. I guess in the low voltage light in the newsagent's the man who was watching me couldn't see them.

I could see him. Every detail, from the rivets on his dark Levi 501s to the tiny red logo on the breast of his long-sleeved black top. Lustrous blue-black hair, falling in waves from a central parting to just above his shoulders. Hypnotic hazel eyes. A freckle like a beauty spot to the left of a mouth that curved slowly into the sexiest of smiles. A much younger and more charismatic version of Antonio Banderas, whose photo on the cover of a film review magazine had held me temporarily spellbound.

I glanced over my shoulder to see who he was looking at – another woman, his girlfriend, even a man – but there was no one else in the shop, apart from Jimmy, the owner, who was out the back. He wasn't looking at himself in the CCTV camera either. My heart turned over and my knees went weak. He was gazing at me in an admiring, hungry way.

He tucked a newspaper under his arm before squeezing past me in the aisle, and walking out to the pavement where I half-expected him to vault onto a jet-black horse and gallop away like Zorro.

'I forgot what I went in for,' I complain.

'I shouldn't get too excited,' says Lorraine, tweaking my fringe. Although it's still damp, I can see that it's striped Copper and Honey Gold, making me look like some bizarre strain of tiger. 'I expect you reminded him of his mother.'

Chapter Two

Did I really remind the stranger of his mother? I hope not, but if I did, I can only console myself with the thought that I cannot possibly remind Andy of his.

I glance towards the postcard beside me on the cork board in the kitchen; it's pinned on top of a history of failed lottery tickets that I should really sort through and throw away. The card has a picture of a château on it, a fairytale palace that appears to be floating on water. A place of escape, but there is no escape from the demands of family life, for it reminds me of Andy's mother who sent it. I am not, as you will see, overly fond of my mother-in-law, Pammy; I call her the Rhino as a reference to her remarkably thick skin. She is impervious to irony or rancour, even to wit.

'Where's my shirt?' I hear Andy yelling from upstairs.

'In the wardrobe!' I yell back. It's been one of those mornings. I've given emergency resuscitation to the

Prayer plant on the kitchen windowsill, repaired My First Barbie's bikini with sticky tape (I knew there was a reason for watching *Blue Peter* all those years ago) and assembled a Lego football pitch without the instructions, all before seven o'clock.

Andy turns up in the kitchen a few minutes later, fastening a blue silk tie, a shade darker than the elusive shirt.

'Found one in the wardrobe,' he grunts, tucking the end of his tie inside the waistband of his dark grey trousers.

I refrain from saying, Told you so.

'I'm off then,' he says.

'Have you had breakfast?'

'You forgot to buy any more marmalade.'

'I'll drop everything and go and get you some right now,' I say.

'No need to do that, Jules,' Andy says, oblivious like his mother to irony, and oblivious too, it seems, to my appearance. He hasn't mentioned my tiger stripes, but then I didn't have my hair coloured for him, or the errant stranger who seemed to have mistaken Jimmy's newsagent's for the Mexican desert, and certainly not to make an impression on Joe. I did it for myself. Okay, I wasn't sure about the stripes at first, but now I like them. I feel different, like a tigress.

'I'm out today,' Andy goes on. 'Car auction in Bristol. You and Gayle can hold the fort. Oh, by the way, Steve's in this morning.'

26

'Steve?'

'The new mechanic.'

Andy has taken out a loan to do up part of the garage into a servicing and MOT centre. He hopes it will increase turnover, and it means he can buy in cheaper cars and have someone get them running without calling on Kevin, an ex-mate who runs his own garage in Addiscombe. Andy and Kevin fell out over some clocked cars and haven't spoken since.

'Daddy, what's shagging?' says Jamie, peering round the door. 'Mum said you'd tell me about it.'

Andy grins. I turn away, trying not to smile myself.

'Lorraine says it's scoring goals,' Jamie persists.

'Come on, Jamie. Daddy's in a hurry,' I say. 'We'll talk about it later.'

'I'll ask Miss Trays.'

'No, no, don't do that,' I say quickly. Miss Trays is Jamie's teacher at the primary school, and she looks about ten, far too young to know about shagging yet.

'Miss Trays knows everything about everything in the whole wide world.'

'No one knows everything about everything,' Andy says. 'Miss Trays knows about dinosaurs and . . .' He hesitates.

'And partitioning and apostrophes,' Jamie helps him out.

Andy pats our growing genius on the head, ruffles his number four haircut with the little piece of fringe left so

27

it can be stuck up or down with gel, and I follow them into the hall where I find Emily trying to wipe something brown off the cream carpet with a roll of toilet paper.

'What are you doing?'

'Milkshake fell down,' she says.

'You dropped it.'

'It fell.'

'Oh, let me do it,' and I glide back into the kitchen to fetch a battery of cloths and stain removers.

'Bye, babe,' Andy calls from the front door.

'Have you got your sandwiches?'

'I'll pick something up.'

'So, why did I bother? Slaving over a cold chicken last night when I could have been watching *EastEnders*?'

'Because you love me!'

'Cheeky so and so!' That's it. Swan off while I get the children ready, remember to ring the doctor to make an appointment for Jamie, although he seems much better, get myself ready for work, and plan dinner for tonight.

A chill runs down the back of my neck. Dinner tonight?

'Andy, you're not going to be late tonight,' I shout through to the hall.

'Is that a question or an order, Jules?'

'Your mother's coming for tea.'

'All right. I'll be there.'

'Don't you dare be late!' I scream, but Andy is on his way, trotting like a mountain goat down the steps to the

28

pavement where he zaps a gleaming black Mercedes
Coupé with a key. It is his car. It has a cardboard cut-out
of a Crystal Palace strip hanging in the rear windscreen.

I imagine Andy not turning up until late, and me
launching myself from the top of the steps and squash-
ing him flat. Death by chocolate, indirectly.

'Mummy, it's half past eight.' Jamie interrupts my
plan for revenge. 'We'll be late.' I turn to find him with
his book folder in one hand, rucksack on his back and
his shoes on with the Velcro straps fastened down. 'Aren't
you even dressed yet?'

Half past eight? Forget the stain. Forget that Emily's
dungarees are plastered with milkshake. I dash up to the
bedroom and grab what comes to hand.

One bra, size 34C. White pants with misleading CUTE
logo on the front. Blue Teflon blouse from a couple of
springs ago. Black trousers. Brown boots. I know, I'm
in a hurry.

'Mum, it's twenty-five to nine,' Jamie yells.

It's amazing what you can do in four and a half
minutes. By twenty to, we're in my car, a three-door
F-reg Peugeot 206. It's off-white, almost the same shade
as the hall carpet. You'd have thought that being a secondhand-car salesman, Andy might have found me a decent
car. I did have one once, a red Ford Fiesta, but Andy
sold it to Joe within five minutes of meeting him at the
Mayday, the hospital where Tyler and Emily were born.

'I need a wee.'

It's Emily.

'We're nearly at Mary's. Can't you hang on?'

'I need a wee-wee. I need one NOW!'

'Emily needs a wee-wee,' Jamie joins in chanting, but we're stuck in a traffic jam along Grange Road.

'You'll have to wait, darling,' I say through gritted teeth as a double decker cuts me up at the traffic lights, and pulls tight in front so I am sitting very close to the advert stuck to its rear end. It shows a desert island, no more than a few paces across, which would make the perfect destination for getting away from it all – at least for the next few years until the carbon dioxide blasting out from all these combustion engines that surround us raises the temperature a couple more degrees, and sea-levels a few more inches.

I wish I was there lying on the beach in the shade of the single palm tree, not with Andy and the kids, but with the gorgeous stranger. I close my eyes. I can hear water lapping at the sand, I can smell coconut oil trickling over the hot skin between my breasts, I can see the stranger's mouth, his lips parted slightly as he leans down to kiss me . . .

Someone hoots. Road rage. The traffic lights are green.

'Who's that man waving at you?' Jamie asks.

'I don't know, do I?' I mutter, avoiding the withering gaze of the driver alongside me who's trying to squeeze into the same lane as I am. I release the brake, but miss the change, and go through on red.

'Mummy, you were naughty,' says Jamie. 'The police will come and put you in prison.'

'They'll have to catch me first,' I say, turning the radio on loud as I put my foot down. Virgin is playing the B52s' 'Love Shack' from a long time ago. I glance at Emily in the rearview mirror. She's looking out of the window, so I guess she's either forgotten about needing a wee, or she didn't want one in the first place.

Outside school, we're too late to find a parking place so I drop Jamie off, and watch him skipping through the school gates without a backward glance. Emily isn't so happy. She bursts into tears and wails that she doesn't want to go to Mary's today.

'You always go to Mary's when Mummy goes to work,' I say firmly. My voice is steady, but my palms are beginning to slip on the steering wheel. Divert. Do not draw attention. 'Can you see that lady over there? She's taking her sausage dog for a walk.'

'Not going to Mary's.'

'It's a cute little dog, all brown and hairy,' I say hopefully, turning into the road where Ms Mary Bacon lives. It's a respectable area, and she lives in a downstairs maisonette with a tiny garden, and a parade of shops across the road.

'Sausages are not hairy like that dog! I not going to Mary's!' Emily starts to shout and scream. I haul her out of her carseat, pick her up and transfer her to Mary's doorstep. She's like a windmill in a hurricane, arms and

legs whirling in all directions and at great speed. Mary
– we have only just reached first-name terms – comes
to the door, looks pityingly at me, and grabs my daughter who kicks and screams.

The children have been coming here for six weeks.
(Our last childminder had a nervous breakdown.) Mary
seems very capable. She wears the uniform of a professional childminder – brightly coloured sweaters with
pictures of Winnie the Pooh on the front, and navy
leggings that bag at the knee because of all the crawl-
ing about on the floor that childcare involves.

Mary's about fifty, and five foot six. She has big
breasts, broad shoulders, and a beer belly, although I'm
sure she doesn't drink, not when she's minding the children. Sometimes her face bears the shadow of a moustache. Sometimes it doesn't.

I don't know why Emily has to kick up quite such a
fuss about coming here. When Andy and I came to meet
Mary before we made a decision, we were impressed.

Mary possesses two working stairgates even though
she has no stairs. She has ethnic minority toys like
Chinese bowls and chopsticks, and her home looks very
clean and smells of Febreze. She said she would collect
Jamie from school along with a couple of other children,
and give them tea from the menu she showed us – broc-
coli lasagne, macaroni cheese made with organic yoghurt,
and sugar-free snacks. As she was convenient, living
near the school and the nursery we have Emily's name

down for, we signed up and paid one month's fees in advance.

'Emily'll be fine, Juliet,' Mary says. Her voice is deep and reverberates like a baritone's as Emily twirls about in one of her big hands. 'Same as usual, is it? And Jamie?'

'Yes, thanks, Mary. I'll see you at six.' I return to the car with Emily's paddy fading into the distance. Suddenly, there is peace, apart from the sound of the traffic, and I'm free to go to work. I catch my reflection in the rearview mirror. I haven't brushed my hair.

Although my appearance leaves much to be desired, I feel a sense of pride as I drive up to work. *Wyevale Autos, Buyers and Sellers of Quality Used Cars. Servicing and Repairs to All Makes, BMWs a Speciality.* I drive up past the side of the building, a relic from the 1960s, rendered white with fine cracks running across it like the threadveins on my thighs. I park in the yard opposite the workshop, and return on foot to the forecourt where Larry is playing a hose on a Toyota Corolla five-door hatchback in metallic red.

Larry waves. 'Morning, Mrs Wyevale.'

I don't know much about Larry, except that he's over sixty, and he rolls his own cigarettes. He wears jeans and a cap, and has a complexion the texture of orange peel. I don't know his full name or where he lives, but it doesn't matter. I pay him weekly, cash in hand.

There are six more cars on the forecourt, sparkling in

the sunlight – a high-mileage Vauxhall Vectra, a Volvo and four BMWs. (I used to think a marque was something you had to remove from your whites.) The black BMW 3 Series (1990) two-door convertible/cabriolet with CD player, ABS brakes, alloy wheels, central locking, alarm and power steering is sold, awaiting collection.

Inside the showroom, beyond a Jag and another BMW, I find Gayle, receptionist and occasional salesperson, at her desk.

'Hi, Juliet,' Gayle says brightly, slamming the phone down much too quickly for my liking.

'Who was that?'

'Oh, just someone making an enquiry.'

'About what?'

Gayle gazes at me, rather blankly. It isn't a difficult question, is it? I almost find myself asking her if she would like to phone a friend, but I suspect that is what she has been doing already. I must remember to check the bill.

Gayle is West Indian, in her thirties, very tall, and voluptuous. She dresses well in up-to-the-minute fitted suits and high heels, and I imagine she's one of those women who sleeps with her storecards under her pillow. She wears designer glasses with bronze rims for close work only, and braids her long hair, and she pities me because she has none of the attachments – husband, kids, business – that I have, whereas I believe it is she who is to be pitied. Whatever, we will never agree on anything.

Gayle keeps a photo of her current boyfriend, a fitness instructor, along with a pair of foam frustration bricks on her desk. On Andy's desk, which is also against the rear wall of the showroom, is a picture of me and the kids eating chips on Brighton Pier, and a bigger one of Crystal Palace FC. Between them is the door to the office where I work, and Andy closes the deals when they happen, which is becoming less frequent. The bottom is falling out of the market with people buying off the Internet and shipping in new cars from the rest of Europe. Maybe Andy is right about diversifying into servicing and MOTs, but there's no sign of the new mechanic.

I log on to the computer in the office, dig out some paperwork, and a packet of milk chocolate HobNobs from the depths of the filing cabinet. I sit down to eat, trying at the same time to settle my conscience about leaving Emily mid-paddy, and reasoning that while Mary has her three days a week, I have her the remaining four and I'm still perfectly sane. Aren't I? I eat a third biscuit, feeling the light trickle of crumbs down the front of my blouse.

A man in a helmet enters the building. He strolls around the Jag and approaches Gayle, but I get there first, eager not to let a customer leave the forecourt without a sales agreement in his hand. Sometimes I think Gayle puts buyers off. Her curvy figure and never-ending legs make them forget what they came in for.

'Can I help? My husband's out at the moment.'

The helmet comes off, revealing a pair of hazel eyes ringed with long, dark lashes and partly hidden behind a curtain of gleaming black hair. Antonio Banderas in well-worn leathers tosses his head and flicks his hair back from his face.

It's him. I gasp like a dying fish. It's the stranger. Does he recognise me? Part of me hopes that he does, part of me hopes he doesn't. He looks me up and down, taking in, no doubt, the unkempt hair, black trousers and brown boots. Recognition dawns.

'It's you,' he says softly, with an audible exhalation of breath. My own breath is stifled. I can hear strident drumming like the bass on a Black Sabbath track. It is my heartbeat.

His eyes fix mine. His lips curve into a smile.

'Hi, I'm Steve, the new mechanic.'

'Er, coffee?' I stammer.

'Thanks, Mrs Wyevale.'

'This way,' I say, directing him into the office, aware that Gayle can't keep her eyes off him either. In fact, she keeps finding excuses to interrupt.

'Phone call for you,' she says, knowing full well she can transfer the call to my desk without leaving her own. 'Not for you, Juliet. For Steve.'

Steve is straddling a chair, elbows out and resting his hands on his thighs. He has cast off his jacket, revealing a dirty white vest which shocked me at first until I remembered that this is Steve the mechanic, not Antonio the movie star.

'Who is it?' he asks quietly.

'She won't give her name. Says you'll know who it is.'

'Well, tell her I'm not here.' As Gayle closes the door behind her, Steve turns back to me. I get the impression he is trying to gather himself together, like Jamie does when he falls off his bike and tries not to cry. I feel an almost overwhelming urge to fling my arms around him and kiss him better.

'It's my ex-girlfriend,' Steve begins.

'Oh, you don't have to explain,' I cut in, wanting to spare his feelings. 'Unless you want to,' I add, because I'd like to know more about Steve and why he's ended up here at Wyevale Autos when he could be fighting bandits or taking beautiful Spanish women hostage and tying them up.

'It's all right. I can talk about it now,' Steve says, gazing towards the toe of one boot. 'She finished with me a couple of months ago, and now, because I'm doing well for myself, she wants us to get back together.'

'I don't think that's a good idea if it didn't work out the first time.' The words come out before I have time to consider whether I am the person best placed to be advising Steve about his love life.

'Oh, I'm not planning to see her again,' he says, looking up and fixing me with wide, yearning eyes. 'She's so bloody immature . . .'

I smile in spite of Steve's apparent regret. He's hardly a grown-up himself.

'Would you like a HobNob, Steve?'

Steve . . . the name lingers on my tongue as I speak his name to the pasta that I have bubbling on the hob when I am back at home after an oddly enervating day. Steve . . . The name is strong, sensual and masculine. There's no ambiguity there. Steve . . . The name that describes the demigod who looked at me and smiled a lot, who kept popping back to the office for coffee.

The water bubbles and boils over. I reach for the knob on the stove and turn down the gas. The pasta shells continue to seethe wildly in the pan.

Leonardo and Kate. Steve and Juliet? That's impossible. Nothing will happen because . . . because I am me. I am the person who never dares step out of line, never jumps the queue when returning unwanted items to Marks & Spencer after Christmas, never pushes her children forward so they can sit in the front row when Mr Hiccup, the entertainer, comes to the park in the summer. I have never considered having an extramarital fling with anyone, let alone a boy of what – twenty?

Whatever my sensible conscience is telling me, the tigress that has been awakened within me is flicking her tail and growling low in her throat. Steve isn't a boy. He's all man. There's a fearsome assurance about him, and a smouldering sexuality. My conscience fights back. What about Andy? Where is Andy anyway?

I drain the pasta.

I shan't think of Steve again . . . I shan't dwell on the smudgy fingerprints he leaves on the mugs in the office. I shan't even begin to picture the sinews of muscle that tighten and swell in his arms when he lifts his tools. (Liar.)

As I stir tomato and herb sauce into the pasta shells, the Rhino comes into the kitchen. I had almost forgotten she was here. She is sixty-two, but looks ten years younger. Petite and slim, she has contact lenses, colours her hair mahogany red, and wears masses of gold jewellery and frothy 'mother-of-the-bride' clothes. Today she is sporting a trouser suit which I can only describe as football-pitch green, with a frilly white blouse. She left the coordinating hat in the hallway.

'I see you've been putting on weight again, Juliet,' she says. 'No wedding ring . . .'

'Oh, it's not that, Pammy. I took it off to do some gardening.'

The Rhino raises one eyebrow. She has a habit of doing that, whether I'm telling the truth or not.

'You'd have been better off attending to that stain on the hall carpet, wouldn't you? I told you that colour wasn't practical for a young family.' She pauses. 'Isn't dinner ready yet, Juliet? Regular meals and regular bowels go hand in hand. Your lack of routine doesn't do the children any good at all. They must be starving.'

How can they be? Mary told me she gave them cheese

and pineapple on sticks, and organic cracker biscuits after school today.

'It's almost ready,' I say, frowning. 'Will you ask the children to sit at the table in the dining room?'

'They must wash their hands first, surely,' the Rhino sniffs.

'Oh, of course.'

'I couldn't help noticing earlier that the soap in your cloakroom appears to be growing mould.'

At this point, Lorraine would crack some joke about having green fingers, whereas I meekly offer the Rhino a drink.

'Have you any of that sherry left?'

'In the cupboard.' I nod towards the sink. The stuff the Rhino gave us is best kept with the household cleaners. Andy and I haven't touched it even for culinary purposes.

The Rhino pours herself a large one. She doesn't offer me any.

I pull out the plates – they're cold, and the garlic bread is still frozen because I forgot to switch the oven on. I spread out the plates and slap the pasta on them. I include one for Andy, cursing him for not being home yet, and for forgetting to tell me he'd employed the most beautiful mechanic in South London.

Jamie and Emily are waiting, cutlery poised, in the dining room with Granny as they call her. I plonk the plates down and fetch the salt- and pepper-pots.

'I haven't added any salt,' I say pointedly. 'It isn't good for the children.' According to the health news on teletext, salt affects your kidneys and gives you high blood pressure, but it hasn't killed the Rhino yet.

She stares at the pasta.

'I don't eat foreign food,' she says flatly.

'It's not foreign,' Jamie assures her. 'It's from Tesco's.'

The Rhino scoops up pasta on her fork and lets it fall back onto the plate. How can she say she dislikes foreign food when she came back from her holiday in Crete raving about stuffed olives and moussaka? I watch her take a mouthful. She chews very slowly, swallows without effort, and takes another.

'I hope you've remembered my allergy, Juliet,' she says.

Oh? My conscience cajoles. Confess. Apologise. There's bound to be something in the freezer. But the tigress is back, claws unsheathed and putting words into my mouth.

'Oh, yes, of course. How could I ever forget?' I sit down and pick at my food. It tastes bland, and I find myself wondering as the Rhino takes it delicately piece by piece into her mean-lipped mouth, what Steve is eating tonight and who he is eating it with.

'What's that smell?' asks Emily, holding her nose.

'It's you,' says Jamie.

'Something's burning, Juliet,' says the Rhino. 'Aren't you going to have a look?'

'I've left the gas on.' I dash out to the kitchen, switch off the hob and plunge the saucepan I'd left on it into the sink where it hisses and spits. When I turn away from inspecting the black gritty remains in the bottom, I realise Jamie, Emily and the Rhino are all at the kitchen door, watching.

'Go back inside and finish your tea,' I snap.

'Wasn't that one of the saucepans we gave you as a wedding present?' says the Rhino.

I take a quick guilt trip around the kitchen, opening the windows and the back door to air the house.

'You seem distracted, Juliet,' the Rhino accuses. 'Perhaps you're having a breakdown?' she adds hopefully.

Clutching the edge of the sink, I take several deep breaths. Can't she see I have everything under control? I am a paragon of domestic virtue, a goddess. Even goddesses are allowed to have an off day once in a while, aren't they? Once I have counted to ten – twice – I return to the dining room to sit down with the Rhino and the children.

'Daddy is going to tell me about shagging, Granny,' Jamie pipes up, having shovelled away all of his dinner.

The Rhino turns red-faced and begins to choke. I hesitate, almost willing that pasta shell to remain lodged in her windpipe but, loyal daughter-in-law that I am, I give her a good thump in the back.

'Miss Trays said shagging's a rude word,' Jamie goes

on once the Rhino has had time to compose herself. I sag forwards and rest my head on my hands. If you're going to dig yourself into a hole, you might as well dig it deep.

'I think you mean shaggy,' says Granny. 'Shaggy dogs.'

'Hairy dogs,' says Emily. 'I saw a sausage dog today. Its tummy touched the ground.'

'Like Mummy's,' says Jamie, laughing.

I scowl at him.

'I'm not very hungry now,' he says. 'Can I get down?'

I glance towards the Rhino to gauge the full extent of her disapproval.

'Surely Jamie should wait until we have all eaten,' she says.

'I don't have much time to play after school.'

The Rhino sniffs as Jamie leaves the table. Emily sniffs too. I hadn't noticed before, but they're quite similar in their characteristics and behaviour. I retire to the kitchen to make coffee and mull over the frightening prospect of Emily growing up to be just like the Rhino.

'Shouldn't the children be in bed?' the Rhino says, popping her head around the door.

'I was hoping they'd stay up till Andy came home.'

'Poor Andrew. Out so late, looking after you all. Oh, you received my cards. You didn't say.'

When she went to France, the Rhino sent us several postcards to remind us of her presence in her absence, I

43

suppose, or to gloat. Andy's younger brother, David, is the apple of her eye. He went to university to study English, and ended up in the travel agency business. It means we can all have cheap holidays, which the Rhino has taken advantage of. However, all Andy and I have managed is a couple of weeks in a wooden chalet near Land's End. Although there was damp seeping up the walls, there was no running water, and we had to fetch and fill buckets from a standpipe half a mile away. Emily was sick, and Jamie broke his arm on the swing in the on-site play area. It was an experience never to be repeated.

'Yes, thanks for the postcards,' I find myself saying. Why am I always so polite? If I had been Lorraine, I would have made some acerbic put-down. 'Jamie liked the one with the castle on it.'

'Oh, that's not a castle. That is a château.'

'I know. You wrote that it was a castle on the back.'

'That is because I assumed you wouldn't know what a château was, Juliet,' the Rhino says superiorly.

The Rhino assumes too much. For example, that because I left a crummy comprehensive at sixteen with three O-levels, I must be thick.

My eyes turn towards the knifeblock beside the hob. It's time the Rhino went home. Home is a narrowboat on a private mooring on the canal in Islington. She says it's cheap, but I know mooring fees are over £300 a month, and the boat is hideous, decorated with painted roses. She bought it after Andy's father died because she had always wanted to live on a narrowboat, and he, wisely, hadn't let her. I make sure I top up the Rhino's coffee with plenty of water straight from the cold tap so she doesn't take too long to drink it. It works. As I show her out ten minutes later, she asks me the question that has been burning on her lips since she noticed that I'm not wearing my wedding ring.

'Have you and Andrew had a falling-out?'

'We never argue,' I say adamantly. We don't. We're very polite to each other and I sometimes wonder if that's where we've been going wrong.

The Rhino arranges her mahogany curls under her hat, and says her goodbyes to Jamie and Emily. Jamie won't kiss her any more, but Emily coos and hugs her, to her smug delight.

'Oh Juliet, I believe you'll find the number for Relate in the front of the Yellow Pages. You should contact them.' The Rhino fires her parting shot. 'Unless it's already too late.'

Chapter Three

Is it already too late to save my marriage? I hope not, and I'm not just saying that to spite the Rhino. Andy fell into bed at midnight last night without even cleaning his teeth. He was out again before eight, off to work, leaving me far too much time alone for my imagination to run riot.

'You remember that man I met in the newsagent's, Lorraine?'

'Juliet, you're obsessed!'

We're on an expedition to feed the ducks in Kelsey Park. There's me, Lorraine, Emily, Tyler and Jamie because he has what he thought was an 'insect' day until I explained that it is an inset day, a day off school when the teachers go shopping.

'You'll never guess, but I've seen him again.'

'I expect he lives nearby,' Lorraine says, her voice softly condescending, 'so it's not surprising that you ran into him again.'

'It's better than that. Steve – that's his name – he's our new mechanic. It has to be more than coincidence. It's fate.'

'You should go and see my psychic.'

'No, I don't think so,' I say. 'I don't believe in all that stuff.'

'She's very accurate. She told me I'd have a baby by the time I was thirty-three, and that I'd live in a house on top of a hill.'

'Same as me. I'd call that a good guess.'

'You don't believe in fate then?' says Lorraine, her brow furrowed but not so deeply that she'd consider Botox yet.

I think of Steve, of the hunger in his eyes, of his thoughtful attentions to me like pouring the milk into my coffee and putting the lid back on the HobNobs to stop them going soggy . . . Fate or coincidence? My heart turns over.

'Do you think I've remembered everything? Bag for baby wipes, bag for purse, bread for ducks,' Lorraine recites a list as she loads the buggy beside the car, 'rain-cover in case of rain, parasol in case of sun.'

'Neither of those seem likely.' It is overcast, dry and chilly for April. Showers aren't forecast until this evening – if you believe GMTV. 'Can't you leave some of it behind? We can always come back to the car if you need anything.'

'You never know,' says Lorraine, squinting skywards

to where a lucent halo in the grey suggests the sun might be attempting an appearance after all. 'Come here, Tyler.'

'Oh, let her walk with Jamie and Emily,' I say, knowing Emily will blow up again because I didn't bring a buggy for her.

Tyler smiles, and takes Emily's hand and they run off ahead of us through the park gates.

'Be careful,' yells Lorraine, and in response, Tyler falls flat on her face, grazing her nose and elbow, which necessitates the unpacking of the first aid kit – the Savlon, the cottonwool, the hypoallergenic plasters, the arnica and then the pouring of an almost colourless orange squash to relieve the pain.

'I want a drink, Mummy,' says Emily.

'I didn't bring one,' I say.

'I want a drink.' Emily stamps her foot.

'We'll buy one later,' I say. 'You can't be thirsty – you had a drink before we left.'

'I are thirsty.' Emily sits down in the gateway, and starts to sob her heart out while another family walks past. Neglectful mother, I can see them thinking. Poor child dehydrating in front of her eyes. How can anyone ignore those pitiful cries? I try to think clearly. I try to remain disconnected and detached as explained in the booklet from the National Family and Parenting Institute about coping with tantrums that Mary Bacon thrust on me last week. How can this yowling creature belong to me?

'What do I do, Lorraine? If I reason with her, she screams. If I ignore her, she screams. If I scream at her, she screams. I can't win, can I?'

'I guess Emily can have some of Tyler's juice once Tyler's finished,' Lorraine offers from the sideline, but the offer I know is tentative as she worries about germs. In the end Tyler hands the cup to Emily who is so mad by now that she throws it down to the ground where it rolls in mud and duck poo.

'I'm so sorry,' I say, retrieving it and rubbing the spout down the sleeve of my jacket. 'Emily, that isn't a kind thing to do when Tyler is offering you some of her drink.'

'I don't want Tyler's drink. I want *my* drink . . .'

'For goodness' sake, Emily, I didn't bring it and that is that.' I begin to walk away.

'Mummy!'

'I'm not listening.'

'Mummy!'

'Come on, Jamie. Come on, Tyler. Let's go and feed the ducks.'

'Joe and I like to walk here,' says Lorraine as we wander along the path towards one of the interlinking ponds. 'Once we did it in the bushes over there by the lake.'

'You didn't!' There's a faint blush on Lorraine's cheeks. She isn't lying. 'Didn't you worry that someone would see you?'

'That's the fun of it,' Lorraine grins.

She and Joe have always been more adventurous than me and Andy. Our idea of the ultimate in lovemaking is sneaking downstairs to do it on the sofa. Don't get me wrong. We've had our moments, but I have to say that I find sex is not all it's cracked up to be. The tigress murmurs, 'But what about Steve?'

A heron is standing on one leg on the small island in the centre of the pond, and three ducks swim over to join it when we arrive. Either they have already been fed, or there's something seriously wrong with the bread. Fortunately, a squirrel and a couple of pigeons do the honours.

'I love Kelsey Park,' says Lorraine, apparently recalling moments of passion among the laurels.

We always go to Kelsey Park. Forget Grangewood Rec right on our doorstep – that's too dirty and attracts the wrong kind of people. Forget South Norwood Lake – it's too small.

I guess Kelsey Park reminds Lorraine not only of passionate times with Joe, but of her youth as she lived in Beckenham when she was a kid. Her parents still live there. Her mother, Ruth, runs a nursing home for the elderly with Lorraine's stepfather, Ron. They won't retire, can't afford to. Lorraine hopes to move back one day. In her opinion, Beckenham is a superior address. Kent is Home Counties, not London.

As for me, I spent my childhood in Hounslow. I

remember lying on my back on the grass watching the planes flying in to Heathrow, plane after plane after plane. The views from Beaulieu Heights, the Crystal Palace mast and the wooded hills towards Croydon are my countryside now. I have no desire to leave South Norwood – unless someone offers me a thatched cottage in the New Forest.

Emily follows us eventually, as we're about to disappear out of sight around the next corner.

'Mum, Emily's got mud on her trousers,' Jamie points out, 'and her hands.'

It's not mud, it's duck poo, and we take Emily to the toilets and wipe her down as best we can. Good old Lorraine lends me a set of spare clothing she's brought for Tyler. It's OshKosh, a floral dress with pink socks trimmed with the same material as the dress. Emily is impressed.

Crisis over, Emily, Jamie and I stroll along hand in hand. Tyler is back in the buggy. Why does Lorraine treat her like a baby? Is it because Tyler is an only child? I've asked Lorraine before why she doesn't have any more children, but she goes quiet. I think maybe she and Joe have been trying for a while, but it hasn't worked out. Maybe that's why they have so much sex. Maybe a kind of desperation sets in when you can't conceive.

'Shall we go to the swingpark?' Lorraine suggests.

Lorraine and I sit on a bench and watch Jamie pushing both the girls on the swings. I remember I've forgotten to ring the doctor. The trouble is, I know that once I've made an appointment Jamie will make a miraculous recovery, worthy of being recorded at Lourdes, and I shall have to sit in the surgery, red as a radish (I don't do beetroot), while Jamie tells the doctor he's never felt better.

'Jamie's pushing Tyler higher than me!' yells Emily. 'Mummy!'

'Do you want to get off that swing?' I say, standing up.

'Noooo.'

'Then stop fussing. You're going just as high as Tyler.' I sit down again, my heartbeat settling to a slower rhythm as I realise Emily is not about to throw another wobbly. At least, not yet.

'Did I tell you about Kaye?' Lorraine asks, scraping one immaculate French-polished nail across an imaginary mark on her linen trousers. They're pale blue, from Next, and a size eight or ten.

'Didn't she meet someone on the Internet?'

Kaye is Lorraine's oldest sister. Sara is the middle one. Kaye is married to Mark, a postman. Sara lives with Tom who is her long-term lover and the brother of Lorraine's stepfather. The family don't speak to Sara any more.

'Kaye's leaving Mark for the boy she used to sit next to at primary school. She found him on a website.'

I have visions of a little boy in grey shorts with

scabs on his knees, sitting on a website, waiting to be found.

'So, talking of complicated relationships,' Lorraine continues, 'tell me more about Steve.'

I don't mind telling her. We became friends in hospital. We were in adjacent beds. Lorraine's first words to me were, 'You look wrecked.' Neither of us dared laugh because of the stitches, hers from a caesarian, mine from a perineal tear. Lorraine didn't apologise and that's what I like about her. You know where you are with Lorraine.

'Steve – he's . . .' I hesitate. I can't find the words to describe him.

'I take it you fancy him.'

'He's gorgeous.' Understatement of the year. 'Like Antonio Banderas.'

'Really?' breathes Lorraine, raising one perfectly sculpted eyebrow. 'Sounds interesting. When am I going to meet him?'

'Oh, he's far too young for us. He looks like he's just left school,' I backtrack, wondering why I don't like the thought of Lorraine meeting Steve.

'We all have to have our fantasies, I suppose.' Lorraine turns away. 'Jamie, please don't push Tyler so high.'

Love is in the air. There's a couple of schoolkids, no more than thirteen, walking along hand in hand. I don't think it's a relationship that will last – the girl, all legs and pierced bellybutton, is on her mobile, laughing to someone else, while the boy, wearing trousers so baggy

they leave everything to the imagination, stares uncomfortably out across the pond.

As the couple pass, I can't help noticing that the girl's
bellybutton is swollen and red around the ring she wears.
It is not attractive. I nudge Lorraine and whisper, 'Did
you see that?'

'Couldn't miss it. It's like a traffic light.'

'I'd never abuse my body like that.'

'It's only a piercing, Juliet.'

'I wouldn't risk anyone, even a doctor, modifying my
body in any way.'

Lorraine smiles. 'You'll change your mind. Come on,
you're almost forty, the time when a woman's thoughts
turn to cosmetic surgery.'

'Thanks a lot.'

'Don't scowl – you'll make those lines so much worse.'
Lorraine laughs then I laugh with her while in the distance
out on the road 'Greensleeves' plays from an ice-cream
van.

'Let's pick up an ice cream on the way home,' Lorraine
suggests. 'The café's closed.' And so is the subject of
Steve, I suppose. I suppress the thrill that runs down my
spine as I breathe his name. I can't help it. It is like a
reflex over which I have no voluntary control.

'Did you say we could have an ice cream? Only we
can't,' Jamie butts in. 'The ice-cream man's run out.'

Lorraine frowns. 'Course he hasn't.'

'He's playing his music. Everyone knows when he's

playing his music he's run out.' Jamie hesitates, sensing there's something wrong. 'That's what Mum says.'

Lorraine looks at me and grins. 'Your mum's a wicked woman,' she says in spite of my frantic mouthing of 'Shh!' and 'NO!'

Emily looks at me curiously too.

'Did you tell a lie, Mum?' says Jamie in awe. 'Mum, you told a lie . . .' His face falls. I know how he is feeling. The first disillusionment. The first realisation that his parents are not perfect. I can only hope he's not going to tell everyone.

'It's not a bad lie,' I say. 'It's a white lie. I said it to preserve your teeth.'

'You have ice cream every night, Mum. I've seen you buy it. I've seen you eat whole buckets of it while you're watching *EastEnders*.'

'How?' I bluster.

'I see you when I go downstairs to fetch a glass of water.'

It's difficult to explain to a six year old the subtle differences between a lie, a half-truth, a white lie, a fib, and a tactful answer. I guess they are all dishonesties. I have lied about the ice-cream van, and I am about to lie to Andy – about the ring, and about my lack of knowledge of the gluten content of quick-cook pasta shells.

Andy doesn't arrive home until eleven. The children have been asleep for hours, and I've been channel-hopping on the telly.

'Where the hell have you been?' I ask as he opens the door. I know I shouldn't jump on him as soon as he arrives. I know I should be the good wife and bring his slippers – if he possessed any – and a cup of tea before I start the inquest into his day.

'Good evening,' he says, slipping his jacket off. 'How was your day?'

'Oh, you know how it is. I've been to the gym, had lunch in town, fended off the advances of hundreds of men.'

Andy smiles. I smile back although I am a little hurt that he doesn't make some chivalrous comment about how he's not surprised I've had to repel so many admirers.

'How was it really?'

'Same as usual,' I shrug. 'Emily's been a nightmare. Jamie's been getting under my feet because there was no school.'

Andy throws his jacket onto the banister at the bottom of the stairs. The jacket bothers me. It is offensive, like a zit on the end of a nose. I have just tidied up – flung Jamie's rucksack, various shoes, Emily's crying, talking, sleeping, walking, almost living doll and half a box of Celebrations chocolates into the understairs cupboard, and now this thing sullies my tidy house. As does Andy, who stands in the hall, looking shattered and grey around the eyes.

'I had to go to my mother's,' he says.

'Oh?' I want to go up and hug him, but a wailing sound from the understairs cupboard stops me.

'What have you done with Emily?'

'It's all right – it's the doll. Baby-what's-her-name? I forgot to switch her off.' I dig about in the cupboard in the dark, grab it by its hair and fumble for the switch in the back of its neck.

'I thought for a moment you'd shut Emily in there. She had a nightmare last night about being locked in the dark with an angry bear.'

'I didn't hear her,' I say, handling the doll more gently. It's so realistic that I find myself laying it face up on the rubble inside the cupboard so it can breathe.

'You rarely do.'

'I rarely do what?'

'You rarely listen to what Emily has to say,' says Andy. He pauses. 'That's why she's like she is.'

The cupboard door closes slowly. The catch clicks shut. I drop my hands to my hips, and squeeze the soft flesh until I can feel bone. I can feel bone. Honest.

'Would you like to leave the house and come back in again?' I ask. 'I have spent all day listening to your daughter . . . *She* won't listen to *me*. And that's not my fault. She's rude. She's stroppy. She's utterly noxious.' The words gush from my mouth like steam from an over-filled kettle. 'It comes from your side of the family, not mine. Emily's genetically programmed to be a pain in the neck.'

'All right, all right,' Andy says, raising his hands in a gesture of conciliation. 'Maybe I'm wrong. Maybe you're wrong. Maybe we're both wrong. I was trying to tell you why I was late.'

'Oh?'

'My mother's bowels are giving her trouble.'

'Oh?'

'The doctor's been in to give her an enema.'

I wonder if Guy Ritchie bothers Madonna with such trifles when he returns home from making a film? Madonna – there's a woman who's reinvented herself over and over again; sometimes she's a virgin, sometimes a cowgirl, sometimes naked in a book for the coffee table, or more precisely for the shelf beneath the coffee table so the Rhino doesn't see it, although I'd like to see what effect Madonna's provocative poses would have on her bowels.

'Would you like me to stick your dinner in the microwave?' I ask.

'Mother says you gave her gluten last night, Juliet.' I know it's bad when Andy calls me Juliet. He usually calls me Jules. 'She says you did it deliberately.'

'I forgot,' I say lamely, hugging my soft belly.

'How could you possibly forget?'

'I have a million and one things to think about. I can't remember everything.'

'Mother's talked about her gluten allergy often enough.'

'You said it.'

'Juliet!' Andy follows me as I march into the kitchen with a mixture of guilt and fury boiling up behind my ears. I pull a dish of desiccated sausage casserole out of the fridge and slam it on the worktop. I yank at the cutlery drawer which comes out halfway and sticks because some kitchen implement has caught inside. I shove it back in, yank it out again, extract a fork and ram it into a lump of sausage where it remains standing up. I could solve our financial problems in one fell swoop if I could make it palatable again. I could market it to NASA for longhaul space trips.

Andy comes up behind me, places his hands on my waist and begins a conversation with the back of my neck.

'Jules, I'm sorry I snapped. I've not had a very good day.'

'Neither have I.' I turn to face him, reach up and rest my hands around the back of his neck.

'Did you meet Mr Parker, the bloke I sold the BMW to?'

I shake my head. Andy gives me a squeeze.

'He's brought it back for a refund. Said he took it to a friend who knows all there is to know about BMWs, and he said he wouldn't have touched it with a bargepole. Guess who that friend is?' Andy doesn't give me the time to answer. 'It's that bastard, Kevin!'

I disentangle myself from Andy's now pythonic

embrace as he vents his fury over Kevin's disloyalty.

'Did you give Mr Parker the money back?' I interrupt.

'I had to in the end. He threatened to call Trading Standards and the local rag and then went on to introduce me to his brothers.'

'Was there enough money in the business account?' I ask, panicking.

'I don't know, do I? I thought you'd sort it out tomorrow.' Andy pauses and rubs his nose with the tip of one finger. 'I had to have a word with Steve today. He was late in this morning, didn't start till eleven.'

'Employ in haste, repent at leisure,' I say brightly.

'I think you're referring to marriage,' Andy says. I argued against taking on a mechanic in the first place, but I find I have warmed to the idea over the past couple of days. 'I took Steve on on trust,' Andy goes on. 'I bet he didn't mess his uncle about like this.'

'His uncle?'

'He worked for his uncle in Walthamstow.'

'That isn't what he told me.' I chew at my lip, wondering how much to reveal. That over coffee and HobNobs Steve told me he had learned his trade from a family friend in Willesden? Perhaps Andy misheard or forgot exactly what Steve said. It is not possible that Steve is lying. He's not that type. If anything, he is like me, capable of no more than the telling of a white lie, a falsehood designed to protect someone else. 'Go gently with

Steve, won't you, Andy? I think he's depressed. He's just broken up with a girlfriend, and you know how traumatic that is at his age.'

'It is at any age,' says Andy. 'Hey, you're not wearing your wedding ring.'

The Rhino's told him, hasn't she? Vengeful old bitch.

'I took it off to wash up the other day. I forgot to put it back on.'

'You never wash up. That's why we had to have a dishwasher.'

'I bleached the mugs,' I insist. 'I'll put it back on when I've cleared up tonight.' I know Andy will be very hurt if I have to confess. When he proposed he went down quietly on one knee. There was no embarrassing public announcement on the radio which is how Joe proposed to Lorraine.

'I'll drop some bread in the toaster and put the bins out for you,' Andy says. 'Then, if you'll forgive me, I'll have a shower and go to bed. I'm knackered.'

When I finally turn away from the casserole, Andy is already on his way.

You can't put the bins out yet, I want to call after him, but I bite my tongue. I haven't had time to check through the rubbish yet. I've checked everywhere else – the windowsills, the sink traps, under the beds, inside the washing machine.

I find myself in the shadows at the bottom of our steps, rummaging in rubber gloves through the bins, torch between my teeth because the streetlamp has gone out. It is not only the ring that is missing from my life. There's something else, like the fizz in a cola or the buzz you don't get from a low-alcohol wine. Life's like one of those jokes Joe tells after he's had a few lagers, when you say, 'Yeah, that's funny,' but you don't laugh.

Making this voyage of self-discovery, I also discover among the foul odours that emanate from the bins a jar of mouldy jam which shouldn't be there at all if I had bothered to rinse it out and take it to the bottle bank for recycling. I am eternally guilty of contributing to the world's mountains of waste. I am eternally guilty of squandering Earth's resources. I am as good as flooding my own home, except, being up on the hill, ours will be one of the last to go under as London disappears beneath the waters.

However, my panic is rising much faster than the water in the Thames. I can't find the ring.

I tip the whole bin out on the pavement. There's an empty bottle of bleach, the last of the Chinese takeaway cartons, and the shoebox Jamie made into a hamster house in the hope Andy and I could be persuaded to take on a hamster. No hope there, I'm afraid.

As I squat down and turn over a rather unpleasant mass of tissue, the plumber from Anerley parks his van. He doesn't give me a second glance. Has his mind on his girlfriend, I expect. I wonder if she is waiting for him, fresh and fragrant from a long soak in a bubblebath, her hair still damp, and I feel guilty because I never wait up for Andy, all fresh and fragrant and seductive, and because I've lost my wedding ring, a circle of plain gold that isn't terribly thick because we didn't have any money at the time we bought it, and because I'm not looking for it because I particularly want it back, but because I don't want Andy going on at me because I've lost it. And when I think of Andy, I don't see Andy at all, but Steve . . .

It's no good. The ring's not here.

'What are you doing out there?' Andy asks from the top of the steps. 'I said I'd put the bins out.'

'I know . . .'

Andy screws up his face. 'You stink.'

I sniff at my sleeve. There's an earthy scent of apple peel and rotting kiwi fruit. It's not exactly Chanel.

'Well?'

Good question. A reasonable question, but how am I to answer it, bearing in mind I haven't found the ring, yet I am still quietly optimistic that it will turn up before I have to tell Andy I've lost it? What else would Andy consider precious enough to warrant digging through the bins for in the middle of the night? A tenner? Fifty?

'I thought I'd thrown your season ticket out by mistake,' I stutter. 'I thought I'd better check.'

Andy frowns. 'Of course you haven't – it's in my wallet. Oh Jules, I haven't been looking after you, have I?' He kisses me on the top of my head like a brother kisses a sister, and leads me by the hand back up the steps. 'I'm sorry for what I said about Emily. You do a great job with the kids.'

Silence.

'Really, you do.'

Silence.

'I'll ask David to find us a holiday. A cheap one. A last-minute deal. We could go at the end of the summer, perhaps, once we've recouped some of the outlay on the new mechanic. Something not too far away. Can you imagine Emily cooped up on a plane?'

I am moved to speak.

'Not Cornwall this time,' I plead, thinking of pasties with sludgy insides, and unremitting rain, and hazardous cliffs that a child could disappear over during a millisecond of parental inattention. 'Not Cornwall.'

'Not Cornwall, I promise.'

I wonder whether a holiday will bring us together or push us further apart.

'We are all right, aren't we, Andy?'

'I hope so,' he says. 'It's going to take time to restore our financial situation to what it was, but we'll do it.'

'I wasn't referring to money or holidays. I was talking about me and you.' I hesitate. Andy smiles.

'You're all I ever wanted, Jules,' he says softly. It's here that I should melt into his arms and tell him how much I love him, except he rather spoils the moment. 'By the way, I've invited my mother for dinner tomorrow night.'

'You've what!'

'You don't mind, do you?'

'Mind?'

'Thanks, Jules. I knew you wouldn't.'

Chapter Four

Did Steve arrive at work before me today because Andy had a word with him about starting late, or because he couldn't wait to see me? Dare I hope that it's the latter?

I park my car alongside his motorbike. I check my make-up in the rearview mirror, fling the door open and slide gingerly out of the driver's seat. Gingerly because the thong I chose to wear with tight black trousers this morning, to prevent a VPL, is in danger of completely disappearing up between my legs.

How is it possible that I possess a thong? It's nylon, not silk. It's bright red, and almost invisible, and Andy loves it. I tell him he should try wearing it if he likes it so much. If he wore it for a day – half a day – he'd soon realise why I don't appreciate him nagging me over not wearing it.

Anyway, the thong came about through Lorraine during one of her many forays into being a party-plan hostess. I felt obliged as always to buy something. (I go for the second cheapest item so as not to appear too mean.) This time I ordered a jar of chocolate spread with a difference, developed for licking off a lover's body. I thought, if I swapped the contents into the Nutella container at home, no one would notice the difference. However, there was a mix-up with the order codes, and Lorraine presented me with the thong with great interest and delight. 'You dark horse, you.'

I digress. I am trying to divert myself from the sensations the sight of Steve removing his leathers at the door to the workshop has aroused within me in my secret and long-forgotten places. Long forgotten until I slipped into this thong, that is.

My knees grow weak. My nipples pearl. (That's a term I picked up from reading a couple of romantic novels from the library when I was pregnant with Jamie. It stuck in my mind because it isn't appropriate. My nipples can't be described as pearls. They've worn badly, ending up more like those ridged brown leather buttons you see on very old three piece suites.) I think I'm in love.

Steve looks up when I slam the car door.

'Hi, Juliet,' he says.

'Morning,' I say breezily. It is breezy too. The wind is catching up pieces of litter, takeaway cartons and crisp packets, from along the Whitehorse Road, and depositing them elsewhere, mainly here in the yard behind

Wyevale Autos. Steve is waiting, watching me as if he expects me to stop and chat. I squeeze between the car and the motorbike. I've parked much too close.

'That your bike?' I ask. Idiot. Of course it's his bike, growls the tigress. You don't see Gayle or Larry striding around in leathers, do you? I am not like everyone else – my mouth has no direct nervous connection with my brain. I try to make up for stating the obvious by showing an interest. 'What make is it?'

Steve moves round towards the bike and points out the lettering I missed on the tank.

'It's a Triumph,' he says, 'a Speed Triple, 900cc.'

'Very nice.' I pause, studying it. 'I like the colour.'

'Do you?'

'It's great.' It is orange. It's bright. Very bright.

'You can see me coming in the dark.'

How innocent a comment is that? The look in Steve's eyes is like a honeytrap, and I am both caught and caught out. A fervid tide washes up my face and neck. I wish the tarmac would open right up along the crack on which I am standing and swallow me up.

'Juliet,' he begins, his voice low and raw.

'Yes?'

Steve looks away. I follow his gaze. Andy is driving up in the Merc. His pinched face lights up when he sees me, and my skin crawls with guilt. I glance towards Steve.

'I'll be in for coffee,' he mutters.

Inside the showroom Gayle is sitting at her desk with

the telephone receiver in one hand. She gives me a long stare.

'Are you well, Juliet?' she asks. 'You look terribly pale.'

'Do I?' I say, running my fingers down my cheeks. 'It's probably my make-up.'

'Ah, yes,' says Gayle. 'It's your foundation. Haven't you heard of the expression, less is more?'

I notice her fingernails are all more than an inch long, and painted in pearlescent purple. How does she do that? Keep them intact, I mean?

'I'll be checking the phone bills from now on,' I say, 'and charging for personal calls.'

'That's entirely fair and reasonable,' Gayle says coolly, dangling the receiver and twirling it on its cable. 'I've been trying to pacify Mr Parker – I'll transfer him to you straight away.'

The phone in the office buzzes. I don't have time to introduce myself or say good morning.

'I want my effing money back,' growls the man at the end of the phone. His manner suggests he is one of those very small men who have to strut about in a black suit and shades to get themselves noticed. As he continues with, 'Who the hell are you?' I see his hands curling into a fist, presenting a row of thick gold rings.

I find it easier in these situations, which don't occur very often, to be someone else. Financial Controller?

Company Director? No, too much responsibility. Switchboard operative? Receptionist? Cleaner?

'Sales,' I mumble. 'Can I help you?'

'You certainly bloody can. I want to speak to that Wyevale geezer right now.'

'I'm sorry, but that's not possible. He's out of the office.'

'Who did you say you were?'

'Sales.'

'Well, Mrs Sales, the cheque's bounced. I want my effing money back.' There's a series of epithets I have never heard used in combination before, and the man at the other end slams the phone down.

My blood runs cold. There is no money in the business account. Even the overdraft facility is overdrawn which explains why the cheque Andy gave to Mr Parker for the BMW has bounced. With a sinking heart, I call the bank before I go and see what state the BMW is in. (And see Steve.)

'I can understand why this Parker bloke felt he'd been shafted,' Steve says. He is in the pit, shining a torch up into the belly of the car in question. 'Want to have a look?'

'At what?'

'The motor.' Steve frowns slightly, wipes his hands on his blue overalls. The press-studs are open down to his waist, revealing a grey T-shirt. I try to force my eyes away from the shadowy dip at the base of his neck.

'It's all right, Juliet,' Steve says, apparently interpreting my hesitation as reluctance to descend into the pit in case I should trip or soil my clothes. 'You don't mind me calling you Juliet, do you?'

'That's fine.' My mouth is dry. You can call me anything you like, I want to add, but I can't. All this poor young boy has done is try to be friendly with the boss's wife. I say boy, because he is young enough to be my son. If, when I was seventeen or eighteen, I had dared to leave my girlfriends on the floor of the disco, and I had found one of the boys who clung to the walls around us attractive, and one of those boys had found me attractive in my Indian cheesecloth blouse and ruckling red stretch jeans, I might have had my first full sexual experience. I might have fallen pregnant to Dexy's Midnight Runners singing 'Come on, Eileen!'.

I am diverting. Steve doesn't mean anything by it. It's my overactive imagination misinterpreting the look in his eyes, the tone of his voice, the words that he chooses . . .

'You're looking at me as if I might bite,' Steve says eventually, reaching out his hand. 'I won't bite . . .' I take his hand and step down, 'unless you ask me to.'

I snatch my hand away and wish I hadn't because when I look up at his face, I catch a flash of even, white teeth. He is smiling. I was right in the first place, wasn't I? Steve's no boy, no innocent child.

'It's rusted right through,' Steve says.

I peer in the direction Steve is pointing the torch, but it doesn't mean anything to me. It is grubby and dark like all cars' underbellies as far as I'm concerned.

'Can you do anything with it?' I ask, granting him omniscience.

'I don't think so.' Steve pulls a screwdriver from the pocket of his overalls, and sticks it through a panel. It slides through like a knife through butter. As if there's already a hole in it. 'It's too far gone. I'd scrap it if I were you.'

'It's not really my decision,' I say slowly before I realise how this looks. I know the business. Why shouldn't I decide? If Steve says it's no good, then it's no good.

I decide to be proactive, hands on, and I reach up and give the nearest part of the underbelly of the car a tap with one finger. There's a dull metallic echo and a shower of what might be rust, or dirt. I muse for a moment, appearing to consider, although I am actually appraising the rate and depth of Steve's breathing. I can hear him. He is very close, and when I speak, I can't control my voice. The words tumble out of my mouth like little fishes, slithering past each other from a fisherman's net.

'What was that, Juliet?' Steve asks.

I press one hand to my breast, trying to still my racing heart. I gather my breath, aware he is watching, waiting. His eyes glitter softly across the pit.

'You okay?'

'Fine. Just thinking.' Thinking how Steve's lips would

feel on mine. How hard, how possessive? Wondering, if I were in a position to do so, how I would respond. Pondering on how many people have made love in inspection pits. Fire burns hot in my belly. I give a nervous cough and wish I hadn't – I don't want Steve thinking I'm infectious in any way.

'You're right, Steve,' I say at last. 'It's a wreck. We'll get rid of it.'

'I've got a friend who'll pick it up, if you like,' he says smoothly. 'I can organise it to save you the bother.'

Thanking him, I clamber out of the pit, my trousers too tight around my hips and the thong cutting me in half. In a dream, I pour myself a coffee back in the office, sloshing it over the rim of the mug. Gayle interrupts.

'Juliet, it's Mr Parker again. He says he wants to speak to Mrs Sales. I guess that must be you.'

'Tell him I'm not here.' Tell him I've died and gone to heaven – I feel like Kate and Leonardo on that ship when they're dancing together in steerage. Gayle rests her hands on her hips. Reluctantly, I pick up the phone.

'If I can't have Mrs Sales, I want Mr bloody Wyevale.'

'We are trying to connect you. Please hold the line.' I try to unscramble the gist of what I am planning to say to pacify Mr Parker. I repeat: 'We are trying to connect you. Please hold the line.'

I jump as I hear someone clear their throat. I was right in assuming that Gayle had left the office. It is Steve and he's trying not to laugh at catching me at a disadvantage.

'This is Juliet Wyevale speaking,' I begin, and before Mr Parker can get a word in edgeways, I jump in with what I feel is a fair offer, considering the state of the car.

Mr Parker blusters like a bulldog at the other end of the phone. He releases another string of epithets that I'm very glad Jamie and Emily cannot hear and therefore repeat to Miss Trays or Mary Bacon.

'The bank will accept the cheque when you re-present it,' I confirm. But Mr Parker doesn't want the cheque. He wants cash and he wants it now.

'I'll make sure it's here tomorrow.'

'It effing better be.'

Breathing sighs of relief, I put the phone down.

'I'll be around tomorrow if there's any trouble,' Steve offers.

'Oh, I'm sure there won't be,' I say. 'Mr Parker sounds like a reasonable man.'

Steve chuckles, and I smile. Steve knows where I'm coming from. He understands me. As he swaggers up to the coffee-maker I realise I could be in for the Big Thing. I could be Kate Winslet, singing out my love for Leonardo from the prow of the *Titanic*. Or I could be Kate Bush, serenading her Heathcliff from *Wuthering Heights*.

Andy goes straight home to meet the Rhino in case she arrives early – she keeps her watch running ten minutes ahead so as never to be late for any appointment. I offer, in spite of the pain I am experiencing from the thong, to collect the children from Mary's.

I find I have to wait for a space to park in front of the parade of shops across the road because there's a van parked outside Mary's maisonette. It's an old green one that's been sold on several times, judging from the state of the panelling, which has had more than one layer of lettering painted out. I walk past it to Mary's doorstep. The door is open.

''Scuse us.' A man carrying a stack of boxes pushes past me and enters Mary's house. 'Thanks, love.'

Mary comes to the door. She doesn't invite me in, but I suppose there isn't much room inside a maisonette with all these boxes that the delivery man continues to carry past us as she calls for Jamie and Emily.

'I find working from home so very convenient,' Mary says. 'It means I can take these few bits and pieces in for number four.' She nods towards the upstairs window. 'They're out all hours.'

'That's the last of it, Mary,' the man interrupts.

A faint blush spreads across Mary's cheeks.

'Thanks, Arnie,' she says.

He waits on the doorstep beside me, arms folded across a T-shirt stained with grease-spots and brown sauce. He's about thirty, and five foot tall, and he sports a dark blue cap, and a goatee beard. He grinds the sole of one boot against the step as if he's extinguishing a cigarette.

'You've got the cash this time?' he growls.

'Oh, I almost forgot,' says Mary, disappearing into

the hall and returning with an envelope which she hands to the delivery man. 'It's all there.'

'It better had be.'

Mary and I watch as he turns and strolls back to the van, trying to tuck the envelope into the back pocket of a pair of skin-tight jeans.

'You'd have thought Arnie was doing *me* the favour from the way he behaves,' Mary observes. 'If I wasn't so accommodating, he'd have to come back later.'

'I hope the people from number four are grateful,' I say. 'What on earth is in all those boxes?'

'Oh, I don't ask,' says Mary, and I find myself warming to her scrupulous sense of discretion. I am even more pleased when she tells me that Emily has been a little angel.

'I hear you've been a good girl, Emily.'

'I been good, Mummy,' she says, sounding slightly dazed as if she's been watching the Fimbles all day.

'I've been good, too,' says Jamie. 'I got a certificate at assembly today. It's for "Excellent Manners at Lunchtime".'

Just as I am about to congratulate him, there is a loud clonk. Mary looks up and waves her fist at the ceiling just inside her front door.

'What was that?' I ask.

'Number four's cat,' she replies, 'a monster of a tabby. I feed it sometimes. They're like you, Juliet. They know they can rely on me.'

Back at home, I nip upstairs to remove the thong as

soon as I can, and replace it with a pair of saggy maxis. The Rhino is in the living room watching the news and sipping sherry. Jamie is reading Harry Potter and Emily is snuggled up against the Rhino on the sofa. I join Andy in the kitchen.

'Hi, babe,' he says. 'Did you manage to sort out that cash for Mr Parker?'

I nod.

'I don't know what we're going to do,' he worries. 'I was relying on that sale to keep us afloat. I guess I'll just have to hope I can sell that BMW again by the end of the month.'

'You can't. Steve's scrapped it.'

'He what?'

'He showed me the rust. He's getting one of his friends to take it away. That's all right, isn't it?'

Andy's eyes darken a shade. 'I think so . . . What do you make of Steve?'

I don't know what to say. What *can* I say?

'Isn't he a little inexperienced? I mean, at mechanics?' I say, blundering. I hope Andy doesn't notice the flush that spreads slowly up from the base of my neck to the roots of my hair.

'He knows his stuff.'

'So, I made the right decision?'

'Yes, of course . . .' Andy rubs his nose with the end of his finger. 'I didn't think there was that much rust, though.'

I worry because Andy doesn't usually make a mistake. He isn't in the habit of selling duds. I know he's desperate to keep us afloat, but he has other things like his mother, Emily and Crystal Palace FC preying on his mind. He's depressed because the Eagles are slipping down the First Division. That always makes him depressed. He hasn't got SAD, but FAD – Football Affective Disorder – and there isn't a cure.

'Perhaps you should have another look at it yourself,' I suggest.

'No, no. I believe you.'

'I didn't see rust exactly because it was pretty dark,' I confess, 'but Steve ran a screwdriver through one of the panels without any effort.' I am beginning to doubt what I saw. Andy sidles up, slips his arm around my waist and plants a kiss on my cheek.

'Don't worry about it now,' he murmurs.

'But you're worried too. I can tell.'

'It's bad enough that Kevin is spreading rumours that we're selling rubbish without discovering that we really are. Wyevale Autos is going down the pan.' Andy sighs. 'We've been through bad times before . . .' Then he changes the subject, although it doesn't stop me worrying that the outcome will be different this time. 'What's for tea?'

'I don't know,' I say in despair. 'Andy, you said you were cooking. She's your mother, not mine.'

'Hey, keep your hair on, Jules. It's a joke.' He points

towards two carrier bags on the worktop. 'I'm doing stir-fried Chinese vegetables and rice.'

I thought stir frying was a quick technique, but it is over an hour before Andy has it ready and we are all sitting around the dining-room table. Andy dishes up and passes the plates round.

The Rhino eyes hers with suspicion.

'It's all right, Mother,' Andy says. 'It's gluten free.'

'Oh Andrew, you are so thoughtful,' the Rhino begins, casting a sideways glance at me, 'but you needn't have bothered. I've brought my own food.' She picks up a large handbag from between her feet and unpacks a couple of rice cakes wrapped in clingfilm and a small bottle of still spring water.

'Andrew, dear, could I have a plate, please,' says the Rhino. 'A clean one.'

'Of course, Mother.' Andy fetches a plate from the kitchen and places it in front of the Rhino. She unwraps the rice cakes and breaks one into pieces.

'How's business at Wyevale Autos?' she asks.

'We're bumping along,' Andy says.

'You're in difficulty again then?'

'We're having a small cashflow problem, that's all,' I interrupt, flashing a warning glance towards Andy. The last thing I need is the Rhino interfering in the business as well as our family life.

'Have you had an accountant look at your financial situation as I suggested?' says the Rhino.

'There's no need,' Andy chips in. 'Juliet does the books.'

The Rhino gazes at me. She tips her head slightly to one side, and scratches one blunt-cut nail across the tablecloth, dislodging some dried cereal that one of the children dropped a couple of days ago.

'No one would believe that Juliet's mother was a cleaner, would they?'

'No, I have a very clever wife,' Andy beams with pride.

It is touching to know that Andy values my hard work, but irritating that he fails to realise what the Rhino really thinks of me.

'You ought to take some exercise, Andrew,' she begins. 'I do believe you're getting a paunch.'

'I'll have to get out and play more football,' Andy says, sitting back and patting his stomach.

'I don't like playing football,' says Jamie.

'You need to practise if you're going to join the Eagles.'

'I don't want to be a footballer when I grow up. I especially don't want to play for Crystal Palace.'

'Quite right, Jamie,' says the Rhino. 'With a brain like yours you could be a doctor or a lawyer.'

'No way. I'm going to design intergalactic space-ships.' Jamie stuffs down his last forkful of rice. 'Granny, did you know that Mum says it's okay to tell lies as long as you don't get found out?'

'I didn't say that.'

'You did – in Kelsey Park.'

'I didn't.' I feel myself growing hot. 'Not exactly.'

'What's that funny noise?' Emily interrupts.

'That's a burp,' says Jamie, chuckling. 'Someone's doing burps.'

'Burp, burp, burp,' chants Emily.

'That's enough,' I snap, looking towards Andy for moral support. It's no wonder the children love him more than me when it's always me who has to tell them off. He should do it, particularly when it's gas being released from the upper end of the Rhino's digestive system that is causing the disturbance. As it is, it is the Rhino herself who provides the distraction.

The Rhino wipes her mouth with a piece of kitchen roll even though she hasn't touched a thing. In fact, she turns as white as the kitchen roll itself, and tiny beads of sweat leak from her powdered forehead.

'I should be going home,' she mutters. She stands up, wobbles slightly and sits down again.

'Mother, are you all right?' Andy jumps up and moves round the table.

'I'm in terrible pain,' she moans. 'I'd like to go home.'

'You can't go home like that,' Andy says. 'We won't let you, will we, Jules?'

What can I say? There's a heap of clothes in the spare room waiting to be ironed, and I haven't dusted in there for months. The Rhino's terrible pain seems to loosen its grip as she contemplates spending a night under the same roof as me. At the same time a terrible pain kicks into my head at the thought of waking up to provide the Rhino with a gluten-free breakfast.

'You must stay, Mother,' Andy insists.

'Thank you, Andrew, but I'd feel much more comfortable in my own bed. Perhaps you would drive me back, if Juliet can spare you?'

'Of course.'

'I don't want to miss my appointment with the allergist tomorrow.' She picks up her handbag from the floor at her feet. 'I managed to get a cancellation with Dr Leaver. *The* Dr Leaver.' She looks at Andy as if she expects him to know who she's talking about, but it's no good, because if Dr Leaver isn't the Eagles' team doctor, he won't have a clue who he is. 'He has a clinic on Harley Street. He's treated several celebrities for gluten allergies like mine.'

'Anyone we've heard of?' I ask.

'Oh no, Dr Leaver's secretary wouldn't divulge that kind of information. That's one of the reasons I picked on him.'

'You can't really describe yourself as a celebrity, Pammy,' I point out, 'not even a minor one.'

'I'm well known about town,' the Rhino says with a withering look.

'You're forgetting that Mother has had two articles published in gardening magazines about container planting for narrowboats,' Andy cuts in quickly.

83

The Rhino smiles fondly at her son while I try to imagine her arranging for Max Clifford to negotiate the best deal for her life story. I picture him throwing his hands up in despair, and saying, 'What life? What story?'

The Rhino pales again, and clutches her stomach, making me afraid she's going to change her mind and stay the night. Andy relieves me of that worry by taking her straight home, but that only allows my other concerns to resurface. That rust, for example.

Chapter Five

I have never been troubled by rust before, and I decide to put my mind at ease at the earliest opportunity. The following morning while Andy is occupied with handing over the cash for the BMW to Mr Parker, who is just as I imagined he would be, I take Steve's coffee to the workshop.

'Steve?'

He looks up from the engine of the Volvo he's working on. He is like one of those calendar hunks, photographed in ultramarine and white. I take in the pectorals that glisten with sweat and smudges of oil, the rippling six-pack, and the smattering of hair across his chest. A dark line starts at his belly button and dives down below the belt of trousers so filthy they would stand up on their own. I want to touch him, to graze my fingertips across his skin, to feel the muscle beneath . . .

'You're making me nervous, staring at me like that.'

'Oh, I'm sorry,' I bluster. 'I've brought you some coffee. I'll leave it here, beside the door.'

'Thanks.'

I hesitate. 'I wondered if I could have another look at the rust on the BMW Mr Parker returned.'

'You could,' Steve says, a smile playing on his lips, 'but you'd have to lie on your back.' He gives the wing of the Volvo a thump. 'This one won't be leaving the workshop for a while, and my mate's picking the BMW up at eleven. I could try calling him to tell him not to bother if you've changed your mind, but I expect he's already on his way.'

'I'd prefer to keep the arrangement as it is.' I am reassured by Steve's attitude. He has nothing to hide.

On my return to the office, I find myself imagining what it would be like to lie on my back, not beneath some rusty old chassis, but beneath Steve with the weight of his body crushing my breasts and his thighs between mine. The HobNobs in the back of the filing cabinet are losing their allure. I no longer crave chocolate, and I realise with regret that I no longer crave my husband's company. When Andy pops his head around the office door to tell me he's off out to look at some Porsche that might just sell for enough profit to put Wyevale Autos back on track, I gaze at him wondering why.

He's put on weight since I married him, but not as much as some of his football mates. He takes care of his appearance without spending a fortune on male grooming products which he considers a girlie thing to do. He still talks to anyone he meets with that easy manner that attracted me to him in the first place.

'You're picking the kids up, aren't you?' Andy says quietly.

I nod.

'I'll see you later then, Jules.' Andy blows me a kiss, and I see and hear no more from him until Gayle interrupts the conversation Steve and I are having over afternoon coffee.

'Juliet,' she says. 'Andy's on line two.'

'Hi, darling,' I say when we connect, but we're not really connected, are we? Not any more.

'It's my mother. She's in hospital on a drip and strong painkillers.'

'Spare me the gory details.'

'She wants you to know.'

'You mean she wants to make me feel guilty.'

'No, she wants you to realise the full consequences of feeding pasta to a person who has a severe allergy to gluten.'

Liar. She wants her suffering to prey on my mind.

'I said I'd go straight to the hospital. I'm trying to park.' Andy's voice breaks up then reassembles. 'I'll tell her you and the kids send your love.'

'Yep.' I mouth the words, laced with gluten, silently. I decide to leave work early. Andy won't be coming back, and Gayle can close up later. I spend money we haven't got on sausages which are on special offer at the super-market before I drive to Mary Bacon's to collect the children.

I knock on Mary's door. A girl of about fifteen opens it. She smiles, revealing a heavy brace on her teeth.

'Come in,' she says.

I step inside, squeezing past the vast bag that's slung over the girl's shoulder.

'Where's your gear?' she asks as she follows me through into Mary's living room where three more teenage girls are perched about the furniture. Jamie and Emily are rummaging through a heap of clothing in the middle of the floor.

'I've come to collect my children.'

'Oh, I'm sorry. I thought you were one of us.'

'One of the family,' Mary cuts in as she walks through from the kitchen. 'These are my nieces – Letitia, Amber, Demi and Jade.'

'Hi, nice to meet you.'

The nieces scowl and turn away, but Jamie looks up.

'Hey, Mum,' he says, his eyes wide with excitement. 'It's Mary's birthday. She's had loads of presents. Look, here's a watch.' He waves what looks like a Rolex – a fake, of course. Mary wouldn't be smiling at him quite so benignly if it was a real one.

I feel terrible.

'I didn't know,' I say, turning to Mary. 'You should have told me. I'd have brought you a card at least.'

'There's no need to waste your money on me, Juliet.'

I notice that Mary is wearing a new sweatshirt of tent-like construction with a bunch of balloons appliquéd to the front. I detect the faint smell of cigarettes overlain by Febreze – I expect the sulky nieces smoke.

'I must apologise,' Mary begins, 'I've been so busy I've only had time to give the children a small sandwich for tea – ham from happy pigs on bread made from organic, unbleached flour. I hope you don't mind.'

'Not at all.' At least, I don't think I do. The trouble is that Emily is still hungry and her mood deteriorates on the drive back.

'Is Daddy at home?' Jamie asks.

'He's at the hospital with Granny. She's not very well.'

'Can we go and see her?'

'Not today.'

'I want to see Granny,' Emily pipes up from behind me.

'No, not today.'

'I want to see Granny!' Emily's feet dig into my back through the driver's seat. I take a deep breath. Divert. Distract. But it's too late. Emily explodes. It's been a long day, and I lose the power of rational thought as she kicks her feet into my kidneys.

'If you don't shut up, I'll stop and put you out on the pavement, and I'll leave you there!' I yell, but it's hopeless. Emily can't hear me. I turn the radio up, Jamie stuffs his fingers into his ears, and Emily paddies all the way home.

Later, I sit slumped on the sofa in the living room. I'm staring at the telly, but not taking it in. It's a hospital drama, bustling with randy doctors and nurses. I half-expect to see the Rhino in Intensive Care.

Andy remains down at the hospital with the Rhino. I don't suppose she will let him go. The children are in bed asleep, Emily clutching Tyler's OshKosh dress because she refuses to give it back, and Jamie lying with his head on pages 74 and 75 of *Harry Potter and the Order of the Phoenix*.

Bored, I switch off the telly, and go into the kitchen where I load Robbie Williams into the CD player. Andy bought him for me for Christmas. Well, he didn't exactly buy me Robbie Williams, although that would have been a highly acceptable gesture. He bought me the CD.

I turn the music up and dance, matching the wild, uninhibited movements of my reflection in the kitchen window. I haven't pulled the blind down – there's no need to up here on the hill. No one can see.

The doorbell rings. Andy? Andy's lost his keys? It's too late for the Jehovah's Witnesses, although they haven't disturbed us recently. Usually it's two elderly women delivering booklets. Lorraine says they're evil, but they look perfectly normal to me. They won't accept blood transfusions which Lorraine says is a sin, but I don't mind because it means there's more blood for everyone else. Anyway, because I felt sorry for them having struggled all the way up our steps, I took their booklet indoors, promising unfaithfully that I'd read it, and now they drop them off on the gate pillar at the bottom without bothering me, so I doubt very much that it is the Jehovah's Witnesses. The doorbell rings again.

I switch off the CD player, run my fingers through my dishevelled hair and head for the door. Could it be the police? I don't think I had the music up loud enough to disturb the neighbours. The bell rings for a third time. I dismiss the fantastical thought that it might be Steve about to declare that he feels the same way about me as I do about him . . . Breathless and hot from dancing, I answer the door.

It's Joe.

'Andy's out.' I stare beyond Joe's shoulder where several sets of aircraft landing lights are blinking in the night sky.

'I know.' Joe's dark eyes glitter. He steps forward into the cone of light from the lantern in the porch. There is a loose thread, I notice, just a small one looping from the front of his Crystal Palace top.

'In that case, why are you here?'

'Can't you guess? Juliet, I'm here to see you . . .' Joe takes a deep breath. 'Has anyone ever told you how incredibly sexy you are?'

'Oh, yes. Hundreds.' (Liar.)

Joe's cool about it. His expression of disbelief is immediately transformed into a big, cheesy smile.

'Of course. How could it be otherwise?' he says smoothly, reaching out to stroke my tiger stripes back behind my left ear. I duck back. Joe tries again. 'I love your hair.'

'So you're not dead yet then?' I say, pulling my arms up inside my sweatshirt. I think anthropologists would describe it as a defensive reaction. The sweatshirt has the name of one of those cheap sports shops across the front, and a dribble of tomato ketchup from when I finished Emily's chips at tea-time.

It's chilly on the doorstep. Joe pushes past, knocking against the terracotta pot of dried earth I've left there since last October when I intended to plant it up with daffodils but didn't, on discovering that daffodil bulbs are highly toxic. Apparently, some poor chap kept bulbs in his larder in a brown paper bag. He cooked and served them up as onions. He's dead now. I don't want any mix-ups like that, even with the Rhino. Death by daffodils wouldn't cause adequate suffering to make up for what she's put me through since I married Andy.

'Andy will be back any time now.'

'Where is he?'

'At his mother's deathbed – I mean, bedside.'

'Pammy? What's up with her?'

'I've killed her. Allegedly.'

'Oh, you poor thing.' Joe makes sympathy an excuse

92

to put his arm around my back, and hold me close. 'You and Pammy have never liked each other, have you?'

'Andy and I have been married for nine years yet she still can't accept me as a Wyevale. She still makes it quite clear I am not the wife she would have chosen for her son.'

'I can't think why. You seem like the perfect wife to me.'

'And how would you describe the perfect wife, Joe?'

'Curvaceous and amenable, I suppose,' then he adds, 'and eager to please.'

I want to hit him, but he's bigger than I am, and I'm not sure how he'd react in his present state of mind.

'Andy's always saying how wonderful you are,' he continues.

'Is he?'

'Doesn't he say it to you?' Joe pauses, leans down and kisses me, this time not on the cheek, or the air that bathes my forehead, but full on the lips. He smells of day-old aftershave and other people's cigarette smoke.

'Joe,' I protest, pushing him back, but he clings on like a limpet, giving me one of those suffocating, but non-penetrative kisses that are *de rigueur* when you're seventeen.

'I need you, Juliet.'

'What about Lorraine?' I say indignantly. Joe pulls back slightly. 'How do you think she'd feel about you coming on to me?'

Joe frowns. 'Don't get me wrong,' he says. 'I care about Lorraine, but she drives me mad. She's always nagging me about the clothes I wear, about going to the pub, about watching footie, about decorating the house . . . When I'm with her I have to act like I'm someone else. I can't do it any more, Juliet. I want to be myself.'

'Have you talked to her?' I ask, but Joe's not listening any more. He has one hand on my left buttock, the other on my left breast, reminding me of the game Twister we used to play at Christmas until Lorraine lost the plastic mat. Or so she says. Makes me wonder about their marriage, even at a moment like this, when Joe is all over me. In fact, viewing Joe entirely dispassionately as I am, he reminds me of Ronnie the rabbit and his relationship with the football. There's no candlelight, no soft music, no foreplay . . .

'I'll die if I can't have you,' he groans, pulling away slightly.

When I glance down I realise he's not wearing anything on his feet, which means he's planned this right down to not having that embarrassing moment when you're not sure whether or how to take your socks off in the heat of passion. I am rational. Switched off by the direct approach.

'I'm sorry if you're going to die,' I begin. There I go apologising again when it should be Joe apologising to me. 'I'm sorry, Joe, but I'd die if I had to make love to you.'

'You know you don't mean that.'

'You can't possibly know what's going on in my head when I don't know myself,' I say, trying to lighten the mood of our encounter as I wonder how I am going to escape. I've already told Joe I'm not interested. How many times does he need telling?

'You're so hot, Juliet.'

'Yes, with fury, not lust.'

'Liar.'

I am about to protest when the phone rings, interrupting Joe's urgent invitation to accompany him upstairs.

'That'll be Andy.' Joe releases his grip, allowing me to head for the phone. 'I expect Pammy's taken a turn for the worse.' But it isn't Andy. It's Lorraine wanting her husband back.

'He's right here.'

'There's no hurry as long as he's making himself useful,' she says.

'He's on his way right now. Speak to you tomorrow.' I put the receiver down. Joe stands downcast in front of me with his hands in his pockets. 'Go on. Back to your wife where you belong.'

'I shall die,' he murmurs.

No one dies. Not Joe. Not the Rhino. The next day she is well enough to discharge herself from hospital so Andy is able to babysit while Lorraine and I go to yoga at the local secondary school.

We are learning how to bend our bodies into various

positions like the dog and grasshopper – which Lorraine thinks would make a good name for a country pub. Our classroom, which smells of old plimsolls, leads out into the corridor opposite the canteen via a glass door, so people from other courses can wander past and see us all with our bums up in the air.

The professionals take their own mats. Lorraine and I make do with those that Kyra, the tutor (I'm not sure that's her real name), brings. Lorraine says it's not worth buying one because if she can't suck her own toes by the end of this term, she's giving up to try Indian head massage.

Kyra takes the register. Three of the nine who began classes this term have already dropped out. Kyra says one of the women has enrolled every term for the past four years and never turned up. She wonders if she tells her husband she's doing yoga, which covers for her going home hot and sweaty from a liaison with a lover.

'Stretch, Juliet,' Kyra urges. 'Stretch out that tension.' Kyra's so skinny I can see every muscle in her arms. She wears a black leotard, short black sarong, and black hair up in a bun, drawing it back severely from her face, giving her a natural facelift. I've tried pulling my hair back like that, but it gives me slit eyes and makes my ears seem bigger. I guess Kyra's about sixty, but she's incredibly fit and supple. When she inhales, her stomach disappears behind the struts of her ribs. She can stand immobile on one leg just like the heron on the pond in Kelsey Park.

'Breathe in, and out. Stre . . . tch.'

'I can't,' I gasp.

Kyra tries to bend my right arm back behind my head. 'Ouch!'

'Relax and breathe, Juliet,' she murmurs. 'You must have had a stressful week. You're so tense.'

I'm not a pipecleaner. I don't bend in that direction. There's a click and a nasty tearing sensation in the back of my neck as I discover that I do.

'Hold it to a count of five,' says Kyra.

I have no choice. My neck and shoulder have locked. On the count of five, Kyra gently straightens me out.

'You see, you can do it,' she says. 'You should have more confidence in yourself.'

Lorraine and I sit alongside each other at breaktime. I sip from the bottle of water I have brought with me. Everyone has a bottle. It's part of the uniform, along with leggings and baggy T-shirt or leotard and tights. You can guess which I'm wearing.

I stretch out my legs. My feet are bare. So are Lorraine's, but her toenails are shaped and polished gold. My big toes, I observe, are sprouting tiny hairs. I wonder if I should take steps to remove them. Do people wax their toes? Mine curl at the thought. I take one last swig of water before the class restarts.

When we are all lined up on our mats, attempting a

position that involves stretching one leg out behind the other, someone releases a fart. Not a riproaring, 'I'm not embarrassed' break of wind, but an 'I'm trying to hold this in, but I can't' squeal.

Who did that? Everyone's casting inquisitive glances at everyone else, apart from Lorraine who's staring at the floor. Her shoulders are shaking. It was her, wasn't it? I giggle. Kyra laughs. Everyone is laughing. I never imagined I would enjoy evening classes this much. I am completely relaxed. I haven't a care in the world, apart from worrying over the question of telling Lorraine about Joe, my concerns for the financial security of the Wyevales and the possibility that Steve is interested in my bodywork.

Afterwards Lorraine and I wander back to my car, talking.

'I'm so embarrassed,' Lorraine whines. 'I can't go back, Juliet.'

'Of course you can. Breaking wind is a natural phenomenon. Everyone does it.'

'Not in the middle of a yoga class.'

'Everyone will have forgotten by next week. Don't worry about it.' I glance towards Lorraine. She will worry. In spite of her sharp tongue and confident exterior, Lorraine cares what other people think about her. 'Hey, do you think that woman who's never turned up to class is really having an affair?' I wonder how easy it would be to arrange. The trouble is, I have Lorraine with me and she knows the ruse, but if she gives up yoga to do Indian head massage which is on Tuesdays, I could meet Steve every Thursday night. Not that he's asked me.

'It seems as if everyone's doing it nowadays,' says Lorraine.

'I'm not,' I say hurriedly.

'How's your washing machine?'

I frown as I hunt through my bag for the car keys. Since when has anybody been interested in the health of my appliances?

'Joe said he got it going last night. You should have told me it wasn't working. You could've used mine.'

'Thanks for the offer.' The keys surface from the depths of my bag. I don't like the thought of contaminating Lorraine's machine with our dirty linen. I don't like the thought of Lorraine folding it for me afterwards and finding the holes. It occurs to me that this is a good time to enlighten her as to her husband's nocturnal activities. There seem to be more holes opening up in her marriage than there are in mine.

'I didn't know Joe was any good at fixing washing machines. He's never been able to repair ours.'

'The more fancy programmes they have on them, the more difficult they are to fix,' I say quickly. 'Ours isn't quite as old as a twin tub, but it's not far off.'

Lorraine smiles. 'Well, I'm glad he was able to help.'

I start the car.

'Would you like to stop in for coffee?' Lorraine asks.

'No, thanks. Not tonight. What with the Rhino going into hospital, and work, I feel as though I've hardly seen Andy the last few days.'

'You haven't found the ring, have you? You haven't told him yet. Really, Juliet, you must tell him.' Lorraine leans back in the passenger seat. 'Joe and I have always been totally honest with each other.'

The engine stalls, jerking us forwards. I curse, put the car into neutral and turn the key. It restarts, but I feel little sense of relief. I am no better than Joe, lusting after someone other than my spouse.

Chapter Six

I don't usually lust after other men – real and available men, that is. It is wrong and I shan't do it any longer. I am the perfect wife and mother. From now on, I have resolved to suppress my own desires, to subjugate them to my family's whims. I am martyring myself on the cross of family life. The Rhino will be proud of me.

I was up an hour early, lining up neat piles of shirts and socks on the guest bed in the spare room for each member of the family. I chose modest clothing – white blouse, black trousers and black shoes. No thong. Ever again. I stuffed it in the rag-bag in the cupboard under the stairs.

I leave the house by eight thirty so I have time to take Emily to Mary's before I drop Jamie at school. This means he can hand over the birthday card he has made for her personally.

I was intending to give Mary the Delia cookery book

that the Rhino returned to me, but I thought I might embarrass her with my largesse, even if I did explain that I bought it from the remainder bookshop. (I also worry that if I'm too generous, Mary might just start asking for a better hourly rate.) I chose a small box of Maltesers from Jimmy's instead. Emily is holding on to it in the back of the car. I don't know if she'll give it up when we reach Mary's, but that's Mary's problem, not mine.

Jamie hands over the card on Mary's doorstep.

'What's this?' she says, frowning.

'Happy late birthday,' Jamie smiles. 'I made it for you because you didn't have any cards.'

Yesterday Jamie told me Mary hadn't had *many* cards. Perhaps I misheard. Now I think about it, I can't remember seeing any in Mary's living room, but I was distracted by the nieces and their eclectic choice of gifts.

Mary opens the card – there's no envelope.

'Thank you, Jamie. You're very kind.'

'We've brought you a present as well,' he says.

'You shouldn't have,' Mary says, glancing towards me.

'Give it here, Emily,' says Jamie, wrestling the box from her hands. Emily screws up her face, turns purple and screams. The window above us flies open and a woman's voice, high-pitched and angry, emerges. I press my hands over Jamie's ears as the voice swears vengeance on the fat cow downstairs.

'I'm so sorry, Juliet,' says Mary.

'Oh, it isn't your fault. It's like family, isn't it? You can't choose your neighbours.'

'Actually, the nieces and I had a bit of a do last night. It didn't go on late, but number four – that's Frank and Doreen – weren't too happy about the noise. Frank is suffering from a terminal illness.' Mary pauses as if she's trying to remember something, then adds, 'That's why they're out all hours down at the hospital, you see.'

I don't see. I am not entirely sure that Mary is telling the truth. Why does a sick man need all those boxes Mary took in for him the other day? Do they contain some kind of medication?

'Now, come on, Emily,' Mary says gruffly. 'Remember that story I told you about what happened to the little girl who wouldn't stop screaming?' She grabs Emily's hand. Whatever story it was, it hasn't had the desired effect, because Emily screams louder.

'You go, Juliet,' Mary says. 'She'll calm down once you've gone. Out of sight, out of mind.'

Out of sight, out of mind. I'm not sure Mary's got that right. When I draw up to work, I park in one of the spaces on the forecourt reserved for customers rather than drive round the back. That way Steve remains out of sight, but he's still very definitely in my mind.

I approach the showroom, pause and look through the glass door. Andy is throwing open the doors of the Jag, trying to sell it to a woman who follows him around, dragging one of those tartan shopping trolleys. It's Nell Cornwell who walks past almost daily to buy cat food. She's in her eighties – nineties maybe – and she wears the same red wool coat and buckle-up shoes every day of the year. Andy thinks she's one of those people who're loaded, but don't show it. I think he's wasting his time.

I love that man, I tell myself, even if he does joke that my hair looks like streaky bacon. We used to laugh all the time. Andy and Juliet BC (Before Children) couldn't keep their hands off each other. It didn't matter which match was on the telly, or what was happening in *EastEnders*. Nothing came between them. So what has happened? How can I recreate that time?

If I close my eyes, I can recall snippets of sensation – anticipation pulsing like fire through my bloodstream, making me lightheaded with lust, the taut ache deep in my pelvis, the moist heat of Andy's breath against my breast . . . I remember running my hands through Andy's hair. I can't bring the hair back, but can I restore the desire?

I push the door open.

'So you'll let me know, Mrs Cornwell?' I hear Andy saying.

'You're a very persuasive young man,' says Mrs Cornwell, apparently trying to extricate herself from Andy's determined handshake, 'but I'd prefer something less ostentatious.'

'It's not flash,' Andy says smoothly. 'It's stylish and

sophisticated, just the thing for cruising along the front at Eastbourne.'

Nell Cornwell pulls her knitted hat down over her ears.

'Good morning, Mr Wyevale,' she says politely before shuffling out with the wheels of her trolley rattling over the bumps in the lino.

'Hi, Jules,' Andy says. 'Nell said she'd think about the Jag.'

'She was being polite.'

'No, she liked it. She said she could see its appeal.'

I wonder if there's something wrong with Andy. It's supposed to be the customers who are gullible. On the other hand I am being disloyal. Lorraine is never disloyal although she has good reason to be. I feel a stab of guilt. How can she be disloyal if she doesn't realise she has something to be disloyal about? In my new role, I am going to have to tell her about Joe, aren't I?

Perhaps I should approach it in another way. Instead of blurting straight out that Joe propositioned me, I should show Lorraine Joe's view of their marriage, that he thinks she's nagging him to death, then they can sit down and talk through their differences.

There is one major hitch in this plan – men don't talk about relationships. In my experience, they prefer to discuss transfer fees and groin strains, attack formations and shin splints.

'Where's Gayle?' I ask, realising Gayle is not at her desk.

'She was here a minute ago.' Andy grins. 'She said she was taking Steve some coffee. He seems like a popular guy.'

My heart stops. 'What do you mean?'

'Look at Gayle's desk,' he says in a conspiratorial whisper. 'What's happened to the photo of her fitness instructor boyfriend?'

'It's gone.'

'No, Jules. It's lying face down. I'd suggest he's on his way out and Gayle's got herself a toyboy.'

I move over, pick up the photo and place it upright on the desk. It's not possible. Gayle and Steve. But why shouldn't it be? I'm not available. Why shouldn't Steve move on to find happiness with someone who is?

Andy says no more about the subject of Gayle's love life because just then Gayle returns to her desk, slinking along in her high heels.

'I'm taking one of Jimmy's mates on a test drive,' Andy says, flinging a jacket over his shirt. 'I'll see you later.' He takes the Toyota off the forecourt into the traffic on the Whitehorse Road, and I try to settle to some paperwork. I can't concentrate. Gayle has turned the photo of her boyfriend back face down, and I'm sure she's filing her nails with more than her usual vigour. Not that my equilibrium should be disturbed in any way by the thought that she might be trying to get off with Steve, because I am the perfect wife and mother.

I am going to prepare a special meal for Andy and,

when he's had a couple of glasses of wine, if I can keep him off the lager, I'll tell him about the ring and it will all be over with. I shall go and ask Lorraine if I can borrow Jamie Oliver. I shall chuck in a bit of this and a bit of that, and I shall bathe and present myself to Andy, fresh and fragrant as a quickfrozen herb.

At twelve-thirty, Gayle goes off for lunch. Andy isn't back yet. I'm starving so I open the cheese and pickle sandwiches I made last night and kept in the freezer by mistake in my new drive for perfection and efficiency. They are hard in the middle and soggy at the edges.

'Hi, Juliet.'

Suddenly, I am no longer hungry, at least not in the conventional sense. Steve is standing in the doorway in a grubby vest that might once have been white, and trousers that might once have been royal blue, but the dirt doesn't detract from his appearance. Not one bit. His dark hair is dishevelled and his face flushed as though he has just jumped out of bed. His eyes flicker across the office from the coffee maker to the sandwiches on my desk, and settle on me.

'You didn't bring me a drink this morning.'

'Gayle did, didn't she?'

'It wasn't the same. I wanted to see you.'

'I'm sorry.' Why do I always do that? The English disease. Constant, unnecessary apologising. 'I'm sorry, but I've been tied up.'

Steve raises one eyebrow.

'Not literally,' I say, dropping my guard enough to smile. 'Er, would you like a sandwich?'

'I don't eat in the middle of the day.'

'You ought to.' What am I saying?

'Never have done,' Steve says, pouring himself a coffee. 'My mother says I should too.'

I bite my lip. It's true what Lorraine said. I do – I have reminded him of his mother. I watch, appalled at myself, yet transfixed as Steve drinks his coffee down in one. He puts the mug back, wipes sweat from his fore-head, and proceeds to strip off his vest. He moves delib-erately, slowly, enjoying me watching him. I mustn't look, but I can't tear my eyes off him.

Steve tosses the vest over one shoulder and rests his fingers on his belt buckle. For one delicious moment, I wonder if he is going to reveal more naked muscle, but the Toyota roars back onto the forecourt, and squeals to a stop. Steve tucks his thumbs inside his belt.

'I'd better get back to work,' he says, leaving the aphrodisiac scent of sweat and engine oil behind him, and smudges on an empty mug. The smudges are inti-mate, ordinary things left behind, like buttons from a shirt, or hairs on a comb. They reveal that Steve has a scar, a broad line that disrupts the whorls of his thumbprint. He's not so young that he doesn't have history.

I have history too, ties I cannot sever for a quick fling with a man I hardly know, even if he does remind me of Antonio Banderas. I have a wonderful, considerate husband. I have two beautiful children. I have a house of solid construction high above a flood plain. I have a car that runs, just about – it's been making a funny squeaking noise recently. My cup overflows.

I am the perfect wife and mother, and from now on I am going to nurture my marriage and try to salvage Lorraine and Joe's. I cannot put this into effect until after seven this evening when, with a brown paper package tucked under my arm, I drop round to Lorraine's.

'I'm sorry it's late, but I've come to borrow Jamie Oliver,' I say, pushing Jamie and Emily forwards through Lorraine's front door, so she can't shut us out.

'Tyler's just going to bed,' Lorraine says, but I am determined.

'I'm planning a romantic meal for Andy tomorrow. I need to make a shopping list.'

'I thought you had a copy of Delia.' Lorraine frowns. She looks as if she is about to go out, her hair brushed, and shining in the light that comes on automatically when someone reaches her front door. It's a good idea, but it's not dark yet.

'I find Delia difficult.'

Lorraine sighs. I am interrupting her evening routines. We don't have those in our house.

'I suppose you'd better come in,' she says, leading us straight to the kitchen where Tyler is wandering about in pink pyjamas. Her ringlets are damp, and she is drinking milk from a baby's bottle.

'I want a bottle,' Emily starts.

'You're out late tonight, Juliet.' Joe pops his head around the door.

'Juliet's cooking a special dinner for Andy,' says Lorraine.

'You could try mixing in some Viagra,' says Joe.

'You're so cruel sometimes,' Lorraine titters. 'Sure you wouldn't prefer Nigella?'

'I would,' says Joe.

'I was talking to Juliet. You could have Jamie and Nigella.'

'I'm not sure they'd get on.'

Lorraine smiles and hands me both TV chefs' books. 'Take your pick.'

Somewhere in this conversation I have gathered that Lorraine has repeated snippets of what I have told her about Andy and our sex life to Joe. I am confused. I have never repeated anything the other way. On the other hand, maybe I have . . .

Joe looks at me, winks and disappears out of the kitchen.

'I want a bottle, Mummy,' Emily tries again.

Tyler's too old to be drinking from a bottle, but I can't come out with that in front of Lorraine. If she's not careful Tyler will make the transition from milk to alcopop without ever having used a proper cup without a lid and spout. I can understand she's worried about her soft furnishings, but you have to take a risk sometime.

'Mummy, I want a bottle!' Emily stamps her foot on the laminate floor.

'You have mine,' Tyler mutters, twisting the silicone teat between her teeth.

'Don't want yours!' Emily says, but she snatches it anyway and Tyler starts to cry. Rather than argue with Emily, I pick Tyler up and hug her. She smells faintly medicated, of tea-tree oil and eucalyptus.

'Why don't you give me the bottle, Emily, and Tyler can show you and Jamie the latest furniture for the dolls-house?' says Lorraine. Tyler gives a sniff, and wriggles down from my arms. Emily meekly hands the bottle over.

'You know, I think Emily's behaviour's improving,' Lorraine says, watching the two girls head out of the kitchen with Jamie in tow.

'She couldn't get any worse.'

'She hasn't turned the new childminder to drink yet?'

'No.' I pause. 'She might have turned her to nicotine though.'

'You don't think she smokes in front of the children? That's criminal.'

'I didn't mean it,' I protest. 'It was a lighthearted remark. Mary takes in deliveries of cigarettes for her neighbours upstairs.' (I had asked Jamie what was in the boxes.)

'You take in deliveries from B&Q for me and Joe, but I'd never suggest that you'd turned to abusing our solvents.' Lorraine grins. 'I need a coffee. Would you like one, Juliet?'

'I'd love one, thanks.'

Lorraine flicks the switch on the kettle, a new one, I notice. It's see-through with an integral filter. Very swish. Joe turns up again, this time wearing a smart camel-coloured fleece I haven't seen before. His hair is different too, spiked up with gel. His eyes twinkle and his skin has a glow about it. I could, if I wasn't obsessing over Steve, consider him rather attractive. He has an air of suppressed excitement about him, like Andy does when he's looking forward to watching a match.

'I'm off then,' he says.

Lorraine raises one eyebrow. 'Tonight? You said you'd stay in and make a start on the bedroom.'

'I didn't.' Joe looks towards me. 'Lorraine wants me to replace the wardrobe doors with reclaimed floorboards. What do you think of that?'

'Sounds interesting, but haven't you just decorated the bedroom?' I recall Lorraine's pine wardrobes standing against freshly painted lilac walls and the four sets of duvet covers – virginal white, romantic white embroidered with stars, an assertive lilac and white check, and lustful lilac satin – which she changes according to her mood.

'That was ages ago,' says Lorraine.

'Lorraine wants olive paint teamed with pale pink wallpaper, and a hessian-covered headboard,' Joe says.

'Soft romantic is so last year,' says Lorraine. 'Organic elemental is what's happening now, and I want it happening in our bedroom, Joe.'

'Well, it's not happening tonight because I'm off out for a drink.'

'Where?'

'I don't know yet. The Portmanor? The Alliance? Anywhere for some peace and quiet.'

The kettle is boiling, breathing steam. As is Lorraine.

'You're not going to be late,' she says. That sounds more like an order than a request to me and it gives me the ideal opportunity once Joe is gone to hand her the brown paper package.

'What's this?'

'A book. *Men are from Mars, Women are from Venus*. Tips for a healthy relationship. My sister recommended it.'

'Oh, I don't have time to read,' Lorraine says, dropping it still wrapped onto the kitchen worktop. 'Besides, why should I need a book on self-improvement?'

I suppose that is the answer one should expect from someone who believes she has the perfect life, but I am not deterred.

'Men don't like being nagged.'

'I go on at Joe sometimes, but that's not surprising considering how he behaves. All I'm asking for is some of his time. He's not a kid any more. He has responsibilities which he needs me to remind him of.' Lorraine pours two coffees. 'It's not nagging, Juliet.'

113

Lorraine and I join the children who are playing with Tyler's dolls-house in the sitting room. Their sitting room is not as comfortable, not as lived in as ours, although I would never say so. The walls are painted coffee and cream. The suite, which is new, is raspberry. The room is dominated by that framed photo of Joe and Lorraine on their wedding day. Lorraine wants to replace the gasfire and surround beneath the picture with one of those ultramodern fires that I can only describe as a bowl of flaming pebbles.

I study the photo as I have done so many times before. Then, I was wondering if it could reveal the secret of attaining the perfect marriage. Now, I wonder if I was missing something all along, something in Joe's wicked smile or the way Lorraine's strangling the blooms in her bouquet, that predicts infidelity and failure.

'Do you believe you're being unfaithful if you imagine being unfaithful, but you don't act it out?' I begin.

'No,' says Lorraine after a pause. 'That's a strange question. Is this meal for Andy not what it seems? Is it a guilt trip?' She lowers her voice. 'Has something happened?'

'What would I do with a lover? I haven't the time or the energy.'

'You would tell me if you had?'

'Yeah.'

'You wouldn't do anything silly, would you, Juliet? I'd hate to see you throw it all away.'

'Throw what away?'

'Your marriage and your family. Andy loves you.'

'All he's done is looked,' I protest. 'He hasn't touched me, not intentionally, not in an amorous kind of way.'

'You mean Steve, the mechanic?' Lorraine pauses. I guess she's going to say more on the subject, but she goes quiet, gazing towards Tyler's dolls-house. It's made of wood, not plastic, and furnished with more items than I'll ever have in my own house. It's everything I dreamed of as a child, and more. The front is painted white with trailing plants and flowers. The roof is red. It even has electric lights.

'I've told Joe I'd like a cottage just like that,' says Lorraine.

'You won't find one of those in Beckenham,' I point out.

'It's my birthday soon,' Jamie interrupts.

'Oh, this wasn't for Tyler's birthday,' says Lorraine.

'It from my grandma,' Tyler chips in.

'One of the old girls at the nursing home left Mum a little cash. She used it to buy us all presents. It's one of the perks of the job.'

'It's my birthday soon,' Jamie repeats.

'In a couple of months,' I say. 'That's ages to wait.'

'I'm going to have a hamster and a big party.'

My heart sinks. I'm not sure we'll have the money this year, and I don't want to waste what we have got on a small brown rodent that I'll end up looking after, although a hamster might be cheaper than his second choice of present, a dog, and not any old dog, but a Dalmatian.

'I'm not sure about the hamster, Jamie.'

'But Mum . . .'

'What use is a hamster?'

'It . . . It . . .'

'You can eat them, can't you?' says Lorraine.

'No. Yuck!' shouts Jamie.

'So, if you can't eat it, what exactly is a hamster for?'

Jamie smiles. His eyes soften.

'To be loved,' he says, and my heart swells. He lets Lorraine ruffle his hair which has grown rapidly from a number four to what I'd guess is a number five. I spread Jamie Oliver across my lap and flick through the pages. I choose cod.

The supermarket has no cod, but they do have pollock which hasn't quite the same ring about it. I buy it anyway. I put the kids to bed early and prepare pollock with prawns, cream, avocado, tomato and basil. I do it the Jamie Oliver way, scattering prawns, tipping cream straight from the container without measuring it out first, hacking at an avocado and ripping up leaves of basil. I have forgotten to buy tomatoes, but I don't think it matters. For someone who's more used to cooking sausage casserole and turkey meatballs, it looks pukka. I boil rice that I can reheat in the microwave, and drizzle olive oil over peppers which I shall roast, as long as

I remember to switch the oven on. I put a Chardonnay in the fridge, glad I resisted eating chicken nuggets and chips with the children.

Andy should be home for seven. I aim to be ready just before. I picture myself taking his jacket, and leading him into the dining room where shadows cast by flaming candles dance on the walls. The music is low. I pour two glasses of wine.

'Sit down, darling.'

'Oh Juliet, you shouldn't have,' and then, 'You're the most remarkable woman, the most wonderful wife a man could have.'

Afterwards we dance, and then, melting in the gaze of his blue eyes, I lead him up to the bedroom where we make love all night long. (Loud so Joe hears, but not so loud that the children wake up.)

It's 7.15 though and Andy's not home. I can't get him at work. I can't reach him on his mobile. I leave a message from the home phone.

I send two texts from my mobile, one at 7.21 and another at 7.30 by which time the dinner has been in the oven twenty minutes longer than Jamie Oliver recommends. It smelled quite pleasant twenty minutes ago, but now it emits the aroma of dried fish and burned wood. I take it out and leave it on the hob. I take the wine from the fridge through to the dining room and unscrew the lid. It smells of lemons and lychees – liquid sunshine. I pour myself a glass.

'Cheers, Juliet,' I say to myself before drinking the whole glass down in one. Who does that remind me of? Steve drinking from a mug, his head tipped back, exposing the muscles in his neck and the vein pulsing in its groove. I pour a second glass, kick off my shoes and sit at the table, running my fingers slowly up and down the stem of the wineglass. How do perfect wives and mothers keep it up? I pour a third then a fourth glass of wine. The room is rotating slowly around me.

I need music. I stumble to the tower from MFI that contains our limited CD collection, and find some Fleetwood Mac which belongs to Andy. There's a song containing lyrics about laying someone down in the tall grass which makes me think of Steve again. Don't ask me why. I don't like men any more. There's another song, in which Stevie Nicks and friends are exhorting someone to go their own way, and it's while this is playing, at 9.23 precisely, that Andy comes home.

'Hi, babe,' he calls from the hall. 'Where are you?'

'In here!'

'I'm bloody knackered,' Andy says, running his hand across his head. I think sometimes he forgets he has no hair. The hair he has got needs clipping. It's too long, and I know that the dark shadow around his jawline will bring me out in a rash, if I ever let him get that close again which, the mood I'm in, is highly unlikely.

'I cooked dinner.'

'Oh, I'm sorry – can you freeze it? Only I had something on the way to—'

'Don't tell me,' I interrupt. A kebab – I can smell curry sauce on his breath. 'Andy, I've been trying to get hold of you. Didn't you check your phone?'

'I tried calling you sometime after seven, but you were engaged. I assumed you were talking to Lorraine.' Andy gazes around the room. 'The candles? The wine? Oh, I'm sorry, Jules, but you didn't tell me.'

'It was a surprise. You don't tell someone you're giving them a surprise, otherwise it wouldn't be a surprise, would it?'

'You can still eat, Jules. I won't mind.'

'I'm not hungry,' I snap.

'What was it anyway?' Andy turns the music off and the lights on. I pinch the candles out.

'Pollock.'

'Enlighten me?'

'Fish.' About £3.50's worth, a 400g pack of frozen prawns at £3.99 and a £5 bottle of wine. All wasted, like my efforts to be the perfect wife and mother. And I still haven't told Andy about the ring. I am perfectly pissed off. I am so angry that the fact that Andy is trying to tell me something while he's backing out of the dining room hardly registers.

'Please keep calm, Jules.'

'I *am* calm.'

'Keep your voice down,' Andy warns. His eyes are

drawn to my hands where I am twisting an imaginary ring around my ring finger. 'Where's your wedding ring?'

'I don't know.' I tip my head back and stroke my throat, which makes my double chin almost completely disappear. If Andy doesn't speak to me again, I don't think I'd care.

'You said you knew where it was.'

'I thought I did. I looked and it isn't where I thought it was.' I've tried everywhere now, even pulled the loose floorboard up alongside the bed in the spare room and hammered it back down again.

'How long's it been missing, Juliet?'

'Ooh, I don't know.' My heart pounds uncomfortably against my ribs. Lying while sober has been going so well, but after all those glasses of wine – nearly a whole bottle – I'm as transparent as microwave and freezer wrap.

'You've been lying to me, haven't you? You haven't worn it for days, weeks . . . That's why you were digging about in the bins, isn't it? You thought you'd thrown it away. You probably have.'

'I didn't mean to mislead you, Andy. I didn't want to upset you.'

'Well, you have upset me. Very much. How could you lose the most precious thing I have ever given you? How could you not tell me? I could've helped you find it.'

I think for a moment that Andy is about to burst into tears. I have seen him cry twice before. When his father died from cancer. When Crystal Palace sold Morrison to Birmingham City. I stand up, holding on to the edge of the table.

'I bet you've told Lorraine. I bet you've told her all about it. You have, haven't you? She knows and I don't!'

'I'm sorry.'

Andy gives me a look that breaks my heart. He stares at me, eyes narrowed, mouth set in a grim line. Every negative emotion is there etched on his face. Hatred, disgust, and anger.

'I really am sorry.'

'Oh, save it, Juliet!' Andy yells loud enough to be heard in Brixton. 'How do I know you're not lying about that as well?'

I don't know how to answer that. The dining-room door creaks open behind him. My first thought is that we've woken the children. My second is that I'm caught up in an impossible nightmare as the Rhino's face, phantom pale, materialises from the darkness beyond. I open my mouth in a gaping scream.

Chapter Seven

If Kyra thought I was tense at yoga the other evening, she should see me now.

'Why does *she* have to stay here?' I ask through gritted teeth, once Andy has tucked his mother up in the spare room where I was intending to sleep tonight.

'She's sick – not that you care,' Andy snaps.

'You could have asked me if I minded.'

'And what would you have said if I'd managed to get through to you?' Andy pauses. 'Yes, I thought so. Well, I've told her she's welcome to stay for as long as she wishes.'

'How long is that?'

Andy shrugs.

Tap. Tap. Tap.

'Andreeeew . . .' The Rhino wanders into the kitchen. She's wearing a kimono-style dressing-gown over a chiffon nightie so pink that Barbie would be envious.

Her face is shiny with cold cream. 'I can't sleep,' she whines.

'Are you in pain, Mother? Should I call the doctor?'

'It's not that. Those curtains in my room aren't lined. They let far too much light through. I'm used to the shutters on the boat.' She pauses. 'I've come down to make myself a nightcap. Where do you keep your camomile?'

'You'll have to settle for PG Tips, I'm afraid,' says Andy.

'Juliet can buy me some tomorrow,' the Rhino says, turning to me. 'I don't like to be a nuisance, but PG Tips aren't my cup of tea.'

'How about some hot water?' Andy suggests. 'I'll bring it up to you.'

'Thank you, Andrew. Goodnight, Juliet.'

''Night,' I mutter.

'I hope you're going to make an effort,' Andy says as the Rhino pads off along the hall. 'Dr Leaver is furious that she discharged herself from the hospital too early.'

So am I.

'He suggested she should stay with friends or relatives for a while,' Andy continues. 'She didn't want to come here, but I insisted.'

'What about David? Why couldn't she stay with him?'

'He's in the Gambia.'

'On holiday again?'

'He's working. He likes to check out the destinations

personally before he recommends them – apparently, some of the hotels are appalling.'

'Poor David,' I taunt. 'I take it he's on an all-inclusive break.'

'How did you know?'

'I guessed.'

It is a difficult time. Andy and I are at war. It's not a missile-firing, mine-dropping, high-mortality conflict, but a quiet advance of enemy lines which, once in sight of each other, leads to a stand-off lasting several weeks. The Rhino remains living with us, acting as Andy's ally.

Initially, she retreats to the spare room and sleeps, as you would expect for someone who claims to have recently enjoyed a near-death experience, but it doesn't last. She is soon up and about, ordering healthy, gluten-free meals, and trying to organise my life.

'I'd love to meet the paragon who minds my grand-children,' she hints several times before persuading Andy to take her into work one afternoon, so she can come with me to collect Jamie and Emily from Mary's.

'I thought we'd be going in the Mercedes,' the Rhino says.

'The children's booster seats are in my car,' I say firmly. 'You don't have to come with me.'

'Oh, I do,' she insists. 'We can have a little chat on the way. Woman to woman.'

'There's no need.'

'I beg to differ.'

Panic grips me by the throat. There is no escape. The Rhino, dressed for the occasion in a black and white spotted skirt, black jacket and black boater-style hat with mock lilies and netting wired to the brim, is belted securely into the passenger seat beside me. Even worse, we are stuck in a queue of traffic on the Whitehorse Road.

'It hasn't escaped my notice that you and Andrew are not happy together, Juliet.'

'We're fine.'

'I'm not criticising the way you treat him with those dark looks and sulks of yours. I'm merely observing that husbands require a certain amount of attention. A neglected husband is vulnerable to straying and theft.'

I want to tell her that she doesn't know anything about my marriage, but I can't get a word in edgeways.

'After all Andrew has been doing for me, I feel that I'd like to help in some way. Perhaps offer to babysit so you can go out together. However,' the Rhino continues, 'it wouldn't be wise considering my precarious state of health. Dr Leaver tells me that the slightest stress could trigger another attack and, although Emily is delightful, she isn't the easiest child for an invalid to cope with.'

The Rhino doesn't let up.

'I wonder if Emily is really happy with this Mary Bacon. That's why I thought I should meet her myself. I realised long ago that Andrew isn't the best judge of character.'

126

'You mean your son has a flaw?' I can't help myself. I've had just about all I can take.

'Innocence and openness are not flaws in themselves,' says the Rhino. 'It is the people who take advantage of those qualities in others who are flawed.'

When we arrive at Mary's, I have to park across the road again, not because of any delivery van, but because there's a sleek, black hearse parked outside her maisonette.

'I wonder who's died,' the Rhino says in a hushed whisper. The excitement in her voice is hardly restrained. She loves ceremonies – christenings, weddings (apart from mine), and funerals.

She walks over to Mary's with me. I knock at the door. A gust of Febreze hits me in the throat as Jamie opens it.

'Hi, Mum. Hi, Granny.'

Four men, carrying a black coffin with chrome fittings, walk up to the hearse and load it into the back. A woman, dressed in black with a fringed hat to rival the Rhino's, follows.

'Frank's dead,' says Mary when she arrives at the door. 'Lung cancer.'

All of a sudden I feel terribly guilty for having doubted Mary when she said that Frank had a terminal illness.

'Are you going to the funeral?' I ask. 'I'd have come earlier if—'

'Hop in, love,' interrupts one of the bearers. 'You'll be late for the crem.'

'Us? Me?' says the Rhino, clasping her neck. 'I never knew the poor man.'

'My mistake. I thought with you being dressed up like that you were one of the mourners.' The bearer slams the rear doors of the hearse, and strolls around to the driver's door.

'An easy error to make,' says Mary, looking the Rhino up and down. The Rhino does the same to Mary while we wait on the doorstep for Jamie and Emily to fetch their coats. I don't need to ask the Rhino her opinion of Mary Bacon. I already know it.

When we return to the car I have to move Jamie's booster seat into the front of the car so Emily can sit next to the Rhino on the way home.

'In my experience,' the Rhino begins, 'people who use air fresheners and fabric deodorisers do so because they have odours they wish to disguise rather than remove. It's disgusting.'

'Andy thought Mary was all right,' I say, but the Rhino's not listening.

'It's a mistake to wear leggings when you're over a certain age. In fact, in my opinion, it's a mistake to wear leggings at any age. They emphasise the thighs and derrière. So unflattering.'

'Yes, but—'

'She wouldn't look me in the eye, Juliet, and that makes me wonder if I can trust her. She seemed ill at ease.'

'You would be if you'd had Emily all day,' I point out.

'It has nothing to do with Emily. What I am saying is that I'd never have left my boys with a woman like that.'

'You didn't have to. You had it easy. You didn't go out to work.'

'I ran my home to the highest standards,' she says sniffily.

Jamie sneezes beside me. The Rhino hasn't finished.

'That boy's always off-colour, Juliet. I know you dismiss his symptoms as just another cold but, given your family situation, I wonder if it's psychosomatic.'

'What's psychosomatic?' Jamie asks.

'Don't ask your mother while she's driving,' the Rhino says quickly. 'I shall tell you later.'

In spite of everything, I smile to myself, and let my fingers play on the steering wheel. The Rhino disapproves of Mary Bacon, therefore, I am even more inclined to like her.

I'm not sure what triggers it – my driving, Jamie's questions, or Emily's demands – but the Rhino takes to her bed with stomach pains. The following day, she makes an urgent appointment with the eminent Dr Leaver. Andy takes her to the narrowboat where the doctor makes a housecall to save her travelling to Harley Street. The doctor decides that living with us is far more stressful for her than living on her own, and the Rhino remains in Islington.

I can't tell you how good that makes me feel. I am more kindly disposed towards Andy although we are still officially at war. I cope with Emily's paddies about going to Mary's with a smile, and I have a spring in my step as I go about my work at Wyevale Autos.

'Hi, Juliet.'

'Morning, Steve.'

There's a catch in his throat, a suppressed chuckle. 'It's afternoon. Two o'clock.'

'You surprise me.' Steve is always able to surprise me. I become more besotted with him the more I discover. At twenty-one, he's travelled the world, bathed naked in hot springs in Iceland, played naked on the beaches in Thailand (I didn't ask who he played with or what he played), hiked (half-naked) through the Australian outback and tried whitewater rafting (not naked) on the foaming waters of the Colorado River.

I pick up a pen, trying to distract myself from thoughts of Steve in various states of undress. Steve perches his rear on the edge of my desk. He's very close and he's peering down my top. I lean back, tipping my chair. The end of the pen drifts between my lips.

'You seem distracted, Juliet. Are you all right?'

'Fine.'

Steve cocks his head to one side like a puppy dog and I can almost see the appeal in owning a puppy dog as a pet.

'You know you can come to me,' he says softly. Come

to me? How's that for an invitation! I could respond. I could leap up and grab him by the shoulders, and yell, 'Yes, yes, yes!' or I could do what I am doing. I smile faintly, regret not taking up the offer, and stab the end of the pen into the top of the desk where it leaves an inky gouge. 'If you want to talk . . .'

I don't know what to say. I don't know how to kick-start the conversation. I don't like to talk about the children. I know just how interesting other people's children can be, and although Jamie is doing brilliantly at school according to Miss Trays, Emily has done little to recommend herself recently apart from paint a red blob holding a big black stick. She told everyone it was a scary pig, a portrait of Mary Bacon, her childminder.

'Lorraine and I go to yoga classes. Have you ever tried yoga?' I ask.

'No,' Steve says, wide-eyed and innocent, but I know he's teasing. 'I bet you could show me some interesting positions.' He leans very close. My face is red hot. His eyes are searching mine. All I can hear is a pulse pounding in my ears and Steve's ragged breathing. 'How about, if you show me, I take you for a ride?' He lowers his eyes, cocks his head and sears my cheek with the imprint of his lips.

I pull away sharply, uttering a wordless protest.

'Hey, hey,' Steve soothes. 'You need to relax . . .'

'I couldn't relax on a bike,' I say stupidly. Motorbikes

are dangerous machines driven by hotheads who fail to respect the rights of other road-users. It's one of the few things that the Rhino and I agree on.

'I'd take care of you, you know that. Oh Juliet, you have lovely eyes.'

'Oh, I haven't,' I say gruffly.

'Trust me, you have, and I know that behind those eyes there's a wicked woman trying to get out.'

Steve may be right, but my wicked alter ego has no opportunity to explore just how wicked she might be because Gayle's voice cuts through the mists of frustrated passion.

'I'm not interrupting, am I?'

Steve stands up very straight. 'I just came to see the boss about some parts,' he says with a grin.

I wonder briefly what, if anything, Gayle thinks she saw, but my mind is concentrated on one of the parts that I think Steve came to see me about, the outline of which is clearly discernible and upstanding to the left of the zip of his fly. Unless it's the handle of an extra large screwdriver.

Gayle clears her throat. 'There's someone to see you, Steve,' she says.

'Oh? Trouble?'

'It's Debs again.'

I glance from Steve to Gayle and back to Steve once more.

'She knows you're here. I've sent her round to the

workshop. I don't want to be party to your complicated love life.'

'Who—' I begin, but Steve interrupts.

'My ex.' He rubs his palms up and down the tops of his thighs.

'She's in quite a state,' says Gayle. 'I said I'd put the kettle on. You can make her a mug of tea.'

'I'll do it.' I stand up and grab the kettle before Gayle can. I want to see this ex of Steve's, see the young lady who has broken his heart. 'You'd better go to her, Steve,' I suggest. 'Gayle, would you phone those ads in to *Auto Trader*?'

Apparently displeased at having to use the phone for a legitimate purpose, Gayle stalks out. Steve follows, head bowed and hands in his pockets. Poor Steve. A clean break is always best. Meeting up to rake over the past, to sift through the bitterness and jealousies of a broken relationship isn't a good idea. It only prolongs the agony for the injured party. I hope this Debs isn't going to try to persuade him to take her back.

I make tea and take it round to the workshop. Who is Debs? What is she like? Sexier than Holly Valance? More beautiful than Catherine Zeta-Jones? I hesitate as I reach the workshop. The double doors are wide open. I can hear Steve's voice. It's definitely not the voice of a man who's intending to get back with his ex.

'Debs, I've told you before, I'm not listening to your sob stories and lies. Now piss off!'

'You bastard!' A woman – no, she's no more than a girl – dressed in very tight jeans, and a black bomber-type jacket comes running out past me. I catch sight of a tearstained face, and hair dyed red. She isn't that attractive. Steve must have fallen in love with her personality, not her looks. I don't know why I'm surprised. Knowing what I do about him, it's what I should have expected.

When I slip into the workshop, Steve is standing beside the open bonnet of the car he's working on.

'Are you all right?' I ask.

Steve moves round, releases the clip on the bar that holds the bonnet up, and slams it down hard. When he turns towards me, his face is pale and his mouth set in a grim line.

'Tea?' I offer him the mug which he takes in shaking hands, I notice.

'Thanks,' he says. 'I don't normally drink the stuff, but I've had a bit of a shock. Debs says she's pregnant.'

'Oh no,' I gasp. 'What are you going to do?'

Steve shrugs. 'Get her to take a DNA test as soon as the baby's born.'

'Isn't that a little harsh?' I blurt out. 'I mean, the poor girl doesn't look much more than seventeen.'

'She's sixteen.'

'She must be terrified.'

'Sweet, innocent Juliet,' Steve says, half-smiling. 'It turns out that, far from being the innocent virgin, Debs

134

slept around while we were supposed to be together. That's why we split up.'

'Oh Steve . . .'

'Oldest trick in the book, isn't it? Debs wants me to believe the baby's mine because she hopes I'll support it. I'm not going to, though . . .' His voice tails off. I leave him to ponder the implications of Debs's visit. Steve seems pretty confident that the baby's not his and, even if it is, he's the kind of man who'll have the courage to face up to his responsibilities.

As I sit back at my computer, I wonder why other people make their lives so complicated . . .

'Flowers for Mrs Wyevale,' I hear someone call from the showroom. Beyond, I can see the bonnet of a green van parked on the road. 'Flowers for Mrs Wyevale!'

Gayle shows a thin, will-o'-the-wisp woman into the office. I can hardly see her for flowers, a profusion of pink and yellow carnations and floaty gypsophila, and more exotic blooms that I can't name. They must have cost a fortune.

'For me?'

'There's a card,' the woman says tersely, leaving the bouquet on my desk.

I notice Gayle is watching as I tease the card from where it is attached by a yellow ribbon, and open the envelope. The message is typed, the letters smudged as if the florist has shed tears over it.

Juliet. We have to talk. All my love. Andy. XXX.

It's silly really, but my eyes start stinging. I think I'm going to cry.

'Quite a day for romance,' Gayle observes as she watches me sniffing into a tissue.

When I collect Jamie and Emily from Mary Bacon's she says they won't need any dinner tonight because they have had two helpings each of cottage pie made with free-range minced beef and organic vegetables, but Emily moans all the way home that she is starving.

'You can't be hungry, Emily. Jamie isn't.'

'I am,' Jamie says as I pull up behind Andy's car outside our house. 'Mary didn't give us much tea.'

'How much is not much?' I ask.

Jamie thinks for a moment. 'Not enough to keep even a hamster alive,' he says.

'Daddy's home,' shrieks Emily.

Jamie pushes through from the back seat to the passenger seat, opens the door, jumps out and runs up the steps to the house. Emily hurries after him. Andy is waiting. He jumps out from behind the front door, shouting, 'Boo!'

'Daddy's home. Daddy. Daddy!'

I carry my flowers up the steps. Andy looks at me, eyebrows raised.

I nod and smile. 'I love them.'

'I've put a vase ready in the kitchen, and I've ordered a pizza for eight o'clock,' he says. 'The wine's in the fridge – I thought you could do with a break after having to put up with my mother for all that time. She can be pretty demanding.'

I want to say that I'm surprised Andy noticed, but I bite my tongue. It would sound ungracious when he is trying so hard to make amends.

He reads Emily a story about a pink ballerina, baths her and Jamie, and puts them to bed while I sit on the sofa, gazing at the flowers on the mantelpiece. How do I feel about the flowers? I would prefer to receive them now and then for no particular reason rather than on the rare occasions of a marital crisis. Flowers to me are more a symbol of discord than of love and affection, but I guess they serve a purpose in breaking the ice.

Andy and I reconcile over a deep-pan, stuffed-crust pizza with extra pepperoni, and two bottles of white wine.

'I'm sorry I overreacted when you told me you'd lost the ring,' Andy says. 'I've been tired, stressed out . . .'

'I should have told you before.'

'I should have asked you if my mother could stay.'

'You had so much on your mind, and I thought the ring would turn up.'

'You know I love you, Jules.'

I wonder if we're holding different conversations here, but Andy seems happy. He shifts along the sofa and rests his arm around my shoulder. I recognise the signs. His pupils seem to fill his eyes, displacing the blue with liquid black ink. Flowers are in the vase. Cellophane's in the bin. War's over. Let's have a shag. But I'm not ready yet. We have things to discuss while we're still on speaking terms. You never know how long a truce will last.

'We ought to think about Jamie's birthday party,' I suggest.

Andy rubs his nose hard with one finger, compressing the blood out of the tip. 'What does he want then, babe?'

'A big party for all his schoolfriends, and a pet.'

'I'd rather he had a new pushbike.'

'So would I.'

'Couldn't we have the party at home? Money's tight,' Andy says.

'He'll be terribly disappointed.' I think of how Jamie'll look when I tell him. He'll be crestfallen, but he'll try to smile and put a brave face on it. My little hero. 'Perhaps we could do something at home – invite a small, select group of his friends instead of half his class.'

'We could give him the strip I bought last month for his birthday.'

'Okay.' I wish Andy would realise that we don't all share the same passions. Jamie likes swimming, not football. He wants a pet to look after, not a glorified shirt and shorts set.

'You know, Jules,' Andy begins. 'We should spend more time together, just the two of us.'

'If only we could find a babysitter.'

'What about Lorraine and Joe's?' Andy suggests.

'No way.'

'Why's that? Are you afraid I'll run off with her?'

I can't help smiling. I can't imagine anything more ridiculous than the sight of my husband skipping off into the sunset hand in hand with some insatiable nymphomaniac.

'You'd never keep up.'

'I suppose not,' he says ruefully.

I sink down so my head rests against Andy's chest. His shirt carries the comfortingly familiar smell of Persil. I hate to admit it, but I've missed him over the past few weeks. I've missed the little things like Andy's backchat, the hugs and kisses, and even the pats on the bottom.

'Did you know Steve's ex came round to see him today?' I begin.

'Must have been while I was out buying the wine for tonight,' Andy says. 'She's a bit of a pain, that Debs.'

'You've met her?'

'She's been round a couple of times before.'

'You didn't tell me.'

'It's none of our business, is it, Jules? It doesn't matter.'

It does because I like a bit of gossip to relay to Lorraine to prove that I have my finger on the pulse, that I am a vibrant part of our local community, and that I have friends other than her.

'She's told Steve she's pregnant,' I say.

'Poor thing.'

139

'You're right. He's far too young to be tied down.'

'Not Steve, Debs. Poor little thing. She's only just turned sixteen. Very naive. I guess Steve's her first proper boyfriend and she's still in love with him.'

'Andy, you're so gullible,' I sigh. 'You always think the best of people, but Debs is telling you what she wants you to hear. The baby isn't Steve's.'

'That's not the impression she gave me.' Andy turns and kisses me on the cheek. 'Let's go upstairs . . .'

Making love isn't so bad. I find that afterwards. You look back and wonder why you've been so resistant for so long. I lie wrapped in Andy's arms with my back against his belly, and my breathing matching his. Me and Andy. Andy and me. In our bedroom where the darkness is broken by the glow from the sky outside, it seems that we are entirely alone.

'I love you, Jules,' he whispers, nuzzling my hair.

'Love you too.'

'Have you any plans for the week?'

'Lorraine and I are going to IKEA as long as the car holds out.'

'Better ask Steve to take a look at it,' Andy says.

'No, I'm sure it's fine.' Other people from the outside intrude on our marriage and break the spell. Andy begins to snore, and I cannot sleep. I stroke the side of his face uppermost on the pillow, feel the spiky growth of his beard and the small ridge of the scar on his jawline where he was glassed when he tried to protect some woman in a fight that broke out in a pub before I met him. I do love this man. I can't imagine living without him.

There are signs of the shared fabric of our marriage all over the house: Cheeks, the Beanie Baby baboon Andy bought for me; the photos, views of Selhurst Park, the Eagles' football ground (capacity 26,309, all seated), that I bought for him. How could I possibly walk away from all this if, and it's a big IF, Steve asked me to?

Far from offering me the chance of the Big Thing, Steve hasn't even kissed me properly, not that I would kiss him back. I know from experience – premarital experience, that is – that the Big Thing isn't always what it's cracked up to be. That the Big Thing can turn out to be really quite small.

I have a pain in my chest. Indigestion or guilt? Probably the latter. I wriggle from Andy's embrace and stumble out of bed. On the way back from the loo, I stop at Jamie's bedroom door. He is sleeping quietly, frowning his way through a bad dream. I check on Emily. She is asleep too, and her face is dark as thunder. Are they unhappy? Am I neglecting them? Are they going to grow up into socially inept adults because of my inadequate mothering? The Furby hiccups as I brush past the shelf it is now sharing with a heap of shredded tissue. (Emily is helping Jamie manufacture hamster bedding. Jamie lives in hope.)

I guess everyone lives in hope of something. Everyone has a dream. Jamie's is that he'll have a hamster, and Andy's is that the Eagles will win the Premiership. Well, some dreams are more likely to come true than others. The question is, will mine?

Chapter Eight

Dreams can come true, but they have a nasty habit of not turning out quite as you expected. When I dreamed of marrying Andy, having two children (even-tempered ones like Jamie) and living happily ever after, I didn't imagine just how many socks would be involved.

'Where's my socks, Mum?'

'Where are my socks, Juliet?'

Like a queen, I find myself holding court with Jamie and Andy while I'm in the bath. The bathroom isn't worthy of a palace though. It is beige all over, apart from subtle lines of pink that run through the tiles to suggest water and flying birds, and the hot tap on the bath drips constantly. Lorraine suggested I should ask the plumber from Anerley to fix it. I asked her if she was offering to pay his fee, because I wasn't going to waste money in the hope he might spill all about his love life. She said, no, she wasn't, but she'd find out what he was up to, and who with, some other way.

If we did have the money to do it up, I'd like our bathroom to be cool, contemporary and quite minimal; a white suite with chrome fittings, aquamarine mosaic tiles and everything put away in shiny white units.

'I have only one sock,' Andy says.

'You'd better buy some more then,' I say lightly. I bet Leonardo wouldn't have gone on at Kate about his socks if their relationship had not been prematurely torn apart by the icy forces of Nature.

'I had hundreds of socks. Where else could they be?' Andy asks.

'On your feet?' I close my eyes, hold my breath and sink my head under the water.

Compared with the great romance that fills my dreams nowadays, socks are really very small, but Andy will be in a bad mood, and Jamie will get cold feet and be teased at school if I don't find them. Is it possible that one day I shall look back on my life and regret wasting so much time? I agreed to go to IKEA this morning with Lorraine and now I wish I hadn't.

'When are we going to get there?' Emily pipes up as soon as I turn out of Ross Road.

'I want to go to the pet shop,' whines Jamie.

I notice Tyler is sitting in her car seat, holding her non-drip cup upside down. I can see a dark stain spreading across her leggings.

'Why are we going to IKEA?' I ask Lorraine. Lorraine is wearing a white T-shirt, denim jacket, and a red and white gypsy skirt with a flounce, the kind of skirt that makes my ankles look thick and my calves very short. 'Is there any particular purpose to this trip?'

'I want to look at bed-linen and kitchenware.' Lorraine tosses her soft, wavy hair. 'I thought you might want to buy a rug to cover that stain on the hall carpet.'

'That's a good idea,' I say, brightening a little. I glimpse my own hair in the rearview mirror. The stripes are growing out.

'Would you do my hair again sometime, Lorraine?'

'You really did like it then,' she says. 'I wasn't sure.'

'I said so, didn't I?'

'Yes, but you don't always say what you mean, Juliet. You're so afraid you'll hurt people's feelings.'

I guess that's why I'm so keen to have my hair retouched. The tigress inside me has mellowed. She's acting more like a pussy cat.

'I could wax your eyebrows at the same time,' Lorraine adds hopefully.

'I'd rather you did a few more practice ones first.'

'The problem is finding models to practise on when you haven't had any experience.'

'I can understand that.' Lorraine looks disappointed. She hasn't had a customer for weeks. 'I'll think about it,' I say, glancing at my reflection in the rearview mirror.

My eyebrows are soft and luxuriant like dark brown pussy willow.

'You have to admit it, Juliet,' Lorraine observes, 'you have brows to make that Winston bloke who makes babies on TV envious.'

I slam on the brake, change down to first instead of second gear in error, and turn sharply into Wellesley Road, Croydon. I'm sure this isn't the quickest route, or the shortest, but I know where I am. I drive carefully, avoiding the trams until we come to the flyover when it's down to Waddon Station, right and right again onto the Purley Way. I drive very fast past Toys 'R' Us without giving the children the chance to spot Geoffrey the giraffe on the front, and drop back down below the speed limit when we're level with Sainsbury's on the opposite side of the road.

'There's the chimneys!' yells Jamie. He is referring to the two tall chimneys with the yellow and blue bands around the top that make IKEA visible for miles around.

'IKEA, IKEA,' chant Emily and Tyler.

We don't dump the kids in the ball pool inside the entrance to the shop, not because we're being good mothers, but because once Emily's in there, I can't get her out.

'If you're good, you can have a McDonald's later,' I announce.

'Can I have milkshake?' Emily asks immediately. She

knows it doesn't come with a Happy Meal and I'll have to pay more for it, but what price is peace?

'If you're exceptionally good,' I say, and she is. We lose Emily just once – in an indoor tent in the toy section – and find her easily, following the screams as she attacks Tyler for not wanting to stay and play.

Lorraine buys two hundred tealights, a pack of dusters, a cuddly panda and a set of cutlery with blue handles to fit in with the contemporary eclectic theme of her kitchen. Not to be outdone, I buy a couple of photo frames, a pack of six beakers which Lorraine assures me will come in useful when the summer weather comes, a chocolate and cream striped rag rug to cover the stain on the hall carpet, and a giant pepper-pot.

I notice it, or rather it jumps at me, as we arrive downstairs among the kitchen equipment. I reach out and pick it up. Six pounds seems good value for a pepper-pot with a bright red shaft, and superbly knobbed end. I have a tight sensation in my throat. It is a bargain indeed.

'Lorraine, what do you think?'

'It's nice, Mum,' says Jamie.

'It's yucky,' says Emily at the same time, and she and Tyler dance around displays of china and glass, chanting, 'Yucky, yucky, yucky.'

'Be careful, Tyler,' says Lorraine. 'If you bought it, you'd be making a statement, Juliet. You'd be taking a stand against the conventions of middle age.'

'What on earth do you mean?'

'You're almost forty. You should be buying glass jars with silver tops for dispensing your condiments.'

'Thanks a lot,' I say, thinking of the ones we already have at home. 'I'll take it.' The tigress inside me purrs that the pepper-pot isn't what I need. It's a representation of what I need . . .

Once we've paid and left the shop, we squeeze the shopping into the boot of the car and drive round to McDonald's. As I lock the car, I hitch up my leggings. Lorraine doesn't miss a thing.

'You've lost weight, Juliet. Why's that?'

'I'm not dieting.'

'What's the secret then?' Lorraine doesn't give up, but I am not inclined to divulge my theory that emotional stress is the cause of my weight loss. 'You must be dieting,' she insists.

'Not at all,' and I order a double cheeseburger, large fries and a chocolate thickshake to prove it while Lorraine sips at a black coffee and picks at Tyler's fries. 'What about you?' I ask, biting into the reassuring mush of bun, cheese and beef.

'Not really.' Lorraine's perfectly curved eyebrows, neither too heavy, nor too light for her unlined face, seem to fuse together as she frowns. I can see her contact lenses – green today – slip up and down across her eyeballs as she blinks. 'Joe's offering to pay for me to have liposuction.'

I wonder about Joe, I really do. If he's going to die

if he doesn't get intimate with my cellulite – and I do consist largely of cellulite – how can he seriously consider having Lorraine resculptured? Lorraine is deluded. She doesn't have cellulite. She hardly has thighs.

'Did I tell you Tyler wrote her name all on her own yesterday?' she says, changing the subject.

'Yes, you did.' Five times actually. Twice while we were on the phone this morning arranging this outing, twice in the car and once beside the high-sleeper beds in IKEA.

'Do you think she's supposed to be able to write her name at this age?' Lorraine's eyes are glazing over. I can see she's booking Tyler's place at university already. 'It's pretty incredible, isn't it?'

'Amazing,' I agree. 'Shall we go home?'

'Are you sure you wouldn't like to stop off at that pet superstore on the way?' Lorraine says, keeping her voice right down so Jamie can't hear.

'Quite sure.'

'You really ought to consider letting him have a pet if he wants one.' Jamie hears her this time and pricks up his ears. 'Look at Tyler and Ronnie. Having a pet teaches so much about responsibility for living creatures—'

'I know how to spell responsibility,' Jamie interrupts, and he spells it out perfectly, as far as I can tell without writing it down on paper.

For once Lorraine is impressed. I am bloating with pride, and a surfeit of cheeseburger.

'Owning a pet,' she continues as I bask in my son's

149

intellectual glory, 'teaches children about caring, about nature, about sha—'

I flash her a warning glance, but it's too late.

'Oh, it's all right, Mum,' says Jamie. 'I don't need to know about shagging yet. Miss Trays says it's the most fantabulous fun, and I'll find out all about it when I'm older.'

'She didn't say that?'

'She did. I asked her.'

I often wonder if Emily is really my child, or whether someone swapped her for mine in the hospital. I sometimes wonder that about Jamie too. He's smarter than I am, and he has this beautiful, almost transparent skin, and clear blue eyes that grow large in his face when he's excited. He has to be a changeling, not a straight swap. He also has angry red bruises on his upper arm that I haven't noticed before.

'How did you do that?' I ask, my mind running through a list of possibilities. Has someone hit him? The kids in the playground? Emily? Mary Bacon?

Jamie twists himself up to look at them. 'That's where you pushed me out of the house this morning,' he says.

'Me?'

'They're your fingermarks, Mum.'

I didn't push him hard, I muse as we sit in a traffic jam on the flyover back into Croydon. But I must have done it harder than I thought. The evidence is there. I must be more careful. I must ensure he wears a longsleeved top for the next few days.

The traffic ahead creeps forward between the tower blocks that the developers in Croydon seem to love so much. I change gear to keep up. The gearstick judders about in my hand, the engine emits a bang, and the car stops dead in the outer lane of the dual carriageway approaching the roundabout. I turn the key in the ignition back and forth, but nothing happens.

'Sod it!'

'What did you say, Mum?' asks Jamie.

'Sausages.'

'You didn't,' he says. 'You said a swear word. Mummy, you swore!'

'Mummy did a swear,' chants Emily. 'Mummy did a swear.'

'Shut up!'

'Why aren't we moving?' Jamie complains.

'Because the car has broken down.' The learner driver behind me beeps her horn. I lean out of my window, gesticulating at her to overtake on the inside because I'm not going anywhere, not until I've called Andy and ripped him off a strip for making me drive around in this poxy, good-for-nothing rust-bucket. I try my mobile, but the battery symbol is flashing. I forgot to charge it.

'Shit!'

'Is that another swear word, Mummy?'

'Oh, for goodness' sake, Jamie.'

'Your mum's a bit stressed,' Lorraine observes calmly. 'Mummies often are. Here, use my phone.'

It's complicated. Andy says he and Steve will come down to pick us up as soon as Steve's back.

'Where is he?'

'Fetching parts,' says Andy.

'Again?'

'A mechanic needs parts,' Andy insists. 'I'll take you all home, and Steve can bring the car back once he gets it going.'

'He can't,' I point out. 'I'm the sole driver on the insurance.'

'I shouldn't worry about it, Jules.'

'I shall, so I'll drive home.'

'You'll have to keep the kids with you then because I have to see my mother. She says her bowel has almost ruptured and she almost has peritonitis.'

'Is she in hospital again?' I ask hopefully.

'No, she's at home, but she can't get out, and she hasn't any food.'

'Eating would be the last thing on your mind if you had peritonitis,' I grumble.

'She hasn't *got* peritonitis – she *almost* has peritonitis. There's a difference. Anyway, Steve's back. We'll be with you asap.'

'Andy's bringing Steve with him to repair the car,' I explain to Lorraine. 'They shouldn't be long.'

'I'm looking forward to meeting this hunk,' she says as big drops of rain begin to hit the windscreen. Emily wants a wee until I tell her she'll have to go in the road. Suddenly she's fine.

When Andy and Steve arrive, pulling up a couple of feet behind us, it's raining cats and dogs. I help Andy unload the children, car seats and shopping into the Merc. Lorraine follows, having offered to take Emily and Jamie to hers until I return, and introduced herself to Steve. Once in the passenger seat, she taps on the window, unwinds it a little way down and speaks through the small gap at the top while Andy and Steve are looking under the Peugeot's bonnet.

'Take that silly grin off your face, Juliet Wyevale,' she hisses. 'If I was on a girls' night out, I wouldn't look at Steve twice. What on earth do you see in him?'

I can't answer that because Andy comes up to give me a peck on the cheek.

'It shouldn't take long to do a temporary fix,' he says. 'I'll leave you in Steve's capable hands.'

I stand in the rain level with the bonnet, watching Steve's capable hands at work. He looks up and smiles. My heart turns over even if the engine doesn't.

'Hop in the car, Juliet. You're getting wet,' he says, and I wonder how he knows . . . I slip into the driver's seat and wait with traffic hooting and swerving around us until Steve taps at the window to catch my attention, and sticks his thumb up. I turn the key. The car starts. I keep my foot hard down on the accelerator until Steve jumps in beside me and slams the door.

'Let's go,' he says, banging the dashboard twice with his fist.

'I'm sorry we had to drag you out,' I say.

'No problem.'

'Thanks anyway.'

'So that was Lorraine, your best friend,' Steve says, 'the one you're always talking about?'

My throat constricts. I want Steve to approve of Lorraine because she's my friend, yet I'm concerned that now he's seen her, he'll no longer be interested in me.

'I thought from the way you described her, she had to be the Kylie of South Norwood,' Steve says.

Any relief I feel that Steve doesn't consider Lorraine the Kylie of South Norwood is swamped by a tidal wave of envy. How can I compete with a woman who has a waxwork of her buttocks displayed at Madame Tussauds?

'Don't get me wrong. Lorraine's pretty enough, and so's Kylie, but pretty isn't the same as . . .' Steve pauses. In some ways he comes across as quite shy. He's one of those people who are better able to express themselves physically than verbally. Maybe it's because he's so young. 'What I'm saying, Juliet, is that pretty isn't the same as sexy.'

'You're saying Kylie isn't sexy?'

'Not like you.'

I want to laugh, but I'm afraid to hurt Steve's

feelings. I glance across. His hair is slicked down against his skull. His eyes are dark pools of desire. His cheeks are flushed. I turn up the fan speed to cool things down.

'You're a real woman, Juliet, with plenty to grab hold of,' Steve begins, leaning closer.

'Thanks a lot. You make me sound like some great whale.'

'I was paying you a compliment.' Steve's voice sounds small and hurt. 'I think you're bloody gorgeous.'

Distract. Divert. I'm not ready to go where Steve's conversation is leading.

'Have you heard any more from that girl who came round the other day?' I can't bring myself to use her name. How petty is that?

Steve hesitates.

'I'm sorry. Tell me not to stick my nose in.'

'There was a time when I couldn't bring myself to talk about Debs,' Steve says carefully as though he's testing the strength of the repairs he's made to old wounds. 'Me and Debs – it wasn't meant to be, and it was time I moved on anyway. Seeing Debs was tearing me apart, and her old man was giving me grief.'

'Her father?'

'He was my boss.'

'Andy said you worked for your uncle?'

'Oh, I did, before I moved on to work for Debs's old man.' Steve pauses. I can't see his face. 'My uncle gave

155

me the boot, said he'd caught me out stealing which is a lie. I never took what wasn't mine.'

'Oh, Steve!'

'My cousin wanted me out of the business, so he could take a bigger cut of the profits. He set me up.'

'Didn't you go to the police?'

'I didn't want the hassle. I took off and travelled the world as you know.'

'What about money? How did you manage?' I can't help asking. I guess I'm hoping for confirmation that Steve isn't a thief.

'I took bar jobs and lived pretty rough most of the time. It wasn't all fun.'

My relief that Steve is a wronged man is tempered by the fact that he has had to dredge up what must be painful memories in the process. I suppress the urge to run my hand along his thigh – in a comforting manner, you understand.

'Would you like me to drop you off anywhere?'

'I need to fetch the bike,' Steve says, 'but thanks.'

By the time we reach the garage, dusk has fallen. I drive up to the workshop. Steve's bike, two BMWs and a red Ford Fiesta that I haven't seen before are parked in the yard.

It is very quiet, apart from the thrum of the engine and the tinny beat of the rain. I am intensely aware of the knobbed gearstick that vibrates between us. I can see the shape of Steve's collarbone diving under the neckline of a T-shirt that leaves nothing to the imagination. Steve's nipples are pert. I can smell wet clothes, and engine oil and cold coffee. We are enveloped by a damp fug. The windows are running with condensation. It crosses my mind that the Peugeot is almost antique. We could be Kate and Leonardo writhing naked in the back seat.

My heart pounds. My mouth is dry. Steve takes my hand, and massages it in his. I imagine if I was wearing my wedding ring, he would feel it and be reminded that any relationship beyond a platonic, working one is out of the question, but as it is . . .

'Gayle's gone home.' Steve leans closer. I lift my hand to touch the side of his face where the muscle in his cheek tautens and relaxes. 'Oh, Juliet,' he murmurs.

My heart keeps pounding. It hurts. It really does. If I could have any man on this earth, I would have you, but I can't and I mustn't. I am married. Only the other night, I stroked Andy's cheek fondly like this.

'Well?' Steve says simply.

'I've got to go. Lorraine's got the children. It's almost Emily's bedtime, and Jamie's got homework, and there's a whole heap of ironing.' I fumble for the doorhandle and almost fall out of the car.

'Juliet! Juliet!' Steve is out, banging the top of the car. 'Juliet! Come back!'

I hesitate. It's still raining.

'You'll want the car to get home,' he calls.

Embarrassed, I slip back inside, watch Steve open up

the workshop, disappear inside, then reappear in his leathers and helmet, visor down so I can't see his face. What have I done? I hope I haven't left Steve believing I turned him down because I don't find him attractive, or because I don't find his attentions flattering . . . I do, but I am a grown woman very close to a certain age, and I can't go around upending my life and longstanding relationships just because I want Steve to upend me and drive me senseless. Can I?

I feel as empty as a cinema at midnight. I turn on the radio. Natalie Imbruglia sings 'Torn' as rain pours down the windscreen. That's me. I know exactly how she feels.

Chapter Nine

What am I doing here? The universal question, the answer to which everyone has a deep psychological need to discover. Some find it in religion, some at the bottom of a wineglass. Others search for ever.

'So, what am I doing here? Remind me,' I say as Lorraine and I stand outside the tattoo parlour – Tyrone's Tattoos, not the London Piercing Clinic, because Lorraine assures me it's cheaper and she has several friends who have been so happy with their body art from here that she'd be happiest having it done here too.

'I am having a tattoo,' says Lorraine, 'and you're being a true friend coming to support me.'

'Why?' We have been through this already while she was persuading me to accompany her to the shop in case Tyrone turns out to be a sex maniac.

'Because I want to surprise Joe.'

I go, grudgingly, because I have chores to do at home,

like planting out my busy Lizzies and geraniums. Lorraine says I've left it a bit late. Her petunias are already dense and leafy.

'I've wanted one for ages.'

'No, you haven't. This is a spontaneous, and let me say, rash decision that you haven't thought through. You've been doing this a lot recently.'

'I haven't.'

'Are you sure everything's all right in your personal life?' I ask, doing my best Trisha impression. I don't watch *Trisha*. (Liar.) Lorraine doesn't respond to my question. 'What will Joe think?'

'Joe wants me to have one. On my right buttock.'

'You'll have to take your pants down,' I gasp.

'That's why I want you with me, Juliet.'

'Why do you really want one?' I have a feeling Lorraine isn't telling me the full story. 'Some people say tattoos are a sign of insecurity and an inadequate person-ality,' I say quietly.

'Well, I don't care,' Lorraine insists. 'I am going to have a heart with *JOE* written underneath.'

'I don't think you write a tattoo on,' I say. 'It's not like a stick-on transfer. I'm not sure you should make a tattoo too personal either. What if the guy in the shop gets it wrong? What if he's dyslexic? What if something happens to you and Joe? What if . . . What if you split up?'

Lorraine looks at me witheringly. 'Till death and

beyond,' she says. 'Me and Joe are like . . .' She ponders for a moment. 'Sonny and Cher?'

'They split up,' I say.

'Leonardo and Kate,' she says, brightening.

'Leonardo died,' I say, brushing an irrational tear from my eye. I have to keep reminding myself that he didn't really die. It was only a film.

'I am not changing my mind.' Lorraine pushes me forwards. 'In we go,' she says brightly as if she's talking to Tyler, not me. With that, I find myself inside the shop, a tiny room in which you couldn't swing a cat or a handbag if you wanted to subdue an over-amorous tattooist. The walls are hung with posters and pictures of all kinds of designs: from tigers to flowers. There is a table with a cash register, a credit-card machine, a phone, and a copy of the Yellow Pages. There's a couch, similar to the one Lorraine uses for her beauty therapy, except this one's covered with a tartan blanket. There are shelves stacked with boxes of inks, and crude models of body parts made of papier-mâché, pierced with rings and spikes to demonstrate the various piercings on offer. It all stinks of stale beer and cold Chinese takeaway from the shop next door.

I've always said I would never let anyone, even a doctor, modify my body, and this place doesn't do anything to convince me otherwise. Tyrone doesn't inspire me with confidence either, for he turns out to be Chris, an ex-Navy man – in his early fifties, I guess. He took on Tyrone's business in lieu of what he says was payment of a gambling debt, although I suspect it was a drugs deal. Chris has tattoos of anchors and sea-serpents up his arms. His belly, which hangs over the waistband of his jeans, is not, I observe, tattooed. He gives the impression of being very busy even though we are the only customers in the shop.

'What can I interest you in, ladies? A Chinese dragon? A Beckham number twenty-three? I've just done a Medusa.'

'Is that a jellyfish?' I ask, but Chris isn't really interested in me because Lorraine is here in one of her push-them-up and squeeze-them-together bras, and I have to say I'm impressed. She's not terribly big, but it makes her look very curvy in an immaculate glo-white shirt. Dead sexy. I think I might buy one.

Chris demonstrates with stained fingers how his needles are all new and sterilised. They are also long, shiny and incredibly sharp. He shows us his certificate.

'I have an MA in skin artistry,' he says proudly.

'And a doctorate in taking the piss, I suppose,' says Lorraine. I can see Chris likes a bit of cheek . . . and a bit of breast. He smiles, and gawps down Lorraine's cleavage. He gives her a bit of cheek back. He suggests an intricate rose, but Lorraine is dead set on a heart, and it has to be a small one, so there aren't too many pricks with the needle.

'There isn't any point in having one that size,' I observe. 'You can hardly see it.'

Lorraine has become pale beneath her skim of foundation. I can smell fear, perspiring through clouds of perfume and deodorant.

Chris is growing impatient. 'It doesn't hurt,' he says.

'You go first, Juliet,' Lorraine says.

'Me? I'm not having a tattoo!'

'You said you liked the dragonfly.'

'I said it's a delicate design, and *if* I was having a tattoo, which I'm not, I would choose that one.'

'But it doesn't hurt, and that tiny little dragonfly is gorgeous, and Andy would like it, I'm sure. And it would be so daring of you, Juliet. You're like me. You never do anything rash, or mad any more.'

I'm not sure I ever did, but in a moment of absolute madness I find myself sitting on Chris's couch with my leg up in his face, with him sticking needles and ink into my ankle. It is agony. I bite my lip to distract myself from the pain. Divert. Imagine giving birth to a tenpounder. Without a *Tens* machine. Without gas and air.

'Well?' asks Lorraine.

'Doesn't hurt at all,' I gasp, but I can tell from Lorraine's face that it is all over. Any pretension she had to wanting a tattoo is finished, and here I am £30 lighter with a dragonfly on my ankle.

'If you can take that,' says Lorraine, 'you must let me wax your eyebrows.'

'I don't understand why you didn't go through with it,' I say, admiring my tattoo in the shop windows as we walk down the street. My ankle is red and stinging, but I love my dragonfly. What will Andy think of it? What about Steve?

Steve has been very quiet since that wild, rainy evening when I rejected his advances. Either he is worried about Debs and the paternity suit, or I have hurt his feelings terribly. Young men don't take rejection well, I know, and I can only console myself with the knowledge that he can't be hurting anywhere near as much as I am.

However, although my heart (and my ankle) aches, my conscience is clear. Almost. I wouldn't be human if I didn't wonder what it would have been like to do a Kate and Leonardo in the Peugeot round the back of Wyevale Autos. I can't bring myself to call it sex. It would have been more than that. Far, far more. Like thick, brandied chocolate sauce to a Milky Bar.

'Come back, Juliet. You're off with the fairies.'

Not the fairies. Steve is definitely not a fairy.

'Juliet! You're not listening . . .'

'You should have had one, Lorraine. It's a work of art, and it can't have hurt any more than having your ears pierced.'

Lorraine twiddles the tiny silver star she has in the topmost piercing of three in her left earlobe.

'I had a couple of glasses of wine before I had them done,' she says.

'Next time then?'

'Yeah, next time.'

'You won't, will you?' I know she won't. 'Some friend you are!' I say aloud.

'I'll make it up to you,' Lorraine smiles. 'I'll help you out with Jamie's party next weekend.'

'And you'll bring a bottle of wine?'

'Several.'

My ankle is much better by the time I collect the children from Mary's after work the following day. As I wait on Mary's doorstep for someone to come to the door, a woman emerges from number four. She glares at me rather fiercely for someone I have never met, but then I recall that she has recently lost her husband. She must be devastated.

'I'm Juliet,' I begin. 'You must be Doreen. I'm so sorry—'

'It was them bloody fags,' the woman interrupts. 'I told Frank he should give them up, but he wouldn't listen. Not until the doctors told him he had less than a year to live, when he gave all the fags he had left to her downstairs.'

'Does Mary smoke?'

'Who?'

'Your neighbour.'

'Her? No, she likes a few pints now and then by all accounts, but I've never seen her smoking. She wouldn't do that with the kiddies about, would she?'

I am beginning to wonder.

'What did she do with the cigarettes then?'

'I imagine she sold them. Me and Frank used to go car-booting on Sundays. We'd see her sometimes.'

'Mary doesn't have a car.'

'She had so much stuff to get rid of, she borrowed a van. I had a microwave off her once. Cheap as chips, as David Dickinson would say. Frank used to love his show . . .' To my consternation, the woman's eyes fill with tears.

'I'm sorry about your husband,' I say gently. 'At least you have your cat for company.'

'Cat? I can't bear the things. I only have to see one and I come out in a rash.'

'Mary said you had a cat. I've heard it thumping about in your flat.'

'I think I'd know if I had a cat,' the woman says unhappily, 'and I haven't. What you heard would have been my poor Frank banging his stick against the floor. Goodbye.'

'Goodbye . . .' Mary told me she had to take delivery of the boxes of cigarettes for number four because they were out. They weren't. Frank almost blew her story by banging on the floor with his stick, but Mary made up the cat as a cover. Why bother? Why not just say she was mistaken, and Frank was at home after all? I could have helped her carry the boxes upstairs. Perhaps though, Mary is like me, prone to covering up one tiny untruth with another until she ends up with one great big lie that she can't backtrack on without looking incredibly foolish.

After I have knocked on the door three more times, Mary finally answers it.

'I've just spoken to your neighbour, Doreen,' I say, building myself up to ask Mary some very awkward questions about her honesty.

'I'd be surprised if you had a sensible conversation with her,' Mary responds. 'Since Frank died, she's gone doolally.'

'I'm sorry?'

'Doolally tap. Mad as a hatter. Nutty as a fruitcake.'

'I see . . .'

Mary turns and yells for Jamie and Emily over the sound of the telly, and a few minutes later, Jamie struggles towards the car with what I suppose you'd describe as a sculpture made from cardboard boxes and tubes, and painted blue and yellow. It reminds me of the pair of chimneys that rise above the Purley Way.

'That's brilliant, Jamie. That looks just like IKEA.'

Jamie's face falls. 'Mum! It's a spaceship. I designed it in Science and Technology. Can't you tell?'

I tip my head to one side. 'Oh yes, I can see it now,' I say, reminding myself to keep my opinions to myself in future.

'I made it ages ago at school, and Mary's just found it behind some boxes in her bedroom.'

I help Emily into the car, and strap her into the booster seat in the back. I know she can do it herself, but I like to feel useful in a motherly kind of way now and then.

As I give the seat belt a quick tug to check it's fastened properly, I notice orange splashes down the front of Emily's T-shirt.

'What did you have for tea?'

'We had sketty oops,' Emily grins. 'They was yummy.'

'Spaghetti hoops? You can't possibly have had spaghetti hoops.'

'And sausages,' says Jamie.

'Is this true?'

'If I was going to tell a lie, Mum,' Jamie says, 'I'd say no.'

I scratch my head. What's happened to the Chinese dishes made with free-range organic chicken, and the pasta with ricotta and tomato sauce, made with fresh organic tomatoes?

'They were from a tin with a white label like the ones you buy sometimes,' says Jamie. 'I was supposed to be watching the telly in the living room, but I sneaked out and watched Mary in the kitchen.' He pauses. 'Are you all right, Mum? You've got crinkles on your forehead.'

'Crinkles?'

'The things that old people get,' he says impatiently.

'You mean wrinkles?'

'That's right.'

'Thank you very much, Jamie.'

He smiles. I try to smile back, but my heart is heavy. I wonder if I should confront Mary about the children's meals today, or wait to see if it happens again, in case it's a one-off. I know from experience that no one can be perfect all of the time – unless you count the Rhino and Lorraine. I shall have to speak to Lorraine. Life is so complicated.

'What are you sighing for, Mum?'

'I'm sighing because you think I'm old, Jamie.' I feel even older when I recall that he is almost seven.

Jamie's birthday on a Sunday in late August dawns bright and much too early, with Jamie coming into our bedroom before 5 a.m. Emily comes too, snuggling into bed between me and Andy, clutching a Barbie flannel, her latest comforter, to her face. Andy buries himself beneath the duvet, pretending he is not here.

Jamie searches through the packages on the floor on my side of the bed, but I can tell the one he is looking for isn't among them. I suspect he is looking for a box with ventilation holes. There is a Harry Potter figure, and money from my parents who came over on Friday evening for tea. There is the football strip from us. Emily wrapped it up herself with paper and half a roll of sticky tape which takes Jamie some time to pull apart.

'It's not a hamster then,' he says sadly as the strip drops out.

'A hamster isn't just for a birthday, or Christmas,' I say. 'Hamsters take a lot of looking after.'

'I'd look after it. I'd call it Becks.'

'But he's never played for Crystal Palace!' Andy

exclaims, emerging from beneath the duvet. 'You can't have a hamster of that name in this house.'

'I can't anyway,' Jamie sighs, 'because I haven't got a hamster. I've already got a Crystal Palace strip, Dad.'

'Last season's.'

'It still fits me.'

'Your mum told me to buy one to last,' Andy insists. 'When I was your age I'd have loved to have had any number of football strips for my birthday. You do like it, don't you?'

Jamie nods. Liar. He's just like me.

'I suppose I'd better get up,' I say, hoping Andy might leap up and offer to fetch me a cup of tea.

'Make us a tea then, babe,' he says, smiling, 'and I wouldn't mind a couple of digestives with it.'

'It's your turn next weekend then,' I say, tossing my pillow at him.

He fumbles and tosses it back, but I am already halfway out of the door on my way to prepare for Jamie's party. I dress in navy cropped trousers that cover my cellulite but not my tattoo. They're new, and while I was buying them I found a red T-shirt with a low V-neck that flatters me, though I say it myself. I am losing weight. Those danger areas, the tops of my arms, are becoming quite shapely like they used to be when I was in my twenties.

Lorraine comes round early as promised with the wine, and we have already finished one bottle when Jamie's friends arrive. Andy answers the door, and controls the flow of small boys. We have invited six, but there seem to be many more.

Lorraine and I remain in the kitchen, not to protect the sensibilities of parents who prefer not to leave their offspring in the protection of two sozzled women, but to continue preparing the food. It's all right. Andy, and Joe who will be round shortly, have promised not to drink until they've all gone home. This is not a truly altruistic gesture on our husbands' behalf – both Andy and Joe have terrible hangovers from last night. If the Eagles win, they celebrate. If they lose, they commiserate. Either option involves consuming copious volumes of lager.

Andy arranges a football match. It's five a side until Emily and Tyler decide football isn't for them, and Emily disrupts the game, running off with the traffic cones they're using as goalposts. I open a packet of cocktail sticks and start stabbing them into sausages while I watch the chaos fondly from the kitchen window, until a sharp rap on the front door disturbs me.

'Where's the party?' Joe calls through.

'Come on in,' I yell back, and Joe appears with the Rhino on his arm. I'd forgotten about the Rhino. Today she is wearing a cream hat with cherries all the way around the brim, a cream blouse with frilled collar, and a burgundy skirt, giving the impression of a cloying trifle.

'I found this gorgeous lady on your doorstep,' says Joe, grinning at the Rhino.

The Rhino tips her head to one side, and pats Joe's chest. 'Flattery will get you nowhere, dear boy,' she smirks.

'Shame,' says Joe. 'Can I get you a drink, Pammy? A glass of wine?'

'I shouldn't, not at this hour,' she says, but she accepts a small glass of sherry from beneath the sink instead. She takes a sip then looks me up and down.

'That colour top suits you, Juliet,' she says, 'but I wonder if you shouldn't have bought it a couple of sizes larger.'

I stab a sausage so hard that the stick snaps in half.

'I think it's perfect. Very sexy,' Joe chips in. 'Now, Pammy, come into the garden, and tell me what you've been getting up to since I last saw you. I'll fetch you a chair.' The Rhino waits in the kitchen while Joe goes outside and shifts a garden chair so that it's in the shade of the parasol I bought last year. The football match breaks up completely with the news that Granny has arrived, and Emily comes running in and flings herself at the Rhino.

'Granny!'

Jamie tries to push her out of the way, but she remains clinging to the Rhino's skirt.

'Here is your present, Jamie,' the Rhino says, taking a package from her handbag.

'Thanks, Granny.' Jamie rips the paper off. 'Oh, it's a video. Is it about hamsters?'

'I don't think so,' says the Rhino.

Jamie hands it over to me. It's from the BBC Wildlife series, probably a film of copulating giraffes and the Rhino's idea of helping Andy and me out with the question of shagging.

'Are you coming outside, Granny?' Jamie asks.

'Yes, but I shan't stay for long.' The Rhino touches her stomach. 'I have my allergy to consider.'

'She looks remarkably well for someone who's supposed to be dying,' Lorraine whispers as the Rhino follows the children outside to the garden. 'She is dying, isn't she?'

'Did I say that?'

'You gave that impression.' Lorraine pauses. 'When are you going to stand up to the silly cow? I'd hate her to die before you tell her what you really think of her. Look at her now, fawning all over Joe.'

The Rhino is sitting on the garden chair beneath the parasol. Joe is standing with one arm around the back of the chair and from here, it appears he is gazing down past the brim of her hat into her eyes. I'm not sure who is fawning over whom.

'Joe told me off last night for not nagging him,' Lorraine begins. 'I read that book you lent me. It made me realise that perhaps I can be a little too demanding at times and that Joe always takes my requests the wrong way. Anyway, I didn't remind him he had a dental appointment so he missed it. The surgery rang and they're charging him a cancellation fee. Serves him bloody well right.'

'What are you going to do?'

'Start nagging him again, of course. Joe can't survive without me, you see. He needs me to organise his life. He can't do it himself.'

'That's men for you, I suppose,' I say, trying to suppress an air of triumph. I knew it. Lorraine and Joe's marriage isn't all that perfect after all, although Joe is proving that he can be the perfect gentleman, kicking the football back to Andy and the boys whenever it rolls towards the Rhino's slender, stockinged legs.

Lorraine tops up our wineglasses.

'Are you still all right to have Jamie and Emily while Mary's on holiday this week?' I ask.

'Yes, of course. Have you spoken to her yet?'

'No.'

'I thought you'd made up your mind to confront her.'

'I don't want her to turn round and tell me to find someone else.'

'She wouldn't do that. You've said it before – she needs the money.' Lorraine hesitates. 'Is this just about the spaghetti hoops, or is something else bothering you?'

I think of the delivery man and the nieces, and shake my head. There's nothing I can put my finger on.

I watch the Rhino curl her fingers around Joe's arm

as he helps her up from the chair. She doesn't stay for the food or birthday cake which Lorraine and I distribute outside in the garden, to save mess.

Andy comes up, and pats my bottom. He's wearing a cap, but his face is catching the sun.

'Did you check the Lottery numbers last night?' he asks.

'Yes, and no we didn't win.' I am not disappointed. It would be somehow cheating to win, not to overcome our temporary cashflow problem by our own efforts, but by chance. 'Did you know your nose is going red?' I fetch the sunblock, rub it on Andy's nose and spread it across his cheeks and his chin.

'Kiss me, Jules,' he murmurs.

I drop a quick kiss on his lips then wipe my mouth with the back of my hand.

Andy frowns. 'What's up?'

'You taste of sunblock.'

Andy takes a step back, runs his fingers inside the waist of his shorts as if to relieve the pressure on his stomach.

'Looks like you need some new shorts,' I comment. I say it lightly, in jest, but Andy doesn't take it that way.

'Can't afford any,' he says sharply. 'The bank account's overdrawn and we've taken the credit cards almost up to the limit. It doesn't help when you go out and spend thirty quid on a tattoo.' He pauses, softens. 'Lorraine told me how much it was. I don't mind as long as you try to be a bit more careful for a while.'

It must be the heat of the sun on the back of my neck, the depressant effect of the wine and the presence of these horrible, noisy boys. I clench my fists at my side. How dare Andy criticise my housekeeping? I'll be more careful, all right.

'I'll restock the cupboards with economy groceries, and go around looking like a dog again. Is that what you want?'

'No, not exactly—' Andy says, but I'm not prepared to listen.

'You'll have to stop going to the pub too,' I snap. 'I bet you spent more than thirty quid last night, and what do you have to show for it? A beer gut and a pasty face!'

Lorraine continues to snuggle Tyler in her lap, but I can see her ears flapping. Joe and Emily are watching. The boys have finished eating and are back racketing around with a football. What's wrong with me and Andy? We don't fight. We never *used* to fight . . .

The boys go home at four. Joe and Lorraine stay on. I offer a barbecue, but I haven't bought quite enough food.

'There'll be some sausages and rolls in the freezer that could go in the microwave,' I say to Andy, who disappears for a while into the kitchen and returns all stiff-backed, and brandishing a packet of frozen sausages.

'How long should you keep stuff in a freezer?' he says.

'What stuff?'

176

'Sausages.'

'Three months? I don't know.'

'I don't even know which year this is. Look!'

I cast an eye over the date stamp that Andy waves beneath my nose. True. There is no indication of the year within the figures, and I don't like to ask at which level in the drawer he found them. If they were at the bottom, July probably refers to last July. If they were at the top, I bought them within the last few weeks.

'What do you think, Juliet?'

'For goodness' sake, just throw them away.' Would Leonardo ever have troubled Kate with the contents of their freezer, if he hadn't frozen to death before freezers were invented? Would he have stood in front of Kate all holier than thou because he had discovered a packet of out-of-date sausages? I doubt it.

I can't understand why Andy is getting into such a flap. Maybe he's annoyed because he thinks if I'm not defrosting the freezer then I'm sitting on my bum, drinking coffee with Lorraine all the time. Maybe it's not that. Maybe it's a symptom of the disease that seems to have infected our marriage, not the cause.

Although I have dismissed him and Andy will never know, the shadow of Steve remains hanging over our relationship like the darkest, most ominous storm cloud. I still want Steve, you see. I can't stop wanting him.

Andy tosses chicken drumsticks onto the racks on the barbecue where they sizzle and smoke. He turns them over, banging forks and skewers about as the sun starts to move off the garden. I know he's upset, but it's only a couple of quid, isn't it? Okay, money's tight, but that's no excuse to rant on about the price of eight beef sausages in front of Lorraine and Joe.

We eat eventually, Lorraine and Andy sitting on the plastic recliners, Joe and I on the lawn.

'We should go home,' Lorraine says.

'Tyler can sleep in the bunkbed,' I cut in quickly. I don't want them to go. I don't want to be left alone with Andy and his niggling. 'I can go into work late tomorrow morning.'

'I think we should go home,' says Lorraine.

'Let's stay. Tyler can sleep in with Emily.' Joe helps himself to another can of lager from the stack at his side and tears off the ring.

'There's jelly to finish,' I offer. It's blue and red. 'The children didn't want it.' No one takes me up. 'It has set.' Last time Lorraine and I made it for Joe's birthday, we added lager and ended up with what was effectively lager and black. Still no takers. I stretch my legs out in front of me. Joe, can in hand, reaches over and traces the outline of the dragonfly on my ankle with one finger. It tickles. It's cheeky. And I wish it was Steve.

Joe says, 'Why don't you have a tattoo, Lorraine? She won't have one.'

'No, I won't, not now I've seen what Juliet had to go

through for the sake of vanity.' Lorraine grins. 'I'd have
to have an anaesthetic.'

'Where's your spirit of adventure? Bloody hell,
Lorraine, you're middle-aged before your time.' Joe aban-
dons my dragonfly and chucks a can to Andy.

'Come on, Tyler. It's time for bed.' Lorraine stands
up and Tyler follows her indoors. I join her, calling Jamie
and Emily. I guess I know why Lorraine wanted that
tattoo – to prove to Joe she could still take a risk, to keep
him hooked.

Once we're in the kitchen, Lorraine lets out a shriek.

'What is it?'

'I forgot to give Jamie his present. Oh, how could I?
Come here, Jamie. Tyler wants to give you something.'
Tyler hands over a package about the size of a 500g bag
of pasta. 'I hope you like it.'

'I love it,' Jamie says, wide-eyed as he unwraps it.
'What is it?'

'Sea-monkeys,' Lorraine explains. 'They're not
monkeys as such, so they're not furry. They swim about
in water.'

'They pets,' says Tyler.

'My own pet!' cries Jamie.

'They're brine shrimps,' Lorraine explains, trying to
stem my rising alarm. 'They're like the shrimps you can
eat at the seaside.'

'I'll never eat them, never ever,' says Jamie, hugging
what I see now is a mini fishtank to his breast. He is

179

over the moon, and that is why, at ten o'clock in the evening, I am at the kitchen sink, mixing little packets of salt and sea-monkey sustenance into lukewarm boiled water. I won't add the sachet of eggs – that's Jamie's department. Andy and Lorraine are on the lawn, Lorraine wrapped up in Emily's fleece throw, picking at her toenails and Andy lying flat on his back watching the stars. Joe is on his way back from the loo. I hear his footsteps padding along the hall, tripping over the rug.

'Shit!'

'You all right?'

'Fatally injured.'

'I hope you haven't bled all over my new rug,' I say, fixing the lid which contains a torch you can switch on and off to the sea-monkeys' tank.

'You're all heart, Juliet.' Joe's voice is soft. He is behind me, his breath gusting hot against the back of my neck. He has me pressed against the sink. I could scream, but Andy and Lorraine would hear, and come rushing in to find out what was wrong.

'Let me go, please,' I say, more politely than circumstance demands.

'Not until you say you'll make love to me.' Joe's hands are inside my T-shirt.

'Just piss off, will you?' I hiss, grappling with his clumsy fingers.

'Hey, keep your hair on,' he mutters. I take advantage of his hesitation, turning round to face him.

'If you touch me once more, I shall tell Lorraine.'

'You wouldn't?' His furrowed brow smooths out. 'You wouldn't.'

'What makes you think that?'

'Because we're friends, Juliet. We're one of a kind. I know you're not happy with Andy. I can tell from the way you look at him.'

'And what way is that?'

'Sort of down your nose as if you've lost respect for him.'

'Like this?' I ask, going cross-eyed, but Joe persists.

'You're like me. Restless. Wanting.' Joe moves in, pressing his lips hard on mine. Something – a small point of slippery flesh – darts between them. Joe's tongue. I can't help it. Fight or flight? I can't flee. There's nowhere to go. I have no option but to bite hard.

'Aargh!' Joe is clutching his mouth. His face is scarlet. 'What the fuck did you do that for?' He waggles his tongue.

'I'm sorry, but no means no,' I insist. I hope I didn't hurt him too much. I watch as Joe pours himself a glass of water. I can't see any blood.

'You've changed,' he says quietly after a rinse and another waggle. 'You've changed your appearance, what with your hair and that tattoo. I don't think I like you quite so much now, Juliet. You're not the same person you were. You're much less generous.'

'You've been here all day, taking advantage of my

hospitality, and you're trying to say I'm ungenerous. You've changed too, Joe. Look at you. All dressed up as if you've somewhere else to go.' It's true. He's wearing a bottle-green polo-shirt and new jeans. Joe doesn't wear shorts, even when he's playing for the veterans – which is a pity because I think we might be missing a treat.

I am trying to keep my voice down because I am aware that Andy has sat up, and both he and Lorraine are looking towards the kitchen window. The blind isn't down. As I've mentioned before, it never is.

'You haven't been wearing your wedding ring. That tells a story in itself.'

'I lost it.'

'So Lorraine said. You know what, Juliet? I believe you have a subconscious desire to free yourself from the shackles of married life.'

'I don't feel shackled.'

'Liar. I bet you have a lover,' Joe whispers. 'Someone else lined up?'

'It's none of your business.' Why did I say that? Why didn't I just deny it straight off? Is it because I suspect Joe won't believe me?

'You have, haven't you? Oh, come on, Juliet. Who is it? Do I know him?'

I don't know about shackles, but my hackles are up. Do I not live at the top of a hill? Do I not hold the moral high ground here? Is it not Joe who is propositioning me?

'As soon as I have the opportunity, I shall speak to Lorraine.'

Joe's face falls. 'Oh, lighten up, Juliet. You take everything so bloody seriously. It was a joke, a bit of fun.'

'I told you if you touched me again, I would tell Lorraine, and I will.' My resolve weakens slightly. Holding the moral high ground is all very well, but since Steve walked into my life, it has become a rocky and dangerous place.

I still think of Steve, you see. All the time. I can't help it. He seems subdued and he has developed a touch of acne. I don't know whether he's worried about Debs and the baby, or whether it's because of me. I hope it's the latter because that would prove I meant something to him, that I wasn't being a foolish middle-aged woman imagining that I did.

Chapter Ten

How would I react if Lorraine told me that my husband had propositioned her? Lorraine is gorgeous, some would say irresistible, to the opposite sex, and she's only a hop, skip and a jump over the picket fence, but Andy's not the hopping, skipping and jumping kind. He's steadfast and loyal like the Labrador the Rhino had put down when Andy's father died because she didn't want it to suffer the same psychological trauma of loss that she was suffering. (And a big dog wouldn't fit on a narrowboat.)

They are qualities I should admire, except I have been wishing in my maddest moments that Andy *would* look at another woman. A real and available woman, not Madonna, or Kylie, or Britney Spears. It would somehow salve my conscience over Steve.

Anyway, the morning after Jamie's party when I deliver Tyler back to Lorraine's after helping Jamie start hatching his new pets, I stop in for coffee. I wonder if

I should wait until next week to tell Lorraine about Joe in case she changes her mind about looking after Jamie and Emily for me while Mary Bacon is on holiday – she's gone to see her sister in Scarborough – but I'm here now and I've planned exactly what I am going to say. I shall hint that Joe has been behaving strangely and channel the conversation towards the subject of 'Husbands who Sleep with their Wives' Best Friends', and let Lorraine draw her own conclusions. However, it doesn't work out that way.

'Joe propositioned me last night,' I blurt out. 'He's done it before.'

Lorraine doesn't even blink. The children run upstairs and I follow Lorraine into the kitchen where she switches the kettle on.

'Doesn't it bother you?'

'Joe fancies you,' she says, betraying nothing. 'He often says so, says he'd like to cuddle up to you. Oh, he doesn't mean anything by it. He knows I'd kill him if he did anything. You can look, but not touch. That's our rule. That's how we run our marriage. That's how we survive.'

'But he did touch me.' I am beginning to wonder if I was hallucinating. 'He kissed me.'

'Oh?'

'On the lips.'

Lorraine stirs the coffees and taps the end of the teaspoon on the rim of the second mug.

'Were there tongues?' she asks.

I shake my head. I could say there were, but that would be stretching a point. It was, after all, the tip of Joe's tongue, not the whole caboodle.

'Then it doesn't matter, Juliet. Joe didn't mean anything by it,' Lorraine continues. 'He was out of his head by the time we left yours last night. We ought to have a girls' night out sometime.' Lorraine is doing what I do with Emily. Diverting. Distracting. Changing the subject. 'If you won't let me wax your eyebrows, you could let me loose on your eyelashes and nails.'

I think for a moment. Lorraine's done a good job touching up my stripes, and my nails are a mess.

'I have a booking next week, Juliet. I need a model to practise on.'

'You promise there's no wax involved?'

'Cross my heart and hope to die.'

'All right then.'

'I'll write you in the appointments book.'

It occurs to me that Lorraine might be going to take revenge on the woman who was propositioned by her husband. It's what I might do in her position, but Lorraine's not like that. If she wanted revenge, she'd tell me straight out.

I gaze out of the kitchen window at the garden beyond as the children thunder around upstairs like a herd of baby elephants. Lorraine doesn't bother planting up pots of petunias at the back of the house, partly because no one sees them, and partly because the rabbit eats them. This morning, I notice that the rabbit is shut in his hutch.

'You haven't let the rabbit out yet,' I observe. He's always out. He gets almost as much attention as Tyler.

'Ronnie isn't shagging the football any more,' says Lorraine. 'He's been dribbling a lot.'

'That's not so bad, is it? Shows he still has a passion for the game.'

'It's not that kind of dribbling. He's not well, poor lamb.'

I hesitate to point out that Lorraine has entirely the wrong species.

'Maybe it's because it's no longer spring, and he's worn himself out. Maybe the football has let itself go, and he doesn't fancy it any more,' I suggest.

'I'm taking him to the vet this morning.' Lorraine joins me at the window. 'The woman I spoke to on the phone when I booked the appointment said he might have to have his teeth clipped.'

'I'd have thought hormone treatment would have been more appropriate.'

'Oh Juliet, Ronnie's not well,' Lorraine says, her voice breaking, and I find myself with my arms around Lorraine's shaking shoulders, patting her back.

'There, there. He'll be all right.'

'I hope so.' She pulls away and grabs a tissue from the box she keeps on the worktop, and smiles through her tears. I've never seen her like this, out of control of her emotions. I am always the first to cry when we're watching the video of *Titanic* – when Kate realises Leonardo has died in that icy sea, it is me who bawls my eyes out, and Lorraine who gives me her last piece of popcorn to shut me up.

'I didn't realise anyone could be that fond of a rabbit,' I say awkwardly.

Lorraine bursts into tears again. 'Neither did I.'

It's strange how she didn't cry like this when I told her about Joe.

I can't imagine that I will form a similar attachment to Jamie's sea-monkeys as they grow in their tank on the kitchen worktop. Of course, it is as I feared. I am the person who aerates their brine and feeds them, but they are otherwise undemanding. They swim about like tiny jerky commas, neither asking for their socks, nor jumping up and down about the shelf life of frozen sausages. They don't sulk either. Not like Steve.

On the Friday morning when the sea-monkeys are a few days old, I move the tank so it will catch the slanting rays of the late summer sun while I'm out, and head off to drop Jamie at school for the third day of the autumn term. You see, I am the perfect pet-keeper, and wife and mother as well. I sewed twenty labels into Jamie's new uniform, including socks, last night.

Steve strolls into the office at nine thirty. He removes his helmet, tosses his hair, and gives me a dark, brooding look. He is magnificent. Untouchable.

'I'd almost given you up,' I begin. 'Coffee?'

'I'm going out,' he says.

'But you've only just arrived.'

'There's some parts I need,' he says, rubbing the back of his neck, 'and then I'm going to the cash and carry. Gayle's given me a list.'

'I guess I shall have to drink coffee on my own.' I try to flash my most wicked smile, but it doesn't persuade Steve to change his mind. He rams his helmet back on his head.

'I'll see you later?' I say.

Steve shrugs and walks out. He doesn't return until after lunch when I find him leaning against the wall outside the workshop, fiddling with his mobile phone.

'I thought you'd like a coffee,' I say, handing him a mug.

'Thanks.' The muscle in his cheek tautens. 'That was Debs.'

'Oh?'

'She's had a scan. The baby's a boy. She says it looks just like me.'

'That's ridiculous. You can't see that kind of detail on a scan.'

'Debs says she can.'

'Wishful thinking, I expect,' I say, thinking wishfully how I'd like to throw my arms around Steve's shoulders, and bury my face in the soft hollow at the base of his neck.

'What are you looking at me like that for?' Steve mutters.

'I'm worried about you. You don't talk to me any more.'

'I thought that's what you wanted.'

Steve's eyes fix mine. My heart contracts. I can hardly control the tremor in my voice.

'I want us to be friends.'

'Is that all?' he asks softly.

'That's all.' (Liar.)

Steve's mobile rings – I don't recognise the ringtone from before. I guess he's taken the time to programme in a new one, something I never get around to doing.

He turns away to answer it, and I return to the office where I spend the rest of the afternoon wondering why doing the right thing feels so wrong. I have broken the ice with Steve, and feel as if I have broken myself in two at the same time. It hasn't been a good day, and it doesn't get any better.

'Mum?'

'Yes, Jamie?' While I have been dealing with the washing that's been in the machine since yesterday, and trying to decide what's for tea, Jamie has been studying the sea-monkey tank on the windowsill.

'Have you taken the sea-monkeys for a walk or something?'

'Of course not.' My heart misses a beat. 'Why?'

'I can't see them.'

'Have you tried looking through the magnifying glass that came with the set?'

'You don't need it any more. They're big enough to see without it,' says Jamie.

'There you go then.' What is it to be tonight? Tuna pasta bake? Andy doesn't like it much, but it reheats well. Or courgette frittata – except that'll have to be just frittata because I haven't any courgettes.

'They aren't here, you know.' There is panic in Jamie's voice.

'They can't have escaped.' I move over to look at the sea-monkeys, but Jamie is quite right. They have disappeared. I lift the tank to the light in the window. The plastic feels very warm, and the sea-monkeys haven't disappeared. They are lurching about at the bottom, moving with the currents I am setting up with my shaking hands, not swimming.

I slam the tank down.

'Be careful, Mum,' warns Jamie.

I grapple around in the cupboard under the sink for the Rhino's sherry. Jamie stares as I open the bottle.

'It isn't for me,' I explain hurriedly. I splash sherry into the tank, grab a drinking straw and blow. It's no good. Sea-monkeys circle up through the bubbling brine, circle and sink. Now I understand how desperate those resuscitation scenes are in *Casualty* and *ER*.

'Stand back, Jamie. I said, stand back!'

'What are you doing, Mum?' he keeps asking.

I pause for a moment. How long do I try for? The tigress says that they're only shrimps, and it's time to get the tea on. My conscience argues that they are living things that deserve a chance and, if I give up on them, Jamie will never forgive me.

Within ten minutes, it is official. The Wyevales are in deep mourning. If we had a flag it would be flying at half-mast. Jamie is inconsolable. He blames me for moving his pets onto the windowsill, for not realising what effect the sun would have on the water, for not knowing that sea-monkeys die if the tank gets too hot and they run out of oxygen. He cries his eyes out when I tip the brine down the sink and bury the sludge that contains the mortal remains in a pot and plant an apple pip in the top in the hope it will grow into a tree. He makes a paper sign, reading, *Sea-Monkeys Rest In Peace*, but it turns to mush in the rain.

'Will I die, Mummy?' Jamie asks the following day.

'Everything has to one day.' I can't lie about that, can I? No one's immortal. 'You don't need to worry about dying yet. You're only six.'

'I'm seven.'

'Sorry, I forgot.'

'Where do you go when you die? Where have the sea-monkeys gone?' he asks, and I wish Jamie didn't think so deeply.

'I don't know,' I say. 'Some people say heaven. Some say you come back as another soul.'

'What's a soul?'

'This is all very complicated, Jamie,' I say, but I can't put him off. 'A soul is the essence of a living thing that leaves the body when it dies.'

'Have sea-monkeys got souls then?'

'I think every living thing has a soul. Some people believe that if you were a cat for instance, and you led a good and pure life, you would come back as a human. If you were bad, you would come back as a slug or a worm.'

Jamie is frowning deeply. 'I'd better warn Emily,' he says.

'She's too young to understand,' I say hastily, and I withhold the other option that some people believe that when you die, that's the end of it.

'I like the idea of heaven,' says Jamie. 'When I die, I'll be able to have my sea-monkeys back. Do you think they'll be waiting for me?'

'Jamie! I wish you wouldn't go on about dying.' The thought of Jamie lying dead makes my blood run cold, and I start to imagine he's paler and less energetic than usual. I imagine taking him to the doctor, and the doctor saying, 'I'm sorry, Mrs Wyevale, but there's no easy way to break this to you . . .'

'Mum, can I have some new sea-monkeys?'

'Yes. I'll ask Lorraine where she bought them from.'

Jamie's face brightens. He thinks he's on to a good thing. 'Can I have a hamster as well?'

'No way,' I say, shaking my head. 'Now, if you're going to football with Daddy, you'd better hurry up and get ready.'

'You'd better,' Andy repeats, having arrived in the kitchen all ready in his Crystal Palace top and jeans. 'The Eagles are playing at home.'

'Who wants to go and see a load of men chasing a ball around a muddy field? It's a senseless, pointless waste of time.' I hear my own words falling from Jamie's mouth. 'And everyone knows the Eagles are crap.'

'Jamie!'

'They're not even in the Premiership.'

'You little rebel.' I try not to smile because Andy is looking to me for support.

'If I was going to bother with supporting a football team, I'd go for Man U,' Jamie continues.

Andy's face is pink with irritation.

'It's just a phase,' I reassure him. 'Go and play with your Lego, Jamie.'

'How about you, Jules? How about I ask Lorraine to babysit and you come to the match?'

My jaw drops. Andy's mouth curves into a big grin.

'Gotcha!' he laughs. 'Don't panic. I'll persuade Jamie somehow.'

'Don't you dare bribe him with the offer of a hamster,' I say firmly, having recovered my composure at the thought that I might have had to spend a Saturday afternoon at Selhurst Park.

'Trust me,' he says, ducking forward and kissing me on the forehead. 'What are you going to do, Jules?'

'The usual, I expect.' Drink champagne with Leonardo in some luxury cabin with views to the sea? Swim in some sparkling country pond with Colin? Sing at Knebworth alongside Robbie? None of these pastimes appeal. The lovers of my imagination are jaded and old and, dare I say it, a little boring, compared with Steve. However, I do have other plans . . .

Andy goes to the match, having failed to persuade Jamie to accompany him and, later, once I have tucked Jamie and Emily up in bed, I flop down in front of the telly with a bar of mint crisp chocolate and a mug of coffee.

'Hi, babe. I'm home.'

I open my eyes, and sit up sharpish. 'What are you doing here?'

'Surprise!'

'Where's Joe? Did he come back with you?'

'I don't know where Joe is. He left the match at half-time, saying he felt sick.'

'Oh?'

Andy's eyes are shining with excitement. 'Forget Lorraine and Joe for a minute. I have a surprise for you.'

My heart jumps. 'What is it?'

'You'll see . . .'

My mind runs riot. Perhaps Andy has bought me a new wedding ring, the one I always wanted, a simple band of polished white gold. I remember though that we have no money, so a ring is unlikely. Perhaps David has found us a cheap holiday at last. I try to picture lazy days on a banana plantation on St Lucia with cocktails for breakfast, lunch and tea. My knowledge of far-flung parts of the world is limited to what Steve has told me, photos in travel agents' brochures, and the vistas shown on *Holiday Nightmares*. Andy did take me to Portugal for our honeymoon, but I was sick after eating some dodgy sardines, and some poor girl drowned in the hotel pool.

'Come with me,' Andy says, taking the mug and the chocolate bar and putting them on the floor. So it isn't a holiday? He grabs my hand and pulls me up from the sofa, ignoring my protests. 'When we get to the front door, put your hands over your eyes, and don't peek.'

I close my eyes and go outside where the air smells of the last barbecues of summer. 'It's not *Ground Force*, is it?'

'Course not. You've been at home all day. I think you'd have noticed if Charlie Dimmock had been out here rearranging your dahlias.'

'They're busy Lizzies and geraniums,' I protest. I know it's difficult to tell one stalk from another when there are no flowerheads, but I'd like Andy to have remembered what they were. I told him several times when I was inspired with the idea of a massive floral display to rival Lorraine's, but we are almost at the end of the summer and there are no flowers. There aren't any leaves either.

'Down you go, Jules.' Andy holds me around the waist,

and leads me awkwardly down the precipice outside our house.

'You can look now,' he says when we reach the pavement.

I open my eyes. What am I supposed to be looking at? The plumber from Anerley's van is here with two wheels parked on the pavement behind the Merc and in front of where I left the Peugeot last time I drove it. The Peugeot has gone. The space has been taken by a Fiesta.

'Someone's nicked my car,' I observe in disbelief. 'Who'd want to steal that?'

'No, look,' Andy says. 'The red car's yours. The Fiesta.'

I can't believe it.

'What do you think, Jules?'

'It's wonderful. Oh Andy, are you sure?'

'It's all yours. Air con, CD player, five doors like you've always wanted. Perfect runner. One owner – an elderly chap, banned for driving the wrong way round the M25.'

'It's all right, you don't have to sell it to me. I love it. I love *you*.' I fling my arms around Andy's neck then hesitate. 'Can we afford it?'

'I did a deal. We're doing better, Jules. Steve's picked up more than enough work.'

'More than he can handle?'

'Yes, and no.' Andy pauses. 'Business is bucking up.'

Only a salesman could describe it as that. The servicing side is just about breaking even if you don't count the repayments on the loan we took out to set it up, and Andy's sold three cars in the past month, nowhere near enough.

'I sold your old Peugeot to Nell Cornwell,' he says, as if to demonstrate he's regaining his touch.

'You didn't?' I feel terrible.

'She said she wanted something smaller, and easier to park than the Jag. I told you she was interested.'

'But it's no good.'

'It'll do her. She can't drive it herself anyway – she hasn't got a licence. She says her son can take her to see her sister down Eastbourne way on Sundays. There's always the historic car rally,' Andy teases. 'It'll be perfect for the London to Brighton run.'

'I wish Nell Cornwell luck. That car can't get to IKEA and back, let alone Brighton.' My face burns with the memory of that day. I see Steve through a rear windscreen, obscured by rain and tears. I see my heart ripped out of my ribcage yet still beating, like something from a horror movie. Filled with guilt that, in spite of Andy's magnanimous gesture, I can think only of Steve, I step back and run my fingers across the gleaming bodywork.

'You did all this for me, Andy.'

'Actually, Steve did it,' Andy confesses.

'Steve?'

'He's been working on it all day. Servicing it and touching it up here and there.'

'But it's Saturday. He doesn't work Saturdays.'

'He didn't mind, especially when I said it was a present for you.'

Andy seems more pleased with my present than I am. It's too little too late, you see. After all those years when I could really have done with a five-door model, Jamie and Emily are able to climb through between the front seats and strap themselves into their booster seats.

'Go on, try it.' Andy holds out the keys. I reach out. He snatches them back. 'Kiss first,' he says, smiling. I kiss him softly on the lips. Andy wraps his arms around me, pulls me against his body and probes my mouth with his tongue and then his teeth. The effect is both arousing and surprising. Andy withdraws, takes my hand and presses the keys into my palm. 'Go on, Jules.'

Once in the driver's seat, I turn on the engine. It purrs. I stroke the upholstery then press all the buttons I can find to see what they do. A song comes floating out of the speakers: 'Baby Come Back To Me'.

'Someone's left a CD in the player,' I shout, but Andy doesn't hear me over the music. I can hear a metallic galloping sound as he drums his fingers on the roof of the car.

'Are you going to take her for a spin, or—'

'Come indoors for a shag?' I interrupt, finishing the sentence for him.

He leans down and smiles. 'If you're offering . . .'

I wasn't actually, but Andy's already opening the door

for me. As we walk up the steps hand in hand, he starts humming the tune of 'Romeo and Juliet', the Dire Straits version.

'*You* used to cry when we made love,' he murmurs. 'Do you remember that?'

'You soppy sod!' I say. I haven't used this term of endearment for a long while. My face burns because I do remember how Andy used to make me feel. It is strange how a song has the power to stir distant memories. *And* not so distant ones.

'You're not just saying you want to do this because of the car?'

'No.'

'I thought perhaps you were getting bored with me. We've been together for a long time.' Andy's hand tightens around mine. 'I've been doing some thinking.'

'Careful,' I say lightly.

'This is a serious matter. I've been neglecting you – romantically, I mean.'

'That's true. You're hardly the lovestruck Romeo any more, are you?'

'I am, Juliet,' he swears. 'I am, and I'm going to make it up to you.'

If I ever dreamed of having six children, Emily has put me off and, if I was planning to have any more – which I'm not – Emily's unannounced presence in the bedroom makes it impossible that I should conceive tonight.

'Mummy! Daddy!' The room floods with light. As I

become aware of Emily's face peering across the bed, Andy stops mid-thrust.

'What are you doing?' Emily asks.

'Nothing,' I say, blinking. 'Go back to bed, will you?'

'Daddy, why are you lying on top of Mummy like that?'

'I'm keeping her warm,' Andy mutters through gritted teeth as he withdraws, and rolls onto his back.

'Emily, will you go back to bed.' I pull the duvet up around my shoulders.

'I had a bad dream,' she says, her voice wavering.

'So did I,' I say. 'I dreamed that a pesky little girl came and disturbed me in the middle of the night. Now will you please go back to bed!'

'*Nooo!*' Emily throws herself onto Andy's side of the bed. 'Daddy, I'm frightened.'

I am inclined to take Emily straight back to her room, but Andy swears her distress is genuine and lets her lie between us. Emily sleeps. Andy sleeps. I cannot, for the tune of the song 'Baby Come Back To Me' swirls around in my head.

It has to be a message from Steve. He has forgiven me for rejecting him and he wants us to start again. It is up to me to make the next move, and I know as I look at my husband's and my daughter's peaceful, sleeping faces what that has to be. To return the CD that Steve left in my car. To make it perfectly clear where I stand.

Chapter Eleven

Where do I stand? With Andy or Steve? With all the care and attention a man demands, one should be more than enough for anyone, yet here I am torn between two.

The question torments me as I drive the family across Waterloo Bridge on Sunday morning to have lunch with the Rhino on her narrowboat. The South Bank is to my left, the National Theatre to my right. The swelling waters of the Thames flow beneath. My new car is more fuel efficient than the old one so I'm making less of a contribution to global warming and rising water levels than I used to, but I can't convince Andy that we should visit the Rhino less often in the interests of the environment.

This morning Andy promised it would be a flying visit and we would leave immediately after lunch.

'Good idea,' I said. 'We don't want to wear the poor old thing out after she's been so ill.'

'You're so thoughtful, Jules,' Andy said, patting my

bottom as I bent over to stack the breakfast dishes in the dishwasher, 'always putting other people first.'

The warm glow I felt wasn't due to the effect of Andy's compliment, but a rush of blood to the head that occurred because I had to reach right over to extract a teaspoon that was caught in the bottom rack. If I did put other people first, I wouldn't be lusting over Steve. I would be devoting myself to Andy, wouldn't I?

I drive on, following a black cab that is moving very slowly, the driver apparently trying to make the most of a fare, something my dad would never have done.

'Juliet, Jamie's been trying to tell you something,' Andy interrupts from beside me.

'I'm concentrating on my driving,' I say hotly.

'Well, try a bit harder, will you?' says Andy. 'You almost hit that police car.'

'What police car?' The car swerves – I make it swerve – just a little, as I search for blue flashing lights.

'Gotcha, Jules.'

I slap Andy's thigh. He grabs my hand and places it back on the steering wheel.

'Your mum's not with us,' he says lightly, but I've been with him long enough to detect the edge to his voice.

'She is,' says Jamie.

'Look!' says Emily, pointing from the back seat.

'Not really,' Andy says.

'I'm here, aren't I?' I protest.

'Yes, but when you're with us, you're always so far away.'

'I'm not. As far as I'm aware, I'm driving this car. Where do you think I am?'

'I don't know and I don't suppose you'll tell me.' Andy pauses. 'What was it you were trying to tell Mummy, Jamie?'

I glance in the rearview mirror. Jamie's eyes are downcast and the corners of his mouth turned down.

'I don't know. I can't remember now,' he says so quietly I can hardly hear him. He might be seven going on seventeen at times, but he's still my little boy. Pain knifes my heart. I can remember that feeling when you're bursting to tell your mum something and she says, 'Sorry, not now, darling.' My mother used to do that when she came in from work, having done an early-morning shift. I always said I would listen to my children, yet look at me. I resolve to make up for my perceived absences by making an effort with Emily, Jamie and Andy, even the Rhino (for Andy's sake).

When we arrive at the narrowboat, Andy hits his head on the hanging basket the Rhino keeps above the door into what she calls the cabin. He always does it. It's a standing joke with the children who squeeze past Granny into the living quarters beyond.

'Hi, Mother,' Andy says, kissing her warmly on the cheek. In return the Rhino catches him by the jowl and gives him a maternal squeeze. I almost expect her to take a handkerchief from the pocket of her turquoise jacket, spit on it and wipe his face. She wears a skirt to match the jacket, and a frilly white blouse with a large opal set in gold at her throat. For someone who was supposed to have been dying, she looks remarkably healthy to me.

'Oh, you shouldn't have done,' she says as Andy hands over the box of Milk Tray I'd covered with my coat in the boot of the car in the hope he'd forget them. The Rhino reverses into the cabin and places the chocolates on the high shelf that runs the full length of the living area and provides storage for her collection of miniature cottages and a handful of books. There's a copy of the Bible, *A Year in Provence, The Shipping News* – which Andy bought her as a joke for her birthday – a world atlas so she can keep up with David and his holiday offers, and a cookery book by Marguerite Patten.

The Rhino disposed of most of Andy's dad's belongings after he died. It was almost as if she wanted to wipe out all evidence she was ever married. It seemed callous at the time. Still does.

'How are you, Pammy?' I ask as Andy and I settle on the less than comfortable bench that runs along the wooden panelling separating the living area from the bedroom at the far end of the boat.

'Could be better, Juliet, but I mustn't grumble.'

'Granny, can I have a chocolate?' says Emily. 'Please . . .'

'Not before lunch,' I say quickly, glancing towards the saucepan that bubbles on the hob in the open-plan galley kitchen.

'Please, Granny,' she begs.

Jamie looks up from where he is playing on the floor with a Lego Bionicle.

'Dear Emily,' says the Rhino. 'She's the only one of you who knows you don't get anywhere in the world today without making a fuss.' She's having a dig at me, naturally, the wimp of a daughter-in-law who doesn't stand up for herself. 'Of course you can have one.'

I look to Andy for support. He shrugs his shoulders and elbows me in the ribs at the same time. (There isn't much room on a narrowboat.) And says, 'Why not? The children eat enough junk already. I don't suppose a chocolate will make much difference.'

'But they won't eat their dinner.'

'It's one chocolate, Juliet, not a whole bar.' The Rhino takes the box back down, tears off the cellophane and passes the chocolates round. She doesn't offer me one. We do get a thimbleful of sherry each though. Andy takes a sip and wrinkles his nose. I look around for a pot plant into which I can tip mine away, but the spider plant the Rhino used to keep in the window nearest me has gone, dead from alcohol poisoning, I expect. In the end I use it to top up Andy's glass, hoping he doesn't go the same way, before we sit down to eat at the pull-out table.

There isn't much – small portions of chicken breast,

roast potatoes and sprouts. I count the sprouts on my plate. It's not difficult. There are three.

'I'm not used to catering for so many,' the Rhino says. 'I haven't had a visitor for weeks, unless you count Dr Leaver, my allergist.'

'Haven't you seen David recently?' Andy asks.

'Oh yes, he's booked me on a cruise around Norway next month.'

'Sounds great,' says Andy.

'Too cold for me,' I say ungraciously.

'When are we going on holiday, Dad?' Jamie asks. 'Everyone in my class has been on holiday except me.'

'I don't like sprouts,' Emily interrupts. 'They yucky.'

'I told you you shouldn't have had that chocolate,' I say.

'I'll have your sprouts, Emily, if you don't want them,' says the Rhino, spearing them one by one and transferring them to her own plate. 'Why don't you ask David about a holiday, Andrew?'

'I can't get away. I'm just too busy at work,' Andy says. 'We'll go next year.'

'Promise?' says Jamie.

'I promise.'

'Where would you like to go, Jamie?' asks the Rhino.

'Paris,' he says.

'How wonderful! You'll be able to see the *Mona Lisa* in the Louvre, and stroll along the banks of the Seine.'

Jamie frowns. 'No, Granny, I mean the other Paris, the one where Mickey Mouse lives, the magical world of Disney.'

'Oh.' The Rhino clears the plates and serves up trifle. 'I made it myself with gluten-free sponge fingers. I hope it's all right.' It must be because she has two helpings. 'I eat like a mouse when I'm on my own, which is most of the time nowadays.' She pats her mouth with a crisp white cotton serviette. (The Rhino calls it a napkin.) Her eyes glimmer with tears, making me wonder if she's hiding an onion inside it.

Andy glances towards me and turns back to his mother. I grimace through a mouthful of trifle.

'Come for lunch at ours next Sunday,' he says.

'Oh, you don't want me getting in the way,' the Rhino simpers. 'I know how busy you are.'

'You wouldn't be in the way, Mother.'

'Please come, Granny,' says Jamie.

'Please,' says Emily.

'If you're sure, Andrew,' the Rhino says, gazing at her son.

'We're quite sure, aren't we, Jules?'

'Absolutely,' I say coldly, unable to find a reasonable excuse why the Rhino can't visit us next Sunday. At least Andy seems to have realised I am not too impressed at the idea, because when we return to the car with Emily and Jamie skipping along ahead of us, he takes my hand and says, 'You look great today, Jules. I mean, you

209

always look great, but . . .' He whistles admiringly between his teeth.

I do feel good. I'm wearing a new push-them-up-and-force-them-together bra underneath a low-cut three-quarter-length-sleeve blouse with a brushed gold finish. Sleek black bootleg trousers and high heels (for me) complete the look. I can't help smiling.

'It's no good trying to suck up to me like this when you've just invited your mother for lunch.'

'I'm sorry about that,' Andy says. 'I know you haven't always got on with her—'

'I've never got on with her,' I interrupt.

'She was upset when you forced her to eat pasta, but that's all.'

'She's never liked me. She hates me for marrying you.'

'That's rubbish, and you know it. She loves you like a daughter.'

'Did she tell you that?'

'Not in so many words.'

'There you go then.'

'My mother would do anything for her family. If she knew about our financial difficulties, she'd be the first person offering help.'

'You wouldn't tell her?'

'No way. With her health being as it is, any further stress could kill her.'

'Good, because let me tell you, Andy, Wyevale Autos

is our business, not your mother's. I will do anything to keep it afloat, and I mean anything, even walk the streets with a sandwich board, but I will never ask your mother for help. It would kill me to think we were obligated to her in any way.'

'Oh, Jules.' Andy thrusts his arm around my waist and pulls me close so his hip bumps against mine as we walk along. 'I adore you. You are the best thing that ever happened to me.' He stops, pulls me round and kisses me long and hard and deep until I forget everything except him and me, and the CD I have to return to Steve, and Jamie, and Emily.

I feel a small hand tugging at my blouse.

'Mummy, can we go home?' Emily begs.

'Mum! Dad!' shouts Jamie from beside the car. 'There are people watching you kissing!'

If there are, I don't see them. Looking back I realise Andy and I are similar in many ways, and our differences are more imagined than real. I am just as guilty as he is of walking around with my eyes closed.

The following day I go to work, determined to show Steve exactly where I stand for the very last time. While Andy is in the office, closing a deal on the Toyota Corolla at last, and Gayle is engrossed in a telephone conversation – so what's new? – I nip out to the workshop to see Steve to give him the ultimatum, the final statement of my lack of intent. I take the CD in its case which I found in the glove compartment of my new car with me.

'Steve?'

Steve emerges from beneath the bonnet of a BMW, not one of ours. He wipes his hands on a rag and tucks it in the pocket of his overalls which he wears with the sleeves tied around his waist. His vest is smeared with oil, and ragged with holes. He looks at me, squinting in the sunlight that slants in from outside. He smiles. My heart somersaults. This isn't going to be easy.

'Thank you,' I begin rather stiffly, 'for the work you did on the Fiesta.'

'It was nothing. I didn't have anything else to do.'

'I'm sorry about that night . . . when I went running off in the rain.'

'You could have shown me some gratitude,' Steve acknowledges.

'You left your CD.' I hold out the case from what I hope is a safe distance. I don't trust myself not to get too close.

'CD?'

'I found it in the player,' I explain, wondering if Steve is being deliberately thick. 'I thought you'd want it back.'

'Oh no, you keep it, Juliet,' he says eventually. 'It's yours. I bought it for you.'

I feel like a teenager in Steve's presence, awkward, unable to speak, unable to articulate my desires, certain of what those desires are, but uncertain as to how to direct them. Or suppress them, which is what I intend to do. What I intended to do . . .

Steve moves closer and reaches not for the CD, but my hand, and leads me past the inspection pit to the far side of the workshop where he keeps his crates of tools and lubricants.

'Juliet,' he whispers. Steve's eyes are wide and black with lust. I can smell his tantalising scent of aftershave overlain with engine oil.

'I don't understand.' My voice quivers.

'Oh yes, you do.'

'Do you realise how old I am?'

'Forty-nine,' Steve says bluntly.

'Who told you that?' I am appalled that I appear that ancient in spite of the stripes in my hair and what Lorraine considers a youthful complexion.

'Gayle told me. I didn't ask her. It came out in conversation.'

'I'm not that old,' I protest. 'I'm thirty-nine, just thirty-nine,' but my conscience nags that I'm old enough to know better. 'I'm old enough to be your mother, Steve.'

'Actually, Juliet, you're older than my mother,' Steve says softly. 'She had her first baby, my brother, at fifteen, and me at seventeen.'

'Poor woman.'

'She says she wouldn't have had it any other way.'

I may be older than Steve's mother, but I don't feel the slightest bit maternal towards her son.

'You know I don't care how old you are,' he continues. 'You're always the same person inside.'

These are seductive words indeed, if I needed any further persuasion, which I don't. Fire burns deep in my pelvis. My heart pounds as Steve snakes his arm around my waist and pulls me so close that I can't tell whether the pulse I can hear is mine or his.

'Relax,' he breathes.

'I can't,' I mutter, making one last desperate attempt to show Steve I am *not* desperate. 'This isn't right. I don't want this . . .'

Steve grins. 'Liar,' he murmurs and he claims possession of my mouth in a hot, probing kiss. At first we are awkward, twisting our necks like courting pigeons, but not for long. Still clutching the CD case, I throw my arms around his neck and press myself against the hard length of his body.

Kate and Leonardo. Steve and Juliet . . . As Steve's teeth graze my tongue, I run my hand through the hair on the back of his head, and catch it in my fingers. More, please. More . . . Dizzy with desire, I close my eyes and concentrate on the sensations Steve is arousing deep inside me as he slips a hand inside my blouse and walks his fingers up my back.

'I want you, Juliet,' he whispers raggedly, tearing his mouth from mine.

How can I refuse? As I take a half-step back to turn my attention towards the zip on Steve's overalls, there is a great clattering sound which pulls me back from the edge of the cliff from which I am just about to jump. Steve jumps too.

'What the hell's that?'

'I dropped the CD.'

'I thought it was your husband,' Steve says, gazing down into the pit where the CD has fallen out of its case and rolled to one corner. I can hear the relief in his voice that it wasn't. I straighten my clothing, and run my fingers through my stripes. Steve goes down and picks up the CD and case.

'There's a note,' he says, sounding surprised.

'I missed that.'

Steve unfolds the piece of paper, studies it and hands it over.

'There you go,' he says, smiling.

The title of the song, 'Baby Come Back To Me', and kisses, XXX, are printed on Wyevale Autos headed stationery. I guess Steve must have sneaked into the office to use the computer, but I don't mind. Not at all. I fold it again, and slip it into my skirt pocket.

'Er, Juliet,' Steve begins.

'Yes?' I say, hopeful that he is about to drag me down into the pit and kiss me again.

'Could you lend us a tenner? Just till Friday.'

'I suppose so. Yes, of course. I'll drop it in on my way to pick up the children.' At this moment I'd give Steve anything he asked for. Anything at all.

'You have grease all over your top, Juliet,' Gayle points out as soon as I return to the showroom. 'You'll never get it out, you know.'

I'm not sure how much Gayle knows or guesses about me and Steve, but I am sure that this isn't a good time to tackle her over the phone bills. I'll have to cross my fingers and hope she doesn't say anything to Andy. In the meantime, I hide the evidence of our passionate encounter with the blue sweat-top I flung into the car this morning in case the summer should be over.

I am so overwhelmed and absorbed by the fact that Steve and I have kissed at last that I almost forget to pick up the children. Mary Bacon pushes them out of her front door with their raincoats on even though there is no sign of rain.

'You're late today, Juliet,' she says sternly.

Emily clings to my leg, scowling up at Mary. Jamie stares at the ground.

'I'm so sorry. I didn't realise what the time was. It won't happen again.'

'I'm glad to hear it. Not that I mind putting myself out occasionally if needs must, but you pay me by the hour, and an extra fifteen minutes here and there adds up to a tidy sum.'

'I understand. I'm sorry.' I begin to fumble in my bag for my purse to offer her some financial compensation to smooth things over, but remember just in time that

I've given my last ten-pound note to Steve. 'Did you enjoy your holiday?'

'It seems a long time ago already,' Mary sighs. She's wearing a Save the Whale sweatshirt, and her leggings have holes in the knees, an indication of how hard she must have been working since she came back. It makes me feel bad that I have to tackle her about the spaghetti hoops, among other things.

'I believe in children being allowed to have a treat now and then,' Mary explains.

I want to say that spaghetti hoops aren't a treat when the children have them pretty often at home, but I keep that opinion to myself.

'I only mentioned it because we agreed that you'd give them meals prepared from fresh, organic ingredients. We also agreed that you'd take them out and about during the school holidays.'

Mary Bacon smiles, making the stubble stand proud from her upper lip like bristles left on a ham.

'It wasn't my fault that I couldn't take them anywhere,' she says.

'Was it because of Emily?'

'No, it was to do with health and safety.' Before I can ask her what she means, she goes on: 'If there's anything else you'd like to discuss, it'll have to wait for another day. I'm expecting my nieces.'

'Is it your birthday again, Mary?' Jamie pipes up.

'No, I'm giving *them* presents this time. Souvenirs

from Scarborough. It costs me a small fortune to keep those girls happy.'

I retreat quickly. It doesn't take a genius to see Mary's planning to ask me for more money. On the way along the road we pass three of the nieces struggling along with heavy bags. I wave. They don't wave back.

I wonder if I should have been more forceful about the spaghetti hoops, but I have more pressing concerns than worrying about Mary Bacon. I have Steve's note in my pocket, evidence of his – if not *my* – indiscretion. I should have shredded it at work. While Jamie and Emily are upstairs changing into their pyjamas, I take it out, smooth it down and read it once more.

I hunt the matches out, recalling that I haven't used them since I lit the candles for the disastrous meal for Andy. I strike one and let the flame lick at the corner of the note. I regret the fact that I have to destroy it, but I can't risk Andy finding it. The paper curls and turns brown, then burns down towards my fingers. When it is too hot to bear, I drop it into the sink and run cold water over the blackened ashes.

There is a scream from behind me and I receive a sound telling-off from Jamie.

'Mum, don't you know it's dangerous to play with fire?'

'I do now, thank you, Jamie,' I say after his lecture. That's just what I've been doing, playing with fire. I like my quiet, ordinary life. I like my tolerable marriage. I must stop this thing, this obsession with Steve, before it's too late.

I haven't by strict definition been unfaithful. A kiss is just a kiss. It doesn't mean anything. I haven't committed adultery just because I let Steve kiss me. Adultery is voluntary sexual intercourse between a married person and a person other than her spouse. I checked the definition in the dictionary. A kiss is a touch with the lips. Sexual intercourse involves considerably more bodily contact than that.

'Jamie, did I give you your vitamin tablet this morning?' I ask while I'm preparing his bedtime drink.

'No, Mum.'

I ask myself if it's possible that I've forgotten to give Jamie a vitamin tablet before – whether it's my fault he's always tired. As I dig about in the kitchen cupboard above the worktop for the Thomas the Tank Engine vitamins, I resolve to try harder, but I am distracted by the pepper-pot I bought from IKEA.

It stands on the worktop, reminding me of the lure of the Big Thing more than ever. Did Kate feel like this, walking on air along the decks of the *Titanic*, her lips aching after Leonardo's bruising kisses? It isn't all physical. I adore everything about Steve. He's happy-go-lucky and passionate, and he never demeans me by patting my bottom or waving packets of out-of-date frozen sausages at me.

'Mum!' Jamie pulls me back from my musings.

'Yes?' I snap.

'You've put the vitamins away.'

'I haven't. I've just given them to you.'

'You took them out of the cupboard and put them away again,' Jamie protests. 'Are you going mad, Mum?'

I shake my head, but I guess I am. I am going mad with love and confusion. I feel for the wedding ring on my finger, and find it's not there.

Later, I read *Sleeping Beauty* to Emily who sits on my lap with her thumb in her mouth and her Barbie flannel pressed against her nose.

'Are you listening, Jamie?' I ask.

'No way. *Sleeping Beauty*'s a girl's story. I'll stick with Harry Potter, thanks.'

'Once upon a time . . .' I see Steve as the prince in chainmail and hose, vaulting from his white charger, bending down to kiss me and waking me up. Emily nudges me.

'Read it, Mummy,' she says impatiently.

Soon afterwards, I take the children upstairs and tuck them up in bed. Jamie will only kiss me if no one is looking. Emily flings her arms around my neck, saying, 'You're the best-est-est mummy in the whole wide world.' Her laughter is thick and sweet like treacle. She smells of strawberry toothpaste. My heart twists.

'I love you, Emily.'

'Love you,' she giggles.

I plug in the nightlight Emily has taken to sleeping with, and switch out the main light in her bedroom.

'Goodnight, darling,' I whisper. 'Sweet dreams,' but I can tell from the sound of quiet breathing that she is already asleep.

How could I contemplate risking losing my family over Steve? Surely Jamie's and Emily's happiness is more important than mine? I couldn't bear the thought of not seeing Jamie at weekends because he's with his dad and, in spite of her paddies, I feel the same way about Emily. The very thought of packing their toothbrushes and flannels, and sending them away makes my eyes prick with tears.

I won't let it happen. Steve and I are finished. Gayle was suspicious before she saw the oil marks all over my blouse. I can't let it go any further. It's gone far enough.

'Hi, Jules. I'm home.' I hear Andy call up the stairs. I take a deep breath.

'Hi, darling. How are you?' I ask, peering over the banister.

'Okay,' he says, frowning. 'What's wrong?'

'Nothing. Nothing at all.' I lope down the last few steps and take Andy's jacket. 'Would you like a cup of tea, or a lager?'

'All right, Jules,' he says rather sharply I think for a husband who is being attended to in the way I imagine that a husband would like to be, 'all in good time.' He pauses. 'Have you crashed the new car, or something?'

'No, of course I haven't.'

'You seem a bit twitchy.'

'There's nothing wrong,' I soothe.

'Are you sure?'

'For goodness' sake, Andy, everything is absolutely fine.'

'Great,' he says, nodding. 'Before I forget, you'll have to use the Merc tomorrow. I want to take your car. There's one or two things need finishing off. Nothing major.'

'Am I allowed to take Jamie to school in it?'

'As long as you make sure he and Emily aren't carrying crisps, drinks or felt-tip pens.'

'I'll pick my car up on the way back from school if it's ready,' I suggest. This isn't a good start to my resolution to break off my liaison with Steve. There is no reason why Andy shouldn't bring my car back after work tomorrow, no reason on earth, apart from me wanting to see Steve.

'I wish I could find my ring,' I say. 'I don't feel right without it. Perhaps—' I begin, but Andy interrupts.

'There's no money for rings. I've just bought you a car.'

'I know that.'

'What do you suddenly want a new ring for anyway? You didn't seem too bothered when you lost the old one.'

'As a talisman against unfaithful thoughts?'

Andy grins. 'Oh, Jules.'

'I might be tempted to run off with another man without it.'

Andy is laughing now.

'What's so funny?'

'The idea of you running off with another man. You don't have time. You're always telling me you don't have time to breathe, let alone find yourself a lover.'

'Other people do,' I say stiffly.

'Yes, but you're my wife. You're *you*.'

'Why is it so ridiculous? Aren't I attractive any more?'

'Well,' says Andy, rubbing his chin. 'You've had two children. Your body's taken quite a battering.'

'Thanks a lot!'

'And – as you keep pointing out – you're almost forty, which narrows down the field of potential lovers.'

'Andy!'

'What's the point in taking a lover anyway? You don't even like sex that much.'

'Are you complaining?'

'Well, I guess I'd like it a little more often than once every six weeks or so, but don't worry. Quality counts as well as quantity.'

'I didn't realise you'd been counting.'

'Cheer up, Jules.' Andy pats me on the bottom. 'I love you. You love me. That should be enough for anyone.'

I unfold Andy's jacket that I have been holding throughout this conversation and hang it over the banister.

'While we're on the subject of infidelity, do you think Joe could be having an affair?' I ask.

Andy raises his eyebrows. He couldn't look more amazed if I'd asked him if Crystal Palace were on course to win the Premiership. They won't, of course, because they're in the First Division. There was a time when I thought the Premiership and the First Division were one and the same, which isn't unreasonable, is it?

'Obviously, you don't.'

'Joe likes women. Who doesn't?' Andy says. 'But he wouldn't have an affair. He's too busy with this training course he's doing.'

'What training course?'

'For work. Hasn't Lorraine told you? I thought she would have done. Joe says she's been going ballistic when he's late home. It isn't fair, is it? Lorraine wants more money to decorate the house, and when Joe tries to improve his chances of earning more, she gets ratty with him.' Andy puts his arm around my shoulders. 'I'll be getting ratty if I don't have something to eat soon. What's for tea, Jules?'

'Egg on toast. I was going to make your favourite, sausage casserole, but there aren't any sausages.'

'I bought two packets the other day and put them in the freezer.'

'You mean those Cumberland ones?'

'They were on special offer.'

I don't know how to tell Andy this.

'I've thrown them away,' I confess.

'What did you go and do that for?'

'I checked the dates on them – I assumed they were last year's. I didn't know, did I? You were supposed to be buying economy sausages, not Sainsbury's best.'

Andy stares at me fiercely.

'I'm sorry,' I mutter.

Andy's mouth twists and his face creases up with laughter. I watch him, biting my lip and holding my shoulders rigid against the wave of giggles that threatens to overwhelm me.

'Come on, Jules, you have to admit that it's bloody funny.'

I give in. It is. It's ridiculous. Almost as ridiculous as imagining I could give up this ordinary life for the love of a boy half my age.

Chapter Twelve

You will be more sensitive than usual. Be prepared for misunderstandings and fallings out. That's what some newspaper astrologer has made up for people born under the sign of Aries, like me, this week. Do I believe it? Lorraine does. She can twist whatever happens to fit the prediction. She says I'm an atypical Aries, meek and sensible, not fiery and impulsive. It has something to do with moons and ascendants, whatever they are.

I smile to myself as I fold up the newspaper. If I believed in horoscopes, I'd stay at home all day.

I fetch Emily from her bedroom where I discover her cutting a doll's hair with the nail scissors that I thought I'd left out of her reach, and find the keys to the Merc so we can collect Jamie from school, and my car from Wyevale Autos. Arriving there half an hour later, I park on the forecourt. Jamie and Emily jump out and run up to the showroom where Andy is walking to and fro, talking on his mobile. I see him press his finger to his lips as the children jump up and down, desperate to tell him what they've been doing today.

I follow them inside, pausing beside Gayle's desk.

'Your car's ready,' Gayle says. I don't like the way she is smiling at me with her mouth, but not her eyes. What does she think she knows about me and Steve? How does she think she can use it?

'Did you ever take a look at the telephone bills?' she asks.

'Oh yes, and I'm not intending to charge you for essential personal calls – even though you have a mobile of your own. It would be petty to argue about a few pence here and there,' I say, almost choking on my magnanimous offer.

Gayle runs one long, pink fingernail across the keyboard on her desk, and flicks away imaginary dust. We have an understanding, I hope. And if I do nothing more to fuel her suspicions that I am having an affair with Steve then there'll be no reason for her to mention them to Andy.

Andy doesn't seem that pleased to see me.

'I've come to collect the car,' I say when he comes off the phone.

'Good,' he says, smiling vaguely and scratching the top of his head.

I let my eyes rove over the cars on the forecourt. There's a red Fiesta, plastered with white lettering like

228

a driving-school car. It's professionally done, no doubt about that, but the words *Wyevale Autos* stand out from every panel.

'What have you done to my car?'

Andy hesitates.

'What have you done?' I am shaking with rage. 'Is this some kind of joke because if it is, it's not funny.'

'I thought it was a good idea,' Andy says sheepishly. 'I mean, you drive all over the place in spite of your environmental principles. It's great advertising.'

'But it's my car!'

'You said you'd do anything for the business. You said you'd wear a sandwich board!'

I did. I can't deny it, but I don't want to be driving to school and Mary Bacon's with *Wyevale Autos* all over my car.

'What if I meet Mr Parker? What about Nell Cornwell? They'll know who I am.'

'I don't suppose Nell will do anything.'

The Peugeot broke down on the way to Eastbourne and Nell no longer speaks to us. Gayle says she's using the Peugeot as a cat shelter in her front garden.

I glare at Andy, seeing a bald, middle-aged man with a paunch, a man who claims he loves me, yet allows the complete mutilation of my car. I turn away looking for a means of revenge, catch sight of the frustration bricks on Gayle's desk, grab them and throw them at him. They bounce off. I would have thrown the photo of the fitness instructor boyfriend, but it's no longer there. I storm outside to the car, and scrape my nails along the sign on the driver's door. It doesn't come off.

It's like the sign I must have written across my forehead.

MUG.

It's my fault, of course. Not only have I succumbed to Gayle's unspoken blackmail over the phone bills, I have gradually by my passive, easygoing nature, led Andy to believe he can do whatever he likes without consulting me first. Well, I have had enough. It's time I stood up for myself.

'Why's Mummy cross?' asks Emily who has followed me out behind Jamie and Andy. 'Is she having a paddy?'

'No, I am not.' I stamp my foot. 'Oh, how could you, Andy?'

'I thought I told you about it. Didn't I tell you?' Andy tries another tack. 'I was going to tell you.'

'No, you bloody well weren't.'

'Mum, you did a swear,' says Jamie.

'Mummy did a swear, Mummy did a swear,' chants Emily.

'Shh, Emily, Mummy's a bit stressed,' Andy says patronisingly. His flushed face contrasts with his salmon-pink shirt. It is not a good look. 'Listen, Juliet. I didn't think you'd mind. You never seem to mind about anything very much.'

I am aware that both Steve and Gayle are watching from the showroom door.

'Emily! Jamie! Get in the car.'

'I want to stay with Daddy,' says Emily.

'The booster seats are in Dad's car,' says Jamie.

'It doesn't matter about the seats.'

'It does,' Jamie insists.

'All right, Daddy'll bring you home.' I jump in, rev the engine and lower the window. 'Don't be late. Jamie has school tomorrow.' I set the car in first gear and put my foot down hard. The car lurches forwards and stops dead.

'You've stalled it,' Andy points out unnecessarily.

There are some things you don't tell your spouse. That you've dropped his toothbrush (by accident, not design) into the loo and neither sterilised it fully in boiling water, nor replaced it with a new one – which is what I would have done if Andy hadn't adulterated my car with advertising. That in spite of being compelled by lack of money to buy economy groceries, you are paying to have your nails done. Lorraine's dreamed up a good offer.

Jamie is at school. Emily and Tyler are upstairs playing in Tyler's bedroom. Lorraine and I are in the spare room that leads off Lorraine's kitchen. She's done it out recently in mango emulsion, and put up posters advertising the benefits of cathiodermie, dermabrasion, and spray-on fake tans. Dressed in a white towelling robe over T-shirt and jeans, I sit perched on a stool, resting my palms flat on a board across my knees.

'I had a strange dream last night,' I begin, 'more of a nightmare—'

'Have another muffin,' says Lorraine quickly, pointing me towards the plate of double chocolate muffins she has left on her therapy couch, and reminding me that other people's dreams are not terribly interesting.

I shake my head.

'I bought them because I thought you needed cheering up after what Andy did to your car,' says Lorraine with mock affront.

'That'll take more than a muffin, I can tell you.'

'Have two or three then.'

'No, thanks. You've seen what Andy's done?'

'Couldn't miss it. Andy has a point though. Pete – the plumber who parks his van outside – says effective advertising is essential when you're setting up a small business.'

'You've spoken to him?'

'He offered to carry the buggy up the steps the other day. Tyler was asleep in it and I didn't want to wake her up.'

'Did you find out who he's seeing?'

'He isn't seeing anyone. He's flat-sitting for a friend.' Lorraine helps herself to a muffin. She peels off the paper case and takes a bite. 'I suppose I should get started. I have to prove to Joe that I can make money working from home before he'll consider a salon on the Portland Road.'

'I can pay you more,' I offer. 'You don't have to do me any favours.'

'Of course I do. You're my best friend, aren't you?' Lorraine screws up the muffin case, and drops it in the brushed-steel bin alongside her. She pulls a wet wipe from the box she has on the couch alongside the muffins, cleans her hands, and dabs at the corners of her mouth.

'How do you do that?' I ask.

'What?'

'Eat a whole muffin without spilling a crumb?'

'It takes practice,' she giggles. Lorraine looks well. She might even be putting on weight. Her top is stretched very taut across her breasts, and her trousers, the linen ones from Next, don't hang straight down at the hips as they did when she first bought them. 'Now, what were we doing? Nails and eyebrows.'

'Not eyebrows. You know that, Lorraine.'

'You really should let me wax them, or at least pluck them,' she wheedles.

'No, absolutely not.'

'Okay, just the nails then,' she sighs. 'Let's see them.'

After much softening, filing and buffing, Lorraine is sticking the last of the new nails on. 'There.' She stands back, one hand on her hip. 'What do you think?'

'Very nice,' I say admiringly. 'Do you realise this is the first time I've had long nails?'

'You'll be able to rake them down Andy's back.'

'Actually, I was thinking of raking them down Steve's.' The words slip out before I can stop them.

Lorraine is silent. Then: 'Are you serious?'

'He kissed me.'

'In a friendly way?'

I shake my head.

'The horny bastard. He did have the horn, didn't he?' Lorraine grabs the plate of muffins, offers one to me which I accept, and takes one herself. 'Oh Juliet, how could you? Steve's half your age. You're old enough to be his mother.'

'I'm older than his mother – he told me – but only by a year or so,' I mumble through a mouthful of chocolate chips. 'Lorraine, I don't know what to do.'

'Of course you do. You tell him to leave you alone.'

'What if *I* can't leave *him* alone? It's not one-sided. I've fallen in love with him.'

'It isn't love, Juliet. It's one of your fantasies.' Lorraine pauses. 'Do you really want to risk everything you have for a quick shag with some randy mechanic?'

'It's not like that.'

'No?' says Lorraine. 'What about Andy? What about Jamie and Emily? How do you think they'd feel if they found out you were screwing around with Steve?'

'It wouldn't be screwing around as you so delicately put it,' I protest.

'Whatever you call it, it's wrong,' Lorraine says firmly.

'You must stop this, Juliet. Don't do it. Promise me.'

'I promise,' I say, but what are promises for if not to be broken? The tigress inside me growls and flicks her tail.

'You're not going to stop, are you? You've already made up your mind. I expect you've already shagged him.'

'I haven't.'

'I don't believe you,' Lorraine snaps back. The sheen of her make-up cannot hide the heat in her face, and her eyes – blue today – glint with fury. I don't think I've ever seen her so mad. 'Do you know what Joe said when I asked him about the time you alleged that he kissed you?'

'There's nothing alleged about it.'

'He said you took it personally that he turned you down. He said that you were coming on to him.'

'Lorraine! You know I wouldn't do a thing like that.'

'Do I? I thought you were a nice, normal person, but you're not. You're a raving nymphomaniac! A scheming temptress!' Lorraine's voice crescendoes. 'A marriage-breaker!'

I slip down from the stool, tug the robe from my shoulders and drop it on the floor.

'I'm going home.'

'Those nails still have to be shaped, and painted and polished,' Lorraine snarls.

'I don't care,' I say, facing up to her. 'I'll do them

myself!' Fired up with anger, I drag Emily away from the game she is playing with Tyler. They are playing 'tattoos' according to Emily, inking images of what might be spiders onto their legs with felt pen and wiping them off with a damp towel. I can't be bothered to tell them off or clear up the mess. Lorraine can do that.

At home, I paint the nails flame red to signify the tigress's bloodied claws. I suppose I shall never speak to Lorraine again. If I were as hardhearted as she has shown herself to be, I wouldn't care, but I'm not. I do care very much, and it's not because I haven't any other friends. I do have other friends, but they're not as close as I thought Lorraine and I were.

Throughout the rest of the week, I am troubled by thoughts of Lorraine. I begin to wonder if I've been unfair on her. There is some truth in what she said, and she really hit a nerve when she asked how Andy and my children would feel if they found out about me and Steve. By the weekend, I'm hoping that she'll ring to apologise, but she doesn't.

I don't mention our falling-out to Andy because I'm not in the mood to speak to him in any depth after the car business. I assumed he would find out from Joe, but he said that Joe didn't turn up to the match or the pub yesterday. Andy didn't stay out late either, and I have to say that he looks quite human without the physical consequences of a Sunday-morning hangover.

'Have you laid the table, Andy?' I ask as I put the

chicken in the oven for the Rhino's lunch. Having checked the gluten content of everything in the cupboards – which isn't much in these days of straitened financial circumstance – I decided to err on the safe side and serve what the Rhino cooked for us last Sunday, but with more sprouts, and peas for Emily. 'Andy,' I snap, 'are you listening?'

Andy looks up from the newspaper he's spread across the worktop where I want to work.

'I'll do it later,' he mutters. 'It doesn't take long to throw a cloth on.'

'It's not just the cloth. You'll need to find glasses and cutlery. You might have to wash up a couple of knives from breakfast.'

'Calm down, Jules.'

'It's all right for you, sitting there with the paper while I do all the preparation. She's your mother, not mine.' I close the oven door, and snatch the pepper-pot from the worktop where I left it beside the red mug I had as a freebie with a purchase of coffee some years before. The mug's cracked, but it's useful for holding the flowers Emily sometimes picks from other people's gardens.

'You can put this on the table too when you get around to it.' I slam the pepper-pot down in the centre of the sports page Andy is reading.

'Hey, don't do that,' he says mildly.

'I'll do what I like,' I huff.

'I don't know why you bought that thing,' Andy says,

pushing the pepper-pot aside. 'We already have a pepper-pot.'

'The old one's not very big,' I counter, 'and it's broken.'

'Oh?' Andy frowns.

'The lid won't screw back down properly. Someone must have cross-threaded it.'

'I hadn't noticed.'

'You wouldn't notice if a crocodile bit you on the nose.'

'I would,' he says, sounding hurt. How much longer are we going to go on hurting each other? 'You're not still in a bad mood about the car?' he asks.

'Yes, I bloody well am!' I go to the cupboard and take the old pepper-pot out. When Andy finally leaves the kitchen to lay the table, I turn the radio up loud, stand on the crossbar of the stool he has vacated, and drop the old pepper-pot from a great height. It wasn't broken, but it is now.

Before the Rhino arrives, announcing her presence with a prolonged buzz on the doorbell, I sweep up the pieces, wrap them in newspaper, and throw them in the bin under the sink. Emily and Jamie greet their grandmother and show her through to the kitchen.

The Rhino's hair is fluffed out around her head in bouffant curls, and she's wearing a brown and cream suit with a pink blouse. She reminds me of a Neapolitan ice cream.

'Would you like a drink, Pammy?' I ask, wiping my hands on a towel. 'Tea? A glass of wine?'

'I'd like a sherry, thank you.'

'I'm afraid we're out of sherry.'

'You liked the one I bought you then?'

'Oh, yes.' I can't confess to having poured most of it into the sea-monkey tank, can I? It hadn't occurred to me before, but it was probably the Rhino's cheap sherry, not the heat, that finished them off.

'I'll buy you another bottle,' she offers generously as Andy joins us in the kitchen. He kisses her on the proffered cheek.

'You look well, Andrew,' she says.

'So do you, Mother.'

'I feel much better than I did, even compared with last Sunday, but I can't say I've made a full recovery yet. Dr Leaver, my allergist, says an attack of colitis as severe and prolonged as the one I've endured isn't something you make a full recovery from. In fact, Ian says—'

'Ian?' Andy interrupts.

The Rhino gives a little smile. 'We're on first-name terms now. I cancelled a lunchdate with him today to be with my family.'

'Oh, you shouldn't have cancelled,' I say. 'You could have come to us another time.'

'It doesn't matter. Ian's taking me to the opera next month. We're going to see a performance of Wagner's *Ring*. That's culture for you, Juliet.'

I open the oven, feel the full force of 200 degrees of fan-assisted heat against my face. The Rhino said she was all alone – that's why Andy invited her. I lift out the roasting tray, and crash it down on the hob where the sprouts are boiling over. Good old Juliet. You can rely on her.

I pick up the carving fork and stab it into the chicken's breast. The juices run out clear.

'I'll carve, shall I?'

'Go ahead,' says Andy.

'Tell the children lunch is ready and make sure they wash their hands before they sit down.'

'Anything else?' he says with sarcasm.

'You needn't make out you're so downtrodden,' I say crossly. 'All you've done so far is prepare the table and read the paper.'

I hear the Rhino's hiss of disapproval of my criticism, not Andy's laziness.

'I'll go and find the children, dear,' she says, sailing out of the kitchen.

'Juliet, please try and make an effort while Mother's here,' Andy says. 'It's not much to ask.'

We sit down at the table in the dining room. Jamie starts eating immediately while Emily claims she likes sprouts better than peas today.

'Poultry?' says the Rhino, prodding her food with a fork. 'It would have been nice to have had something more exotic.'

'You've always said you don't like foreign food, Mother,' Andy says gallantly.

'Ian has been showing me that an allergy doesn't necessarily restrict one's gastronomic experience. He has been most enlightening.'

After lunch, Jamie and Emily run off to play – Jamie planning to assemble his Scalextric set, and Emily to feed her dolls. I follow Andy into the kitchen to make coffee, and avoid having to make conversation with the Rhino.

'Are you sure this allergist of hers is all right?' I ask Andy. 'You hear of unscrupulous people who go round conning old women out of their savings.'

'You're not counting my mother in that category, are you?' Andy says quickly. 'You'd hardly describe her as old.'

'She left the chicken saying it was undercooked, the sprouts bitter, the potatoes green and the gravy out of a packet, and she took the last helping of trifle which Jamie had his eye on.' I can't help it. 'I'd describe her as an old bitch.'

Too late I realise that Andy is frantically waving at me to stop.

'Juliet!' he groans.

I turn. The Rhino is right behind me.

'It's all right, Andrew. Juliet's entitled to her opinion. It's quite a relief to hear that she *has* an opinion about anything, she's such a mouse,' the Rhino taunts.

I didn't mean the Rhino to hear me. It's true. I didn't.

Shaking off Andy's restraining hand, I step up close to her until I can see the pink eyeshadow caught in the creases of her eyelids. I stare at her. Her gaze wavers slightly.

'You've never liked me,' I begin. 'You've never wanted my marriage to succeed.'

The Rhino raises one hand to her throat, and strokes skin that appears more birdlike than human.

'I didn't come from the right background, did I?' I continue. 'My family lived in a council flat in the wrong part of town. My father was a cabbie, and my mother was a cleaner, the lowest of the low. And I left school at sixteen.' I take a deep breath. 'I worked hard to make up for it, but you don't give a damn about that, do you?'

'Juliet!' Andy warns.

'It's not just the matter of your inappropriate upbringing, and lack of intellect and education, is it?' says the Rhino. 'There's the matter of your insincere nature. You were living out of wedlock with some lowlife when you met my Andrew, and I don't know how you did it, but you dug your claws into him and lured him away.'

'He didn't take much luring.' I recall standing beside my car one Saturday at the side of the A4, wishing I'd had the money to join the AA or the RAC. I was supposed to be cooking lunch for the current boyfriend's parents and I had been out shopping for ingredients. It was half past twelve and I was stuck with a puncture and no phone. Anyway, this young man pulled up in a Golf GTi. He opened the door of his car, jumped out and strolled towards me, hands in his pockets. There was something about him. Was it the cheeky chappie smile or the gorgeous blue eyes? I don't know, but our eyes locked.

'Can I help?' he asked.

'I've got a flat,' I muttered, aware of the flush spreading up my neck.

'Got a spare?'

'I don't know.' Before I knew it, he had changed the wheel and we were sitting side by side against some railings up the bank, sharing wafers and a tub of melted ice cream, and details of our lives. He asked me out and the rest, as they say, is history.

'Another week and Andrew would have been married to the girl of his dreams, his childhood sweetheart.'

'Oh, don't be ridiculous,' I protest. 'He wouldn't have been married to her for long.'

'Andrew called the wedding off the night before. Poor Tanya was in pieces. "Pammy," she said, "your son must be deranged to run off with that tart when he could have had me."'

I glance towards Andy, expecting him to defend my honour, but he's staring out of the kitchen window at the fence that divides our garden from Lorraine and Joe's as if he's planning to sit on it.

'Andy, say something.'

'Er, I think I should help Jamie with the Scalextric set.'

'Tanya's a shining star in Public Relations now,' says the Rhino. 'She's beautiful, charming and a great success.'

'I don't care. Andy and I love each other.'

'Don't take anything for granted. Remember, Juliet, a man's first love and loyalty lies with his mother, not his wife.'

I stand firm. 'I've had enough of your snide remarks, and trying to pitch Andy against me. I want you to go home and not come back.'

'It will be a pleasure not to set foot in this house again.' The Rhino sniffs. 'I don't appreciate being poisoned, and I never did like your steps.' She turns to Andy who hasn't yet left to fix the Scalextric, and says, 'Andrew, you must bring my grandchildren to visit me in future. I'd like to introduce you to Ian who has become the new man in my life. You see, I'm not too old for romance. Goodbye.'

I wait, shaking all over, while Andy shows the Rhino out. When he returns, he starts loading the dishwasher, jamming the plates and pans in so they won't wash properly, and then overfilling the salt reservoir without using the funnel, which is so unlike him.

'Aren't you going to say anything?' I ask eventually. 'I'd prefer to be yelled at than frozen out like this.'

He doesn't look at me, just switches the dishwasher on and mutters, 'You're pathetic, Juliet,' and he doesn't speak to me for the rest of the day, communicating through Jamie and Emily and the occasional unpleasant gesture. I don't think I have been unreasonable. I behaved no more rudely to the Rhino than she did to me.

At some early hour of the morning, about three o'clock according to my radio alarm, there is a ringing at our doorbell. I emerge slowly from a dream in which I am trying to protect Steve from a herd of Rhinos (not the rhinoceros type).

'Who the hell is that at this time of night?' Andy yawns, swinging himself to a sitting position on the edge of the bed.

I reach for the switch on the bedside lamp. The light hurts my eyes. I let Andy grab his pyjama top (he only wears the bottom half in bed) and go downstairs. The next thing I hear is him yelling, 'It's Lorraine! You'd better come down!'

I grab my dressing-gown and shuffle down the stairs. Lorraine must have been unable to sleep. She's realised her mistake in accusing me of leading Joe into temptation, and has come to apologise for the way she's treated me. But I am wrong. It isn't just Lorraine on our doorstep. Emily and Jamie are with her, Emily clutching one hand, Jamie the other.

'What's happening? Why aren't you in bed?' I stammer.

Lorraine pushes my children in through the door. I realise that Emily is dragging her suitcase trolley and Jamie is carrying his school rucksack. A teddy bear looks out of the top.

'I'm returning your children,' says Lorraine. 'They told me they'd left home.'

'I put them to bed,' Andy keeps repeating. 'I kissed them goodnight.'

I explode. 'Jamie, what did you think you were doing, wandering about in the dark without telling anyone where you were? I've told you never to leave the house without telling Mummy.'

To my horror Jamie begins to cry.

'Oh, come here.' I squat down and open my arms, but he won't come to me. 'I'm not cross with you. I'm upset. Anything could have happened.' I start crying too. What if someone had picked them up and carried them away? I might never have seen them again. 'Jamie . . .' He trips forwards into my arms and I hug him so hard, he starts wriggling in a futile attempt to escape.

'Emily says she wants to live somewhere happy like Teletubbyland,' Lorraine says. She is still prickly, which I suppose isn't surprising when someone else's children have just tried to move in with you at some ungodly hour of the morning, and you've fallen out with one of their parents. 'She says she wants to come and live with Tyler because Mummy and Daddy fight all the time. Poor little mites.'

I loosen my grip slightly on Jamie, realising that Andy has picked Emily up.

I don't know what to do or what to say. In the end I thank Lorraine for bringing them back, offer her a glass of wine for her trouble, which she declines, and take the children inside.

'Why, Jamie?' I ask, my voice still husky with tears, when I tuck him back up in bed where he's supposed to be.

'You and Dad,' he says. 'You're being horrible to each other and to Granny.'

I stroke his forehead. 'It's been difficult,' I say, 'but we'll sort it out. It'll be all right.'

'Promise, Mum?'

What can I say? I cross my fingers in the dark and wander back to bed. Andy is still awake.

'You didn't tell me you'd fallen out with Lorraine as well as my mother,' he says.

'How do you know?'

'She didn't stay for a drink. What have you fallen out about?'

'Nothing.'

'Juliet, in less than a week, you have fallen out with me, your best friend and your mother-in-law. What's wrong with you?'

'Nothing. Everything. I don't know.' I turn away from him, and pull the duvet up around my ears. I can't talk to Andy any more. We have nothing in common, apart from the children. Does this mean our marriage is over? I can't help wondering if I might be more inclined to find a way to resolve our differences if it wasn't for Steve . . .

Chapter Thirteen

It turns out that our marriage isn't the only one under pressure. On the following Tuesday morning, I am at the kitchen sink with the plunger when the phone rings.

'Juliet, it's Lorraine. Are you doing anything?'

'I'm trying to unblock the sink. Jamie poured his modelling compound away before reading the packet, which warns you not to dispose of it down a drain because it sets.' I stop abruptly. I'd forgotten that Lorraine and I aren't speaking.

'Can I come round?' she says.

I should say no, but her voice is taut. She sounds as if she might snap.

'Can me and Tyler come round to yours?'

'Yes, of course. Give me ten minutes.' I gaze around, panicking. Give me ten hours. I'm not houseproud, but the sitting room looks like a zoo where Emily has assembled every fluffy toy in the house (including mine) on the floor. I toss the toys into a mound against the wall by the door, and I am vacuuming the carpet when Lorraine appears at the front door with Tyler.

'Off you go, there's a good girl,' Lorraine says. She is wearing glasses. She *never* wears glasses. Tyler looks at her mum, wide-eyed and uncertain as if, like me, she hardly recognises her. 'Go on.'

Tyler runs off, piping, 'Emily, Emily, let's play dollies.' Normally Lorraine likes to keep hold of her for a while – to settle her in, she calls it. That's normally though, and Lorraine isn't normal. I don't think she'd notice if I hadn't tidied up. She walks straight into the sitting room and stares out of the window.

'Joe and I had a row. He walked out.'

'When?'

'This morning. Before he went to work. He said some terrible things.' Lorraine pauses as if she's trying to pull herself together. 'He said I was a fat cow. That I was boring. That all I ever thought of was Tyler and my appearance. That all I go on about is the shop he can't afford on the Portland Road.'

'Joe needs his eyes testing. You're not fat. You're pretty well the slimmest person I know.' I move over and take her arm. 'Come on, Lorraine. Come and sit down.'

Lorraine curls up small on the end of the sofa. I sit at the other end. Lorraine looks terrible. Her face is puffy, her hair is limp and lifeless, and her foundation stops in an abrupt line on the line of her jawbone. She must be upset if she's forgotten to blend.

'I'm sure it's not your fault, Lorraine,' I begin. 'Joe's been working long hours recently with this course he's doing.' I notice her jaw drop slightly. 'Andy told me about it.'

'It's supposed to help advance his career, but I'm not sure it's worth it,' Lorraine says. 'He's exhausted all the time. He's short-tempered with Tyler, refuses to do anything round the house, and hardly speaks to me unless it's to argue about our finances. He's annoyed because I put a deposit down on that new sofa, and I can't understand why because it's on the never-never.'

'You have to pay the money back in the end though.'

Lorraine frowns as if she hasn't thought of that.

'Yes, but I don't understand it. Joe's never gone on about money before. He even complained when I took Ronnie to the vet. He said we hadn't any money left in the bank this month, so I said, what are credit cards for, and he said he'd taken mine out of my purse and cut them up.'

I don't know what to say. I am not qualified to counsel Lorraine on the subject of marriage.

'Like a drink?' I ask instead. 'There's half a bottle of Sauvignon Blanc in the fridge.'

'No, I mustn't. I have to take Ronnie to the vet at eleven for a check-up.'

'Would you like me to have Tyler for you?'

Lorraine brightens a little. 'Would you?'

'What would you do without me?' I say drily.

'I'm sorry for what I said the other day, Juliet.'

'That's all right.'

'I like the nails, by the way. Love the colour.'

'I didn't shape them properly,' I say, looking down at my hands. 'Would you like a coffee?'

'I'm off coffee. I wouldn't mind a glass of water instead.'

I return from the kitchen with a mug of black coffee, and a glass of water.

'I think Joe's having an affair,' Lorraine says.

'Not with me,' I cut in quickly.

'He is having an affair. I know it.' Lorraine grabs a cushion and hugs it to her chest. 'When I look back over the past few months,' she begins, 'I realise what a fool I've been, believing Joe's excuses.'

'Give me an example.'

'I'm always catching him on his mobile at odd times of the day. And night.'

'It's work.'

'That's what Joe says.'

'Do you love him?'

'He's my life.'

I'm envious that Lorraine has that conviction after years of marriage. I am filled with admiration, but Lorraine doesn't appreciate it. She sits all forlorn with her hands in her lap.

'Oh Juliet, he's stopped wanting to make love to me.'

'That doesn't mean anything.'

'Shagging is Joe's way of showing he loves me,' Lorraine sniffs, 'so he doesn't love me any more.' Her eyes stream with tears. Her mascara remains adhered to her lashes. 'Have you any chocolate?'

I shake my head. 'There's some cocoa in the cupboard. We could make crispie cakes with the girls and give ourselves a fix.'

Lorraine glances at her watch and swears. 'I'm going to be late,' she sighs, dragging herself up from the sofa. 'You can make crispie cakes while I take Ronnie to the vet.'

By the time Lorraine returns to collect Tyler, I have three batches lined up on the kitchen worktop.

'You'll never guess,' Lorraine grins as she swans in and places a plastic pet carrier alongside the cakes. 'Joe's rung and apologised for what he said.'

'That's quite a turnaround,' I observe when she explains that Joe confessed to having had a migraine this morning, not an affair. He's coming home early to take her out tonight, so I offer to babysit as long as Andy's home in time, but Lorraine says no, Joe's already arranged for her mum to come round and put Tyler to bed.

'He is so relieved about Ronnie too,' Lorraine breathes ecstatically.

I peer cautiously into the box. Ronnie the rabbit's whiskers are twitching furiously.

'The vet says he's fine now. He'll need regular check-ups and this specially formulated food.' Lorraine slaps a small packet of green pellets onto the worktop.

'Don't rabbits eat grass?' I say, naively as it turns out.

'This food contains everything a rabbit requires.'

'So it is grass?' I pick up and sniff at the sample pack. 'Smells like grass. It's a bit of a rip-off if it *is* grass.'

Lorraine snatches the packet back, insisting she doesn't care how much it costs as long as Ronnie is all right. Are Lorraine and I all right now though? I wonder. How about Lorraine and Joe?

At about four thirty, I see Joe jogging up the steps next door. He carries a laptop in one hand and a bunch of flowers in the other – which just goes to show I was right all along. A wife never receives flowers for no reason at all. I can't help wondering if Joe is trying to lull Lorraine into a false sense of security. It is what I would do if I were planning to meet Steve, which I might do, if he should ask me.

It is the third Monday in September and Jamie has already been back at school for two weeks after the summer holiday. He has a new teacher, Mr Harris, who seems even younger than Miss Trays. Emily is with Mary Bacon because no one has dropped out of the nursery I want to send her to yet. I am at work, and Steve is with me, his legs extended in front of him as he leans against the filing cabinet, HobNob in hand. He raises the biscuit to his mouth, and bites into it with suppressed aggression.

My throat tightens at the thought of all that unsatisfied sexual hunger, and I can't help comparing the way Steve treats HobNobs with Andy's. Andy dunks them in his coffee and bits drop off, leaving crud at the bottom of the mug. Not sexy.

Although I am trying to convince myself that my eyes are on the computer screen, I am aware of Steve glancing out towards the showroom where Gayle and Andy are at their posts. Gayle is reading a magazine. Andy is on his mobile.

'Hey, Juliet,' Steve says in a low voice. 'Tell me when we can meet.'

'We can't,' I murmur. 'It's not possible.' I mean that. How can I meet Steve? When do I have any time to myself? I can't even go to the loo without a child turning up to ask me where the sticky tape is, or when tea will be ready. At all times, day and night, someone knows exactly where I am and what I am doing.

'Go on. Please, Juliet.'

The phone on my desk buzzes, almost making me jump out of my skin.

'I need an answer.'

'So does Gayle,' I say, disappointed that we've been interrupted. I pick up the phone so I have Gayle at one ear, and Steve breathing down the other.

'It's the school for you, Juliet.'

My hands start shaking. I picture all kinds of

possibilities – Jamie falling from the playground equipment and fracturing his skull, or playing truant, or smoking cannabis. I know he's only seven, but you hear rumours of drugs being sold in playgrounds all over the country.

'I'd better go,' says Steve softly, his lips touching my cheek in a brief caress before he straightens and leaves the office.

'This is the school secretary speaking, Mrs Wyevale,' says a cultured voice on the phone. 'Would you come and pick up your son straight away? He's not well.' The voice loses its veneer, revealing its owner to be a born and bred South Londoner. 'Get down here right now, will you?'

'I'll be there in five minutes.' I slam the phone down, grab my bag and my car keys, and rush out to Andy who looks up from his conversation.

'It's Jamie,' I gasp.

'Hold on a sec.' Andy presses the mute button on his mobile. 'Problem, Jules?'

'Jamie's not well.'

'You knew that this morning,' he accuses. 'Poor boy had tummy ache. I heard him tell you.'

The skin on the back of my neck begins to prickle and sweat. 'I sent him because I have to come to work.'

'You didn't have to. I could've managed. I'm not exactly rushed off my feet. Neither's Gayle.'

'I had some urgent paperwork.' I must stop lying not

only to Andy, but to myself. I came because of Steve. I recall how big Jamie's eyes were in his face this morning. I told him he was tired because he stayed up too late reading Harry Potter, and he had tummy ache because he wouldn't eat his tea the night before. Either way, he wasn't staying at home to watch videos all day because I had to go to work.

I neglected my child so I could indulge in some sad, middle-aged fantasy, except it isn't entirely fantasy, is it? Steve asked me when we could meet. I have to remind myself that he might wish me to meet him for something more mundane than a passionate encounter, like helping him choose a birthday present for his mother.

There is no parking left within easy walking distance of the school so I end up parking on double yellow lines. This is an emergency, after all. The secretary, a large woman in a tiny skirt, escorts me from the office in the main building to the Headmaster's room where the Head, Mr Dart, greets me, shaking my hand rather too hard, and offering me a chair on the far side of a grand wooden desk that's almost the size of a football pitch, or so it seems to me. Perhaps my distorted perception is down to Mr Dart's ability to make me feel very small and insignificant, just one of the many difficult parents he has to deal with every day.

Physically, he reminds me of the giant pictured in the book about Jack and the Beanstalk that I read to Emily sometimes. His nose and lips are unnaturally swollen as if he has suffered an attack by a swarm of bees. His hair is straight and grey. His presence seems to fill the room.

There are medals and trophies in a display cabinet on the wall, and the carpet is springy underfoot. Mr Dart is a whizz at financial management, apparently.

'There's been some concern about Jamie,' he begins, then he sits there, his hands forming an upturned V and the tips of his fingers pressed together, waiting for his words to sink in.

'His schoolwork's okay?'

'Quite brilliant.' I bask in my son's reflected glory but not for long, for Mr Dart continues: 'It's his physical welfare I am worried about.' He pulls a file from the top of a pile of files on his desk. It's quite thick, yet Jamie's only in Year 2.

'Mr Harris, Jamie's class teacher for this year, has reported bruising about Jamie's body, on his shin and upper arms. I'm not accusing you of any wrongdoing, Mrs Wyevale, but you must understand the school's position. Our pupils' welfare is paramount.'

I feel as though I am about seven myself. I feel as though I must write out 100 times, *Mrs Wyevale is an unfit mother – she must try harder*. I never used to do lines. I used to do other people's. They would persuade, cajole and bully me into it.

'There's this as well.' Mr Dart extracts a sheet of paper, a photocopy of Jamie's work. Above some lines of handwriting is a drawing. The subject is quite clear.

'Jamie has recorded in his weekly journal how you – his mother – punched his granny.'

'That isn't entirely true,' I protest.

'You mean you didn't punch Jamie's granny?'

'I did hit her, but it isn't how it looks. She was choking on a pasta shell, so I patted her on the back to dislodge it.'

'We know all about Jamie's granny, how she's had to go to hospital for stress-related illnesses, how you attempted to poison her. We know quite a lot about you and your temper, Mrs Wyevale. We know you tried to set fire to your house, playing with matches in the kitchen. I don't want to involve the Police and Social Services, but—'

'It's all in Jamie's imagination,' I bluster.

Mr Dart looks at me, his eyebrows bristling halfway up his forehead, taken aback that I have dared to interrupt him.

'Mr Harris gave him a certificate the other day for his work in Creative Writing. He wrote about alien dinosaurs taking over the universe, for goodness' sake.' I struggle to breathe. I can't bear the thought of anyone taking my kids away from me. 'Look, I know I shouldn't have sent him to school this morning. I'm sorry. I gave him a dose of Calpol and hoped he'd be all right.'

Mr Dart replaces the sheet of paper in the file, takes another sheet from the stack on his desk, pulls a pen from his jacket pocket and begins writing notes in a hand so untidy I can't decipher them.

'It's always the same,' he says as he writes. 'We've had a parent dose a child with Calpol and send it to school with malaria after a foreign holiday.'

'Jamie can't possibly have malaria. We haven't been further than Cornwall in the past two years.'

'I'm not interested in your holidays unless they're taken during school time. We're here to give your child an education, Mrs Wyevale, not to act as childminders.' Mr Dart stands up. I follow suit. 'I suggest you take Jamie to the doctor and come and see me tomorrow to let me know the outcome. Maybe there'll be no need to take this any further . . .'

I leave the Headmaster's office, feeling very sick myself. I collect Jamie who isn't looking as bad as I expected. He is the first to point out the fixed penalty notice stuck to the windscreen of my car. I don't mind. I deserve it. I am a hopeless mother, driven by my own selfish desire to spend time with Steve rather than attend to my son's welfare. I mustn't think of Steve, of the touch of his lips on my cheek and the husky tone of his voice as he said, 'I need an answer . . .' I cannot meet him. My children come first.

The receptionist must have recognised the urgency in my voice, for I manage to get a same-day appointment with the doctor. Usually she guards him fiercely like Fluffy, the three-headed dog, guards the Philosopher's Stone in one of the Harry Potter books that Jamie's been reading.

It occurs to me that I could pick Emily up from Mary Bacon's early, but I can't bear the thought of her running riot around the surgery again. Last time I was asked – politely, but in a way I knew I couldn't refuse – if I'd like to sit outside in the car until Emily's appointment was due. She'd hit another little girl over the head with a plastic elephant, one of the toys they keep in the waiting room, and the resulting injury had needed treatment from the nurse.

Instead I decide to ask Lorraine to pick Emily up – she owes me a favour, and she's been wanting to see what Mary Bacon is like for herself – while I take Jamie to the surgery to see Dr Finch. I'm glad it's him, not Dr Chandler because he's old and wears bifocals. It's not that I have anything against aged bifocal wearers. It's the way he looks through them, down the narrow ridge of his nose as though I'm some hypochondriac mother. Munchausen's by proxy.

'How are you, young Jamie?' Dr Finch asks cheerfully. I sit down on one seat, Jamie on the other.

'Fine,' says Jamie, hanging his head. I've coached him well.

'He's not been eating his breakfast,' I say.

'Have.'

'You didn't this morning.' I aim what I hope is a mouth-stopping frown at Jamie. 'You didn't touch your cereal.'

'I had toast. Two pieces. With butter and strawberry jam.'

I grow feverish. My face, I am sure, is as red as a radish. The floor, I observe, as I try to hide my embarrassment, is covered with ribbed grey carpet and stains from the bodily fluids I assume that people have to be interested in if they want to be doctors. Recovering slightly, I demonstrate Jamie's bruises.

'The Headmaster thought I should have them checked out.'

'Bruises often look worse before they get better,' says Dr Finch. 'I expect you play football, don't you, Jamie?'

'Football's crap,' Jamie sighs.

'You run about with your friends?'

'Oh, yes. The girls chase us all the time.'

Dr Finch turns to Jamie's notes which he's called up on his computer as if he's decided that the consultation is over.

'He has tummy ache. He did have tummy ache this morning,' I insist.

Sighing, Dr Finch turns back to Jamie and shines a torch down his throat. Jamie winces as he places the end of his stethoscope on his chest. Dr Finch listens for a moment then offers Jamie a sticker.

'I'm too old for stickers. Can I have a balloon instead?'

'I'll see what we've got.' Dr Finch smiles, and buzzes for a nurse to fetch a balloon from the treatment room.

'I'm sorry we've wasted your time,' I say stiffly as we get up to leave. Jamie still doesn't look right, but Dr Finch says he is, and that's good enough for me. I am furious with Jamie though. On the way out I have a go at him. 'When I take you to the doctor's in future, you are to keep your mouth shut and let me do the talking.'

'Why?'

I try to explain.

'But Mummy, you told the doctor a lie,' says Jamie. 'It's wrong to lie, isn't it?' Doubt has crept into his voice. I have confused him. 'Granny says you mustn't ever, ever lie, but you say you can.'

'It was a white lie. I wanted you to say how you felt this morning so the doctor could tell us what was wrong with you. It's no good going to a doctor and telling him you've never felt fitter, is it? Doctors need to feel useful when you go to see them.'

'Do you think I've upset Dr Finch?'

'Possibly.' I picture Dr Finch's weary smile as he types up his notes – child fine, mother slightly peculiar – and a reminder to the receptionist to strike me off the patient list for wasting NHS time. I pause in the lobby at the entrance to the doctor's surgery where I ring Andy on the mobile.

'What did the doctor say?'

'Jamie's fine, nothing wrong with him. Dr Finch advised me to give him more iron-rich meat and fruit juice. Do I look like the kind of mother who feeds him chicken nuggets every day?'

'The children do have quite a lot of convenience food,' Andy begins.

I cut him off. The mobile bleats out the tune of 'Old MacDonald Had a Farm' but I ignore it. I'm not even allowed to choose my own ringtone. Andy programmed it in, and Emily flew into a paddy when I threatened to replace it with Robbie Williams. I decided to leave it as it is for the sake of world peace.

As I slip the mobile back into my bag, Jamie points to a poster on the wall. It's a picture of a young woman stroking her rounded belly. I stare at it, wondering how I could have been so thick. The symptoms of pregnancy match the mood swings, weight gain and variable appetite that Lorraine has been suffering. Is it possible that she is pregnant?

'Has that lady been shagging, Mum?' Jamie asks. 'She must have been shagging.'

'Come on. We mustn't be late,' I say more brightly than I am feeling.

'Miss Trays is leaving school at Christmas because she's been shagging so much she's going to have a baby.'

'Jamie! Please stop using that word. The technical term is—' I am lost for words as various unsatisfactory euphemisms run through my head. 'The technical term is . . .'

'Copulation,' Jamie finishes for me. 'It was on the video Granny gave me. Mum, are we ever going to see Granny again? I miss her so much.'

'I miss her too,' I say, 'but not in quite the same way. Hurry up, Jamie. Let's go home.'

We arrive back just before Lorraine, and we wait while she parks her car behind the plumber from Anerley's van.

'How's Jamie?' Lorraine asks as she gets out of the car.

'He's fine.'

'Well, that's a relief, isn't it?'

'I suppose so, but I wouldn't have felt such an idiot if he'd really been ill.' I eye Lorraine up and down, pausing on the slight, but convincing swell of her stomach. 'Are you pregnant?'

She assures me she isn't. It turns out that she and Joe haven't used any contraception since before Tyler was born, and she doesn't see why she should have fallen pregnant now.

'Thanks for your concern, Juliet, but I know my own body. I've lived with it for long enough.' Lorraine smiles. I know that look. Subject closed.

'What did you think of Mary Bacon?' I ask.

'She's a bit masculine. I wanted to offer to wax her top lip, but I thought that was a little rude, so I gave her my card instead.'

'I meant, what did you think of her as a childminder? Do you think she's capable of hitting a child?'

'That's a very serious accusation, Juliet. Do you have any proof?'

'I was wondering about Jamie's bruises.'

'Have you asked him?'

'He says he got them playing chase with the girls at school.'

Lorraine stares at me. 'You do believe him?' she says.

'Yes.' I glance towards Emily who is sitting in the passenger seat, holding a packet of low fat, low salt, organic crisps scrunched up in her fist. 'Jamie doesn't lie unless he's asked me first.'

'I guess Mary Bacon would be as good a childminder as any if I had to have one,' Lorraine says, opening Emily's door. 'If you're worried about her, why don't you ring the Council and have a chat with someone?'

'Mummy!' Emily wails. 'I don't like organ crisps.'

'They're organic, not organ—' I begin. I watch appalled as she tips the packet upside down and showers the inside of Lorraine's car with crumbs.

'I'm so sorry, Lorraine. Oh, Emily . . .'

'It doesn't matter,' Lorraine says, but her lips are pursed, and I can tell that it does.

'If you take the car down to Wyevale Autos tomorrow morning at nine, I'll ask Larry to vacuum it out,' I offer.

'Don't worry. I'll do it,' Lorraine sighs.

As Emily clambers out of the car, hooking her dress up on the seat-belt attachment, my fingers itch to hit her, but I don't. I lean down and growl in her ear: 'If you ever do anything like that again, I'll . . . I'll lock you in the cupboard under the stairs and never let you go.'

Her eyes widen with fear. 'Mummy, I wet myself!'

It's the first time I've said anything that's had any great effect on Emily, but I'm not pleased with myself. I can just imagine what Jamie's going to write in his journal at school next week.

'You're so cruel, Juliet,' says Lorraine, lifting Tyler out of the car. 'Mummy doesn't mean it, Emily. She's pulling your leg.'

Emily can't be consoled, and I end up carrying her, sobbing and soggy both ends, and clinging to my neck, all the way up the steps to the house.

'I want my granny,' she cries. 'I want my granny.'

I kiss Emily's salt tears and bury my face in her tangled hair. My eyes cross, focusing on a tiny grey bug just to one side of her parting. A nit! That's all I need.

Once indoors, after I've washed Emily down and found her some clean pants, I make two phone calls. The first to Lorraine who doesn't seem surprised to hear from me even though I last saw her two minutes before.

'It's nothing major,' I say quickly, 'but I thought I'd better let you know . . .'

'What is it?' Lorraine sighs.

'Emily has nits.'

'Well, she didn't catch them from Tyler,' Lorraine says sharply.

I hesitate. 'Speak to you tomorrow?'

I am answered with a non-committal snort. I put the phone down, leaving Lorraine to search out the tea-tree oil remedy she uses for nits, and ring the Council. The bored-sounding woman I get on the other end tells me they've never had a single complaint about Mary Bacon, only praise, and if she had any children of her own she would be proud to call Mary Bacon her childminder because Mary Bacon is an exemplary childminder with her attention to detail such as the availability of ethnic toys, and cleanliness. Suitably squashed, I ring off.

It occurs to me later that I really should have another word with Mary Bacon to discuss my concerns and to see whether she actually possesses a cupboard suitable for the imprisonment of difficult children. I realise that I don't know very much about the woman to whom I entrust my children. It takes a long time to get to know someone properly, doesn't it? Something I should perhaps bear in mind in relation to Steve . . .

Chapter Fourteen

Kate didn't take long to get to know Leonardo, did she? In less time than it takes a liner to cross the Atlantic they were lovers, and I guess the moral of that story is that if you hang around too long making up your mind whether to consummate a relationship or not, you may well lose out to a monster iceberg.

Do all great love affairs come to tragic ends? Mine might well do, for as I arrive at work one Monday morning, parking my car around the back as I usually do, I hear raised voices from the workshop. As I move closer, I catch sight of three figures inside.

'I'll bloody well kill you, you little shit!' It's a man's voice. Not Steve's.

I hesitate. Andy's out this morning, so I can't call on him to referee what is clearly a serious disagreement.

'My daughter's in trouble, and you're pretending you didn't have anything to do with it!'

'Ask your daughter who the father is,' I hear Steve shout back. 'She doesn't know, does she? She's a—' Steve grunts and doubles up as the man lays into him.

'Dad! Dad! Leave him alone.' The third, much smaller figure joins in, trying to pull the man off Steve who falls to the ground in front of the car that's parked inside the workshop. I run to help.

'Stop! Stop!' I scream. 'You're killing him!' There's blood everywhere. The man – I assume he's Debs's father, for the third figure is Debs – is banging Steve's head against the concrete floor. Steve's trying to fight back, but the other man is bigger than him. 'Stop it!'

'Dad! Think of the baby!' Debs shrieks. This seems to bring her father to his senses for he hesitates, gives Steve one more slap about the face, and gets up. He takes Debs's arm, and turns her to face me.

'Look what that bastard's done,' he growls.

I can't doubt Debs's condition. She is obviously pregnant now, and she possesses that healthy glow I remember having during the middle of my own pregnancies. She looks much better than when I last saw her, dressed this time in a black sweater, long denim skirt and heels. With her hair tied back and a slash of red lipstick, she's quite a pretty little thing.

'Look what you've done, Dad,' she says. 'I need you to be around when this baby comes, not locked up for GBH.'

'You should have let me finish him off, you silly cow,' he snaps, and he strides out, dragging Debs with him.

I watch them go, afraid he might return for another pop at Steve, before I squat down beside him to assess the damage. He lies curled up with his knees against his chest. Bloodstained saliva trickles from his mouth and his eyelid is swelling up around his left eye. His hair is dishevelled and sticky with blood.

I dig around in my bag for my mobile, and dial.

'No, Juliet,' Steve moans.

'I'm calling the police.'

Somehow he finds the strength to grab me by the wrist, and yank the phone away from my ear.

'No, don't!'

'Why not? He's beaten the hell out of you.' I am confused by the vehemence of Steve's response.

'*No.*'

'You're not the father of that baby,' I say, reluctantly cancelling the call. 'You said yourself that Debs is a tramp.'

Steve straightens his legs, and props himself up on one elbow, wincing with every movement. His vest is spattered with blood and dirt.

'I can understand why Debs's old man wanted to hit me. He's angry. Upset. He'd have hit anyone in the state he's in.'

'That's no reason to let him half-kill you and not do anything about it.'

'He was good to me once,' says Steve, running his fingertips slowly across his forehead.

'I still think we should call the police.'

'Oh – and what will they do?'

'Take a statement, and go and arrest Debs's dad,' I suggest.

'Juliet, do you really think the police will be interested in a little punch-up?' Steve tries to sit up.

'No, don't move. I'll call you an ambulance.'

'There's no need.' Steve reaches out one hand. I take it, letting him interlink his fingers with mine. It's a small, yet intimate gesture, a suggestion of how our bodies might fit together. My heart begins to beat fiercely at the thought.

'I'll take you to Casualty then,' I murmur.

'Don't fuss.' Steve fixes me with one eye. The other is completely closed up. 'I could do with a clean-up, that's all.'

'Stay there,' I say, tearing myself away. 'I'll fetch the first aid box.' When I return Steve is already on his feet beside the car, a BMW he is supposed to be working on. I blow the dust off the first aid box before I place it on the bonnet, and open it up.

'Are you any good at first aid?' I hear Steve ask.

'I have my Brownie badge. Will that do?' While I'm fumbling for cottonwool and Savlon, a shadow falls over my shoulder.

'Juliet, come here.' It is an order, not a request. 'Kiss me.'

I turn. Steve slips his hands around my back and pulls me towards him. His breathing is rhythmic and strong. His good eye glints softly. His lower lip is swollen, but I don't do what I do next because I feel sorry for him. I do it because I can resist temptation no longer. I lean up and slowly press my lips to his.

'Oh, Juliet . . .' Steve gives a low moan. His mouth claims mine in a kiss laced with the taste of hot metal. He crushes me against his chest and presses the length of the Big Thing against my belly. Blood rushes to my head. Heat pools in my pelvis. Steve's hand is inside my blouse, his fingers dancing circles up the flesh that covers my ribs to my breast. I hear the rip of eighty-eight per cent polyamide and twelve per cent elastane as he dips his fingers inside one cup and catches my nipple between them. I gasp. I can't help it. Something that has been asleep inside me, a sexual animal, flickers to life.

Andy's face flickers too – briefly before my eyes – but it's too late. Desire overwhelms my conscience.

I find Steve's belt, unfasten the buckle and pull the leather through. I unzip his fly. The Big Thing leaps out, hot, hard and throbbing like a V6 that's slightly out of tune. Steve gives a growl of impatience as he hitches my skirt up my thighs and pushes me down on the bonnet. This is it. Me and Steve. At last . . .

'Er, Steve?'

There is an attack of coughing, and it doesn't take a

genius to work out that neither Steve nor myself are afflicted.

'Stop!' I hiss, my whole body stiffening.

'I can't,' Steve mutters as he tears at my knickers. 'Don't be a tease.'

'Steve—'

'Oh, you want me, Juliet. You know you want me.'

'It's not that,' I gasp. 'There's someone else.'

Steve hesitates, frowning.

'Gayle!' I point wildly towards the workshop doorway where Gayle stands silhouetted against the white light of day. Steve is cool, much cooler than I am. While I sit up and rearrange my clothing, Steve starts passing the time of day with Gayle.

'Who are you looking for?' he asks, zipping up his fly.

'Juliet,' she says. 'Her husband's on the phone, but I'll tell him you're otherwise engaged, shall I?' She approaches Steve, and looks him up and down. 'Indulging in some mutual first aid, are we?'

I stand up slowly on shaking legs, and face the brick wall at the back of the workshop. I can't face Gayle. I can't face anyone. In fact, I shall never leave this building again. My face is on fire. My palms are wet with panic.

'Shall I ask Andy to hold?'

'Tell him I'll call him back,' I hear myself say.

'Will that give you enough time for a quickie?'

'That's enough, Gayle,' Steve says firmly. 'It's none of your business.'

'I'm not so sure about that . . .' Gayle's voice fades out with the tapping of her heels as she marches off across the yard back towards the showroom.

'Are you okay, Juliet?' Steve asks. 'Hey, look at me.' I feel the pressure of his fingers cupping my chin and turning my face to his. A smile lights up his battered features. 'That'll give her something to talk about at last.'

'It's not funny.' Steve doesn't seem to appreciate the possible consequences of Gayle talking. If she tells Andy, he'll be devastated, Steve will lose his job, and I will lose everything because, mild-mannered as Andy is, I can't see him standing by while his mechanic shags his wife. 'Oh Steve, I wish we'd never met.'

'How can you say that?' he says indignantly. 'As soon as I saw you I knew we were meant for each other.'

'I'm too old for you,' I begin, swallowing back the sharp taste of bile that must have refluxed into my gullet when I sat up too quickly at the sight of Gayle. 'And I'm married.'

'No excuses,' Steve murmurs, moving closer until his breath is hot against my cheek. 'I want to give you the time of your life . . .'

'Not here. Not now.'

'You tell me where and when, Juliet.' His voice goes husky. 'Just make it soon.'

'I don't know if I can,' I say through tears. I love my

275

husband. I don't want to hurt him. I push Steve away and head straight for the phone in my office to prove that fact to myself. I dial Andy's mobile number. When he answers, I hesitate. I don't know what to say, afraid that my voice will reveal my guilt at how close I came to betraying our marriage.

'It's me, Juliet,' I begin. 'Gayle told me you rang.'

'I just wanted to let you know that I'll be late back tonight.' He sounds apprehensive, as well he might, because I usually snap at him when he's late home. 'Is that all right?'

'That's fine.'

'You don't mind?'

'It'll give me time to do the ironing,' I say, planning penance for my close shave with infidelity.

'In that case I'll pick up a takeaway on the way back to save you cooking. Chinese or Indian? Which would you prefer?'

'You choose.' Any food would choke me.

'I'll see you later then.'

I put the phone down very slowly, breathing a sigh of relief that Gayle didn't mention my moment of madness with Steve in the workshop. I've been given a second chance, but do I possess the strength to take advantage of it?

Later, when Steve strolls into the office and presses a piece of paper with his mobile number on it into my hand, any strength I thought I had evaporates, and, instead of throwing it in the bin as I should do, I find myself memorising the number on the way to Mary's.

'Could I have a word with you?' I ask as I collect Emily and Jamie from Mary's doorstep.

'You'll have to be quick,' Mary says, glancing at her watch, the fake Rolex that the nieces gave her for her birthday.

'Emily's been upset. Something to do with being locked in a cupboard?'

Mary smiles, reaches out and softly boxes Emily's ears.

'Emily got herself locked in the shoe cupboard when we were enjoying a game of hide and seek. She screamed blue murder.' Mary pauses. 'You're not suggesting I locked her in there deliberately?'

'No, not at all.'

'Is there anything else?'

'I'm worried about Jamie too. He's been getting these awful bruises.'

Mary frowns. 'You've seen my references, haven't you? I wouldn't hurt a fly.'

I recall Mary's references. They don't glow – they are aflame with praise.

'If you don't trust me to mind your children, Juliet,' Mary goes on, 'perhaps—'

'No, it's fine,' I interrupt. 'I'm sure everything's fine.' This morning I'd accepted that I would have to give Mary notice and find a new childminder for the sake of my peace of mind. Now, it doesn't seem such a good idea when I'm trying to make arrangements to meet Steve.

When can I meet Steve? Nights aren't good for me. Neither are weekends. Days aren't too brilliant either. I don't do anything, or go anywhere without someone knowing where I am. Lorraine knows exactly where I am now. I've left Emily playing with Tyler while I nip out and pick up some bits and pieces from Fishers, the chemist in Enmore Road. I trawl along the shelves, holding one of those collapsible baskets that looks like it's made from a fishnet stocking but, distracted by my plans for meeting Steve, I can't remember what I was intending to buy.

Tiny shudders of excitement run down my spine at the thought of lying naked beneath the weight of Steve's body, of the sound of Steve's ragged breathing, and the full force of the Big Thing in the slick, burning hollow between my legs.

I don't feel guilty about lusting after Steve. (Liar.) It's all very well buying me the odd takeaway, but if Andy really loved me, he'd buy me flowers for no reason, and stop going on about frozen sausages. He'd spare some of the emotional energy he wastes on the Eagles for me. He'd understand why I have to find out if loving Steve is my destiny.

'Can I help you?' says the woman who is standing behind the counter, hugging a mug that emits breaths of lemony scent, a cold remedy, maybe.

'Er, no, thanks.' I don't like people watching over my

shoulder while I'm shopping, but perhaps I'm being oversensitive. Sensitive? That's one of the things I'm looking for. Condoms. The choice is immense: ultra-sensitive, ribbed, coloured, flavoured, glow-in-the-dark. I'm sure Steve is a sensible young man, but you can't be too careful, can you? I drop a pack of three into the basket, hoping it will be enough for one session, change my mind and add a second.

I splash out on a lipstick, not just for Steve, but for the night out Lorraine has planned for us to celebrate the renewal of our friendship. I also take a pregnancy test kit. Lorraine hasn't asked me to, but I need to know, even if she doesn't. When I return to Lorraine's, I hand it over.

'I don't know why you wasted your money, Juliet,' Lorraine says but, perhaps realising she has hurt my feelings, she adds, 'You're such a good friend to me. What would I do without you?' It strikes me that for the first time, Lorraine is becoming more dependent on me than I am on her, and I am pleased.

'You ought to make sure,' I suggest, declining her offer of tuna and mayonnaise on toast for a mid-morning snack.

Lorraine wraps the kit in a plastic bag and puts it aside before filling the kettle.

'I went to see my psychic yesterday,' she says. 'She says my marriage is over.' She backtracks slightly. 'Well, what she actually said was that she saw turbulent times ahead for my relationship with Joe.'

'How can you believe all that stuff?' I can't see how the movement of the sun in relation to Jupiter and the other planets can have any bearing on whether or not Joe and Lorraine will still be married in ten years' time. According to Jamie, Jupiter is nothing more than a giant ice cube in space. We're sending a hydrobot there, for goodness' sake. Science has advanced.

'How much silver did you have to cross her palm with?' I ask.

Lorraine looks surprised. 'Myrtle takes Switch and Visa.'

'You should have let me come with you.'

'Myrtle doesn't like having anyone else present. It disrupts the lines of mystic energy. I couldn't risk upsetting the reading. I want to know if Joe's having an affair. I *need* to know, Juliet . . .' She pauses. 'Coffee?'

'Please.' I'm sure there are better ways to discover if Joe is having an affair. 'What makes you think he's seeing someone else anyway?'

Lorraine hands me a coffee, and picks up a squash for herself that is at least ten times the strength she allows Tyler to have. She looks at me, tears welling in her eyes.

'Joe was unfaithful before we got married.'

I stare towards the wedding photo on the cork board beside the kitchen door.

'Yep,' says Lorraine curtly. 'The picture's posed. My whole marriage has been a sham.'

I can't believe my ears. 'You never told me.'

'It's not the kind of thing you want everyone to know about, is it?'

'But I'm not everyone,' I frown. 'I'm your friend.' I feel betrayed.

'Joe and I were happy enough. There didn't seem any point in digging it all up. I have my pride.'

'How did you find out?' I ask, leaning against the kitchen worktop, trying to take this revelation in.

'There were rumours which I chose not to believe.' Lorraine pauses. 'I found Joe at it when I went round to Mandy's to find out why she hadn't turned up for her final dress fitting.'

'Who's Mandy?'

'My chief bridesmaid and, from that moment, my ex-best friend.'

'Oh, Lorraine. How terrible.'

'We cancelled the wedding. Mum told everyone I was ill. I was too. I threw up every day for weeks.'

'But you married Joe in the end.'

'Three months later.'

'Why on earth did you take him back?'

'Because I love him.' Lorraine starts to cry as if her heart will break. I put my coffee down and give her a big hug.

'You poor thing,' I soothe.

Lorraine steps back and dabs at the corners of her eyes with the tips of her fingers.

281

'Do you want to talk about it?' I perch on one of Lorraine's kitchen chairs while she paces up and down. 'What makes you think Joe is having an affair?'

'Keep your voice down, Juliet. I don't want Tyler hearing any of this. Not yet.'

'Well?' I say, moderating my voice.

'Joe's been different recently. He's quiet. Withdrawn.'

I feel a pang of guilt, recognising myself in this picture of a spouse who might be having an affair. It's how I've been with Andy while I've been dreaming of being with Steve.

'He's still doing this course at work, isn't he? He's probably preoccupied. It isn't easy returning to study after a break. I know that.'

'I'm not sure there *is* a course.'

'Have you any proof?' I ask impatiently. 'Have you found any lipstick, any unusual perfume clinging to Joe's clothing? Have you checked the phone bills?'

'No.'

'As far as I can tell, all you have against him is your psychic's suggestion that you're about to hit a rough patch, and I'll bet she says that to everyone.'

'Myrtle also said I'd find happiness with a man who drives a van and whose name begins with P.'

'Oh, for goodness' sake, Lorraine.'

'It must be Pete, the plumber from Anerley.'

'Lorraine! You're not going to run off with someone else on the offchance that Joe is having an affair?'

'I guess not.' Lorraine gazes out of the window to where Ronnie the rabbit is nuzzling the football. 'I don't know why you're on Joe's side all of a sudden, Juliet.'

'I'm not.' I'm not on Joe's side for Joe's sake. By finding a plausible explanation for every slip an unfaithful spouse might make when having an affair, I'm hoping to prove to myself that I have what it takes to take the next step in my relationship with Steve. 'I'm trying to help.'

'I don't know what to do.'

'You have to find out the truth, and I have some idea of how you can do it. How about having that girls' night out this Saturday?'

Lorraine agrees to my plan, and on Saturday night while the rain is lashing at my bedroom window, I dig my new lipstick out from the drawer in the dressing-table. Before I have a chance to apply it, the phone rings. It's Lorraine.

'You're not copping out, are you?' I ask.

'No, I'm raring to go.'

I listen for a wavering in Lorraine's resolve, a weakness I can work on, because I don't really want to go out in the rain. But there isn't one. Lorraine is determined.

'Did you do it? The pregnancy test?'

'I'm not pregnant, Juliet. I've been pregnant before and I assure you I'd know if I was pregnant again. I'm under pressure – that's why my period's late.'

'If you did the test, you'd put my mind at rest.'

'Stop fussing, and listen to me,' Lorraine says. 'I'm ringing to ask your advice. I have sixteen outfits on the bed, and I don't know what to wear.'

I can't help smiling. Life's so much easier when you have a limited wardrobe like mine.

'Grab the first thing that comes to hand, Lorraine. It's time we were going.' I drop the phone onto the bed, and turn to the mirror on the dressing-table. I brave myself to look into it so I can put my lipstick on without decorating my teeth at the same time. I pout, making the lines above my upper lip deepen. (I make a mental note to remember not to pout in front of Steve.)

What does Steve see in me? Age? Experience? Attributes that are not generally considered attractive in a woman. However, there is a sparkle in my eyes, a natural colour in my complexion, and a hint of wickedness in my smile and, although I'm less than seven months away from my fortieth birthday, I feel as if I'm eighteen again. It is strange what stress does to people, isn't it? There's Lorraine turning to food, albeit in a small way, to soothe her fears for her marriage, while there's me, in a state of heightened sexual tension, looking like an advert for *Slimming World*.

We haven't been out on the razzle for some time, me and Lorraine. Not since Emily and Tyler turned three years old. That's almost a year ago. Sad, isn't it? Andy doesn't approve, I can tell, even though I have put the kids to bed, and left him a microwave meal ready on the kitchen worktop with its cardboard removed and cling-film pierced.

'Where did you say you're going?' Andy asks.

'Clubbing.'

'Just you and Lorraine?'

'Would you like me to call you a few times during the evening?' My neck is growing hot. Why does Andy's questioning make me feel guilty? Because Lorraine and I are planning to catch Joe out? Because somewhere deep in my soul, I am hoping I shall see Steve? I know he won't be there, but the flame of hope remains, burning in my breast.

'Well, a couple of times would be nice.'

'Andy! You're jealous, aren't you?'

'Me?'

'You're afraid I'll run off with someone at a night-club?' I laugh. I can't help it. The whole idea is ridiculous, but then Andy doesn't know that, does he?

'I don't like the idea of you going down there without a wedding ring.'

'Oh, don't be silly!'

'You are looking particularly . . .' Andy moves towards me, moves up close. His hands are on my waist. His eyes gaze into mine. ' . . . beautiful, Jules.' I can't remember Andy ever describing me as beautiful before. He's used the words 'gorgeous' and 'great', but not 'beautiful'. It's the kind of compliment Leonardo would have offered

Kate without hesitation and many times over, but these are the desperate words of an insecure, middle-aged, suspicious and neglectful husband.

'I mean it, Juliet,' Andy says softly, and my heart – the heart of a spiteful and deceitful wife – almost melts, and I almost say, 'I'll stay at home with you, my darling.'

'I promised Lorraine that we'd have a girls' night out, so there's no point in trying to charm me to stay in with you.'

Andy kisses me.

'Mind my lipstick,' I say, ungraciously pushing him away. The doorbell rings. 'That'll be Lorraine.'

We have a drink in the kitchen before we leave. Andy joins us. Lorraine looks amazing in a skimpy top in a deep sage green, dotted with gold flowers, and a pair of velvet trousers. She is like one of the faces on the cover of *Bella* magazine and I can't understand why Joe wants anyone else.

'Don't let Juliet drink too much while she's out, will you?' says Andy.

'Andy!' I pour two large glasses of white wine which I forgot to put in the fridge to cool, and hand one to Lorraine.

'Don't I get one?' says Andy.

'You're babysitting.'

'It's not much fun watching other people having a good time,' he says ruefully.

'Now you know how I feel when you're down at the Portmanor with Joe.'

'Have you got any ice?' Lorraine asks. 'It's a bit warm for me.'

'Ice?' says Andy. 'This woman is asking for ice. Have we ice, Juliet?'

'Andy's pointing out that I haven't managed to defrost the freezer yet.'

'I'll get it,' Lorraine says, as I reach to take her glass.

She opens the freezer door. There's plenty of ice, but not in the form of ice cubes, which is what she's looking for.

'Did you know,' she says, pulling a pink object from the top drawer, 'that you have a Furby in your freezer?'

Andy looks at me, bemused. 'Must have been Emily,' he says, rubbing his forehead.

'No, it was me,' I confess. 'It wouldn't stop talking.'

'You should have taken the batteries out,' says Lorraine with the voice of experience. She places the Furby on the worktop. 'You'd better try defrosting it, but I don't suppose it'll work again, poor thing.'

'Aren't you supposed to be going?' says Andy. 'There's a film on the telly.'

'Don't let us stop you,' says Lorraine. 'We'll be off when we've finished our drinks. Oh Juliet, I'll have to drop in to pick up my purse. I've left it behind.'

That's part of the plan. The theory as expounded on daytime TV goes like this. Arrange a night out, step out

for half an hour to give the cheating partner time to call
their lover, then nip back and press redial on the phone
to discover the lover's number.

While Lorraine fetches her purse and distracts Joe, I
press redial on their phone, write the number down on
a piece of paper and give it to Lorraine. It's an 0208
number and, according to Lorraine, not the last one she
dialled.

'Do you recognise it?'

Lorraine shakes her head. I leave her standing in the
hall, chewing at her lip, while I pop my head around the
door of the sitting room to say goodbye to Joe.

'Have a good time,' he says quietly. He has dark rings
around his eyes and his face is unusually pale. I almost
feel sorry for him. It isn't easy having an affair, and
anyone who says it is has obviously never tried.

Clubbing as a pastime doesn't appear to have changed
much in the past year. There are lots of people my age
and older, strutting their stuff to music that is reassur-
ingly familiar.

'Keep hold of your drink so no one can spike it, and
don't take tablets if you're offered any,' Lorraine warns
as she waves a tenner in the direction of the barman
who's caught her eye.

The drinks are so sweet they make you believe you're
not drinking alcohol at all. We have a second and a third,
and then I read the bottle: forty per cent proof. Next time
round I have a Diet Coke. Lorraine has another alcopop.

I have never seen her behave like this, and I don't like it. She is flirtatious too, begging a cigarette from one of two men who ask us to dance.

'I didn't know you smoked,' I hiss.

'I don't. Don't tell Joe. He hates it.'

'Is there anything else you'd like me not to tell Joe?' I ask, but Lorraine tugs on her chosen partner's arm and pulls him onto the dance floor.

'I'm married,' I say to the man I'm left with, the shorter and chubbier of the two.

'So'm I,' he says. 'How about a dance?'

'I have two children,' I say, doing my best to put him off his pursuit of love.

'I had six at the last count,' he says. His mouth is smiling, but a more sinister emotion lurks behind his eyes. A desire for control? For violence? I shudder as he moves in closer, jostling me as he is jostled from behind. (I'd forgotten about all the jostling.) 'Do you come here often?'

I begin to smile at the worst chat-up line in the world, but he is perfectly serious.

'I haven't seen you here before. I'd have noticed you if you had, darlin'.' He shows me his tattoo of a tiger on his left arm, but I'm not inclined to show him mine. He takes my hand in a sweaty grip.

'I've got a lock-up near the railway bridge. Done up nice, it is.'

'I've got to go,' I mutter, pulling my hand away sharply.

I push through the mass of gyrating bodies, and find Lorraine dancing up close and personal with her partner. I grab her by the elbow.

'Juliet! Would you mind leaving me alone?'

'Let's go.'

'Where? I'm having a good time, enjoying myself.'

'Well, I'm not!'

Lorraine's partner pulls her back, whispers something I can't hear. I drag her by the arm.

'Getting off with someone else won't help,' I hiss in her ear.

'If Joe can do it, so can I.'

'We haven't proved he's done anything yet.' I push Lorraine ahead of me towards the Ladies. I don't like this place. It smells of requited lust and the stains that go with it, of vodka and vomit. Is it a warning to me of what my life could be like if Andy finds out about me and Steve, and if Steve turns out not to be what I expected at all?

'Have you got that number?' I ask Lorraine as she retouches her lips. I run my fingers through my tiger stripes which have become rather dishevelled. My face is pink, and my forehead sticky with sweat.

'It's in my bag.'

'I'll try it if you like.'

'Would you?'

'It'll be all right, Lorraine,' I say, taking her mobile and the number from her bag. 'It's probably the number of a pizza delivery firm.' I dial. The phone at the other end of the line rings once.

'Who's that? Who's there?' comes a voice.

She – for it is a she – is going to cut me off, so I have to make a quick decision.

'This is Kirby International, Holidays with a Difference. You have won a super prize in our draw.'

Lorraine is staring at me as if I have gone quite mad.

'What prize? What draw?' says the voice.

'You ticked the box on the Royal Mail postal survey that qualified you for entry.' I pause. 'I need to confirm your full name and address before we can dispatch the details of your prize.' I'm sure that Kirby International wouldn't use the word 'send'. 'Dispatch' makes the prize seem much more impressive.

'Can you tell me what the prize is?'

'It's a holiday.' I give a little giggle. 'We are a holiday company, after all. It's a trip for two to watch whales off the coast of the Isle of Wight.'

'That's abroad, isn't it?'

'Of course. We deal solely in international travel.' Inspiration flashes through my mind like quicksilver. It is a sensation I am not familiar with. 'Could you confirm the name of the person who will be accompanying you?'

The voice gives me her own name, Toni Knight, and her address, but before she can supply me with any further information, someone rushes into the Ladies, slamming doors and swearing. The game's up. Toni Knight cuts me off.

'Well?' says Lorraine as I scribble the details beneath the phone number.

'Do you recognise the name Toni Knight?'

Lorraine frowns, and shakes her head. 'What's she like? Young? Old?'

'She didn't sound very old,' I begin.

'Younger than me?'

'It was difficult to tell. She sounded a little hoarse.'

'Sexy, you mean?'

'No, as if she had a sore throat.' I hand Lorraine the piece of paper, but she's in such a state she screws it up and drops it back in her bag without looking at it. 'Lorraine, this doesn't prove anything.'

'Why did Joe call her then?'

'You'll have to ask him.'

'I shall. Tonight.' Lorraine hesitates, her eyes glazing with tears. 'I told Joe that if he was ever unfaithful to me again, I'd divorce him on the spot.'

Chapter Fifteen

What would Andy do if he found out about me and Steve? Would his impulse be the same as Lorraine's? To divorce me on the spot? I couldn't blame him if it was. I'm just going to have to make sure he doesn't find out.

Andy has taken Jamie and Emily to see the Rhino, so the house is empty apart from the second generation of sea-monkeys, who don't really count as company. Although I sometimes find myself talking to them, they don't talk back. The Furby, now defrosted, has made one or two comments in Furbish which don't count either. I silence it for good by removing its batteries as Lorraine suggested, as I shall commit battery if I don't.

The phone rings.

'Hello?' I feel as if I have the fibres from a deep-pile carpet stuck to my tongue, and my head jars with the beat of last night's music. Finding out that it is the Rhino on the other end of the phone doesn't help my hangover.

'I want to speak to Andrew,' she says.

'You can't. He's on his way to you now.'

'Oh, good. Ian's here already. He's brought smoked salmon, and a lovely box of Belgian chocolates.' The Rhino pauses, but I refuse to respond. She's telling me what a great day they're all going to have without me.

'They should be with you by twelve.' I cut the Rhino off, and stare down at the phone in my hand. It occurs to me that I have at least five more hours of social isolation stretching out in front of me. I could have arranged to meet Steve if Andy had told me that he was going to his mother's before this morning. I could still arrange to meet Steve . . . I dial his mobile number.

'Hi!'

'Steve?'

'Leave a message after the tone, and I'll get back to you, sex life permitting.'

'Damn!' I don't leave a message. I dial 118 118 and cut them off before they answer, in case Andy should decide to press redial when he comes home this afternoon, like I did for Lorraine last night. I don't suppose he will, but you can't be too careful.

I wonder what Steve is doing. I picture him sprawled out on his back on a bed with a single, very thin sheet rumpled across his groin, and his hands up behind his neck, revealing thick tufts of dark hair in his armpits. I dial the number again.

'Hi! Leave a message . . .'

My heart sinks. What a waste of a day. Catching sight of movement in the garden next door, I unlock the back door and step outside where the sunlight splits tiny rainbows from the dew. The fence panel between our gardens is as tall as I am, but I can see Lorraine through a gap where the slats have fallen out.

Lorraine, being one of those irritating people who don't get hangovers, is pegging out washing as if last night never happened. She is dressed in stonewashed denim jeans, matching jacket with detachable fake fur collar, and pink mule slippers. Her hair is streaked damp.

'Hiya!' I call.

She frowns slightly, then smiles when she catches sight of me through the gap in the fence. 'You look wrecked, Juliet.'

'Thanks a lot.' If I look that bad, it's a good thing I didn't go chasing off to see Steve this morning.

'Before I forget,' Lorraine says, 'Joe and I are inviting you and Andy to dinner next weekend.'

'Are you?'

'It's our wedding anniversary. Joe's decided we should have a theme – bring something black.'

'Are you sure you want to celebrate? Yesterday you were convinced Joe was having an affair.'

'I asked him about Toni Knight. She's some old bat with bug eyes and dreadful halitosis who's running this training course. He rang to ask her about a project he's working on.'

'On a Saturday night? You don't believe that, do you?'

Lorraine shrugs and returns to her washing. I return inside. So Joe denied any romantic involvement with Toni Knight, did he? And Lorraine is clinging to normality like Spiderman to the sheer face of a tower block, throwing her energies into arranging an anniversary dinner. I fear that it will be a night to remember for all the wrong reasons.

'Bring something black – that's what Lorraine said,' I tell Andy later when we're watching telly in the evening.

'What did Lorraine have to invite us for? Don't you two see enough of each other during the week?'

'I thought you enjoyed having a few drinks with Joe.'

'Not so much now.' Andy pauses. 'I haven't seen a lot of Joe recently.'

'Have you fallen out?'

'No, he's been putting in extra hours for that computer company he works for. Listening to him talk you'd think he was the CEO, but what does Joe know about the cut and thrust of big business?'

'What do you know about it, small businessman?' I counter.

'Plenty,' Andy smiles, chucking a cushion at me.

I catch it, and throw it back. Andy is in a good mood. It seems like a good time to broach the subject of Emily and Mary Bacon, to do some of the groundwork that needs to be done before I can meet Steve.

'I'm thinking of sending Emily to Mary Bacon's for an extra session each week,' I begin.

'What do you want to do that for? Emily needs you, and I'm not sure we can afford it.'

'What cost is my sanity? I'd find it easier to give Emily some quality time if I had some quality time to myself.'

'You have loads of time to yourself.'

'When?'

'When Jamie's at school.'

'I still have Emily.'

'You go to yoga. You go out clubbing.'

'With Lorraine. Not on my own.' I stand up and move to the window. The moon outside is small, mean and fiercely white like my heart. I draw the curtains and shut it out. As I arrange the folds in the cream linen, Andy comes up behind me and slides his hands around my waist.

'You'd better book that extra session for Emily,' he murmurs into my ear. 'I can't have my wife worn to shreds when I need her in my bed, can I?' He presses up closer. 'How about an early night?'

'Good idea,' I say, pulling away and turning to face him. 'I'm very tired.' I yawn to reinforce the point.

'I don't mean for you to go straight to sleep.'

'Not tonight, I'm shattered.' I can't bear the thought of Andy making love to me when I'm craving Steve's touch.

A shadow crosses Andy's eyes, letting me know he's disappointed.

'Goodnight, Jules,' he says softly.

'Goodnight.' I feel terrible. Is this how it's going to be, living the biggest lie I've ever created?

Andy and I don't share things any more. I discovered that he'd eaten a whole tub of mint-choc-chip ice cream while I was out last night, and didn't save a single spoonful for me. He hasn't talked about his trip to see the Rhino either. When I asked him how she was in the hope she might have expressed some hint of regret that I wasn't there, he changed the subject.

I decide to ask Emily instead while she's helping me get organised the following morning. She is bouncing on my bed while I sort through my clothes.

'Emily, stop that, please.'

She redoubles her efforts at bouncing while I continue looking through the wardrobe for something suitable for work. Something grown-up yet not frumpy? Something restrained yet fabulously sexy? Instead, I find the suit that I wore to my wedding. My wedding day was one of the happiest of my life. Everyone came to the register office – Mum, Dad, my sister, and my then best friend, Cheryl. (Not only am I serially monogamous, I have serial best friends. Is that a sign of a faithless nature?) Andy's dad was alive then, counteracting the Rhino's tightlipped disapproval with a generous contribution to the alcohol supply for the evening do.

I turn to Emily. 'Did you have a nice time with Granny yesterday?'

Emily carries on bouncing.

'Was her friend Ian there?'

Emily does one more bounce then lands on her bottom in the centre of the mattress.

'Ian drank six glasses of wine, Mummy.'

'Was he nice?'

'I don't know. He went to sleep. He snoreded and snoreded.'

I give up trying to extract any more information out of Emily, and hang my wedding suit back in the wardrobe.

It strikes me that it must be easier for Joe to carry on his affair – if he's having one – than it is for me. Although Joe claims to do his bit with Tyler, he doesn't have to cook and clean, and iron his clothes. Joe doesn't have to say to his lover, 'I'm sorry, I can't see you today because there's nothing for tea, and I have to fit the supermarket run in between finishing work and the children's bathtime,' does he?

Andy is the same. His preoccupations are different from mine. When I'm at work on Wednesday, he doesn't seem to be able to leave me alone. He comes into the office, leaving the door open. He pulls up a chair alongside mine, and starts shuffling through my papers.

'What are you doing?'

'There are a lot of bills here,' he says, examining one from the cash and carry. 'What's this? Why do we need a new mobile phone? And three packs of tea-towels? And fifteen torches along with enough batteries to power fifty more?'

'Steve needed equipment for the workshop,' I say quickly.

'But fifteen torches?'

'There must have been a mistake.'

'Steve should have asked me first.' Andy picks out another sheet and runs his eyes down the column of purchases. This time, the invoice is for parts.

'You can't complain about that one. A mechanic can't work without parts.' A delicious tingle spreads across my back as I picture Steve working on mine.

Andy's frown brings me back to the matter in hand. I am forced to admit that Steve does buy a few more bits and pieces for BMWs than one might expect for the number of BMWs he works on, but he says he likes to keep some spares in stock so he doesn't have to keep popping out, which seems entirely reasonable to me. However, Andy isn't in any mood to be reasonable.

'You said you'd have a word with Steve about the invoices before.'

'I will,' I promise.

'I can't understand why you haven't already done it. You've had plenty of opportunity. He's always in here drinking coffee when he's supposed to be working.'

I turn to the computer and log in. 'Would you like me to monitor the length of everyone's coffee breaks?'

I ask as coolly as I can. 'I can record them on a spread-sheet if you like.'

'Don't be silly, Jules.' Andy picks up another sheet of paper. 'Look at the phone bill!' he exclaims. 'Is it always as much as this?'

I snatch it from him. He snatches it back.

'I'm going to have a word with Gayle,' he says, standing up.

I stand up too. 'No, don't, Andy. I can't let you do that.'

'Why not?'

'It's been an exceptional quarter.'

'What on earth do you mean?'

'Shh!' I am aware that Gayle is watching us from the showroom. I push the door to. 'I'll speak to Gayle, woman to woman. She's been in a terrible state over losing this fitness instructor boyfriend. I think she's been using our phone to call the Samaritans.'

'She's hidden her feelings well,' says Andy. 'I wouldn't have noticed.'

'She didn't want to let us down. She's good at her job.'

Andy sits down again and reaches for my hand as I breathe deep sighs of relief.

'I'm sorry for being snappy with you, Jules,' he begins. 'I just don't know how we're going to survive. If something doesn't turn up soon, I'm going to have to take drastic measures.'

'Ask your mother for a loan, you mean? Don't you dare, Andy.'

Andy stares down at my hand, and strokes my fingers. 'I wish you'd reconsider your decision not to see her again. She's very sorry that you fell out with her.'

'*I* fell out with *her*? That's typical of her, blaming me for everything. Everyone blames me for everything. Look at you this morning, blaming me for the amount we're having to pay in interest on the credit card. You buy stuff too.'

'Necessities,' Andy says, looking up.

'You spent two hundred and fifty quid and you won't tell me what it was for!'

'Shirts and socks.' For an experienced liar like me, it's not difficult to spot that Andy is lying. It isn't like him, but before I can pursue the question further, there is a knock and the door opens. It's Steve.

'Time for coffee,' he says.

Andy drops my hand, stands up and kisses me on the cheek. 'I'll leave you to it,' he murmurs.

Steve pushes the door shut behind him and takes Andy's chair, stretching his legs out in front of him. He looks tired with dark rings around his eyes, and a couple of spots on his unshaven chin. His hair is untidy, yet these flaws emphasise rather than detract from his fierce masculinity. If an alien asked me to describe what sex was, I would show them Steve.

I prepare the coffee. Four mugs.

'I thought of you on Sunday,' I say quietly. 'I couldn't stop thinking about you. I tried your mobile.'

'You didn't leave a message.'

'I didn't like to.'

'I have to keep it switched off because of Debs,' Steve says. 'She keeps pestering me.'

'Is that why you bought a new mobile on the business last week?'

He fixes my eyes, curls his lips into a smile. He's good, he is. Very good. He raises his hands, turns them palms up.

'Oh God, I'm sorry, Juliet. I forgot to give you the new number.'

Forgot? I want to ask him how he could possibly forget something that is so important to me. To us. But I don't because, as I pour milk into the mugs, I feel Steve's arms around my waist, the heat of his body against my back, and the unrelenting power of the Big Thing.

'I'm so sorry.'

I can feel his breath damp against my skin as his tongue traces the contours of the back of my neck. I can feel the prick of stubble too.

'I'll give it to you now.'

All thoughts of tackling Steve about the invoices, and the fact that he appears to have bought himself a mobile with our money are banished.

'We can't. Not here,' I gasp.

Steve steps back, chuckling softly. 'I meant I'll give you

the number,' he says, 'but make sure you use it, Juliet.'

'Do you doubt me?' I ask, turning to face him. 'You mustn't doubt me. We will be together. I promise.'

'Women don't always keep their promises.'

'I do.'

I do. I do. I realise that I am beginning to think beyond our first assignation to the happy ever after. It is what I did when I first met Andy, and what Lorraine must have done when she met Joe, but it seems that those days are long gone.

'I've brought some Carling Black Label,' Andy says when we settle in at Lorraine and Joe's for dinner on the Saturday evening. 'Does that count? Why did we have to bring something black anyway?'

'Because it's our bloody anniversary, that's why,' says Joe. He's dressed up tonight in a shirt with the top button unfastened, and a tightly knotted tie dangling around his neck. He's already half-cut. 'Lorraine's in one of her moods.'

'Don't you dare suggest it's down to my hormones,' Lorraine says sharply. 'It has more to do with having to live with you.'

'Come here,' Joe teases, putting his arm around Lorraine's shoulder. She keeps her body taut, pulling away from his embrace, and when he plants a kiss on her lips, she wrinkles her nose and turns away.

'We bought you a present,' I offer. 'It's only small.'

'Oh, you shouldn't have.' Lorraine, apparently relieved to have an excuse to move away from Joe, carries the present which I persuaded Jamie to wrap for 50p towards his hamster fund, into the sitting room and sits on the raspberry sofa to open it.

'It's a black cat for good luck,' I explain as she takes a small cat, about three inches tall and made from some kind of metal, from the parcel.

'Jules thought you might need it,' says Andy. 'Some luck, I mean.'

I cast him a warning glance. I'm not sure how much he's supposed to know about Lorraine and Joe's marital difficulties.

'It's lovely,' Lorraine says. 'Isn't it, Joe?'

'Yeah, great,' he says without looking. 'Anyone want a drink?'

Lorraine puts the cat at one end of the mantelpiece while I read the printed note that came with it. It isn't any ordinary black cat. It's Bast, the Egyptian Goddess of Fertility.

'Have you done that test yet?' I ask quietly when Lorraine and I are upstairs checking on the children. Emily tops and tails with Tyler, while Jamie sleeps on Lorraine and Joe's bed. We'll take him home with us when we leave.

'I keep telling you, Juliet, it's not necessary.' Lorraine's hair is tangled across her forehead, and her foundation is too dark. 'I'm tired, that's all.'

I wonder if she's been crying. If Joe has made her cry.

'Joe's surpassed himself,' Lorraine continues. 'He's bought me flowers, Next vouchers, and this.' She points to the sapphire droplet suspended above her cleavage on a delicate gold chain.

'You see?' she smiles. 'Joe must love me, otherwise he wouldn't be doing all this.'

I hesitate to point out that it's exactly what I would do in Joe's position. Overcompensate. Go for the big gestures. Right down to the rather tart champagne he's bought to toast his wife.

Lorraine plugs a nightlight in the socket on the landing so the children can find their way to the bathroom if they get up in the night.

'I'd better check the dinner,' she says. 'I'm cooking.'

The idea of Lorraine cooking sends a shudder down my spine.

'It's all right, Juliet. I've been practising. There's a starter from Nigella, main course from Jamie, and dessert from Delia. I'll show you.'

We sit at the table in the contemporary eclectic kitchen, illuminated by three candles and the tealight in Lorraine's oil burner. She's burning lemon-grass which fails to disguise the all-pervading scent of garlic. There's garlic in the starter, garlic in the main course which resembles a mass of stewed offal that might have come straight out of Hugh Fearnley-Whittingstall's cottage kitchen, and garlic in the banoffee pie.

'That was delicious, Lorraine,' Andy says, gagging on his last mouthful.

'It was bloody awful,' says Joe.

Lorraine looks at me.

'It was very nice,' I say, draining my glass of red wine in an attempt to take the taste away.

'Thank you, Juliet,' she says. 'It's a pity my husband isn't able to appreciate contemporary cuisine.'

'It's a pity my wife isn't able to cook it,' Joe retorts.

I think that perhaps Andy and I should go home and leave Lorraine and Joe to their own devices, but I know Lorraine will be offended if we dash off straight after dinner. In Lorraine's opinion, the length of time you spend with your guests is more important than its quality. The longer you spend in each other's company, the deeper and more valuable the friendship.

Joe stands up, and raises a glass.

'I'd like to propose a toast to my beloved wife. To marriage. To best friends.' He sways slightly then turns to me. 'Here's to you, Juliet!'

'Happy Anniversary,' I say as cheerfully as I can. I glance towards Andy who purses his lips and shrugs.

'Let's have some music,' Joe says, slamming his glass down on the table. 'Let's dance. Leave the dishes, Lorraine.'

Joe and Andy move the furniture in the sitting room against the walls. Joe turns up the amplifier, dims the lights and grabs my hand.

'Dance, Juliet?'

'No, I couldn't. I'm stuffed.' I collapse onto the raspberry sofa.

'I wonder who's been doing the stuffing,' Joe says, sitting down beside me. He presses the length of his thigh against mine and starts massaging my knee. I don't think I've ever seen him so drunk, unruly and unpredictable.

Andy and Lorraine get down to Toploader, Lorraine mouthing the words to 'Dancing in the Moonlight', and Andy standing on one spot, jiggling his paunch from side to side with his elbows fixed at right angles. It's not exactly *Top of the Pops*, but I didn't marry Andy for his dancing talent. I married him because he made me laugh, and cry, and because I loved him.

I close my eyes which is a mistake because the image of Steve jumps into my head, and I'm dancing with him – dirty dancing with Steve grinding his hips against my soft curves, not Andy.

'Juliet,' hisses Joe from beside me, 'don't try to tell me you still fancy that husband of yours. Who is it? Who's ringing your bell?'

I open my eyes and turn to face Joe. 'Are you having an affair?'

'No.' Joe's eyes hold steady. Not a blink. But the muscle in his cheek twitches.

'Liar.'

'Takes one to know one,' he says coolly.

The song finishes. Lorraine presses the previous track button on the CD player, and it starts again.

'You'd better dance with your wife, Joe,' I suggest. 'It *is* your anniversary.'

Joe staggers up. Lorraine looks pleased. She rests her hands around his neck, and they begin to dance. Andy pulls me up. I shake my head.

'Come on, Jules. You can't hate me for ever,' he urges, his breath hot and pungent with garlic.

'I'll hate you for as long as I like,' I say, unable to suppress a smile. 'Oh Andy, I don't hate you.'

'You don't love me either.'

'Oh, come here.' We dance like a couple of penguins on an ice-rink until Lorraine switches to a slow, smoochy number. Andy holds me close, and kisses me hard as if he's misinterpreted my breathlessness for passion. I rest my head against his shoulder to catch my breath, wondering how I'm going to be able to keep up with Steve, a much younger and more energetic man.

'I thought you were having a thing with Joe for a while,' Andy murmurs.

'I am *not* having a thing with Joe. Or anyone else,' I add quickly.

'I thought that you'd mislaid your wedding ring to make yourself seem more available.'

'I haven't mislaid it. I've lost it.'

'And there's that tattoo.'

'Andy, I am not having a thing, as you call it, with Joe.'

'Has he ever asked you to? I mean, he claims he has a libido to match that rabbit of Lorraine's.'

How do I answer that? It's not exactly a lie, more a half-truth, if I deny it. If I confess that Joe made an indecent proposal and kissed me, I don't know how Andy will react. He might nod and say, 'How nice,' or he might turn round and thump him one. Either way, discussing Joe's extra-marital adventures on his wedding anniversary doesn't strike me as being a good idea.

'Well, has he?'

'No.' I try to make a joke of it, nudging Andy in the ribs. 'I'm quite disappointed.'

Andy grins and holds me tight. Out of the corner of my eye, I can see Lorraine and Joe clinging to each other and shuffling around in small circles. Marital peace, if not bliss, appears to have been restored, but not for long. Andy and I decide to sit down. He sits first and I fall onto his lap. There is a sharp snapping sound and one end of the raspberry sofa drops to the floor.

'Oh, no.' My hand flies to my mouth. Andy apologises. Joe says it doesn't matter. He'll get the money back on the household insurance or go back to the company who sold it because it should still be under guarantee. Lorraine isn't quite so understanding.

'I hope they still stock this colour with the free set

of washable covers,' she says stiffly. She turns the music down, and the lights up.

'We'd better make a move,' I suggest.

'No, no,' Joe slurs. 'We're celebrating. We must have another drink.' He gets up, and slaps Andy on the shoulder as he heads out of the room, returning a few minutes later with four cans of lager and a bottle of wine.

'Haven't you had enough, darling?' Lorraine says as Joe snaps the ringpull from a can. I can see Joe's face turning red. 'Are you sure you haven't had enough?'

Joe explodes. 'Yes, I've had enough! I've had enough of *you*! Nag, nag, nag.' He raises one hand, flaps his fingers against his thumb in the manner of a quacking duck. 'Nag, nag, bloody nag.'

'Joe!'

'I can't stand living with you any more. I can't stand coming home and having to decorate the house, and mow the lawn, and see the people you want me to see . . . And as for the sofa, I don't even like the bloody thing.'

'But you said—'

'I know what I said, but I lied. I said it to please you, because you kept going on about it, and you had to have it, and now we're saddled with a credit agreement with clauses as long as my fucking arm that we can't get out of for the next four years. Just because you wanted a red one. The old one was fine. I liked it. But that thing . . . Comfortable? My ass! And then there's that rabbit. Why did you have to pay two hundred quid in vets' bills when you could have had a new one for a tenner?'

'Joe, how could you?' Lorraine wails.

Joe steps up close to her, grabs her by the wrist and twists her arm. 'You're a leech, Lorraine!' he growls.

'Let me go!' Lorraine shrieks. 'Get your hands off me!'

'I'll do what I bloody well like for a change.'

'Joe, that's enough.' Andy shoves me off his lap, and stands up. 'Calm down, will you?'

Joe releases Lorraine, turns round and pops Andy one on the chin. Andy hits him back. Joe rocks and sways on his feet. Blood pours out of his nose. Lorraine runs out, and returns with a roll of kitchen paper. She throws it at Andy, saying, 'Don't let the bastard bleed all over the house,' and runs off again in tears. I follow her out through the kitchen.

'Joe's drunk,' I say, trying to soften the blows Joe has just inflicted on Lorraine's self-esteem. It isn't every day that your husband tells you you are a leech in front of your friends.

Lorraine opens the back door and runs into the garden. It's cold outside. Dead chilly. But Lorraine seems oblivious as she kneels in front of the rabbit hutch, and pulls out the peg that keeps the door secured. The door swings open.

'Ronnie. Ronnie?' Her voice rises to a scream. 'Oh,

my poor lamb . . .' She comes running past me back into the kitchen, clutching Ronnie to her breast.

'What's wrong?'

I spread a tea-towel across the draining board, and Lorraine lays Ronnie out on top of it. She leans over him and presses her ear to his chest. It's pretty obvious from the way Ronnie's legs are sticking up in the air that he can no longer be with us in anything but the spiritual sense of the word.

Andy and Joe wander into the kitchen to join us, Joe holding a bloodied piece of kitchen paper to his nose.

'Ronnie's not breathing,' Lorraine wails. 'Call the vet, Joe. The number's by the phone.'

'I'm not taking a dead rabbit to the vet,' Joe says, picking the rabbit up by one leg and dropping it back down. 'Look, it's as stiff as a bloody board.'

The colour drains from Lorraine's face. She lurches towards the sink and throws up. Andy and Joe turn a sympathetic green.

'I'll stay with her,' I sigh as they stroll out of the kitchen, Joe complaining loudly that he'd have had rabbit for dinner if he'd known.

'Unfeeling bastard,' Lorraine mutters through a curtain of hair and dribble.

I make her sit down before I clean the sink with bleach, and cover Ronnie's remains with a second tea-towel. Once I've put the generous portion of banoffee pie that remains on the table out of view, because that alone is enough to make anyone feel sick, I sit down with her.

'It is only a rabbit,' I venture.

'How can you say that, Juliet? Ronnie's like a child, my firstborn. You don't understand.'

'Try me.'

'Joe gave him to me when I was pregnant with Tyler.' Lorraine's lip quivers and she bursts into tears. 'This is an omen. Joe's going to leave me.'

'You can't tell me that a rabbit can hold a marriage together. You're the one who told me that a relationship is cemented by mutual respect, love, and,' I fumble for the word and its meaning, 'trust.'

Lorraine looks at me, eyebrows raised and tears threatening to spill over her cheeks once more, as if I'm speaking Furbish.

'I'll open another bottle of wine,' I say, glancing towards the shroud on the draining board. 'We'll have a couple of glasses and then decide what to do with Ronnie's mortal remains.'

Half an hour later, Andy comes in from the garden, sweat pouring down his cheeks from the exertion of digging a hole in one of the flowerbeds.

'It's ready,' he says quietly. We are all sombre. It is as if something more than Ronnie has died tonight. Andy carries the body out because Joe is in no fit state to do so. He lowers Ronnie into the grave. Lorraine stifles a sob as she bends down and picks up a handful of stones and earth and tosses it after him. I am almost in tears myself.

Joe wants Ronnie's football to go in too, but Lorraine says it's all too final, and Jamie might like to play with it when he comes round, and Andy says mournfully that he doubts it since his son appears to have been fathered by an alien, and Joe looks at me as if he thinks I've been sleeping around with aliens, and Andy explains that Jamie doesn't like football any more.

'We should sing a hymn,' Joe suggests.

'Can you remember any from school?' says Lorraine.

'"Onward Christian Soldiers", or "We Plough the Fields and Scatter",' says Andy.

'An Easter hymn would be more appropriate for a rabbit, wouldn't it?' I mutter.

Joe begins to hum a football anthem, the 'Three Lions'.

Andy and I take up the strain, and Lorraine inserts a soft soprano. We sing together in harmony until someone a couple of doors down opens their window and shouts something obscene along the lines of, 'Keep the noise down, I'm trying to sleep.'

Andy slips his arm around my back. I turn slightly and reach up and stroke the bruise that Joe has inflicted on his chin. I am aware that Joe is watching me, and I wonder if he too is wishing he was elsewhere tonight.

Chapter Sixteen

'Steve, have you been listening to me?' I am speaking into my mobile, hoping the battery will hold out. While I've been trying to explain the difficulties I'm having arranging to meet him, he's been telling me to picture him naked in the workshop, smeared with grease and sweat. 'I can't just drop everything and disappear.'

'I can't wait,' he whispers.

'You'll have to. Just a few more days. I promise.' It's difficult to keep everyone happy all of the time, isn't it, and I worry that Steve is backing off, wondering if I am capable of handling the great romance, and everything that goes with it.

'Who's that you're talking to?' Jamie interrupts. I'd forgotten he and Emily were at home. I cut Steve off, promising I'll call him later.

'Who is it?'

'No one.'

'You've been speaking to them for ages.'

'I haven't.'

'Why do you speak to the phone if there's no one there?'

'Because no one listens to me.' I try wallowing in self-pity in an attempt to dismiss that picture of Steve naked. 'Have you tidied your room like I asked you to?'

'No.'

'You see? You don't listen to me.'

'It's Emily's fault that my room's a mess. She tipped the Lego out.'

'Well, you and Emily go and clear it up together.'

I watch Jamie go, his shoulders sagging, and I realise I'm being a cow, and it's not Jamie's fault. I go and help sort hundreds of tiny pieces of Lego into the correct boxes.

'Are you feeling all right?' I ask.

'I'm a bit tired,' he sighs, 'and I've got a sore throat.'

'You're still taking your vitamins?'

'I haven't had them today, Mum. You keep forgetting to remind me.'

I study his face. There's no colour, and his cheekbones seem more prominent, as if the flesh that covered them has melted away. I make up my mind. It's time I made some more phone calls.

I try the doctors' surgery first. Dr Finch is on leave for a week. I could make an appointment with Dr Chandler if it's urgent. Is it urgent? I make an appointment for eleven the following day, but Jamie says he can't possibly take time off school then because he's making a fire engine with moving wheels out of an After Eights' box, so I ring back and make a new appointment for ten days' time with Dr Finch. Ten days is a long time to worry about what is wrong with Jamie, but I'm not worried. Not very. If Jamie gets worse, I'll brave the receptionist's ire and change the appointment again.

I tackle the childcare problem second. As I may have said before, for some reason – Emily perhaps – no one ever offers to have our children, and means it. The Rhino offers in such a way that you feel you can't possibly accept. My parents have offered – three times in seven years. However, I decide to give the grandparents first refusal in case they have changed their minds about spending quality time with their grandchildren.

I try my mother. My mother is busy. She doesn't say what she's doing, but she's busy. All next week and the week after.

I try the Rhino. The conversation goes something like this.

'It's Juliet.'

'Who?'

'Juliet, the mother of your grandchildren.'

'Oh, I thought you were the woman who's coming to do my pedicure.'

'I wondered if you'd like to take the children out for the day next week?'

319

'Take them off your hands, you mean?'

'Next Tuesday or Thursday, perhaps.'

'Did you know my consultant's booked me in for a colostomy? Didn't my Andrew tell you?'

I think for a moment. He might have done. He probably did. I accuse Andy and my children of not listening to me. Is it because I don't make enough effort to listen to them?

'I take it that's a no then.'

There's a disturbance, a change in the tone of the Rhino's voice, a fading then a coming back.

'Boat's just come through – there's a bit of a wake.'

I refrain from wishing out loud that the wake was hers. So much for grandparents . . . I try Mary Bacon and ask her if she can have Emily for an extra day.

'Would that be every week?' Mary enquires.

'Yes.'

Mary goes very quiet.

'I'll pay you extra.'

I can picture her stroking her moustache, mulling the offer over.

'How much extra?'

'A little.' I'd pay her anything so I can meet Steve and have his tongue walking down my back, but I don't want Mary Bacon thinking she can take advantage of my weakness.

'What day were you thinking of, Juliet?'

'Tuesday or Thursday.'

'Well, I already have Josh and little Jake on Tuesdays.'

The phone begins to slip in my palm. My mouth goes dry. There's no one else I can ask. Lorraine's already made it quite clear that she's not interested in looking after Emily so I can see Steve, and, although the woman at the Council sent me a list of childminders with spaces available so I could move Jamie and Emily from Mary Bacon's if I really wanted to, the two in our area suddenly recalled they were up to quota when I mentioned Emily's challenging behaviour. Having learned that dishonesty is the best policy when trying to acquire a childminder, I tried the last one on the list, but she was on holiday for three weeks.

'I was thinking of an extra pound an hour,' I suggest.

'I normally do my big shop on a Thursday.'

'How about two pounds?'

Mary Bacon sounds positively orgasmic.

'Cash up front for next Thursday then. Drop Emily round to me at ten.' She pauses. 'May I ask where you'll be for my records, Juliet?'

You may ask, I think, but I'm not telling. I'm not telling Mary Bacon that I am arranging an assignation with my lover.

'I'm doing my carpets,' I say. 'I'm hiring a wet and dry vacuum cleaner for the day. I'll leave my mobile switched on in case I don't hear the phone. You know how noisy those things are.' (Liar.) I've never used one. I don't care though. I am almost ready to meet Steve. I feel young and beautiful like Kate was when she set out on her maiden voyage. Alas, I shall have to start my journey in a far less glamorous mode of transport than the *Titanic* . . .

The following day at work I ask Steve to check the tyre pressures on my car.

'Can you take the day off next Thursday?' I whisper over the hiss of the air that rushes out of the offside front tyre as Steve attaches a gauge. He looks up from his squatting position and smiles.

'Are you saying what I think you're saying?' Steve reaches out one hand, and strokes my ankle where the dragonfly tattoo peeks out from the hem of my black trousers. 'Have you found a space for me in your busy schedule at last?'

I reach down and run my fingers through his hair. It is thick and warm, like an animal's. The bruises on his face have faded to dull yellow and grey. Antonio Banderas, bearing the scars of a skirmish. Steve, the hero, who could have done Debs's dad some serious damage if he hadn't restrained himself from fighting back.

'I'll be with you soon after ten.' Steve's invited me to his place, a flat in Upper Norwood. I don't suppose he can afford the grand gesture of a room in a luxury hotel on his wages and, considering what happened to Kate and Leonardo, I wouldn't contemplate anything more exotic like a boat trip, not even a cruise on the Thames.

'I'll be waiting to strip you down, and kiss you all over,' Steve murmurs. 'Don't let me down, Juliet.'

'I shan't,' I promise. I've been waiting for this for far too long to duck out now.

'Don't go yet.' Steve's hand encircles my ankle.

'I have to,' I say, trying to pull away.

'Kiss first.' Steve's eyes are wide, and beseeching. For a moment I see a boy, closer in age to Jamie than he is to me, but the moment doesn't last.

'Not now. Not here,' I hiss, trying to shake him off.

'Juliet . . .'

I drop my arm around his shoulder, lean down and kiss him firmly on the lips.

'More,' he murmurs, releasing his grip.

'That's it – till Thursday,' I say, backing off. I can hardly stop myself skipping back round to the showroom where Gayle stares disapprovingly at my lightness of step. Andy looks up and waves me to his desk.

'I forgot to ask you if you'd managed to book Emily in at Mary's for that extra session,' he says.

'She's going there every Thursday starting next week.'

'Good.' Andy picks up a business card from the desk in front of him. 'Because we've been invited to lunch.'

'Lunch?' No, no, that's not part of the plan. I hadn't envisaged that at all.

'It's all paid for,' he says, 'drinks included.'

'Who's paying?'

'Some development company.' He shows me the card.

O'Connor & Partners. 'Some men in suits called here the other day. They're looking for plots of land to re-develop. Ours is a prime site.'

'You're not considering selling up, are you?'

'Maybe. I thought you'd like to come with me on Thursday and find out what they're offering.'

'I can't.'

'I know the business means a lot to you. To us,' Andy corrects himself, 'but the rewards aren't great, and I can't see turnover improving much in the near future. Selling up might be the answer. If there's enough money in it, we can buy something else.'

'It's not that, Andy. Thursday's no good for me. I'm going shopping. I want to get you something special for your birthday. And I need to start thinking about Christmas.'

'It's only September!'

'There are cards and crackers in the shops already.'

'All right, Jules. I can see you're not interested. I shall go anyway.'

'That's fine by me,' I say, but I'm not really listening any more. I have other things on my mind. In less than a week, I shall be with Steve.

The following morning, I am scrutinising my appearance in the long mirror on the bedroom wall. I suck my tummy in and thrust my breasts out. Not bad. I push my hair back and examine my eyebrows. Not good.

'Mummy!' I hear Emily scream from the cloakroom. 'I've finished my poo!'

The phone rings at the same time. I pick it up, tuck it under my chin and go and attend to Emily.

'Drop everything, Juliet,' Lorraine says. 'I've decided to take that test. I'll be round in five minutes.'

Lorraine turns up with Tyler clutching tight to Lorraine's new black suede-look skirt. Next, size eight, or ten. Maybe a ten, I note without satisfaction. (Liar.) Tyler won't let go until I untangle her fingers, pick her up and take her off to feed the sea-monkeys with Emily while Lorraine goes upstairs to the bathroom.

I watch the clock in the kitchen, and wait. Emily and Tyler start arguing over how many sea-monkeys there are in the tank. There is a yelp, and when I look down, Emily is holding Tyler's neck in an armlock. Tyler's face turns from red to purple.

'Stop that! Let go!'

Emily releases Tyler who takes a gulp of air.

'Tyler says there's six sea-monkeys,' Emily protests, 'but there's hundreds and thousands.'

Neither of them are right. I suggest we count them together, but Tyler interrupts.

'You can't count, Emily, because you're a baby.'

'I not a baby.'

'My mummy says you're a baby.'

Emily grabs an apple from the fruit bowl and throws

325

it at Tyler. It bounces off her forehead, leaving no mark, but she bawls anyway.

'Emily!' I say, unsure which one to turn to first.

'You said I was a baby, but I'm not.' Emily turns to me for support. 'Am I, Mummy?'

'You behave like one,' I say icily.

'Babies can't talk!' Emily screams. 'I'm not a baby!' and she flounces out of the kitchen at the same time as Lorraine comes charging down from the bathroom, brandishing a white wand.

'Juliet. Juliet! What do you think?' Lorraine's expression tells it all, and I have to restrain her from dancing up and down the kitchen and going into premature labour.

'Lorraine, sit down,' I urge, directing her towards a stool. 'You haven't booked a midwife yet.'

'I'm pregnant!' she shrieks. 'I can't believe it.' She sits down and stares hungrily at her belly. 'You won't tell anyone, will you?'

'You've already told half of South Norwood, yelling like that.'

'I must tell Joe first.' She looks up. 'I'll have to pretend that he knew before you did.'

The thought of Lorraine bringing a new life into the world makes my belly screw up into a knot with envy. I want one too, until Emily storms in, screaming, 'I hate you, Mummy!' She runs up and kicks me in the shin.

'Emily! No! You mustn't kick.'

She kicks out again. I suppress my instinct to pick

her up and drop her out in the garden. Divert. Distract.

'Lorraine's having a baby.'

Emily looks up at Lorraine curiously. 'Where is it then?' she asks.

'In my tummy,' says Lorraine, stroking her belly.

'Can you get it out?'

'Not yet.'

'It's not cooked properly,' I explain.

'But I want to see it. I want to see it now.'

'Well, you can't.'

Lorraine and I end up in the sitting room with our respective children on our laps, Emily sobbing because she can't see the baby, and Tyler because she doesn't want a new baby brother or sister.

'How far gone are you?' I ask Lorraine.

'I'm not sure. Thirteen or fourteen weeks maybe? Joe's going to be over the moon. We've been trying for another baby since I stopped breastfeeding Tyler.'

I wonder whether Lorraine is right about Joe's reaction. His enthusiasm was evident back then, but this is now. If Joe *is* having an affair, I wonder how he will react at the news that his wife is expecting their baby?

'I must call him.'

'Use our phone,' I offer.

'Thanks. I was in such a flap, I forgot my bag, and my housekeys.'

'Don't worry. I have your spare set in the cupboard.' I let Emily slide off my lap. 'Go and fetch the phone, please, Emily, then you and Tyler can go and play upstairs.' Emily skips into the hall and returns with the phone, dropping it on Lorraine's lap, before she and Tyler run up to her bedroom with strict instructions not to draw on ANYTHING.

Lorraine rings Joe's work. Joe is off sick with the flu – which is news to Lorraine. So is Toni Knight, the bug-eyed trainer with the bad breath. Lorraine turns to me, her face pale, her lower lip trembling.

'Joe's been lying to me, the bastard.' Her voice is hoarse. 'I'm going to kill him. I am.'

'I can believe it.' I try to calm Lorraine down because, as much as I'd hoped Joe would die when I wouldn't let him make love to me, I'm not a violent or vengeful person. (Unless the Rhino is concerned.) I struggle to find explanations for Joe's lie that he is tucked up in bed at home, but I can't. Even a practised liar like me can't find any alternative to the option that Joe is tucked up in bed at Toni Knight's.

Lorraine and I leave Tyler and Emily with Lorraine's mum, and head off to stake out Toni Knight's place. I drive, and Lorraine holds the *London A–Z* open on her lap. I feel like a TV detective. Starsky and Hutch. Dalziel and Pascoe. Lorraine and Juliet. I want to suggest that we stop and grab a couple of hamburgers, a bag of doughnuts, and some shades, but Lorraine isn't in the mood for having a laugh.

We head out of London and find ourselves in South

Croydon, just off the edge of the map. We stop at the Forestdale Arms, where I buy Lorraine a drink. I'm not sure she should be having alcohol in her condition, but one small rum and Coke isn't going to hurt, is it?

'I'm going to kill him,' Lorraine repeats as she drains her glass.

'This is a mistake. We should go home,' I suggest gently, but Lorraine insists that as we've made it this far, we may as well keep going, and I ask the woman behind the bar for directions.

It turns out that Toni Knight lives in one of a terrace of modern brick and tile houses that is set back from the road. I park the car some way down, afraid that Joe may catch sight of it from the window, if he is there. It isn't the ideal vehicle for a detective, is it?

'I can see Joe's car,' Lorraine wails suddenly. 'Look!' She jumps out, and runs up the paved path that leads up through a patchy lawn to the obscure-glazed front door of number thirteen. I follow, cutting the corner by ducking beneath the dark boughs of a yew tree to catch up with her on the doorstep.

Lorraine hammers at the door. I ring the bell. Nothing happens. I step back and look into the window that stretches almost the full width of the house, but all I can see is the pattern in the net curtain that hangs behind it. Lorraine tries banging on the door again.

'I'm going to bash this bloody door in.'

'Let's try something a little more subtle, shall we?' I

push her out of my way, bend down and lift the flap on the letterbox. 'Ms Knight,' I call, 'do you want me to take this package all the way back to the depot?'

'Juliet?' says Lorraine.

'I'll handle this. Now, shut up. Someone's coming down the stairs.'

I straighten as I see a figure behind the door, its shape distorted by the glass. The door opens a few inches and a hand emerges.

'You'll have to sign for it.'

The door opens wide. It's Joe. His jaw drops then quickly snaps shut. He gives a disarming smile, and runs one hand through his rumpled hair.

'Hi, Juliet.' He glances past me. 'Hi, Lorraine.'

I try to keep between Joe and Lorraine, who is trying to claw her way past me.

'What the hell are you doing here?' Lorraine shouts.

'I have to ask the same of you,' says Joe. I admire his cheek. It can't be easy to stand there like that, naked apart from a towel around your midriff, and a sheen of sweat across your sex-flushed chest.

'I rang you at work this morning. They said you were off with flu.'

'They must have confused me with someone else, mustn't they? I've just popped round to fix Toni's washing machine during my lunchbreak.'

'It's a bit early for lunch,' I point out, looking at my watch.

'I took an early lunch.'

'What happened to your clothes?' says Lorraine more quietly as if she's beginning to believe Joe's story.

'The machine sprung a leak. My suit got wet. Toni lent me a towel.'

'Nice one,' I suggest. 'Try again.'

'It's the truth,' he says, gazing past me.

'Do you believe him, Lorraine?'

'No, I bloody well don't.'

'Who's that, Joe?' comes a voice huskier than Mariella Frostrup's from the hallway behind him. I catch a glimpse of a young woman in a white sweat top and jog pants, and I know immediately that she has no children. No one who has children chooses to wear white. 'Who is this?' She pushes Joe aside, places her hands on her hips, and looks us up and down. 'Have you come to pick up the envelope for Help the Aged?'

'No, we're collecting for battered husbands,' I say quickly.

'You're not?' says the young woman, staring at me.

'I'm Joe's wife,' says Lorraine, stepping past me. 'You must be Toni.'

Lorraine can't have relied on Joe's description of Toni Knight in making this assumption. This woman is stunning. She has long blonde hair, big, babydoll eyes, and the glowing complexion that goes along with just having been shagged by someone else's husband. She's in her mid-twenties, I guess, and much like I imagine Lorraine was when she first met Joe.

'You've overcome the bad breath, have you, Joe?' Lorraine spits.

Toni's eyes flash dangerously.

'I never said—' Joe blusters.

'Why don't you come in?' Toni interrupts. 'It might be a good idea if we talked.'

How civilised! Can I imagine Steve making that suggestion to Andy, if Andy should turn up on his doorstep while I am with Steve? I think not.

I follow Toni, Joe and Lorraine into a living room. I stand beside Lorraine, ready to restrain her if necessary, in front of one of those ubiquitous posters of waterlilies. Toni stands with her arms folded, facing Lorraine. Joe stands in the doorway, fiddling with the top of his towel. No one speaks. I wonder if Joe has found the love of his life with Toni Knight? If he has, and he's thinking of moving in with her, he's committing himself to a lot more DIY, judging by the state of the decor.

Eventually, Lorraine turns to Joe.

'I came to tell you I'm pregnant,' she says softly.

Joe steps back into the doorframe. Toni goes berserk. Any pretence at civilised behaviour flies out of the jumbo-sized front window as Toni marches up and grabs Joe by the arm.

'You said you didn't sleep with her any more!' she screams.

'I d-don't,' Joe stammers.

'My husband has a short memory,' Lorraine butts in.

'How pregnant are you?' Toni says, turning to Lorraine.

'Thirteen or fourteen weeks.'

Toni appears to be making a quick mental calculation.

'That's not possible.' She turns back to Joe. 'You said your wife hadn't been able to bear to have you kiss her, let alone screw her, for years.'

I contribute the fact that Toni's washing-machine repair man has a three-year-old daughter as well.

'Piss off, Juliet,' Joe snaps. 'This is none of your business.'

'Lorraine's my friend. I don't like seeing her get hurt.'

'Jealous bitch! Just because I wouldn't have you, you're going out of your way to make sure I can't have anyone else.'

'That's not true. I turned you down.' I turn to Toni. '"I'll die if I can't make love to you . . . " Do you recognise those words? It's flattering, isn't it, to think that someone fancies you that much?'

'Not her as well!' Toni shrieks. She starts pummelling Joe in the belly, and driving him backwards out into the hall, out of the front door which is still open, and onto the path outside.

'I never want to see you again.'

'You'll see me at work.'

'I'll get a transfer.'

'Please, Toni – I can explain.'

'Explain to your wife.'

Lorraine and I follow Joe and Toni out. Toni slips back into the house.

'Get the hell out of my life!' she screams as she slams the door on us all.

'Toni? My clothes?' Joe runs up and bangs on the door. 'My keys are in there.' He is answered by the beat of music played so loud that the garden path seems to vibrate underfoot.

'Let's go home.' I tug at Lorraine's sleeve and she comes with me to the car, keeping half an eye on Joe who follows behind.

'Give us a lift home, will you?'

Lorraine turns, lets Joe walk right up to her, and slaps him in the face. Taking advantage of his temporary loss of concentration as he rubs at his cheek, I grab the towel at his waist and pull. Joe takes a grip on both of my wrists.

'Go for it, Lorraine,' I yell.

She takes hold of the towel, and runs for the car.

'Hey, give that back.' Joe tries to cover his modesty with his hands as he follows me to the car. I jump in, start the engine, and pull away from the kerb. Lorraine opens the window. I brake, but keep the engine revving ready to go in case Joe should try to jump in with us.

'Give us that towel!'

'No way.'

'You can't do this to me. I'll be arrested. Lorraine,

please,' Joe begs. 'This has all been one great misunderstanding.'

'You mean you weren't shagging that slag just now?'

'It wasn't like that.' Joe raises his hands. 'Okay, I confess. I was attracted to Toni—'

'What, by her personality or her enormous bottom?' says Lorraine sharply.

'I made a mistake, but it's over now. We'll make a fresh start with Tyler and the baby.'

'I'm not listening,' Lorraine says. 'Take me home, Juliet.'

I put my foot down. Joe runs alongside the car, trying to open Lorraine's door but, after a few yards, he bangs a fist on the roof, and I see him in the rearview mirror standing in the middle of the road with his hands on top of his head. Resigned. Defeated. And nowhere near as big as Andy in the non-extended state, which surprises me since Lorraine has always maintained that Joe is hung like a donkey.

Lorraine sobs into the towel. 'How could Joe do this to me when he has Tyler and an unborn child to consider?'

I point out that Joe didn't know about the unborn child before Lorraine told him a few minutes ago, but she's not listening.

'I'll bet that woman never exfoliates. Didn't you see the pimples on her neck? It must have been like shagging a limp chicken.'

Lorraine's wrong, of course, but a wife is never going

to accept that her husband's lover is more attractive than she is, is she?

I don't try to justify Joe's actions in any way, nor do I lie to console Lorraine. Nothing I can say will lessen the pain she must be feeling – even when I make an appointment for her to wax my eyebrows at last.

Chapter Seventeen

My eyebrows might be described as natural, or flourishing, but they don't need attention. They especially don't need waxing, yet here I am, sitting in Lorraine's spare room, propped up on the couch so that I can see out of the window. Jamie and the girls are playing in the garden. Ronnie's hutch is empty. Tyler holds the door open while Jamie shows Emily how to make a complex walkway from Duplo in the hope that they can entice a hedgehog, or more likely a rat, in to replace poor Ronnie. The football lies deflated in the flowerbed. There's a paving slab with *Angel* written across it in black marker pen. Ronnie's memorial.

'Do you think you'll ever have another one?' I ask.

'No way. They're all lying toe-rags.'

'Rabbits?'

'Husbands. I thought you were talking about Joe . . .' Lorraine's voice peters out. 'Did Joe stay at yours again last night?'

'Yes, he did. Oh Lorraine, I feel really bad about it, but he came round to us, saying you'd had the locks changed. I told him to go away, but Andy invited him in.'

'I suppose they've been mates for a long time,' Lorraine says quietly.

'They drank a lot of lager, and Joe crashed out on the sofa.'

'What's new?' Lorraine shrugs. 'Is he coming back to yours tonight?'

'He's taken all his stuff with him, including the bin-liners of things you threw down the steps. He had to get rid of the portable telly, or what was left of it.'

'Good.' Lorraine drapes me in white towelling up to my chin, and gives me a headband to tuck my hair up from my forehead.

'I didn't realise this would be such a messy business. Wouldn't you prefer to pluck them?' I suggest.

'Oh, no. Waxing's the thing nowadays. I could do your bikini line too.' She grins suddenly, and the old Lorraine is back. Temporarily. 'It's all right, I know you wouldn't let me. Juliet, will you please keep still?'

Lorraine prepares my skin, massaging my face with oil that carries the faint scent of almonds. I try to relax and enjoy the attention, but I can't. Tomorrow, I shall be with Steve.

'You know I shan't have Joe back,' Lorraine begins. Her touch goes light and ticklish. I stifle a giggle.

'It's no laughing matter, Juliet. As far as I'm concerned it's over. I think our marriage was over before it began.'

'But you have a child.' I glance at her belly, which pushes the buttons of the tunic that she's thrown over her clothes slightly apart. 'Two. Almost.'

Lorraine shrugs again. 'Joe can see them whenever he likes, but I want nothing more to do with him.'

Lorraine's not as controlled as she sounds. Her eyes, one blue and one green where she appears to have muddled her pairs of contact lenses, fill with tears. She blows her nose on a ragged piece of tissue.

'Oh Juliet, I don't know what's going to happen. I don't know what to do.' She drops the tissue in the bin.

'Why don't you take some more time to think about it? It isn't inevitable that your marriage is over because Joe's been unfaithful. You read magazine articles all the time about how an affair can revive a marriage,' I add hopefully.

'You can't revive something that's already dead,' says Lorraine.

There is a pause.

'We don't have to do this now,' I suggest. 'Why don't we leave it?'

'There is no way I'm going to let you duck out. I'm ready. Here is the wax. Here is a waxing strip. Now, close your eyes.'

I close my eyes, and Lorraine strokes on some warm

sticky wax below each brow then presses the strips on top. It's not unpleasant.

'Is that it?'

'Oh, no. I've got to remove the strips yet. This is when it might sting just a little.'

'You said it didn't hurt.'

'The pain doesn't last.' Lorraine pauses. 'Would you like something to bite on?'

I can't tell whether she is joking, or not. I keep my eyes closed, praying that the two aspirin I took earlier will be enough. I can feel Lorraine using a fingernail to scrape up one end of the strip below my right eyebrow so she can get a grip on it. I feel her give a testing tug then a quick rip. My skin feels as if it has been torn from the bone underneath.

'That's one,' Lorraine says brightly. 'One more to go.'

It's the same again, a tug and a rip, but it hurts twice as much. I open my eyes, and scream. So does Lorraine.

She is holding the waxing strip, complete with what appears to be my entire left eyebrow, between her fingers and thumbs. She begins to laugh hysterically. I don't know whether to laugh or cry. This would be funny if it was happening to someone else, but it's happening to me, and I have arranged to meet Steve for a day of passion tomorrow.

Lorraine gives me a stiff drink, vodka topped up with green Sunny Delight, to help me calm down. She makes herself two slices of tuna and mayonnaise on toast, and we sit side by side on the couch in her spare room. Lorraine holds my eyebrow in one hand, and a pair of tweezers in the other.

'How long does it take for an eyebrow to grow back?'

'I don't know. I guess you're going to find out. At least that grey hair's gone,' says Lorraine, tweezing it out of the strip. 'I didn't realise you had grey hairs. You didn't tell me.'

'It's not something to brag about,' I say. 'For goodness' sake, Lorraine, I thought you said you'd done this before.'

'I have. I don't know what happened.'

'Can you stick it back on?'

'I don't think so. I could draw you another one.' Lorraine tries various eyebrow pencils. First, she draws a smooth brown line.

'That's too curved,' she says. 'It makes you look surprised.' The next attempt is too flat.

'Here, let me do it,' I say, grabbing the pencil. The result is even worse, even though I've tried to make the eyebrow more realistic by feathering the lower edge.

Lorraine has another go, and another. She tries drawing individual hairs in brown, copper and gold to match the tiger stripes in my hair. She tries smudging them until I look as if I've walked into an iron bar. I cry. Lorraine cries too. I'm in a state over my eyebrows. Lorraine's in a state over Joe.

While we're sharing out the last of Lorraine's tissues, the children wander in from the garden.

'We're thirsty,' says Jamie, spreading mud all over the floor.

'You haven't taken off your shoes.'

'Why are you crying?' He kicks off his shoes, then gives me a second look. 'Wow, Mum, you've done a David Beckham. You're so,' he pauses, 'you're so yesterday.'

Andy isn't as observant as Jamie when he comes home later the same evening. I am stirring the sausage casserole that I prepared last night on the hob. Andy looks at me as if he suspects something is not quite right, yet he can't work out what it is.

'Did you have a good time at Lorraine's?'

I keep my face averted. Steam rises from the saucepan as the gravy bubbles up around the sausages. I flick the switch on the extractor hood above the hob, turn and wipe my forehead.

Andy grins. 'What have you let her do to you this time, Jules?'

I look down at my left eyebrow, which is smeared across the back of my hand, and burst into tears. Andy pulls me into his arms, and hugs me so tight I can hardly breathe.

'Don't be upset,' he soothes. 'Hair grows back, doesn't it?'

'Yours didn't,' I sniff. I look up at his head, which

gleams under the kitchen lights, and I pity him for having lost his hair, and for having such a deceitful wife.

'Look on the bright side,' Andy says. 'At least I don't have to worry about you running off with someone else.'

He's right, isn't he? People who have no eyebrows are not generally attractive to the opposite sex.

Would Leonardo have dismissed Kate if she had had the misfortune to lose an eyebrow? Would she have told him that he would have to wait to make love to her until it grew back? I turn these questions over and over in my mind as I lie in bed some time later.

'What's wrong, Jules?' Andy asks. He's lying beside me, fighting for the duvet, pulling it up and across to his side of the bed so my feet stick out.

'You've taken all the duvet, and I'm getting cold feet.' Cold feet in the literal, not the metaphorical sense. Eyebrow or no eyebrow, I am going to meet Steve tomorrow.

'Don't blame me. You've been fidgeting since I came to bed.'

'I have things on my mind.' I think quickly. 'I was wondering how Lorraine is going to manage without Joe.'

'Pretty well, I'd imagine. He's behaved like a complete idiot. Did you know he blames you for him and Lorraine splitting up?'

'*Me?*'

'He says Lorraine would never have found out about

Toni if you hadn't helped her. He says he was about to tell her their affair was over.'

'Do you believe him?'

'I don't know what to believe any more.' Andy sighs, and wriggles up close to me. His hand rests heavy on the curve of my waist. 'I'm going to meet those developers tomorrow. Won't you reconsider coming with me?'

'Not without an eyebrow. They wouldn't take me seriously.'

'I suppose not.' Andy's hand slips around my back, runs down and cups my buttock. His breathing quickens. 'Do you want to make love?'

I hesitate.

Andy rolls over onto his back. 'No, I thought you wouldn't,' he says. 'I guess you'll need all your energies for your shopping expedition.'

'Andy! It's not that. I'm tired . . .'

'Go to sleep then.'

I lie awake, stiff and straight, so I don't disturb him any more. I listen to the hollow banging of my heart, and wonder if Steve is awake too. I imagine how he will undress me, first with those hypnotic eyes of his, then for real. He is tearing at my bra strap with his teeth when there is a loud scream from Emily's room along the landing. I am prepared to wait for a moment to see if there is another, but Andy leaps straight out of bed to find out what is wrong.

He brings Emily back with him, and drops her in the bed between us.

'She's not staying there,' I point out. 'You know how long it took to break Emily of the habit of sleeping with us.'

'She was having a nightmare about being locked in a dark cupboard with an angry bear,' says Andy. 'She's been having them since she's been going to Mary Bacon's.'

'I did ask Mary about the cupboard,' I say. 'She told me that Emily locked herself in by accident while they were playing hide and seek.'

'Do you believe her?'

'You were the one who said you trusted Mary. You said she was the kind of person you were happy to leave your kids with.'

'I know, but Emily's really upset.'

An icy fingertip slides down my back. I turn to Emily who is lying quietly on her back, eyes open and listening to everything we say.

'Emily, does Mary Bacon ever lock you in a cupboard?' I ask gently.

Emily nods. Her eyes grow large in her face.

'It's behind the naughty door,' she whimpers. 'I hate Mary. I don't want to go there.'

'Juliet, she's scared stiff,' Andy says.

'I know. I suppose I should give Mary notice tomorrow.'

'You aren't thinking of leaving Emily with her?'

'I don't want to, but it's not that simple.' Emily must never go to Mary's again, but I need someone to mind her while I look for alternative childcare. And I can't afford to pay Mary's notice *and* another childminder at the same time. And I must see Steve tomorrow otherwise I shall die. I recall wondering if it was possible to die of unrequited love when Joe first raised the possibility with me, and I realise now that it is.

I lie back. My back grows warm, and wet. Emily has flooded the bed.

Emily and I share a bath, using some of Jamie's Soldier Bubblebath which smells of lime and chlorine. I check the label. It's nasty stuff. May sting. May irritate. May stain. Nowhere does it suggest that it's fragrant or seductive, or that it drives men wild.

'Why did you use my bubblebath?' Jamie complains when he wanders into the bathroom where I am washing my hair in the morning. 'Couldn't you have used Emily's instead?'

'If you remember, she emptied the entire bottle into the bath on the day I bought it.' I pause. 'Have you ever played hide and seek at Mary's?'

'I haven't. I don't know about Emily.' Jamie shrugs. 'I don't think Mary likes children. She doesn't let us play anything much in case we knock her boxes over.'

'What boxes?'

'The ones Arnie delivers with the cigarettes inside

them, and the ones she uses to store the presents that the nieces bring. Mary lets me help her cut the labels off the clothes sometimes.' He smiles. 'She says I'm a good worker.'

'Why haven't you told me any of this before?'

'You haven't asked.' Jamie frowns. 'I'm not sure I should have told you. Mary will be cross. It's supposed to be a secret.'

'Don't worry, Jamie.' I don't tell him that it will be me who will be doing the worrying. Mary's dealings sound a little more involved than dabbling in a few car boot sales. 'Why don't you go downstairs for breakfast?'

'I feel sick.'

'Come here.' I reach for a towel, dry my hands and feel Jamie's forehead. It's burning. This is just what I need. How am I going to tell Steve that I can't see him today because I've had to keep Jamie at home?

'My legs ache.' Jamie lifts one pyjama leg up so I can see the fresh bruise on his shin.

'How did you do that?'

'I knocked it on a chair.'

Jamie's eyes fill with tears. I kneel down beside him and give him a hug. He pushes me away.

'You're making my pyjamas wet with your hair,' he mutters. He looks so pale beneath his flushed cheeks that I force myself to go along with my conscience, not the tigress who growls that I should put my desires ahead of my family's welfare for once.

'You don't have to go to school today.'

'I want to go to school, Mum,' Jamie says manfully. 'We're doing Science and Technology.'

I stand up, and ruffle his hair. Jamie has an appointment to see Dr Finch tomorrow, and Dr Finch will tell me it's just a virus, and viruses are only to be expected as the weather changes.

Outside, the trees are changing colour and the children are playing conkers in the playground when I take Jamie to school. They're not supposed to. I think it has something to do with conker fights being considered a competitive sport.

Emily and I take Jamie into the playground for a change, instead of leaving him outside the school gates, or wherever I manage to stop the car.

'I'll see you later, darling,' I say, kissing him on the forehead.

He ducks back, flushing. 'Oh, Mum!'

Tears prick my eyes. I don't know why.

'You haven't cried like that since my first day at school,' Jamie says accusingly.

'I'm sorry. I'm tired. I didn't sleep very well last night.' I feel as if I have let Jamie down, embarrassing him in front of his friends. Why am I in such a state? Is it because I'm afraid that Steve will discover that I'm an ordinary middle-aged woman with an ordinary middle-aged body and not want me any more? Is it because I'm afraid that Andy will find me out, and I will lose everything?

'Come here, Emily. Let's go.' I take her hand. She sticks one finger up her nose, and refuses to budge.

'I not going,' she says.

I bend down, and tuck the strands of her hair that have strayed across her face back behind her ears. I forgot to help her to brush it this morning.

'Come on, Emily.'

'I not going to Mary's.'

'Well, that's right,' I say bravely. 'You're not going to Mary's straight away. We're going to pick up a few things in Sainsbury's first. We could buy some of those sweets that you like.'

Emily removes her finger from her nose, and examines the bogey on the end of it. Before I can snatch a tissue from my bulging handbag which I packed three days ago, she's transferred it into her mouth.

'I not going.'

'Please, Emily. I can do without this.'

Emily stamps her foot. I stamp mine, but it's no good. By the time we reach Mary Bacon's, Emily is in mid-paddy. I drag her up to the door and ring the bell. No one answers. I give the door a push. It swings open.

'Mary?' I pull Emily into the hallway where the first thing I notice is the cupboard. Emily stops screaming, and clings to my leg.

'I not go in there today,' she says. 'I'll be good now, Mummy. I'll be the best-est-est girl in the whole wide world.'

I bend down and pick her up.

'I'm sorry, Emily.' I don't know what to do. I need to confront Mary about how she's treating Emily, but she isn't here. I check through the rest of the maisonette which appears to have been stripped of Mary's belongings, apart from the telly. It is switched off which is unusual because Mary likes to leave it on all the time for educational purposes. I'm not sure what she expects the children to learn from the likes of Basil Brush and Bob the Builder.

A couple of tins of the cheapest, white-labelled spaghetti hoops stand on the kitchen worktop beside a basket of fruit. In front of the basket lie the silver corpses of flies in a sheen of juice that has run out through the bottom. I guess from the smell that emanates from the carpets that Mary Bacon's Febreze has run out too.

I carry Emily outside, and drop her back down on the pavement. What now? It's ten past ten, and I am supposed to be on my way to Steve's. We wait. I haven't any choice.

'Mary not coming,' says Emily.

'She's out shopping. She'll be here soon.'

A skinny man with flowing blond hair comes along with a white bull terrier. Emily wants to stroke it. It strains against a thick studded leather collar and lead, and growls.

'Oi, Sikes, leave it!'

Emily is fearless. She goes in again.

'I'd keep that child under control if I were you,' the man cautions. 'This dog eats children.'

Emily shuts up, and I wish she would do that for me. Perhaps I should borrow a dog.

'If you're waiting for that one, you might be a while,' the man says, nodding towards the door behind me.

'Oh?'

'The police came round this morning and took her away.'

The police?

'Where did they take her?'

'I dunno, do I? Police station, maybe.'

I am furious with Mary for not keeping this appointment. When someone says they're going to hire a wet and dry vacuum cleaner for the day, you make sure you're at home so they can use it without their children paddling about in the foam it makes. I see my plans for me and Steve dissolving into the rain that is beginning to spit down from the misty sky. The sun tried to break through, but didn't make it.

'Excuse me,' I call.

The man turns back. 'Yeah?'

'Do you know why Mary was arrested?'

'Nah, sorry, love,' and off he goes. His legs, I observe, are bowed just like the dog's.

I thought I was prepared for every eventuality, but I was wrong. Who would have imagined that their child-minder would be arrested on the very day you needed her? I guess that's what happens to the best laid plans of mice and men and silly, infatuated women of a certain age. I don't dwell too long on what Mary Bacon might have done. If she's been arrested for child cruelty, I shall ring the woman at the Council and wallow in self-vindication. I shall tell her about Emily and the cupboard. I might even sue.

'Mummy, can we go now?' Emily is tugging at my skirt. 'Mummy, your eyebrow's gone away again.'

I glance at my watch. It's twenty past ten. What am I going to do with Emily? My heart is as heavy as a 5kg box of Persil with 33 per cent extra free. Emily and I return to my car. I strap her into her booster seat in the front, and redraw my left eyebrow. It's not as good as the one I drew first thing, but it'll have to do. I don't suppose Leonardo was particularly interested in Kate's eyebrows.

'Where are we going?' Emily asks.

'To Granny's.' I am desperate. I pick up a bottle of sherry on the way, and we arrive at the houseboat just in time to discover the Rhino on her way out. She walks towards us, carrying a large brown handbag. She's dressed in a fur hat, gloves, long coat, and brown lace-up boots, which is strange because it's quite warm for the end of September.

'Granny!' shouts Emily, running up and flinging her arms around her.

'Emily, my dearest grandchild!' The Rhino bends stiffly, and plants a kiss on Emily's upturned face.

'Pammy,' I say, holding out the bottle just as I catch sight of the man who is walking along behind her, dragging an overburdened suitcase trolley. 'Oh, you're going somewhere,' I falter.

'You always were so terribly observant, Juliet,' she says, snatching the bottle of sherry. 'How kind of you to think of me.'

She looks me up and down, and I know she's taking in the tiger stripes, the eyebrows, or lack of them, the lowcut blouse, and hip-hugging skirt, and the tattoo on my ankle. In the Rhino's opinion, it is a sin not to wear tights with a skirt. What must I look like? A woman of almost forty, trying to look like she's twenty again. And I didn't even look like this when I *was* twenty. How sad is that? How sad am I?

'Where are you going?'

'I have a plane to catch.'

'I thought you were going into hospital?'

'I am, but I'm taking one last trip with my bowel before it is removed. Didn't Andrew tell you?'

Andy might have done. I do remember him muttering something about the cruise to Norway being confirmed.

'This is Ian, my allergist, who has kindly agreed to accompany me,' the Rhino says, gesturing towards the man with the suitcase trolley.

The man stops just behind her, and smiles. He's short and bulky like a troll, and he sports a ginger moustache, which I find surprising considering the Rhino's deep dislike of facial hair. He's wearing a well-cut tweed suit with a striped waistcoat and yellow tie.

'Ian, this is Juliet, my daughter-in-law, who has given me such attention during my life-threatening illness.'

'I believe I have reason to be forever in your debt, Juliet,' Ian says pompously. 'If it wasn't for you I might never have met this wonderful lady.' He turns to the Rhino. 'I am honoured to be travelling with you, Pamela,' he says. 'We must hurry though. Our cab is waiting.'

'So, you can't look after Emily for me this morning?'

'It's almost midday.' The Rhino stuffs the sherry bottle lengthwise into her handbag, then tries to look at her watch beneath layers of clothing and fur. 'There's not much morning left, is there?'

She turns to Emily. 'Goodbye, Emily, dear. I'll bring you something back from Norway. Give Jamie my love.'

Emily beams and waves, as the Rhino takes Ian's arm, and lets him walk her along the towpath to the road with the trolley squeaking along behind them.

Now what? Emily looks up at me hopefully. I can't ask Andy – he hates having Emily running around at work, jumping in and out of the cars, and answering the phones, and he has a lunch appointment with the developers. Not that I'm expecting any developments to arise from that.

I try Lorraine. She's changed the message on her answerphone. 'This is Lorraine, hair and beauty consultant, specialising in hair colouring, waxing and nail extensions.' Cheeky cow. I try her mobile.

'Lorraine, hair and beauty consultant,' she says sweetly.

'It's me, Juliet.'

'Oh, hi.'

'What's all this consultant stuff?'

'I'm a single parent – I have to support myself now.'

'You couldn't have Emily for a couple of hours, could you?'

'I can have her tomorrow.'

'Tomorrow's no good – I'm working. It has to be today. I want to buy Andy's birthday present, and you know what Emily's like when it comes to shopping.'

'Hasn't it occurred to you, Juliet, that Emily might like to choose her daddy's birthday present with you?' There's a pause during which I picture Lorraine wiping a tear, but not the mascara from her eye, as she thinks of Tyler and her unborn child, and wonders whether their daddy will stick around so that they can buy presents for him.

'Please, Lorraine. I'm desperate.'

'I can't. I'm down at the wholesalers, buying in supplies, then I have an appointment with the solicitor.'

'What about after that?'

'I'm meeting the midwife.' Lorraine pauses. 'Give me a ring later, and I'll see what I can sort out for next week.'

I thank her, even though she hasn't been able to help me out of my predicament, and then I check the text messages on my mobile. There are two.

Luv u, A. xxx, and *Whr th hll r u?*

There's only one thing for it.

'Come on, Emily. I'll have to take you with me.'

'Where are we going?' she asks as we jump back into the car.

'We're just going to pop in to see a friend of Mummy's.'

Emily looks at me, her eyes wide with surprise. 'Lorraine?'

I'm going to have to tell her. She'll find out soon enough.

'No, Steve from work. He's off sick. I'm going to see if he's okay.'

'Are you going to give him some Calpol?'

'Something like that.' I gaze at my daughter beside me, marvelling at how she can look so dignified in spite of her untidy hair and the OshKosh dress tucked up under her bottom.

'This is a 'venture, isn't it, Mummy?' she keeps saying over the repetitive clunk and swipe of the windscreen wipers. 'This is a 'venture.'

Being stuck in traffic on Waterloo Bridge doesn't feel like an adventure to me. It's a bloody nightmare. I try to recall my yoga training. Exhale stressful thoughts, let the ribcage expand, and inhale calm ones. It doesn't work.

356

I glance down the front of my blouse. I am breaking out into a rash. I want to cry, but I'm afraid that my mascara will run.

'When are we going to get there?'

'Soon.' It takes us longer than I thought it would to reach Steve's address. It is 2.15 p.m. when I turn into a small car park made, it appears, by pouring tarmac over a grassed front garden, and driving a bulldozer through part of the wall that formed the boundary to allow access. I park beside a car without wheels that is jacked up and covered with a blue tarpaulin. I can't see any sign of Steve's bike.

'Are we there yet, Mummy?'

'I think so.'

I peer up through the drizzle at the dark, three-storey house. The paint is peeling from the windowframes, and there are a few tiles missing from the roof. One of the windows is boarded up. It isn't how I imagined it would be. I know Steve told me that he lived in a bedsit, but I still pictured a fairytale castle rising from a mountain swathed in pink mist. I pictured myself arriving in a horse-drawn carriage, and presenting myself to Steve, as fresh and fragrant as a Glade plug-in. Instead, I roll up in a car covered in adverts, and present myself all itchy, perspiring and stinking of London streets. Even worse, I have Emily with me.

She trots along beside me as we make our way up the steps to the front door which is unlocked, and into a hallway which reminds me of a pub with its red flock wallpaper and deep green carpet. Upstairs we find a door with a seven splashed on it in white paint.

I knock. The door flies open.

'Juliet, my darling.'

'My love.'

The sight of Steve takes my breath away. His pupils are dark and dilated with lust. I let my eyes track down his body; past the curve of his lips, past the pulse that beats in the side of his neck, past the slabs of his pectorals, past his navel to the grey towel that hardly hides the Big Thing in its fully extended state.

'Where have you been? I've been waiting for ages.' Steve steps up, takes both my hands and pulls me close, ignoring my urgent protestations. He covers my mouth with his.

'Hello, Steve,' Emily pipes up from behind me. 'Are you better? Mummy says you're sick.'

Steve looks over my shoulder, and explodes.

'What the fuck's she doing here?' He pushes me away, quite roughly.

'Steve, please, calm down and let me explain. There's been a hitch.'

'What kind of hitch?' Steve runs his hands through his hair, gathers it together and twists it up behind his head.

'The childminder's been arrested.'

'Isn't there anyone else you can dump her with? What

about that friend of yours – Lorraine?' Steve lets his hair fall back. 'There must be someone.'

'I've tried everyone I can think of, even my mother-in-law, and it's no good. We'll have to do this another time.'

'Can't she sit outside in the car, or go to the shop? There's a park along the road.'

'Emily's three years old. I can't leave her outside on her own.' My mind races. 'Have you got any videos? *Bananas in Pyjamas*, *Postman Pat*, or *The Wiggles*?'

'I borrowed *Terminator II* from a friend the other day, but the telly's bust.' Steve scowls at me. 'Bloody hell, Juliet, I've lost out on a day's pay for you, and you're here trying to tell me you can't find anyone to look after your kid.'

'It's not my fault.' Of course it's my fault. Emily is my child, my baggage, my impediment.

'I don't like being fucked around,' Steve growls.

I glance from the deep flush that has erupted across his face, to his clenched fists, to his waist and down. The towel has slipped, revealing the insolence of the Big Thing and the black screwcurls that surround its base.

'Mummy?' Emily whispers, pushing her hand into mine.

'I'm really sorry, Steve.' He is so angry that I think he might spontaneously combust. 'I'll make it up to you. I promise.'

'That's what they all say.'

'I'll call you.'

'They say that as well.'

'Oh Steve, please don't be like this. I'm as disappointed as you are.' More so, probably. I thought we had a special connection, a relationship that transcended the physical.

Steve's eyes soften slightly. His shoulders relax. He rearranges the towel, pulling it tight around his waist.

'Make it next Thursday then, Juliet. Ten thirty sharp.'

My heart leaps. For a moment I thought Steve and I were finished, but I see now that his anger is merely a manifestation of his frustration and regret that we failed to consummate our relationship today. I am also consoled by the fact that he has omitted to mention my eyebrows out of respect for my feelings.

'I'll be here,' I confirm. I don't kiss Steve. He doesn't try to kiss me.

Back at the car, I check Emily is strapped into her seat, and kiss her on the cheek.

'What did you do that for?' she asks.

'Because I love you.'

She slips her arms around my neck and kisses me back before nuzzling up against my ear, and whispering, 'Can we go to McDonald's?'

'I don't see why not.'

'Can I have a flurry?'

'You can have as many McFlurries as you like. Now, we aren't going to tell Daddy or Jamie about this adventure of ours. It's our secret. Girls together. Promise?'

Emily nods solemnly, but I realise that nothing I do can guarantee that she won't mention today's entertainment to Andy. As I mull over plausible explanations for how we ran into the Rhino, Ian and Steve while I was supposed to be shopping at Bluewater or Lakeside, my mobile rings. I pick it up from where I left it on the dashboard.

'Where the hell are you?'

'Problem?' My heart stops. I don't need to ask. I can tell by the tone of Andy's voice.

'Everything's okay,' he says, but I know it isn't. 'I'm down at the hospital—'

'But I've just seen your mother,' I interrupt.

'It's not my mother.' Andy pauses. 'It's Jamie.'

Chapter Eighteen

It must be bad. Only the dying are seen this quickly in A&E. Jamie and Andy have been through the Paediatric Admissions procedure, and Jamie's already tucked up in bed in a side-room on the ward. To my relief, he is sitting up and, although he's on a drip, there are no breathing machines or blipping monitors in sight. Andy is perched on the edge of the bed.

'Jamie!' I walk up to the other side of the bed and fling my arms around him, but he ducks back.

'I'm all right, Mum,' he insists.

'You don't look it, darling.' I glance at Andy who looks almost as pale as Jamie does.

'He's okay, Juliet,' Andy says quietly. He can't quite look me in the eye.

'What's he doing in hospital if he's okay?'

'He collapsed at school.'

CATHY WOODMAN

'In the playground,' Jamie interrupts. 'Mr Dart called an ambulance.'

'An ambulance?' Emily squeaks. 'Mummy, I want to go in an ambulance.'

'The paramedics switched the flashing lights on for me,' Jamie says. 'It was great.'

Emily jumps up and down. Andy snaps at her to shut up and calm down, which isn't really fair since she doesn't understand the gravity of the situation.

'I had a ride on a trolley,' Jamie goes on. 'A whole gang of doctors and nurses whizzed me through miles and miles of corridors. We nearly crashed . . .'

Emily's mouth is wide open as she hangs on to Jamie's every word.

'Then a nurse stuck a massive needle into my arm . . .' His lip trembles almost imperceptibly. 'That wasn't so great.'

'They're doing some tests,' Andy says. He ushers me aside while Emily bounces on her knees on the end of Jamie's bed. 'Where were you?' he whispers. 'Mother says you went all the way to Islington.'

'You've spoken to your mother?'

'She's on her way.'

'Yes, to Norway. With Ian.'

'She's cancelled her cruise. She's coming here to be with us.'

'So it is bad? Jamie, I mean?' I try to swallow past a lump in my throat that feels as big as a football.

'Shh.' Andy takes my elbow and guides me out into the corridor.

'Dr Finch made out I was a neurotic mother. He said it was nothing.'

'We don't know anything yet,' Andy says firmly, 'and we mustn't alarm Jamie by speculating in front of him. You know how sensitive he is.'

'When will we know what's wrong? Why isn't anyone doing anything?'

'It's all in hand. The doctor's coming back later.'

'Oh, Andreeeew . . .' A wailing, like the siren on some great ship, announces the Rhino's arrival. She heads towards us at full pelt, still rugged up in her fur hat and coat. 'Is he dead?' She takes her hat off and wrings it in her hands. 'He's dead, isn't he?'

I am doing quite well until the Rhino utters the word 'dead'; then I lose my grip entirely, and break down in a gibbering heap.

'I knew it,' the Rhino sobs.

'Jamie's fine, Mother,' Andy soothes. 'Come and see for yourself.' He turns to me briefly. 'For goodness' sake, Juliet, pull yourself together.'

I grab a handful of tissues from my handbag, blow my nose, and follow Andy and the Rhino back into the side-room. Emily leaps off the bed and throws herself at the Rhino who is staring at Jamie as if she's seen a ghost.

'Granny, Granny! We had a 'venture. And, do you

know, me and Mummy . . .' She hesitates. 'Mummy and me have a secret.'

'No, Emily. We don't want to hear about that right now,' I warn, but Emily ignores me.

'I'm not allowed to tell you, but we went to see Steve, and he didn't have any clothes on.' She giggles. 'Do you know what?'

'That's enough, Emily.' I turn to Andy and the Rhino who are both paying great attention. 'I don't know where she gets her imagination from. Always making up stories.' I grab Emily by her arm, and give it a good squeeze, but there's no stopping her.

'Do you know what? Mummy kissed him. To make him better.'

I don't know where to look. My eyes focus on the temperature chart clipped to a file that is hooked on the rail at the bottom of Jamie's bed. If a nurse took my temperature just now, it would shoot off the top of the scale.

Whatever Andy and the Rhino make of Emily's revelations they say nothing.

'Mother, Juliet and I will have to stay here for some time,' Andy says, taking charge of the situation. 'I wonder if you'd mind taking Emily home? I can give you a lift and come back.'

The Rhino looks from me to Andy, and back to me. She knows, doesn't she, about me, and the great romance I've been chasing after with someone other than my husband. Jamie being in hospital is punishment for what I wanted to do with Steve, but didn't, not because I recovered my conscience and changed my mind, but because I had no one to look after Emily.

I kiss Emily goodbye before she and the Rhino, who is looking almost as flushed in her fur coat as I feel, leave. Not long afterwards Dr Anneka, as Jamie calls her, arrives to see him. She reminds me of Gwyneth Paltrow in appearance. In fact, considering how Gwyneth Paltrow seems to pop up everywhere, she probably *is* Gwyneth Paltrow.

'How are you feeling, Jamie?' she asks.

'Fine,' he says.

'He's not fine,' I interrupt.

'This is my mum,' Jamie says apologetically. 'She's lost one of her eyebrows.'

'I see. Good afternoon, Mrs Wyevale. Your son is not well.'

'I can see that. Anyone can see that. It doesn't take years of medical training to see that my son is seriously ill.' Andy casts me a warning glance, reminding me that it was me who failed to notice how sick Jamie was before I sent him to school this morning.

'Is there anything you'd like to ask me?' Dr Anneka fingers the stethoscope that she carries around her neck. She looks very young – not much older than Steve.

'How long have you been qualified? I mean, *are* you qualified?'

'Juliet, let me deal with this.' Andy takes over, apologising profusely to Dr Anneka, while Jamie pulls his bedsheet up over his face. Dr Anneka seems unfazed by my outburst.

'Jamie will be staying in the hospital tonight,' she says, looking towards the head of the bed. 'Your mum and dad can stay with you.'

Jamie lowers the sheet. 'I'd like to go home,' he says hopefully.

'We need to keep an eye on you until we have the results of the blood tests tomorrow.'

'Thank you, Dr Anneka,' Andy says. He seems just as interested in Dr Anneka's figure as he is in her medical knowledge.

When she's gone, Jamie asks for his pyjamas. Andy drives home to fetch them, along with a couple of Lego Bionicles, and clean clothes for us.

'Is Emily all right?' I ask when he returns too late with the pyjamas – Jamie has fallen asleep, and I don't want to disturb him.

'She and Granny have been making green jelly frogs.' Andy falls silent. Weighed down by our concerns for Jamie and my deceit, we find we have nothing to say to each other.

'Would you like some tea?' I suggest eventually.

'I'll get it,' Andy offers. He feels in his pocket. 'Have you got any change?'

'My purse is in my bag.' I nod towards my handbag

which I left on the chair Andy vacated earlier. Andy picks it up. The catch comes undone, and I realise too late what I've done. My blood runs cold as all the evidence of my attempt at infidelity scatters across the floor. One purse. One eyebrow pencil. One mobile phone. Nothing incriminating so far. Not one, but two boxes of condoms. One tube of vaginal lubricant in case I should, like an old car, take some time to warm up.

Andy picks the items up one by one, and studies them before he drops them back into the bag, all except the purse which he squeezes into his trouser pocket. He moves very slowly. It is worse than stripping off in front of him with the lights on. Much, much worse.

I want Andy to react, to yell at me, but he says nothing. He walks out of the room, returning five minutes later with two teas. He hands me one. I open my mouth to confess. It would make me feel better. I want to feel better than this.

'Save it,' Andy says sharply. 'Not now.'

My world turns black and suffocating. I feel like I am fighting my way through rows and rows of coats inside a locked wardrobe. Everything has gone wrong. I excuse myself, and escape outside for some fresh air. I grab my mobile from my bag and start to dial Lorraine's number. I stop halfway through. What can Lorraine do, apart from offer a shoulder to cry on? I can do my crying on my own.

* * *

I spend a long night worrying about Jamie, and Andy who has clearly resolved never to speak to me again. The following morning a nurse ushers me and Andy out along the corridor from Jamie's bedside to another side-room. I've come to associate side-rooms with the hushed delivery of bad news from watching too many hospital dramas, so my heart is already kicking like a donkey when I take one chair, and Andy another. He shifts it pointedly away from mine. He sits down, sits forward, sits back, clears his throat, chews the skin at the side of his thumb.

'I wish they'd hurry up,' I mutter. 'Jamie will be wondering where we are.'

'Don't try telling me you don't like to leave him,' Andy growls back, 'because you don't give a toss about anyone else but yourself.'

Tears prick my eyes, and I am about to protest when Dr Anneka pushes the door open and joins us. She perches on the edge of the table and flicks through some papers on a clipboard, picks one, and clips it back on top of all the others. She looks up, unsmiling, fearful even.

'Mr and Mrs Wyevale, I want to have a chat with you about Jamie's blood results.'

I take a deep breath, and screw up my eyes, praying for the all-clear, as she continues.

'There are some changes . . . We would like to run some more tests.'

Dr Anneka pauses again. The silence is unbearable.

'What changes? What tests?' Andy asks hoarsely.

'It is possible that Jamie has a form of leukaemia.'

Leukaemia? With that one word my world collapses completely. I cannot speak, yet I am screaming inside. *Not Jamie. Not my little boy.*

Jamie is referred to the Children's Unit at the Royal Marsden where the diagnosis is confirmed. He'll have to undergo chemotherapy, but the consultant says he has a good chance of making a full recovery. It's not going to be easy though. If ever I needed Andy, and he needed me, it is now, but he can hardly bring himself to look at me, let alone touch me.

Jamie is asleep, his face pale against the pillow. I lean over and plant a kiss on his cheek. He stirs, mutters something about 'gangsta' hamsters, and rolls over onto his front.

'Leave him alone, Juliet,' Andy murmurs from behind me. 'It's no wonder he's so tired when you keep disturbing him.'

I turn to find Andy's hand hovering above my shoulder. I reach up to take it, but he moves away to the other side of Jamie's bed.

'It isn't me that's making him tired,' I say. 'He's tired because he's ill.'

'You don't help.'

I know, but how can I explain that I can't stop myself?

I can't bear to see Jamie asleep in case he fails to wake up again.

'I have to do something.'

'Shh. Keep your voice down!' Andy warns.

'This is all my fault,' I say in a choked whisper. 'I should have taken Jamie to see the doctor earlier, and when Dr Finch said there was nothing wrong with him, I should have insisted. I should have taken him back.'

'Juliet!' Andy admonishes. 'You're disturbing him again.'

Andy's right. I have my hand resting on Jamie's back, feeling for the rise and fall of his breathing. Very gently, I withdraw it.

'It's not your fault.' Andy's voice softens. 'You know what the consultant said. No one knows for certain how long Jamie's had this thing. The first signs of leukaemia are vague. The significance of the symptoms can be missed on a single visit to a GP, or they can be mistaken for something else, like a virus.' Andy takes a deep breath. 'If any blame can be said to lie with you, it lies with me too. I should have realised how sick he was. I'm his,' tears spring to his eyes, but he blinks them back, 'I'm his dad.'

My chest tightens. I've been so preoccupied with Jamie that I've hardly had time to consider how Andy is feeling. I remember how devastated he was when he lost his father to cancer. Now he's terrified that he's going to lose his son. Our son.

'Whatever has happened between us, Juliet,' Andy goes on, 'we are going to do everything possible to make Jamie better. He is going to get better. One day soon, he'll be back making models of intergalactic spaceships at school, he'll be back playing football—'

'He hates football,' I cut in.

'All right. Maybe I'll have to accept that footie isn't his game.' Andy's lips curve into a brief, wry smile, and for one blissful moment I can almost imagine that there is nothing wrong, and we're chatting together at home like we used to.

The moment doesn't last. I remain at the hospital, while Andy shuttles between the hospital, home and work. He talks about Jamie. He talks about selling our business to the developers. He refuses to talk about us. I suppose I should be grateful because it means I can throw all my energy into looking after Jamie.

'How are you feeling?' I ask him one morning after his admission to hospital.

'Fine,' he mumbles.

'Are you sure?'

'A bit sick . . . Mum, I wish you'd stop asking.'

'Is there anything you'd like to do this morning? Play Hangman, or Bingo?'

'Not again,' Jamie sighs. 'I'm going to read Harry Potter.'

'Oh, no you're not.' It's Lorraine, clutching an armful of magazines.

373

'What are you doing here?' I ask.

'Andy's asked me to come and sit with Jamie for a while to give you a break. He wants to take you out somewhere.'

'Where?'

'He didn't say.'

'I can't leave Jamie.'

'Yes, you can. Andy's waiting for you in the car park. Go on. Off you go.'

Out in the car park, I find Andy sitting in the passenger seat of the Mercedes. He waves me towards the driver's door. I open it.

'You're driving,' he says coldly.

'Why?' I slide into the driver's seat, and turn the key in the ignition.

'You know where Steve lives. You've been there before.'

'What—'

'I'm going there to take back what's mine.' Andy pauses. I can hear a pulse beating about inside my skull as I picture Steve's hard belly run through with a knife, and Andy covered with blood. 'Relax, Juliet. I'm not going there to fight for your honour. Gayle tells me she's seen Steve driving about in a black BMW 3 Series convertible.'

'So?' I drive slowly. I am in no hurry. I haven't had a chance to tell Steve that we're finished yet. I don't know how he'll react when I turn up with Andy.

'You're going to go inside to ask him for the keys, while I wire it,' Andy says.

'Won't Steve be at work?'

'I fired him.'

I turn into the car park at the front of the house where Steve rents the bedsit. There's a car on the tarmac, a highly polished black BMW with gleaming alloy wheels.

'Do you recognise it?' Andy says.

I nod. The BMW that Mr Parker returned wasn't so rusty after all. Steve lied to me, didn't he? I feel betrayed.

'There'll be no question of me having stolen it since you somehow omitted to send the documentation off to the DVLA to inform them that it had been scrapped, so it's still registered in my name,' Andy continues. 'Mr Parker didn't bother to register a change of ownership either.'

I switch off the ignition.

'Off you go then. You know where to find him.'

I walk up to the house, push the front door open, and step inside. There are voices on the stairs. One of them is Steve's, husky, honeyed and dripping with sex appeal. He is saying, 'I always knew we'd be together.'

A pair of legs sheathed in denim appears behind the banister, then a second pair clad in black boots up to the knee.

'You bastard!' I dash towards them.

'What's that, Mrs Wyevale?' Steve says, standing a couple of stairs above where I am, incandescent with fury, on the bottom step. 'You've met Mrs Wyevale, haven't you, Debs? Mrs Wyevale, meet my wife.'

'What?' I stammer.

Steve grins. 'Me and Debs got married yesterday. Her old man's found us a flat, and given me my job back.'

'We're going to be one happy family,' Debs says, stroking her swollen belly.

What can I say? I was going to break the news to Steve that we were finished, even though we never really began, but I can see I am too late. As far as Steve's concerned, we're already finished. He doesn't even have the grace to look sheepish about marrying Debs so soon after making out that I was the woman he wanted to be with. At that moment, I feel like Kate must have done when Leonardo slipped away into the icy depths of the ocean, except I have nothing left to cling to – no bitter-sweet memories of the romance of a lifetime, no wreck-age, no frosted overcoat. I cannot mourn losing Steve, only losing the man I thought Steve to be.

'I suppose you've come round for your ten quid,' Steve says. 'Have you got a tenner on you, Debs?'

'I've got a fiver somewhere,' she says, smirking at me. I expect Steve's told her about me, about how I've been slavering at his heels like a bitch on heat.

'Actually, Mr Wyevale and I have come round for our car.'

'What car?' Steve says.

'That rusty old BMW outside.'

'You can't do that. I've spent hours doing it up.'

'I noticed. Thanks for that. Now, I'd like the keys.'

'Not bloody likely,' Steve grins. 'I'm taking my wife back to Willesden in it today. In fact, we're just off.'

There is a roar from an engine outside, and a couple of bleats from a horn. Andy must have worked quickly. Steve pushes past me, swearing. Debs and I follow. Andy is performing a three-point turn in the car park. He accelerates in reverse, stops sharply just as the BMW's rear bumper touches the wall of the house, changes gear and waits, revving the engine, as Steve runs in front of him.

'Get out of my car!' Steve yells.

'Get out of my way!' Andy leans out of the window, and gives him a two-fingered salute.

'You've got my stuff in there. My phone . . .' Steve jumps onto the bonnet, and bangs on the windscreen.

The engine growls. The car moves forwards very slowly. Steve clings on.

'No! You'll kill him!' screams Debs.

'Andy! Stop!' I join in, not because I'm concerned for Steve, but for Debs and the baby. The car accelerates, and shoots out onto the pavement, where it stops, tipping Steve off to one side. I wait no longer than it takes to see that Steve is still very much alive, jump into the Mercedes and follow Andy back to Wyevale Autos.

'It didn't take you long to wire it,' I comment as Andy drives me back to the hospital.

'I didn't. That idiot left it unlocked with the key inside.'

Andy changes the subject. 'I'm going home to check how my mother's getting on with Emily. I'll be back to see Jamie this afternoon.'

'Won't you stop for a coffee?'

'No, thanks. I don't want to spend any more time than I have to with you, Juliet.' Andy shrugs. 'Anyway, Lorraine's with Jamie. You'll want to have a chat with her, won't you? Have a good laugh at my expense.' Andy almost pushes me out of the car. I shan't be laughing. Neither will Lorraine.

Lorraine is sitting with Jamie.

'How could you neglect to tell me that my favourite young man was in hospital?' she accuses. 'Pammy told me the other day. I've left Tyler with her. She's doing a great job with Emily. And she's defrosted your freezer, you lucky so and so.'

'Lucky? If this is luck, I don't need it.'

'I'm sorry, Juliet,' Lorraine says, lowering her voice. 'I didn't mean to sound flippant. How's Jamie?'

'I told you,' he cuts in. 'I'm fine.'

We leave Jamie reading the *Beano* and make our way to the coffee lounge next to the restaurant. Lorraine has orange juice. I have black coffee, and sit down, wishing I could have something stronger.

'How is Jamie really?' Lorraine sits down opposite me, the other side of a low table.

'He's very bad.' I fight the tears that are welling up in my eyes. 'Lorraine, he could die.'

'No . . . I don't know what to say.'

'Don't say anything,' I mutter, trying to keep control of my emotions, but I don't think Lorraine hears me.

'How are *you*?' she goes on.

I break down.

'That was a stupid question,' Lorraine says quietly.

'The doctor's arranging Jamie's first course of chemo,' I blubber. 'My marriage is in tatters—'

'Your marriage?' Lorraine interrupts.

'Andy found out about me and Steve.'

'Oh, Juliet.' Lorraine reaches out and clasps my hand across the table. 'I won't say I told you so.'

'You just did.' I pause to wipe my face with a tissue. 'How about you?'

'Joe's gone back to that slag.'

'Oh, I'm sorry.'

'She's pregnant. With twins.'

I think of Joe, and his fantasy that life should be fun. Some fun he's going to have with four children to support. Some fun Lorraine's going to have living on her own with Tyler and a new baby. I wonder how she can remain so calm at the prospect?

Lorraine releases my hand, and sits up straight. 'Have you heard about that childminder of yours?'

'Mary Bacon?' Having been thrown into this new role of mother of a child who has cancer, I'd forgotten all about Mary.

'She's been charged with handling stolen goods.'

'Is that all?'

'I thought you'd be pleased that she wasn't charged with child abuse, after all you said about her. Haven't the police been in touch?'

I shake my head. 'Why should they?'

'In case you'd seen anything suspicious while you were dropping the children off. Stolen goods? Dodgy characters lurking outside her maisonette? Apparently, she was running a shoplifting ring.' Lorraine stares at me. 'You did see something, didn't you? Juliet, what was it? Tell me.'

I tell her about the nieces and the presents they brought, including the Rolex which, in retrospect, was probably the real thing. I tell her about Arnie and the cigarettes.

'You dopey cow,' Lorraine chuckles. 'What are you going to do?'

'Tell the police, of course.' It'll be sweet revenge on Emily's behalf. With a bit of luck, Mary Bacon will find out just how unpleasant it is to be locked up against her will.

I'd rather be locked up in prison than see Jamie suffering like this. He's always tired, and he's still losing weight, but he's incredibly brave. Unlike me. A couple of days later, Andy tears me away from his bedside, and takes me home to see Emily. On the way in the car, I notice how white Andy's knuckles are on the steering wheel.

'You can't just forget Emily exists while Jamie's in hospital,' Andy says.

'I haven't forgotten her,' I protest. 'Jamie needs me.'

'Emily needs you too.' Andy pauses. 'My mother's being very kind, looking after Emily for us, so mind how you speak to her.'

'You don't need to lecture me on how to behave.'

'I think I do.' Andy pulls in alongside the pavement outside our house. The front wheel catches the kerb with a grating sound that suggests he's going to need a new trim, if not a new tyre. 'That was your bloody fault, Juliet,' Andy snaps.

'I didn't do—'

'It was your fault. Everything's your fault,' Andy interrupts, his face red with fury. 'If it hadn't been for Jamie, I'd have sent you packing.'

'Andy, calm down. Please. You'll have a heart attack.'

'I don't care. You don't care. You've never cared for me. If you had, you wouldn't have gone off with that –' Andy shoves the door open – 'that wanker!' He gets out, slams the door so hard that the car rocks, and storms off along Ross Road.

'Andy!' I sit for a few minutes with my hand pressed to my chest, trying to regain control over my breathing so that I can climb our steps without having a heart attack myself. Emily and the Rhino are waiting for me at the top.

'Mummy. Mummy!' Emily runs at me, and jumps into my arms, and half-strangles me with joy. 'Where's Daddy?'

'He's gone for a walk.'

'Where's Jamie?'

'I keep telling her he's not coming home yet,' the Rhino butts in.

I press a kiss onto the top of Emily's head.

'Why don't you show me some of the things you've been doing while I've been at the hospital?' I suggest. Emily shows me the fresh soap and citrus pot-pourri she has helped Granny put in the cloakroom. She shows me the gingerbread men, and the sweet-wrapper and rice collage of an ambulance that they've made.

The contrast between Emily's enthusiasm and vigour, and Jamie's exhaustion and pallor is suddenly very painful. Tears prick my eyelids. I excuse myself, saying I'm going to fetch some of Jamie's things to take back to the hospital, and retreat to Jamie's bedroom. It doesn't feel right with all the toys tidied away and the duvet pulled neatly up over the bed. I pick a sweatshirt out of a drawer and press it to my face. It still bears Jamie's smell, not the scent of the hospital.

I want my son back home. I want my family back together. I want to feel Andy's arms around me . . . I am *not* going to cry. I turn and look out of the window, and catch sight of Ronnie's memorial in Lorraine's garden. My lip quivers. Tears run hot down my cheeks.

'Juliet?' The Rhino is with me. She takes the sweatshirt, and pushes a mug of steaming liquid into my hands. She hangs the sweatshirt over the radiator under the window and pulls the curtains. She doesn't say anything. Doesn't tell me to pull myself together. Just sits on the edge of Jamie's bed.

I swallow hard, and take a sip from the mug. I don't know what it's supposed to be, but it's foul.

'It's camomile, Juliet,' the Rhino says. 'I find it very soothing.'

'Thanks.'

'There's no need to thank me for anything.'

'There is,' I sniff. 'I can't thank you enough for stepping in to look after Emily. I don't know how we'd manage without you.'

'You must tell me if there is anything else I can do.'

'There is, actually. I thought Jamie might like a hat. Would you be able to go shopping for one, something that's quite plain, and in a muted colour?'

'Of course,' the Rhino says. 'I'm aware that you consider me a devotee of extreme millinery – that's hats to you, Juliet – but Emily and I will find something that suits him.'

'I had to tell Jamie that he's going to lose his hair,' I explain. 'Do you know what he said? He said it didn't matter because he's always wanted to look like his dad . . .'

Chapter Nineteen

Jamie pulls the baseball cap the Rhino bought for him onto his head. It's plain, not muted, but Jamie says he likes the colour – tangerine.

'Is that everything?' I ask, taking the last Get Well card from his bedside cabinet. It's from Emily, and it depicts a small stick person with a telegraph pole stuck through its middle. I think it's supposed to be Jamie and a hypodermic needle.

'Yes, Mum,' he says, checking underneath the bed. 'Don't worry, I have to come back so if we forget anything, I'll pick it up then.'

I pretend to fiddle with the zip on the suitcase so Jamie can't see how upset I am at being reminded that the nightmare we are living is not over. Jamie has completed his first course of chemotherapy, but he has to return for more tests and more treatment. He's showing signs of remission, but it's far too early to be talking of a cure.

'Let's go,' I say eventually. 'Dad'll be waiting for us in the car park.'

'Great,' says Jamie. 'Did you know Dad says I can have a hamster?'

'No.'

'He said I could have anything I wanted.' Jamie looks at me, his mouth set in a determined line as he assesses the extent of my disapproval. 'I really, really want a hamster, Mum.'

'I know, but we can't always have what we want, can we?' I begin. 'I don't think it's such a good idea—'

'I want a hamster,' Jamie interrupts, 'and it doesn't matter what you say because Dad says I can have one. And he's going to buy a cage like a space station with lots of chambers joined up with tubes, and I'm going to keep it in my bedroom.'

'You have the sea-monkeys to look after already.'

'You can't stroke a sea-monkey, Mum,' Jamie sighs.

I'm not being mean. It's just I don't think I can cope with having to look after a hamster on top of everything else, but I can see that if I put my foot down now, Jamie might take a very long time to forgive me. I wish Andy had spoken to me first. I wish Andy had spoken to me at all. He yells at me quite a lot, but doesn't speak.

The hamster arrives in our household in spite of my arguments against it. Emily suggests that she would like a hamster of her own for her fourth birthday, but I put my foot down, and pacify her with the idea of planning a party instead. Lorraine agrees that Emily should have a joint birthday celebration with Tyler as we have done in previous years, so we can halve the hassle of organising it. At least, that's the theory.

I am in the kitchen with Emily who sits on a stool with her arms folded, reminding me of how she used to sit on her potty, pink-faced with earnest effort.

'What are you doing?' I ask.

'I'm trying to be good.'

'Why don't you go upstairs and play with your birthday present? It's hours until your party.'

Emily slides down from the stool, gives me a big grin, and skips off to play with the doll's cot and car seat we gave her in the hope it will encourage her to treat Baby what's-her-name in a kindly manner. I return to stirring the jelly which won't set. It's had three hours in the fridge already.

'Why does everything I touch go wrong?' I wail, not realising Andy has turned up in the kitchen.

'You've put pineapple in the jelly,' he observes. 'Everyone knows jelly doesn't set when you mix it with pineapple.'

Do they? I didn't.

'Would you like some help?' Andy continues.

'I wouldn't like you to think that I'm a burden on you in any way,' I begin fiercely.

'You're beginning to sound like my mother.' Andy smirks. When he first found out about me and Steve he froze me out, then he went through a phase of yelling at me, and now he sneers. He hates me, and I don't blame him. 'Well, would you like me to help, or not?'

'Not. I'll ask Lorraine.' I try ringing her, but the phone's engaged. After a second attempt, I go round to hers.

At the bottom of the steps, the estate agents' For Sale sign has been altered to Sold, so I guess Lorraine will be leaving soon. I don't know where she's going. Neither does Lorraine yet. Outside Lorraine's gate, there is a white van parked with its offside wheels on the pavement. It's the one that belongs to Pete, the plumber, and since Joe's been gone, he's taken over the space Joe used to park in.

I trot up the steps to Lorraine's front door, and ring the bell.

'I could do with some help,' I say when Lorraine finally answers.

'I've got to get ready.'

'You are ready.'

'Oh no, I need to change, and do my make-up.' Lorraine's hair is tied back, and her lips have been outlined, painted and glossed. She has a sparkle in her eyes. Pregnancy suits her. 'Give me ten minutes.'

It's more like half an hour, and then she turns up with Tyler, and Pete, the plumber.

'I thought Pete could fix that washer in your bathroom,' she says as she breezes through the house, carrying the cake that she's collected from the baker's. 'I don't suppose Andy's had time to replace it.'

I take her aside while Andy offers Pete a lager.

'I know the real reason you've brought him here. To find out what I think of him.'

She grins. 'I respect your opinion, Juliet.'

'Don't ask me. I'm a poor judge of men. And women.'

'Please.'

'Okay.'

While Lorraine takes the cake out of the box and arranges candles on the top, I run my eye over Pete's assets. Do I admire Lorraine's determination to set herself up with another man so soon after Joe? I don't think so. Pete is over six foot tall. He has bulging muscles in his arms that remind me of Popeye, and his lower lip juts out too far to be considered attractive. He says he is forty-six, but I reckon he's the other side of fifty. He says he's been married twice before, and he has two children that he knows of. He jokes too much, like Joe did.

I advise caution, but Lorraine doesn't like it.

'Aren't you doing this on the rebound?' I query.

'You can't talk. What do you know about relationships?'

I refrain from explaining that I know a lot more than I did, while Lorraine continues, 'You're bound to be suspicious, Juliet, after what happened with you and you know who, but Pete's different. He's kind, considerate, and great with Tyler. He makes me feel good. He makes me laugh.' She pauses. 'Give him a chance – for my sake?'

'I'll try,' I say. I owe Lorraine that at least. She was right about Steve, so why shouldn't she be right about Pete?

'I'm sorry if you think I kept you in the dark about Pete,' Lorraine says. 'I didn't want to say anything in case it didn't work out.'

'What do you mean?'

'He's asked me to move in with him.'

'Are you going to?'

'Yes. First we'll move into his place in Anerley. Then Pete says we can look for a house together in Beckenham. It's what I've always wanted.'

I find myself being caught up in Lorraine's enthusiasm. Beckenham isn't far from South Norwood.

'That's wonderful. I'll be able to come and see the new baby.'

'We'll be able to meet up in Kelsey Park for picnics,' Lorraine smiles, 'and you don't have to worry about finding another hair and beauty consultant because I can still colour your hair for you.'

'There's no need,' I say quickly. My stripes have almost grown out, and the tigress that they awakened inside me has padded away without a growl, and that's the way I want it to stay. 'I like my natural colour.'

'I could wax your eyebrows instead . . .'

'There's no way—' I begin before I realise that

Lorraine is pulling my leg. I find myself laughing with her. 'I couldn't go through that again,' I gasp. 'Oh Lorraine, I'm going to miss you being next door.'

It's true. Of the best friends I have had in my life, Lorraine – as Emily would put it – has to be the best-est-est. I shall never consign her to the list of serial best friends I have had in the past. 'We've had some fun together, haven't we?'

'And we'll have a lot more.' Lorraine holds out her hand, gives a little pout, and puts on an American accent that's more *Rugrats* than *Friends*. 'Come on, Juliet. Let's go party.'

We didn't invite any extra children to the party because the chemotherapy makes Jamie vulnerable to infections that other children might bring with them. The adults and the hamster give us enough to deal with anyway.

My mother and father arrive at three, and leave at four-thirty to get back across London before nightfall, as if they have no headlamps on their car. Lorraine's mum drops in before returning to the nursing home to help her husband tuck the old people up in bed and make their cocoa. As she leaves, there is a scream from upstairs.

'Mummy!' It's Emily. I dash up to Jamie's room where I find Emily clutching her hand, and Jamie clutching the hamster, or Hammy as he's imaginatively christened him. (It turns out that Andy made a deal with him that he could have a hamster on condition he didn't call it Becks.)

'Hammy bit me,' Emily cries. 'I have to go to hospital.'

'Let me see.' I reach for her hand, and pull it away from where she holds it tight to her body. 'Look, he hasn't even broken the skin.'

'But I want to go to hospital.'

'Emily wants to go to hospital,' Tyler confirms.

'Hammy will have to go to hospital,' says Jamie, almost in tears. 'I told Emily to be gentle, but she didn't listen, and now Hammy's dead.'

'He can't be dead.' I bend down to look. The hamster's long, rust-coloured fur is more ruffled than usual, but his eyes are open, and his whiskers are twitching in a highly threatening manner, warning me not to inspect him too closely. 'He's fine. Why don't we put him back in his house, and go downstairs to cut the cake?'

The Rhino arrives at five after the excitement of the hamster bite is over, her lips stiff and set and the same livid pink as the icing on the Barbie birthday cake. She must have put her lipstick on in a hurry because a smear has missed her upper lip entirely and spread across her teeth.

'I'm so sorry I'm late, Juliet,' she says. 'I was racked by several agonising spasms, and had to lie down for a while. It's been a stressful time for me, worrying about Jamie. And you and Andrew.'

I ignore that last remark. 'Can I get you anything?'

'A small sherry, thank you.'

'Where's Ian? I thought you were bringing him with you.'

'There are some men worth fighting for, and it turned out that Ian isn't one of them.' She hands me her coat and a hat, trimmed with purple feathers that make me sneeze. 'It goes without saying that I knew as soon as I saw him that he wasn't all that he seemed. The clinic at Harley Street turned out to be a postal address.'

'You liked him though?'

'I had feelings for him.' She pauses. 'At least there's no harm done. Women of my generation don't hop into bed with a man as soon as they meet him.' She eyes me up and down. The skin at the corners of her mouth and eyes creases slightly. I sense a flicker of warmth. 'Of course, it might have been interesting. You know, I used to think you were such a mouse, Juliet, but you're turning out to be a true Wyevale. Stick with it, and you and Andrew will get through this rough patch. I know you will.'

'You'd better go and join the others in the kitchen. We're about to cut the cake.' I hang up the Rhino's coat and hat, and follow her through, wondering if she is suffering an attack of senility. I think she has just paid me a compliment for the very first time, and the very last, once she finds out that there is no hope for my and Andy's marriage.

I get to light the candles. The kids blow and spit. Light, blow and spit. Twice each for Tyler and Emily, and once for Jamie to have a go. The children then disappear to set up a disco in the dining room. The girls dance to Mis-Teeq, S Club 8 and the Sugababes. Jamie DJs in his tangerine baseball cap.

The Rhino goes home, and Pete drives off in his van. At seven, Lorraine declares that it is Tyler's bedtime and prepares to leave.

On the doorstep, she stops.

'Thanks for organising the party,' she says. 'We'll have one with Emily at our new house next year, won't we, Tyler?' she adds, looking down towards Tyler who is trying to manoeuvre one of her birthday presents, a Glamour Gear Waycool Weekender, down the steps. It's a suitcase with wheels and a pull-along handle that Tyler's planning to use for the weekends when she goes to stay with her daddy. If she takes after Lorraine, she'll need something considerably bigger in which to pack her essentials.

Tyler is too busy to answer.

'When do you think you'll move out?' I ask.

'Pete's going to hire a van to shift our things next weekend.' Lorraine pauses. 'Don't look so worried, Juliet. I'll ring you as soon as we've settled in.'

I watch her walk down the steps to catch up with Tyler who is fighting to extract her suitcase from where it is caught by one wheel in a gap between the last step and the gate pillar. I stroll across to the mini picket fence and wait until she and Tyler have climbed the steps back up to their front door.

'You promise you'll ring me?' I say as she puts the key in the lock.

Lorraine turns back to me and grins. She steps up close, and gives me a hug across the fence.

'I promise, Juliet,' she says firmly. 'Now I've got to go – I think the baby's dancing the salsa on my bladder.'

As I watch her disappear into the house with Tyler, my heart sinks at the thought of going back indoors myself, to spend another evening trying to keep out of Andy's way.

When I get in, Andy is upstairs putting Emily and Jamie to bed. I finish clearing up in the kitchen, and I am wiping down the worktop when I notice that my thong is draped across the pepper-pot that I bought in IKEA. There is a note in the Rhino's handwriting with it. I don't know how I missed it before.

Found this in the rag-bag under the stairs when looking for a duster. Thought you might want it back. The phone number for Relate is printed in bold letters beneath. I screw up the note, and throw it in the bin. It is too late. Far too late. Andy has made it clear that our marriage is over, and he wants no more to do with me. When the sale of the business goes through, we'll have enough money for us to go our separate ways. Andy will fight to keep the kids with him, and I will fight to keep them with me, and our lives will be in a terrible mess . . .

'Juliet?' Andy comes into the kitchen. 'Are you busy?'

'Yes,' I say quickly, biting back tears. 'I haven't said goodnight to the kids.'

'They're both asleep.'

'I like to check on them.'

'Go on then.'

I creep upstairs, and pop into Emily's room, knocking into her bookshelf on the way to her bed.

'Haaaa,' wails a familiar voice. 'Me hungry.'

It's the Furby. The Rhino must have replaced the batteries. I place my hand across its eyes, and it begins to snore. Emily is snoring too. I am so proud of her. Since she stopped going to Mary Bacon's, she has been positively angelic.

'Haaa . . . Me hungry.'

I grab the Furby, slip Emily's window open, and throw it out. I hear it rattling down the steps before it falls silent, then I go to Jamie's room, and sit on the edge of his bed, listening to him breathing.

'Juliet?' I feel Andy's hand on my shoulder. 'You can't watch over him all the time. I know you want to. I feel the same.' He pauses. 'Jamie's going to beat this. We have to believe that.'

'I know.'

'Come downstairs. We need to talk.'

A shiver runs down my spine. I have been dreading this moment. I follow Andy slowly downstairs to the sitting room where we sit at opposite ends of the sofa. The telly is on with the sound turned down. I examine my hands. No ring, and now no husband. How could I have been so careless?

'Look at me, Juliet,' he says softly. 'I can't bear it when you won't look at me.'

I look up. Andy's mouth is taut, and his eyes dark with apprehension.

'Just tell me one thing,' he says. 'Did you sleep with him?'

'Does it matter?'

'Yes, it does. Well?'

'No.'

'Think carefully.'

It isn't surprising that Andy doesn't believe me after all the lies I've told. What is surprising is that he believes it is important to know whether Steve and I had sex or not. Relationships are about emotional involvement, not shagging.

'I would have slept with him,' I admit.

'But you didn't?'

'I wanted to.' I stand up. 'There, I've said it.' Andy sits with his head bowed, staring at the carpet. 'If you want a divorce, I'll understand.'

Andy looks up sharply. His eyes are glittering with tears. 'Don't you love me any more?' he says, his voice breaking.

'I do . . . I do love you.' I find myself kneeling on the floor with my arms around Andy's neck. He tries to push me away, but I won't let go. 'If you never believe anything else that I say, you must believe that.'

'You have a strange way of showing it,' Andy says gruffly.

'I made a terrible mistake. Will you forgive me?'

A tear glistens on his cheek. He sniffs and falls silent for what seems like for ever, and then he rests his hands around my shoulders, and pulls me close. We rub noses, but don't kiss.

'I knew something was going on,' Andy begins. 'You drifted away, and I didn't try hard enough to bring you back. I thought it might be Joe at first, but once he was out of the picture, I guessed it had to be Steve. You were like a little kid when he was around, dressing up in new clothes, and giggling over private jokes.'

'Oh, Andy. Why didn't you confront me? Stop me?'

'Would it have made any difference? Would you have stopped?' Andy pauses. 'Steve's nothing like I am. He's young, fit and completely irresponsible. He's a liar and a cheat. I hoped that you'd find out that what you felt for him was just lust, and that you'd come back to me . . .'

'Come back?'

Andy hums the tune of 'Baby Come Back To Me'.

It is as if someone has dropped an ice cube down the back of my neck.

'It was you who bought the CD I found in my car?'

Andy nods. 'Don't tell me I never buy you anything,' he says. 'Wait here a moment.'

I wait on the sofa, curling myself up into a cringing

ball of regret as I recall how I gave the CD to Steve, and Steve let me go on believing it was a present from him.

'Andy,' I begin when he returns, all flushed and smiling. I don't continue with what I was about to say because he falls down on one knee in front of me, and pulls a small box from his pocket.

'Let me speak, Jules.'

I sit up straight. I'm listening.

'I've never stopped loving you,' Andy says. 'I know I haven't always made it clear—'

'Andy—'

'I know I'm not Richard Gere, or—'

'He's too old,' I say softly.

'Robbie Williams?'

'He strikes me as being unreliable, not a man you could depend on.'

'I'm bald and overweight, I'm obsessed with football . . .'

'You do have positive features,' I remind him. 'You're kind, patient, goodlooking. You're great with the children. You have—' I correct myself, 'You *did* have a fantastic sense of humour.'

'I suppose I let everything get on top of me.'

'It isn't your fault. It's all down to me. I've been such a cow.' I take a deep breath. 'I'll understand if you can't forgive me.'

'But I have forgiven you.' Andy takes my hand and

presses the box into my palm. 'I'd like us to make a fresh start. I love you, Jules. Always have and always will.'

Could Leonardo have said that to Kate if the men on the bridge had managed to spot that iceberg in time, and they had stayed together for as long as Andy and I have? Well, *could* he? My eyes brim with tears. I lean forward and throw my arms around Andy's neck, and this time, we kiss.

'Aren't you going to look inside the box?' Andy murmurs.

I lift the lid very slowly. Inside is a ring of white gold.

'It's beautiful . . .'

'I wanted to give it to you ages ago, but it never seemed to be the right time.' Andy reaches over, takes it out and slips it on the third finger of my left hand. 'Don't cry. You're crying again. Please don't be sad.'

'I'm not sad,' I sniffle. 'I'm over the moon . . .' I stare at the ring, and recall the two hundred and fifty pounds that went onto our credit card, and how Andy wouldn't tell me what he'd spent it on. I look up. 'You could have had a couple of ties as well as shirts and socks, if you hadn't bought this. I am right, aren't I?'

Andy smiles.

'I can't wait to show it off to Lorraine,' I continue. 'Not this minute, of course. Tomorrow morning will do.'

'Good, because I haven't finished yet,' Andy says. 'I've been thinking that when Jamie's better—'

'If,' I interrupt.

'*When* Jamie's better, we'll go on holiday. Not Cornwall – somewhere hot where you can strut about in that thong of yours.'

'If we can afford it . . .'

'Didn't I tell you? The letter from O'Connor and Partners' solicitor arrived here this morning. Wyevale Autos is no more.' Andy kisses my hand. 'We'll have more time to look after Jamie. You won't have to work, and I can take a nine-to-five job for a while. When he's better, we can put the money into something else.'

'What about Gayle and Larry? What will they do?'

'Larry says he's going to retire, and Gayle's going to work somewhere up town as a PA. Do you remember how she replaced the photo of the fitness instructor boyfriend with a photo of a woman? That's her new partner.' Andy smiles. 'Everyone's happy . . . How about celebrating with some ice cream?'

'No, I don't fancy it.'

'Not double chocolate chip?'

'What double chocolate chip?'

'The tub you put in the freezer the other day. I saw you.'

'Oh, go on then.'

Andy sits next to me, opens the tub, and turns the lid upside down on the carpet. He digs the spoon into the tub, scoops out a melting mound of ice cream and

3

chocolate chips, and raises it to my lips. I open my mouth and suck the ice cream from the spoon. Andy leans close and kisses me. The inside of my cheeks and my tongue are cold, yet my lips are burning. My heart starts to pound with anticipation.

I curve my body to fit against his, pressing my breasts against his chest.

'Let's make love,' he whispers.

It feels right. I want Andy to strip me naked. I want to feel his skin against mine. I want him to shag me senseless. Juliet and Andy. The survivors. I fumble for Andy's belt. He groans softly, reaching under my blouse with one hand, and keeping the ice-cream tub and spoon in the other.

'Oh, Juliet!'

'Andy . . .'

'Mummy!' Emily is standing in the doorway. Andy smiles ruefully, and refastens his belt as Emily creeps in. Jamie follows, wearing his baseball cap with his pyjamas. He appears to have more colour in his cheeks than he has had for some time, and it isn't a trick of the light.

'What are you two doing downstairs?' I ask.

'I'm thirsty,' says Emily.

'I can't sleep because Hammy's scampering around,' says Jamie. Pet shops don't tell you that hamsters like to run around by night, sleep by day, and bite people, do they? I guess they wouldn't sell many hamsters if they did.

Jamie squeezes onto the sofa between us. Emily clambers onto Andy's lap.

'Can I have some ice cream?' she asks.

'No, it's mine,' Andy says, snatching it up above her head. He grins as Emily screws up her face with annoyance, then gives in and hands her the spoon. 'You first,' he says.

Emily flicks a spoonful of ice cream across the room. It hits the wall, and slides down to form a small pool on the edge of the carpet.

'Emily! No!' I yell.

'I didn't mean to,' she wails.

'It's all right,' I soothe, sorry now that I shouted at her. 'I know you didn't. Come here.'

Emily slips down Andy's outstretched legs to the floor, and scrambles onto my lap. I wrap my arms around her, and kiss the top of her head.

'I love you, Mummy,' she says.

'I love you too.'

I tell her how grown-up she's been today, especially being so brave when Tyler was bragging about the Snack Attack Scooby that her grandma gave her for her birthday. The Rhino gave Emily a set of phonics books to kickstart her education. Some things never change . . .

Emily wriggles as if to escape, but I'm reluctant to let her go. When I think of the danger I put her and Jamie in by entrusting them to Mary Bacon, I feel sick. Mary terrified Emily by locking her in that cupboard. She encouraged Jamie to mix with criminals. She betrayed my trust, just as I betrayed my children by leaving them with her while I chased after some ridiculous fantasy.

I know I wasn't the only person Mary misled, but I should have taken the trouble to look beyond the stair-gates, the organic menu, and all that Febreze. I didn't, because just as Mary wasn't the perfect childminder, I am not the perfect mother. I squeeze Emily tighter, making a silent promise to try harder from now on.

'Mummy, let me go,' Emily grumbles. 'I want some ice cream.'

I let her jump down, and Andy hands her the ice-cream tub. She sits down on the floor with the tub between her knees, and starts eating.

'Where's the remote control?' Jamie asks.

'It was on the sofa last time I saw it,' says Andy.

Jamie digs around the edges of the sofa cushions while we're still sitting on them. He finds a tissue that belongs to me, a fifty-pence piece which both Jamie and Andy lay claim to, and a sticky Fruity Pop lolly.

'That's not mine,' Emily says quickly.

'It is,' says Jamie.

'Isn't.'

'Is!'

'That's enough,' Andy warns, but Jamie's found the remote, and he's searching through teletext for the chil-dren's joke page.

They – my family – are all facing the telly. Andy is

leaning back with one hand behind his head, his scalp shining in the light. Jamie is frowning as he tries to angle the remote to change the page. Emily's eyes are flickering across the screen as she sits there with her hair in tangles, and ice cream dripping from her chin. As I watch them, I realise how close I came to losing them, and how lucky I am to be given a second chance. I shall make sure it never happens again, of course. I love them all far too much.

If Antonio Banderas himself strode into my life and offered to tie me up, or tie me down, or whisk me off through the desert on his horse, I would say, 'No, thanks.' My ordinary life is adventure enough for me. I am the happiest woman on earth.

'I've found it,' Jamie pipes up. 'Hey, Mum, Dad, when's the best time to buy a bird?'

'I don't know,' says Andy. 'When's the best time to buy a bird?'

'How do you find the answer, Mum?' Jamie whispers to me.

'Press reveal.'

'Ha,' says Jamie. 'When it's going cheep. That's not funny, is it, Dad?'

'No, it isn't,' says Andy, but the more he tries to explain the joke, the more we all laugh. We laugh until our sides ache. We laugh until we think we can never stop.

The Pride of Park Street

Pamela Evans

When Jess Mollitt gains a place with the famous Burton Girls dance troupe, appearing on the West End stage, it seems her dreams have finally come true. But then a family outing ends in tragedy, killing her mother and leaving her father a broken man. Jess is forced to give up the career she loves to look after her younger siblings and manage the newsagents her father is no longer capable of running.

Working in the shop is a far cry from the glamorous existence she has left behind and, unable to contemplate a life without dance, Jess searches for a way to bring a little of that joy back into her days. It's not long before she's running a hugely popular Saturday dance class for local children and this, combined with her blossoming friendship with neighbour Don Day, provides Jess with the saving grace she needs. But when the brother Don hates arrives on the scene, it seems Jess's problems may be only beginning . . .

'A good traditional romance, and its author has a feeling for the atmosphere of postwar London' *Sunday Express*

'The leading characters are finely drawn . . . crisp prose . . . a superb and heartwarming read' *Irish Independent*

'Very readable' *Bella*

0 7553 0041 6

headline

Now you can buy any of these other bestselling
Headline books from your bookshop or
direct from the publisher.